Anything done in love, will las
Pick up Ghandi's talk 2 week

SIGNATURE
MORMON CLASSICS

Drawing on a rich literary heritage, Signature Books is pleased to make available a new series of classic Mormon works reprinted with specially commissioned introductions. Each book has left an indelible impression on the LDS church and its members, while also having influenced non-Mormon perceptions of the Saints. The authors, whether believers or skeptics, occupy an important place in the development of LDS culture and identity. The reissue of their works offers readers today an opportunity to better appreciate the origins and growth of a major religious and social movement.

SIGNATURE MORMON CLASSICS

Virginia Sorensen

A Little Lower than the Angels

With a Foreword by
Mary Lythgoe Bradford

SIGNATURE BOOKS ❧ SALT LAKE CITY

A NOTE ON THE TEXT
Except for the front matter and foreword,
this Signature Mormon Classics edition of *A Little Lower than the Angels*,
by Virginia Sorensen, is an exact reprint of the 1942
first edition published in New York City
by Alfred A. Knopf.

First published in the United States of America
by Alfred A. Knopf 1942.

Signature Mormon Classics
reprint edition with a foreword by Mary Lythgoe Bradford
published by Signature Books 1997.

Library of Congress Cataloging-In-Publication Data
Sorensen, Virginia Eggertsen
A little lower than the angels / by Virginia Sorensen,
with a foreword by Mary Lythgoe Bradford.
p. cm. — (Signature Mormon classics)
ISBN 1-56085-103-1 (pap.)
I. Title. II. Series.
PS3537.0594L58 1997
813'.52—dc21 97-39403
CIP

FOREWORD

Mary Lythgoe Bradford

WHEN I THINK OF VIRGINIA SORENSEN (1912-1991) and her first novel, *A Little Lower than the Angels*, I picture a young faculty wife and mother gathering up her typewriter and paper and trekking across campus to a small tower office where she could write eight hours a day. A fulfillment of her writer's dream, it was at the same time an act of self-defense. Her mother-in-law had lived with her and her husband Frederick (Fred) since their wedding six years before. Emma Baker Sorensen not only took charge of the household, but she also contributed the pioneer history of her grandmother, Mercy French Baker. Mother Sorensen's degree in domestic science from Columbia made her "right in everything, and I could tell that she would continue to be right into the future,"[1] Virginia said many years later. Fred, with whom Virginia was deeply in love, also showed signs of being right as she began her peripatetic life with this "stormy petrol" of a husband. His problems with his mother, his drinking, his unrealized ambitions would mean a change of job every two or three years for the next twenty years. Virginia, who had considered herself a writer since childhood, decided to turn the situation to her advantage.

Virginia Eggertsen was the third child and second daughter of six children born to Helen ElDeva Blackett and Claude Eggertsen, both descendants of Mormon pioneers. Although her mother was a Christian Scientist and her father a self-avowed "jack" (i.e., nonpracticing) Mormon, she was reared in the Mormon church in Manti, American Fork, and Provo, Utah. She was a student at Brigham Young University when she met Fred who was already teaching English at a local high school. After their wedding for time and eternity in the Salt Lake temple, they departed for Stanford University in Palo Alto, California, where he earned a Ph.D. in English, and she took poetry workshops from Ivor Winters. Her diploma in journalism and English arrived at the birth of their first child, Elizabeth.

Two years later Frederick Jr. was born, and after Fred's graduation, the family departed for Indiana State Teachers College in Terre Haute. Mother Sorensen brought along the only remaining relics of Mercy Baker's life: a sewing chest and a silhouette. Virginia studied these and the Baker family history, and a property deed left by Mercy's husband, Simon Baker, and signed by Joseph Smith. Virginia searched newspapers of the Nauvoo, Illinois, period and sent away to "good old BYU for a few precious books." These probably included the Nauvoo portions of B. H. Roberts's multi-volume *History of the Church*. She may have seen the works of local historians in Illinois and Indiana and the works of Harry Beardsley, a non-Mormon historian.

It was easy to arrange a month in Nauvoo to soak up local color. One old-timer "knew intimately about the flowers, trees, and the layout of the city" as well as stories of his region. "Legends that remain are almost as important as historical documents," she said, "because they throw light upon how the people lived during the period of 1829-1846."[2] "I am a family chronicler, not a historian," she said later. She dedicated the book to Mother Sorensen, and in spite of their difficulties she was grateful for "the gift of time" and for the discipline that developed into a lifelong refuge.

As the manuscript neared completion, she attended a faculty writers' conference where one of the English teachers showed it to guest lecturer Burgess Johnson. He then passed it on to Alfred Knopf in New York who believed, along with his enthusiastic staff, that he had discovered a new star that would shine its brightest in the Western sky. Virginia's editor, Harold Strass, and the Borzoi publicists, were attentive, even affectionate. In fact, the quality of their attention seems to give the lie to the stereotype that all New York publishers are ill-informed and prejudiced against Mormons and Westerners.

After his first meeting with Virginia, Strauss wrote her, "Your visit here I remember as a fresh breeze blowing aside the sultry schemes of too clever contrivers among which I have to pick my way." He found her "exactly the sort of person that your manuscript hinted you might be—a person in love with life for its own simple and wonderful sake."[3] Virginia marveled later that he and Knopf had accepted the manuscript in its simple, wonderful, and *unpunctuated* state. "I had such a romance with e.e. cummings' style that I sent *[Angels]* out without any punctuation! Alec Waugh [her second husband] thought it amazing that a 'little girl from Utah [could] actually sell to Knopf without a capital letter or comma or period.' I explained to Harold Strauss ... that I wanted my words to flow without interruptions. So they sent me a ticket to New York and put me up at the Barbican Plaza over the ducks of Central Park. I was thrilled to hear ducks as I labored."[4]

In May 1942 *A Little Lower than the Angels* (a title suggested by Fred) was published under the Borzoi imprint to favorable, even delighted reviews in the Eastern press, as well as in her midwestern home. Walter Prescott of the *New York Times* noted its "rare subtlety and literary stature,"[5] and a year later included Virginia as one of a "handful of rising stars" for her "poetic imagination, her sensitive, artful writing, and her fresh picture of Mormonism ... all rare and unusual."[6]

Wallace Stegner, writing in *The Saturday Review,* invoked Utahn Bernard DeVoto, who had despaired of writers ever being equal to the Mormon story because God had already written it. "Up to now, nobody has proved Mr. DeVoto wrong, but Virginia Sorensen, in this admirable first novel, comes very close to doing just that ... Instead of trying to cover the whole panorama of Mormon history ... she confines herself to the story of Nauvoo ... [but] even that history she subordinates to the story of a family ... every member of it is real enough to make the average historical novel look like Grandfather's stuffed Sunday shirt." He pronounced her portrait of Joseph Smith "too kind ... She endows the Prophet with some of her own gifts."[7]

Milton Rugoff called it "a novel of distinction" in the *New York Herald Tribune.* "What goes on as Mercy fights a desperate rear guard action from her sickbed as Simon and the elders face the loaded guns and torches of the good people of Illinois makes a double-barreled narrative that is everywhere vigorous and yet finely wrought ... the intimate studies of the Baker children ... and of Mercy's reactions and perceptions ... make the narrative continuously stimulating."[8] *Newsweek* weighed in: "Poignantly human,"[9] while Louis B. Salmon of *The Nation* pronounced it "a stirring tale of quiet heroism," yet praised her for creating not simply a "historical pageant" but showing instead the "travail of a desperate band of believers through the mind and heart of Mercy Baker." He found her style "poetic without being pretentious ... showing sympathy for the spiritual and physical yearnings of the Saints."[10]

In the Sorensens' home state, *The Indianapolis Star* called *Angels* "one of the most important first novels of the season."[11] Citizens of Terre Haute honored her with one of the most elaborate literary events in the city's history, and Fred's English department bulletin reviewed a reading Virginia gave to the faculty. "Those who heard Virginia Sorensen read in her low melodious voice [said] it would not be too far-fetched to hear on of her rapt audience say 'Almost thou persuadest me to be a Mormon.'" *The Chicago Sun* also showed sympathy with the Mormons, calling them a "devout people heroically defending their integrity and the holiness of their goals. Unlike other Christian sects, the Mormons do not stress the inferiority of man to God."[12]

New York reviewers noted her ability to dramatize intimate family scenes against an epic background, while keeping the epic securely in the background. Lewis Gannett's review in *The New York Herald Tribune* prompted Strauss to scrawl "Whoopee" across the pages before sending it on to Virginia. "Her essence is more than outward plot," said Gannett. "Mercy Baker, Jarvie, and Menzo, the boy who wanted to be an Indian, are worth knowing." Gannett also praised a technique that allowed her to "write stories within the longer narrative so complete they could stand alone."[13] He found her treatment of children and women especially convincing. Clifton Fadiman of *The New Yorker* agreed: "I have read a number of Mormon novels but none that more convincingly explores the mind of Mormon women confronted with the tragic, comic, and grotesque problems of plural marriage."[14]

Some of the "short stories" imbedded in the narrative foreshadowed Virginia's later career as a prize-winning writer of children's books. "Your children are your best characters," a friend told her after reading such vignettes as young Betsy listening to a sermon by Wilford Woodruff: "Brother Wilford Woodruff stood before the little ones in Sunday School and spoke to them with the disarming simplicity that had won for him thousands of converts in England." He asks the children to "suppose there are one hundred and thousand millions of fallen spirits sent down from heaven to earth—that makes one hundred evil spirits for every one of us. The whole mission and labor of these spirits is to lead all the children of men to do evil and effect their destruction." He admonishes them to "see what danger they're in" and refers to "these thousands of evil spirits hovering over us night and day" (p. 263). Little Betsy tries to count in her mind the enormity of the number *one hundred.* "Because she could not count so far, using both hands full of fingers surreptiously among her dresses. The other numbers ... had no meaning except a terrible vista of endless black wings, beating and suffocating ..." Woodruff advises them to be watchful at all times "lest evil spirits catch you unawares," and Betsy is "flooded with a feeling of terrible helplessness." She asks herself how God could watch over so many. "One little girl and one hundred—*If only it weren't so many*" (p. 264).

In another "short story," Betsy and her small sister Becky accidentally smother some kittens, causing another moral dilemma. Explorations into the minds of children were to become one of Virginia's trademarks. She was in many ways a little girl grown up who never hardened nor cut herself away from her roots. All of her novels seem unified by a consuming curiosity by which she was able to understand the problems of childhood.

At first the glow in the Eastern sky lulled Virginia and her publishers into high expectations from the Utah Saints. Her hometown paper, the Provo *Herald*, praised it, as did the *The Salt Lake Tribune* and the *Ogden Standard Examiner*. But word from the Mormon church's most influential publications, *The Improvement Era,* the *Deseret News,* and Deseret Book Company caused Alfred Knopf to write to Virginia: "I am very sorry about the news we had from Salt Lake City. And I confess rather puzzled by it."[15] Knopf had assured Virginia that she would outstrip Vardis Fisher's *Children of God*, published in 1939 by Harper and Brothers. "I think your novel so much better that the two simply cannot be mentioned in the same breath ... I think Fisher's a very pedestrian, unexciting performance which must have sold solely because of its sheer overwhelming bulk."[16] When a friend reported to Virginia that Knopf's ad for her book in *The Salt Lake Tribune* had motivated people to "line up at libraries to get the book," a Knopf publicist replied, "Rushing to libraries rather than to bookselling counters is not too pleasant for us ... but is perfectly understandable. ... The average person will read lots of novels, but not wish to own more than a few."[17]

John A. Widtsoe was not a literary critic, but his high office as an apostle in the LDS church gave him the power to review novels in *The Improvement Era*, the church's house organ. While crediting her "gifted style," he accused her of misunderstanding the "compelling forces" that had motivated the pioneers. She had portrayed Joseph Smith and his associates as "ordinary, rather insipid milk and water figures [that do not] comport with the historical achievements of the Mormon pioneers."[18]

The *Deseret News* weighed in on 15 May 1942: "Mrs. Sorensen has chosen a subject too often exploited and with which she appears to have little sympathy and understanding." The reviewer followed with an ad hominem attack. She was "a propagandist" who had committed the unpardonable sin of creating a doubter protagonist. "Mercy is not typical of those who believed in the doctrine." She patronizingly judges her for "her desire to avenge her own feelings ... [upon] a subject she so thoroughly despises."[19]

When the director of the Deseret Book Company wrote to cancel an order, he critiqued the book: "We think Virginia Sorensen has lost an opportunity. Our people have very high ideals ... The organizations have been of an exalted nature ... nothing of a base character ... like she portrays." Instead of citing the sexual or bed-wetting scenes that had shocked Widtsoe, he attacked a Relief Society gossiping bee, which he deemed unworthy "for one of our faith."[20] With the copy of this letter, a Knopf spokesman wrote: "[This] will explain to you why it is practically impossible for us to do anything for you in Utah ... But you may be sure that we will do everything we can for your book everywhere else." Virginia wrote across the letter: "The Powers have spoken! A virtual excommunique!"

That these three responses could be seen as killing sales in Utah makes Samuel Taylor's comment in 1967 especially appropriate: "I recently re-read four books that caused an uproar 25 years ago [Fisher, Whipple, Brodie, and Sorensen] and I stand utterly amazed. I wondered if these books weren't mainly the victims of bad timing. ... If they were published today ... with a little luck they might find themselves upon the shelves at Deseret Book .. [*A Little Lower than the Angels*] reads like something the *Improvement Era* would love to serialize."[21]

Utah notwithstanding, *Angels* had sold 7,800 copies by the end of May 1942, and it was reprinted a year later by Grosset and Dunlap. "A very respectable sale for anyone, particularly a first novel," said Knopf. "The times are out of joint and anyway, I think the book is going to sell, even if slowly, for a very long time." Indeed, it was successful enough that Virginia had trouble moving on to new subjects and new themes.[22]

Looking back, I am almost persuaded that non-Mormon reviewers of the 1940s understood Virginia's Mormon themes better than Mormons did. At the time the only acceptable fiction seemed to be that of "home literature"; anything else was judged to be "anti-Mormon." The term "Home Literature" was coined by Orson Whitney, an LDS apostle (1855-1931) who wrote biographies of church leaders and poetry of an "exalted" type. He urged the Saints to write a powerful literature that would at all times be "subservient to the building up of Zion."[23] In some minds literature that presented the weaknesses and the foibles of human beings could not be seen as building Zion. It was, therefore, judged "anti-Mormon" by a people still smarting from persecution.

In 1947 Ray West, a Utah critic and historian, declared that "the popular Mormon story is unavailable to the writer of fiction because it does not admit human error. The perceptive mind, which is the creative mind, is caught always between man's aspiration and his achievement. The imaginative writer ... may depict the tragic fact, the actual achievement. The unimaginative writer reproduces the myth ... and the result ... is cliché."[24]

As Leonard Arrington astutely put it, "By not producing their own imaginative literature, the LDS lost the image battle during the period of their Western pioneering. Not until the 1950s [did] the image begin to change." He cites the publication of pioneer diaries and histories by Juanita Brooks, Preston Nibley, and Dale Morgan. "Above all ... our image changed as a result of our production of a significant body of high quality imaginative literature by a number of people reared in our own culture."[25] He cites Virginia along with Vardis Fisher, Maureen Whipple, Richard Scowcroft, and Ray West. A poet might have cried out, "Give me critics to match my novelists!"

I believe that the god who raised up good novelists and historians in the late 1930s and 1940s had not yet called enough critics and publishers to accompany them. From my perspective in the 1990s, it appears that Virginia Sorensen was the first novelist to write seriously and movingly about the Nauvoo period. Instead of epic characters set down in exotic places to learn religious lessons from their trials, she had the nerve to place a young mother much like herself in a turbulent setting that asked the question, What happens to a happy family when the wife is required to share her husband with another woman? What happens to the adolescent children? Valid questions whenever any woman is forced to share her husband with another wife, with a mistress, or with a mother-in-law. This theme occupied Virginia throughout her career, and it mirrored another question: What happens when a woman is forced to share her husband with a faith, a church, a charismatic prophet?

For *Angels*'s heroine, Mercy Baker, a true insider-outsider, these are painful questions. She joins the church and follows her husband out of love for him. He in turn follows the prophet, and his loyalty to the church exceeds his love for Mercy. Indeed, he is constitutionally incapable of understanding her sensitive soul. Like the land, women are to be cultivated and made fruitful. It is one of the triumphs of *Angels* that Simon emerges as a sympathetic character.

Virginia's portrayal of better-known historical characters—Joseph Smith and Eliza Snow—posit the idea that the words *poet* and *prophet* were once joined; therefore, love between the woman that Nauvoo Saints crowned "Zion's Poetess" and the founder of the true church presents a dramatic paradox. I believe that Virginia identified with Eliza, having amassed a collection of her own poetry since childhood, added upon each year when she presented Fred with a hand-made book of these poems. Ivor Winters at Stanford encouraged her to produce a verse play. When former classmate Sam Taylor visited her at the birth of Elizabeth, he urged her to write for pulp magazines in order to make money. She replied that she was a poet. Years later Taylor paid tribute to her "lyrical gift [which] marked her as a modern Eliza Snow."[26]

Her portrayal of Eliza's love affair with Joseph shocked some

Mormons since it was difficult to imagine the prophet whispering words of love to a mortal woman—a fair-haired Romeo who quotes scripture as he kisses her eyes. Eliza says, "I don't like people to call me a poet because they ... expect me to go around spilling poetry and I can't. Poetic things just don't come to me while I'm talking" (p. 85). The prophet understands: "I know how it is. They're always expecting me to say beautiful things too. And I can't. Prophecies don't always just come to me when I'm talking either."

The prophet/poet theme mirrors another theme that became recurrent in her novels. "In heaven, Eliza," he tells her, "there will be lips and hands. Men and woman will love one another there." He takes her hand in his and says, "I will love you there Eliza!" (p. 97) Eliza feels the overpowering emotion of a quotation from Crenshaw that Mercy has given her: "Happy proof! she shall discover/ What joy, what bliss,/ How many heavens at once it is/ To have her God become her lover." This theme also provides impetus for Virginia's sixth novel, *Many Heavens.*

The relationship of Mercy and Simon echoes the ones between Joseph and Emma, Joseph and Eliza. Mercy loves Simon with worshipful loyalty as he worships his God. It would be tempting to deconstruct a text from Virginia's personal life—the romantic and dangerous temptation to make of one's lover a God, and vice versa.

Modern readers who fault Eliza Snow as a mere versifier also fault Virginia's portrayal of *Angels*'s lovers as too sentimental. But critic/historian Dale Morgan believed that a tendency toward sentimentalization was offset by her dramatization of the "age-old questions that are always new: on what terms a man and a woman may live together, what they can possess of life, and what life can do to their possession of each other."[27] I agree with Morgan that although her characters seem authentic in their setting, they exceed mere regionalism and could be set down anywhere else. Richard Scowcroft, another Mormon novelist of the 1940s, believed that "all literature is in a sense regional—that is, a writer writes from the social and geographical climate with which he's familiar ... Fiction comes out of human experience, and the Southerness of it, the Westerness, the Mormoness of it, is significant only as a meant of portraying human character."[28] Virginia decided that "It is not new sights that are important in writing, but new seeing." She learned to feel the "equal validity" of different, but co-existing patterns of life. She maintained that "Once we have recognized ... the great human struggle ... we may move in any crowd of strange or familiar faces but never again be unaware of the struggle—and of the importance of each individual."[29]

Some critics fault her historical research, however. For instance, Eliza was not Joseph's first polygamous wife in an unconsummated union. Considering that Virginia anticipated Fawn Brodie by three years and research and writing on Nauvoo and its heros by twenty-five years, she was quite successful in recreating a part of the brief idyll highlighted by historian Carol Cornwall Madsen in a study of Nauvoo women: "These women built homes that breathed permanence ... Latter-day Saint Marys and Marthas pooled their talents to introduce refinement and grace ... developing visiting rituals of friendship that became the basis of health and welfare services ... that would be transferred to Utah."[30] Like Madsen's women, Mercy was "often left alone with a farm and small children." Mercy joins a thousand Nauvoo women in signing the "brilliant defense of the Mormon cause, written by Eliza Snow and Emma Smith and presented to the governor of Illinois."[31] Virginia alternated such historical vignettes with intimate family scenes, at the same time avoiding the historian's label. "All my life I was escaping into poetry and stories, and I liked to embroider everything." When accused of writing "unsavory" scenes, she replied, "I didn't think they were unsavory ... I saw what was around me ..." When members of the family complained that certain details were wrong, she countered that the novel was a work of her imagination, based on her own experience. She said that "Some of [her] experiences can't be bettered, but I've never been able to satisfy myself with any description of how it felt to be in love."[32]

A writer can never render a living historical character as he or she really was. The writer must make the character fit the purpose of the story itself. Joseph Smith may have been vastly different from Virginia's conception of him, but as a character in *Angels* he is authentic. Mercy Baker was a real person, but she was probably not exactly the woman of Virginia's story. Indeed, in "real life" she was not a polygamous wife at all.

I think Virginia's use of historical background is quite sophisticated, slipping unobtrusively into the narrative. In her first meeting with Eliza Snow, Mercy is told that "when Brother Joseph first chose this place, some said he couldn't be right this time; they told him he'd need a boat to survey it. And he said, 'All right, then, build me a boat.'" Eliza adds that "it was Commerce when we came ... Brother Joseph said Commerce would be a name for a rowdy, whiskey selling settlement, and Nauvoo means 'beautiful place' and implies a place to rest.' And that's what we want—all of us" (p. 24). The story of Nauvoo's naming becomes part of Eliza's tone of voice, subtly explaining the lives of the people, and the prophet is introduced in a vital, human way. The persecutions of the Mormons, their trials in Nauvoo, so violently portrayed by Vardis Fisher, are not important to Virginia's characters except when the Mormons are preparing to leave Nauvoo. Then she has Simon set upon by Mormon haters. Brigham Young's conversation with Stephen Douglas, which results in the ousting of the Mormons from Nauvoo, is recounted when Simon asks his son to read the proclamation that "we propose to leave this country next Spring" (p. 375). (Virginia found a copy of this proclamation in Mercy Baker's sewing chest.) Polygamy is used to develop Virginia's belief that Mercy in the final analysis was always alone in her own skin. Polygamy, a test of her faith, becomes a lesson in life's more painful truths.

A speech given by a character in *Many Heavens* applies here. The hero, Zina, says, "The queer thing is the way our story is tied into that one peculiar little knot of Mormon history. It couldn't have happened just the way it did ten years before or ten years afterward. Yet the fundamentals—the love and the marriage—could have happened anywhere; they go back to the Prophets and ahead to the Millennium" (p. 10). Virginia loved a peculiar people, but she loved them for the traits they shared with the rest of humankind.

In an article written in 1955, Virginia summed up her philosophy: "For writers ... what is the lesson? The necessity for creating freely, certainly, but something more, the responsibility of preserving some web of significance that men can live by. And this too is only a part—for it demands not only freedom within a *tradition*, but an ever-widening tolerance for the traditional values of others."[33]

As for me, I think I know what it was like to live in that little city in a swamp, a city obsessed by grandiose dreams and in love with its prophet-king.

Ever since I was introduced to Virginia Sorensen's world in 1955 by my thesis chair, William Mulder, at the University of Utah, I have been her grateful friend. Mulder convinced me that she was a fit subject—a living, breathing Mormon novelist representative of a host of others I had not yet read. It is a clue to the culture that I could pass through graduate school without reading Maureen Whipple, Sam Taylor, Vardis Fisher, Fawn Brodie. Virginia was very productive, having written six novels with Mormon themes and three children's books. I was drawn to her characters and landscapes so much like those of my childhood. She had a Danish, Old World charm, a seeking spirit, and an observant eye. A year later, after reading her books and meeting her and her family, I finished my thesis, "Virginia Sorensen: An Introduction," and embarked on a mini-career as an introducer of her works at conferences, study groups, and in the newly-minted *Dialogue: A Journal of Mormon Thought.* Fifteen years later I was still introducing her in my role as editor of *Dialogue*. I had the privilege of introducing her in person to readers of *Exponent II* at a retreat that also featured her cousin, Esther Peterson. She had become part of Mormonism's "Lost Generation," a term bequeathed her and the other novelists of the 1930s and 1940s by the brilliant critic Edward L. Geary. These were those writers who felt unappreciated by their natural audience. Virginia felt keenly that lack of appreciation as was clear in a letter she wrote to Edward L. Hart in 1987: "I felt deeply the lack of sympathy out home and perhaps rather more deeply, the booing. Even the family said, 'Can't you let Grandma lie in peace?' When I had hoped to give her a kind of eternal life."[34]

In the world outside Utah, Virginia had been recognized for her superior children's books while her adult novels were being reprinted in other countries. She went out of print in America at about the time readers and critics were discovering her in Utah. In the 1980s and 1990s young scholars and teachers at Brigham Young University and other universities discovered what the critics and writers of the 1960s and 1970s already knew. But they added fresh new insights, some feminist, to the earlier considerations of

Edward Geary, Bruce Jorgensen, Eugene England, Linda Sillitoe, and John Sillito. They were published in independent journals and in the proceedings of the Association of Mormon Letters who presented her with a lifetime membership.[35]

Upon learning that she was being rediscovered by a new generation of Mormons and Westerners, she told me that she considered herself "now forever introduced. ... I have been your favorite windmill, but bringing forth sweet water."[36] When I asked her in 1980 what she felt about being read again, she said, "When your books are out of print and you've given them up to find that someone is reading a book that came out over 25 years ago is very hopeful. When I learned that *Dialogue* readers and professors and writers at BYU and in Salt Lake were reading me again, it made me very much want to do a good modern Mormon novel."[37]

At the end of the decade she was much in demand, invited to speak at Brigham Young University, Weber State, and at the Utah Librarians Association. Eugene England declared her to be "Foremother of the Mormon personal essay," and Dennis Rowley, archivist at BYU's Archives and Manuscripts library, announced that he was working on a book of "Conversations with Virginia Sorensen." (Unfortunately, both Rowley and Virginia died before the project could get underway.) She visited the scenes of her childhood in Manti and the graves of her parents in Provo, and decided to be buried near them.

When Bill Mulder inducted her into Phi Beta Kappa at the University of Utah on 8 June 1988, he declared that "Virginia Sorensen may be out of print but not out of mind." His perusal of the checkout record at the Salt Lake Public Library showed that she had been read enough to require rebinding of the books. Calling her Utah's First Lady of Letters, Mulder decided that at least one member of the Lost Generation had been found.[38]

All this leads us to the fulfillment of one of Virginia's dreams—to see her books reprinted. It is also one of mine—for the simple and wonderful reason that they make such good reading.

Notes

1. Virginia Sorensen, "Autobiography," *Something About the Author Autobiography Series, Volume 15* (Detroit, MI: Gale Research, 1983). All of the reviews and correspondence from publishers quoted in this foreword may be found in the Virginia Sorensen Archive, Department of Special Collections, Boston University Library, Boston, Massachusetts.

2. Gertrude Cronin, "Have You Heard about This?" *Terre Haute Sunday Star*, 28 Sept. 1941.

3. Harold Strauss to Virginia Sorensen, 27 Nov. 1941, copy in my possession.

4. Virginia Sorensen to Newell Bringhurst, 2 Feb. 1988, copy in my possession.

5. Orville Prescott, Review, *New York Times,* Wednesday, 13 May 1942.

6. Walter Prescott, "A Handful of Rising Stars," *Spring Book Supplement, New York Times Review,* 21 Mar. 1943, 13.

7. Wallace Stegner, Review of *A Little Lower than the Angels*, *Saturday Review of Literature*, 9 May 1942, 11.

8. Milton Rugoff, "The Mormon Paradise," *New York Herald Tribune Books*, Sunday, 10 May 1942.

9. Unsigned review, *Newsweek,* 18 May 1942.

10. Louis B. Salmon, "Mormon Family Portrait," *The Nation,* 10 May 1942.

11. Corbin Patrick, "Important First Novel by Hoosier," *Indianapolis Sunday Star,* 10 May 1942.

12. Marion Fradon, "Early Mormon Settlers on the Mississippi," *Chicago Sun*, "Books and Art," Sunday, 24 May 1942, 33.

13. Lewis Gannett, "Books and Things," *New York Herald Tribune*, Tuesday, 10 May 1942.

14. Clifton Fadiman, "Books: Three Novels," *The New Yorker*, 16 May 1942, 60.

15. Alfred Knopf to Virginia Sorensen, 12 May 1942, copy in my possession.

16. Alfred Knopf to Virginia Sorensen, 7 Jan. 1942, copy in my possession.

17. J. R. de la Torre Bueno, Jr., to Virginia Sorensen, 17 June 1942, copy in my possession.

18. John A. Widstoe, "On the Book Rack," *Improvement Era,* June

1942, 380.

19. Frank Winn, "The Bookrack," *Deseret News*, 15 May 1942.

20. Axel J. Andresen to Everett Stuart, 1 May 1942, copy in my possession.

21. Samuel W. Taylor, *Dialogue: A Journal of Mormon Thought* 2 (Summer 1967): 29-30.

22. She was never able to please Knopf again. Mother Sorensen had advised a joint project, so she and Fred worked on a combination biography/novel on Sam Brannan which finally reached 1,426 pages. Virginia was awarded a Guggenheim to Mexico to study Brannan's activities there, and instead wrote her 1951 novel, *The Proper Gods.* Knopf refused the Brannan book. "I did two versions of Sam ... before I put the whole mess in a box along with my marriage," she wrote (letter to Newell Bringhurst, 21 Mar. 1988). The fact is she stayed with the marriage through seven adult novels and four children's books, but that is another story.

23. Orson F. Whitney, "Home Literature," *A Believing People: Literature of the Latter-day Saints*, ed. Richard Cracroft and Neal Lambert (Salt Lake City: Bookcraft, 1979), 129.

24. Ray West, Review of *Sweet Love Remembered*, *Western Humanities Review*, July 1947, 303.

25. Leonard Arrington, "Mormonism: Views from Without and Within," *Brigham Young University Studies* 14 (Winter 1974): 150.

26. S. Taylor.

27. Dale Morgan, "Mormon Storytellers," *Tending the Garden: Essays on Mormon Literature*, ed. Eugene England and Lavina Fielding Anderson (Salt Lake City: Signature Books, 1996), 10, first published in *Rocky Mountain Review*, Fall 1942.

28. Richard Scowcroft to Don D. Walker, 25 Oct. 1946, copy in my possession.

29. Virginia Sorensen, "Is It True? The Novelist and His Materials," *Western Humanities Review* 7 (Autumn 1953): 284.

30. Lynne Watkins Jorgensen, Review of *In Their Own Words: Women and the Story of Nauvoo,* by Carol Cornwall Madsen, in *Journal of Mormon History* 21 (Spring 1995): 169.

31. Ibid.

32. "When You Are a Writer, You Write," Interview with Virginia Sorensen by Mary L. Bradford, *Dialogue: A Journal of Mormon Thought* 13 (Fall 1980): 29-30.

33. Sorensen, "Is It True," 283.

34. Edward L. Hart, "Writing: The Most Hazardous Craft," *Brigham Young University Studies* 26 (Summer 1986): 84.

35. See, especially, the *Proceedings of the Association for Mormon Studies* for 1994 (Vols. 1 and 2) and 1995.

36. Virginia Sorensen to Mary L. Bradford, 12 Nov. 1980.

37. Interview in *Dialogue* 13 (Fall 1980): 36.

38. William Mulder, "Citation Honoring Virginia Sorensen on the Occasion of Her Election to Membership in Phi Beta Kappa Alpha Chapter of Utah, June 8, 1988," typescript in my possession.

A LITTLE LOWER THAN THE ANGELS

BY

VIRGINIA SORENSEN

To

Mother S.

Who – like one divine –
Dispenses Truth
And Time.

What is man, that thou art mindful of him? and the son of man, that thou visitest him?

For thou hast made him a little lower than the angels, and hast crowned him with glory and honour.

Thou madest him to have dominion over the works of thy hands; thou hast put all things under his feet.

Psalms viii. 4–6.

The characters and situations in this work, except those drawn directly from history, are wholly fictional and imaginary, and do not portray and are not intended to portray any actual persons or parties.

A LITTLE LOWER THAN THE ANGELS

Chapter I

It must have been two o'clock in the morning when Mercy sat up, disturbed by a new light, and saw the red moon. Carefully, not to disturb Simon, she rolled off the tick and went to the window, leaning her elbows on the sill to watch it coming. Feeling her two heavy braids slip forward silently over her shoulders, she had a strange sense of having lived this moment before, the whole moment, the hour, the moon, the braids, even the sound of Simon sleeping. Perhaps she had lived it that night when she had first seen the prairie moon, leaning forward to put out the supper fire. On the endless road, only a few weeks ago. She remembered how she had scattered dust over a last blue blaze, and the braids slipped forward, and then, as she looked up – the red moon.

Looking back over the Mississippi and beyond over Illinois prairie, moonrise was a drama after dust and heat, and space was as terrible in extent as the sea at home. But here there was not the pallor that made the sea-moon a human thing. Here red, not white like a sensible natural moon. This moon stared at you like blood upon a sheet.

And the great river answered with a shaken scarlet line.

Mercy looked at the moon accusingly, distrustfully, as though blaming it for being different, as everything was different out here on the edge of civilization. Old blear-eyed Peeping-Tom of a moon, red-Indian of a moon. But as it rose higher, it paled, and presently was the moon she knew. There, that was better. After all, the moon had no right to be different anywhere. Even if a woman came west with her family, looking for home, and everything else changed, the land and the people and the talk even, and living grew to be an intense and difficult thing, she should still be able to look up and see the moon the same. And the sun and the stars. She needed them to steady her.

She heard Simon turn over, and as his breath became rhythmic once more, he began to snore, little quarter-circles of sound with a quality of abrupt breaking just as they were completing an ascent. She could trace part way around the edge of the moon with them.

Presently she went back to the tick, stretched yet upon the bare floor. The room was as bare as the prairies now, but she knew fullness awaited it, and was content. Like Simon said yesterday, the shapes for need come first, the beds and the cradles and the two benches and the plank table — then the gradual gathering together of things to make a body proud of home. She stood still, hearing a stir in the loft where the boys slept, but it ceased at once, and only a faint splashing of river broke the silence.

She could see Simon now, in the moonlight, and stood looking down at him as she loved to do. He was stretched full-length and his arms were flung out, as though in his sleep he welcomed all the world. His beard had grown long during the weeks of traveling and clearing land and building, weeks when a man labored every daytime hour and thought of nothing else; it made him look older than he did when he was clean-shaven. But even so, his mouth was young and pliant, tender almost, parted a little as he slept, and she loved it. She had always loved it, and the little swirl to his whiskers, and the width of shoulder and the blond hair heavy on his arms to the wrist. Even Simon's height she loved, beyond her so that from the beginning her spine must be stretched, kindling, for his kisses. A silly thing to think about, some might say, and it would never do for telling, but still, after all this married time, it was one of the things that mattered most. All the little things that made him Simon and nobody else, they were mighty important. The one Simon.

Queer what things a woman will think about when she wakes up at night and sees a moon!

As she looked down at him, affection was turbulent in her, the same, unchanged, as that night when he sat with his hat on his knee meeting the folks, and Father said, just to scare up talk: "There's history a-making out west." And Simon's face had suddenly turned to light and he said: "Yes, sir, and I'm aiming to help make it!" The same affection, but with a sharper point now, that made passion a better word, even for every day. That wouldn't do to tell folks, either, and she had never said a word when the silly women in the New York settlement used to come to sew and whispered in pious shocked voices how when they were pregnant they were cold under their husbands. With Mercy nothing had ever made her feel any different. She lived like a waiting and was always half-ready; after all, there's no knowing in this life when a moment is likely to come to you.

She leaned down and drew another cover over him; sometimes, here by the river, it cooled toward morning.

Through the window (unglazed yet because the glass must come up the river from New Orleans) a late firefly came and blinked curiously about the room. They had amazed the children out on the prairie, the millions and millions of them. Like a sky of stars come down for a holiday, and sometimes, as Jarvie said, looking as though a whole dipperful might have been dumped in one willow tree.

She opened the door softly and went outside to squat on the ground. Sometimes when a baby got heavy like this, there had to be relief two or three times a night. She saw that the moon was far up now, with a mist around it, a loose garment trailing ribbons. There was a little sound behind her in the shadows of the trees and she stood up quickly, her heart suddenly excited and her knees weak. Silly, some little creature—but she hurried as she moved to the house. Silly—but you couldn't know out here, after all. Iowa was still Indian country.

Yet she scolded herself: "When a woman is getting along the way I am, there should be no fear of night left in her"; a grown woman didn't go on peopling every dark corner with mysterious and terrifying images; and a mother must be up in the night, often without time for finding a candle. Yet never did Mercy walk in the dark without stumbling, without a feeling at her back that some creature was close, almost close enough to reach out and touch. Whenever she climbed down the loft steps from seeing to the boys, she felt something reaching down after her and would duck her head quickly, and when she climbed into bed again she would be conscious of a hurrying bend in her back as though she escaped by sheer quickness the design of a secret thing. It was a part of childhood, never ended. Even with four walls and a thick door bolted, her spine hurried, bending inward, and her head ducked, like the rear of an army, pursued and last exposed. And here in Iowa, with Simon's ax cutting at the wilderness and the cabin still unfinished and folks full of scary talk—

When she entered the door, she stopped abruptly and felt the door-frame sharp against her shoulder. Someone was coming down the ladder from the loft. Surely, surely taller than any of the boys. She could not move or speak, but stood gazing into the shadow. To the floor it came and then turned toward her. She shrank back, slinking around the frame. The figure came through the door, a hand stretched out, and when it entered the full moonlight she saw with sickening relief that it was Jarvie. Him, all right. But he was seeing nothing, she could see that. He walked steadily, his hand reaching, until he came into the clump of sloes at the edge of the clearing. He stumbled then and made a little sound, and she ran to him.

"Jarvie! What you doing?"

He turned his head but said nothing, and when she took his hand and led him into the house again, he came along like a little child. "You lie here by your father," she said, and he sank down on the tick, gone at once like falling down a well. She saw that he was almost as tall as Simon, stretched out like that. Traveling and working, you stopped noticing, you got so busy living you forgot to live. She knelt down and felt his forehead and found that he was very hot.

It had been – let's see, that summer Father came out to west New York to visit – three years this past June since Jarvis had walked in the night. When he was a child it had happened often. Never would she forget the first time, finding him in the dark, trying to climb onto the washstand, reaching, reaching. And after he got to be bigger, embarrassed when she told him next morning, not wanting to speak of it.

Well, there was always a reason if you could find it. He'd been working like a man, getting out timber. Sometimes Simon was likely to forget Jarvie wasn't a man yet. And that noon when he said he was tired, Simon had grinned and said: "Maybe Betsy better go help; Jarvie's tired." And when he overslept, Simon had shaken him and said: "Wanta stay home with the fat women, Jarv?" To Mercy he had said significantly: "Maybe there's another book that wants reading."

The one cross thing between her and Simon was that difference – and Jarvie was like her in it. When they wanted to bring all the books west, Simon said: "They want folks that'll work, not folks sitting around on their hinders reading books."

But it had been important to her, and the books had come. She had told Simon she'd rather leave her initialed silver, her bed-linen, anything else. You can't make a life out of things like that, or out of air or out of all that space on the frontier. You've got to take your life along with you.

She ran her hand down around the boy's cheeks and felt the hot neck and the rapid beating of the pulse in his throat.

Queer how many things a woman can worry about in the night.

The moon moved up past the window and on west until it turned to lusterless milk with dawn. She still sat on the edge of the tick. When it was quite light, she got up and made the fire. Simon heard her and arose, stretching, and she said to him, trying to keep the accusation from her voice: " Jarvie walked last night."

Simon raised his brows and touched the boy's shoulder. " Jarv! " he said.

" Let him sleep, Simon."

" Maybe if he works harder he'll sleep better," Simon said. " The rest of us don't have enough power left to be walking nights."

She said nothing, knowing anything she said would not help Jarvie's case any. But when he went off that morning, she did not like the look of his face.

ALL the morning of work, Mercy looked at the river. When she was in the house, it beckoned there at the window. When she was outside, it dominated the world. Especially since it was autumn and the sap was down and the leaves turning. Autumn was doubled in the river, and the sun was repeated with millions of bright motions, and these Iowa bluffs were in it, and over the river a great curve of Illinois was in it, too. Over there the river half-claimed the land itself, seeping up into swamp for a good distance, but here he encountered the bluffs and only where they gave out did he manage to crawl up into backwater.

Anyone near a river must look at it constantly. And the Mississippi, river of rivers, even folks born a stone's throw away look always at him, not aware that they are looking. If you exclaim, saying: "Beautiful!" they are likely to stare at you and say: "I guess we're used to it." But you see them looking.

To Mercy this river was yet a stranger, and her eyes embraced it with absorbed contemplation, aware of the full width and the mimicry of trees and the two excited furrows that followed the ferry. Awareness of all loveliness was implicit in her, as fear was implicit, as love was implicit. Wherever she had lived, the surrounding world had mattered much to her. She had a capacity for looking fully, for appreciating richly. There were those who said she was very lovely herself, and those who said she was only different, but nobody denied that the very way she looked at anything seemed subtly to enrich it. She was slight-boned and so small of stature that her husband liked to hold his arm out and show how she could stand under it, but she always seemed tiptoe with the force of her pleasure or concerns, as though, to carry all the emotion she must carry upon so slight a physical being, she must be sharpened and intensified. Her hair was heavier than it should have been for one of her stature, and dusky; massed as she wore it, it appeared darker than it really was. Women always envied her skin, for it had a shiny quality, very clear and very white, like the hinge of a clam shell. Her nose was slender and a little overlong in profile and her cheekbones stood at an unusual height, close under her eyes. Her father had considered her most beautiful in silhouette, and had her likeness made in Boston when she was eighteen and the two of them had traveled down to see Macready play *Hamlet*. She always kept it after her father died, between the leaves of her Bible, and for years it had been there, pressing the page in an oval at the story of Leah.

This morning she was restless and her natural discomfort was exaggerated by her feeling. She tried to think of this room as it would be. There the big bed, and it would be the same kind of bed, silly to keep thinking of another one back in New York – getting used to a new corner now and different bones. "The lowboy will stand close (like it used to) so's the linen will be handy. And the washstand right by the door so the boys will fairly fall over it to remind them."

The wind made free with her in her own house this morning, blowing out the comfortable smells of hoecakes and salt pork and bringing in swamp-smell and river.

It was getting on toward noon. She put potatoes to bake in the ashes and used the last of the meal for pone. As she straightened slowly from the hearth, she heard Georgie's furious voice. "You stepped on it!" And then he came running. "Mother, she stepped on my bake-cakes!"

Betsy peered in. "How'd I know they were bake-cakes? They didn't look like anything –"

"Be more careful, Betsy, you might know it was *something* he was making. Perhaps she didn't know, Georgie."

He started to protest, but she silenced him sharply. Through the open door she could see a woman coming up the path. A picture-lady without a wrinkle on her and wearing the proper little smile for calling. For a moment Mercy was aware only of a sharp recognition, and then she realized who her caller was and ran her hand down over her skirts to smooth them, rapidly worried her fingers with the wisps of hair that had escaped from pins. Eliza Snow, of all people, Eliza the poetess whose hymns everybody had been singing at the meeting last Sunday.

Eliza stood framed in the doorway.

" How do you do? " Mercy's fingers still tucked the long wisps under.

" Please don't trouble for me — " Eliza came forward, her hand outstretched, and when Mercy lifted her own hand a fervent pressure claimed it.

Georgie stood irresolute, then he dragged against Mercy's skirt and said: " She did, too, Mother, she knew."

" Hush," Mercy said. And to Eliza: " I don't know whatever to do, they're always at each other."

" Well — even Lucifer and Christ had a good argument! " Eliza said seriously.

" Won't you sit down? There's not much to sit on yet, but — " Eliza gathered her skirts forward with one hand and sat upon the bench. She looked up at Mercy.

" I can't stay long, Sister Baker, but I wanted to extend a hand of welcome to you and your family. We all hope that our troubles are over now, and that there'll be nothing for Zion but growing."

" Simon says Nauvoo is going to be the most beautiful city in the world! "

" All of us say it. Sometimes it's discouraging, but everything worth doing is like that. Remember the day you came in — that was the low point in our fortunes, there never can be a day more hard than that."

" The day we met you." Vividly the picture crossed Mercy's mind. She had been too tired to care about anything, but the children had been wild with excitement, and when they scrambled out to stretch their legs she had looked out and had seen the Mormon people for the first time. The people whose fortunes Simon had made the Baker fortunes. They were stretched out over the grass as far as she could see, and they were not sleeping; they were bitterly ill. She heard them crying out, she saw their heads lolling. When Brother Joseph came to the wagon with Simon, he told them about the swamp fever and how the people were too weak to fight it after that winter coming out of Missouri. Exposure and hunger start telling when the fever strikes, he said. She had sat and stared at them over their Prophet's head as he stood talking about the land to Simon. Hundreds of them, big and little, on the open ground and in little wide-mouthed tents, and in wagon-boxes. Eliza had come up from the river with other women, carrying wet cloths to soothe the fever. And Brother Joseph Smith said: "This is Eliza Snow – our poetess."

"The day we met you," Mercy said again. "Simon kept saying: 'So they were mobbed from their homes because they thought different – in this country!' He couldn't believe it. And I sat there thinking over and over: *Like this at the pool Bethesda. . . .*"

Eliza's face lighted. "I thought of that too, many times. And then I'd think: the Prophet Joseph is the angel sent down to move the water."

She spoke with restrained emotion as those speak who are accustomed to stern personal vigilance. Even her dress, painful in its simplicity, confirmed this impression, having a neatness of texture and line and a quality of minute perfection. Her narrow chest had little besides her precise breathing to lift it up; her arms were very long and slender, so that her whole identity was a flowing line in the consciousness, a line straight and yet flowing. Mercy had a feeling that she would like to loosen the brown hair, push it forward to release the sober mouth; then, as though to pass judgment for such a thought, the mouth curled easily.

"You're far along to have come clear from New York." Eliza looked into Mercy's face and not at her burden, even as she spoke of it.

"You know the saying – a baby rides easier in the belly than on the hip!"

" It was likely a man that said it."

Mercy laughed. " It likely was." Then she said, because something in Eliza seemed to compel complete honesty: " I didn't want to come. But Simon had to. The Elders came on a Wednesday and by Friday Simon was getting ready to move." She did not say how it had hurt her that a new devotion could suddenly supplant everything stable and settled in their lives. She did not say how it had hurt that Simon could drag her out over the same doorstep he had carried her over, going in. She had said nothing, even to Simon, and it had never seemed to occur to him how she might be feeling. His job was building the wagons and packing and getting good horses; hers had been demolishing and giving away and making the narrow choices that would fit in two wagon-boxes. He had been too full of the Prophet's message to think of anything but going to Zion. The Faithful were to gather in one place, the place had been chosen, every Saint with two hands was to hasten to Zion and build up the City of God. She understood that to Simon it was an edict.

" Sometimes," Eliza was saying, " a testimony of the work comes very quickly, and sometimes it grows slowly. I think folks have to lose something for it before they really know how much it matters. All those Saints you saw in Nauvoo have lost something for it, some of them have lost everything; and they're home-folks, too – they're not the kind that want to keep moving."

Abruptly she stood up and walked to the great space that would be Mercy's east window; the drama in her outstretched arm was not ludicrous in her as it might have been in some women, but belonged to her.

" When Brother Joseph first chose this place, some said he couldn't be right this time, they told him he'd need a boat to survey it. And he said: ' All right, then, build me a boat.' "

" Simon says the swamp can be drained all right."

"They're draining it, but of course it's slow, and there'll be fever till it's done." She stood still, looking, and when she spoke again her voice was gentle. "It was Commerce when we came, a couple of old shacks, but Brother Joseph said Commerce would be a name for a rowdy whisky-selling settlement. Nauvoo means 'beautiful place' and implies 'a place to rest.' And that's what we want, all of us. After he named it, folks began believing in it more."

"Nauvoo. All of us like it."

"I told Brother Joseph he got it from the two notes of a turtle dove, just before sun-up." She looked briefly at Mercy. "But of course it's from the Greek, as he says."

She looked out again. "At Kirtland and Far West we settled in other men's cities, and we grew faster than they'd ever grown and they were afraid of us. They didn't seem to like God so close, either, watching their ways!" There was an edge of bitterness in her voice. "So they pushed us out, they didn't even bother to pay us for our land or our houses. But now we've a city of our own – we're buying every foot of land we settle on and we're going to push back over the prairie and over the river here and north and south, every Saint on his own land." Her face was bright with pride and hope. "On that highest hill in Nauvoo the Temple will stand in God's name."

"Nobody will molest people who are building a city," Mercy said. "Goodness knows, there are plenty a-building all across the country. Every mud-spot we passed was going to be the biggest city in the West if you'd believe the folks building it."

Eliza stood very straight. "Remember, Sister Baker, we aren't building only a city – it's God's kingdom we're building."

She moved from the window and sat down again, searching in a petit-point bag she carried for a little record book. When she found it, she looked up, smiling. "I'm the Zion question-box. It's for the records."

Mercy answered her questions carefully. " Simon was baptized in New York, Chautauqua County, two years ago. Elder Benjamin Brown converted and baptized him, and he was ordained an Elder the same day. Jarvis Young Baker, our eldest son, was baptized that day, too, by his father. Amenzo and Albert, they're both past the age, but they'll be baptized when I am. I had to wait for the baby."

Eliza looked sharply up into her face. " Two years? " she asked.

Mercy flushed. " I'm not like Simon, I guess," she said. " Things go more slowly for me, the way you just said – "

" But don't put it off." Eliza's voice was sharp and anxious. " For one reason, it's a good thing to have waited. Now you can have the ordinance at Joseph's own hands, but go as soon as you're able. It will give you strength, it will give you power you've never dreamed of having. And then, besides, there won't be any suspicion – "

Mercy stared at her incredulously. So every gentile was under suspicion. Even now it was as bad as that.

Eliza hastened to explain. " It isn't that I wouldn't understand, of course, but the others have got so they don't trust anybody that doesn't belong. There's still a reward for the Prophet, you know, and somebody's always trying to get him back over the border to Missouri. Every man and woman and child in Zion must be aware of that danger before we're fully armed. Even among ourselves we have to be careful; there've been traitors before and there'll be traitors again."

They were silent for a moment, and then Eliza went on with her questions. When Mercy answered, her voice was unsteady. " I was born in Providence, Rhode Island, but we lived for a time in Massachusetts. Mother was Methodist. Father – well, he was Methodist, too, I guess. Simon was born in New York. I was teaching school when we met; he'd come to visit some of his folks and I was there to dinner – I went around, you know, to the homes of the children. Simon was eighteen then, and I was twenty-one. He was running a mill for a man in west New York, and already had a house he'd built. We lived there until we left for Nauvoo."

"It's a long time to have lived in one place."

"Yes. All the children were born there."

Eliza rose, smiling. "You'll live longer here, we hope," she said. "And there'll be some children born here, too."

When Eliza went to the door, Betsy and George were there, close together as loving as anything. Mercy saw that Eliza did not treat them as children but as she might treat people of her own stature and importance. She said: "How do you do, Miss Betsy?" and "How do you do, Master George?" Betsy curtsied deeply as she had been taught to do, but George ducked his head and ran around the house.

Eliza pressed Mercy's hand. "You and I are going to be friends," she said. "When your boy is born, I'll come see him."

Mercy raised her brows. "A boy?" she asked, laughing. "I have four boys already, and we thought a sister for Betsy –"

"A boy, this time," Eliza said certainly. "You'll name him Joseph."

There was nothing strained or self-conscious about her words; they simply came out of her. Mercy said: "Brother Joseph Smith isn't the only Prophet in Nauvoo, then?"

But Eliza was serious. "The spirit of God is prophecy, you know," she said. "Anybody with the spirit of God is a prophet." Her fingers slipped away from Mercy's fingers, and she was gone.

Mercy watched her until she disappeared down the bluff. "I know just what kind of poetry she writes," she thought. "Without ever seeing any, I know. Iambics as crisp as a pair of starched shams, and rhythms so sure and obvious there'd be no changing them in this world or another. Popey couplets, careful as egg-walking."

Onto the coals with the cornpone. But she still thought of Eliza. "Her religion is like a cloak over her, and when she speaks the Prophet's name there's something in her voice like reverence. If she was like any other woman, I'd say she was head-over-heels in love with her Prophet!" But you couldn't think of Eliza being head-over-heels in anything. Love, or anything else, would have to come over her slowly and decorously.

Then she forgot Eliza, forgot everything, because Simon came in and he was carrying Jarvie. He did not look at Mercy until he had laid the boy on the tick, and then she saw that his face was stricken. "He went right out," he said. "I've been trying to bring him out of it."

She was aware of her heart, beating sickeningly, sending waves of fear to her thighs, her calves, weakening her knees. "He shouldn't have gone this morning," she said, and was instantly sorry because Simon's face whitened and she knew he suffered enough remorse already.

Jarvis did not wake, but lay in a stupor all day long, only moaning sometimes. It was swamp fever, like the folks had in Nauvoo, and sometimes he shuddered with chills and sometimes sweat flowed off him like water.

"I thought if we built on the bluff, swamp fever couldn't get us," Simon said once.

"It's in the air," Mercy said, and shivered.

Chapter II

It is always the one who is sick that you are sure you love the most. Simon spent the afternoon getting the bed finished and the ropes bound on. When he lifted Jarvie up onto it, Mercy stood with her hands hanging and wondered whenever Jarvie's legs had grown out of Simon's arms like that. Simon stood looking down at him. "I should've known," he said. "Menzo and Bert were outworking him, two to one, and I wouldn't give him any peace. I kept saying I'd as soon have Betsy – "

"Fever hits sudden," Mercy said.

"If anything happens to him, it's my fault," Simon insisted. "I knew he was a worker and I knew he could stick, because he worked and he stuck on the way out here. I should've known."

"No use worrying over what's done; just do better another time."

Simon's voice was low and persistent. "Last night just before quitting, he said he'd sure be glad when the wood was all in and ranked and it was winter and we'd have to stay in. I said: 'Crosspatch, draw the latch,' and Menzo said: 'Sit by the fire and spin.' "

Menzo, his freckles sharp today against a white seriousness, wriggled on the bench. "How'd I know he was sick? "

"He never liked cutting trees, anyway," Mercy said. She had thought a thousand times today about what Jarvie said once on the trip west, after they had passed for endless æons of time through nothing but prairie grass, opening before the horses and closing in after the wagons like a great green eternal funnel. They had found a few trees at last, along a little river, and Jarvie lay under them, looking up. "If I had my way," he had said, "I'd never cut a tree down, never."

She had asked, smiling: "What'd we use to build our houses, then?"

"I don't know. Rocks. Bricks. Anything. Seems like it's awful to kill a tree. Seems like they're made just to stand there like that in the sun, turning the sun off you with their leaves –"

"I suppose they're glad to be of use," Mercy had said. "You know, Jarvie, there's nothing so wonderful as having a firm use in the world."

But he shook his head and mused. "Just standing there, making the ground cool under and stirring the air around," he said. Then he had looked at her in a way he had, different from any of the others. "I don't like the noise they make when they fall, either," he said. "They groan and the branches sort of sigh, settling down, and then they crack and it sickens you. It's worse than hog-killing."

And now for weeks, she reflected, he had been felling trees in woods where trees had never been felled before.

MERCY did not really believe the Prophet himself would come to bless Jarvie. Maybe a messenger or one of the Elders or somebody, but surely not the Prophet himself. But Simon said confidently that he would come and went over the river to fetch him.

Until she saw him coming up the road, she did not believe he would come. Even then she stood in the doorway straining her eyes to be sure. Simon, some stranger shorter than Simon, and then – she could not believe it. And yet she knew it could be nobody else. She had seen him only once, the day Simon bought this land and Joseph had signed the deed, *Isaac Galland, by Joseph Smith, Agent;* but once you had seen him, you knew him when you saw him again. The great shoulders, slightly stooped as though with the world's burdens on them, and bright hair that caught the light and made folks think significantly of halos. She stood and waited.

When he reached the door and held out his hand, her eyes met his and she was stirred as she had been at their first meeting. Luminous eyes, almost wild, yellow lashes falling over them like a curtain. Some called them shrewd, others called them glorious. His cheeks were pale, almost transparent, and she was aware of the long and delicate fingers that enclosed her hand.

Simon's face was triumphant; you'd have thought Jarvie was well already.

"In here," he said, and she stood back and allowed him to lead the Prophet to Jarvie's bed.

"This is Bishop Ripley, Mercy." Simon's voice was low, but she caught the pride in his voice. The Prophet and the Bishop of Montrose; now might not Simon be certain that he had found the Church of the True Democracy?

Simon, himself an Elder and entitled to administer, stood with the two others, and each laid his left hand upon the next shoulder and made a circle, their right hands upon Jarvie's quiet head. With the contact of the four bodies, the four powers would be fused. While Mercy stood watching, she saw Jarvie's body begin the ritual of the fever. Long shuddering chill, teeth chattering as though they rattled in an empty skull, and then swift engulfing heat.

"Your eldest son?" the Prophet asked.

"Yes, our eldest. Jarvis Young Baker."

"Has he been baptized?"

" Yes. I baptized him myself. Elder Brown was there; he confirmed him."

" Back home," Mercy said. The Prophet looked at her quickly and then smiled.

" Jarvis Young Baker, by the authority of the Priesthood vested in me I rebuke the weakness of thy flesh and command you in the name of Jesus Christ to rise and be made whole."

Jarvie moaned.

" Amen. Amen. Amen." And Mercy said, very quietly: " Amen."

Sometimes, the stories said, especially the Great Day of Healing in Nauvoo, the sick ones rose under Joseph's hands as though his hands were a magnet lifting them from their beds. Some of them even got up, folks said, and followed him to heal others. Sometimes it was like that. She looked at Jarvie hopefully, but he did not move, did not open his eyes.

The three men stood awkwardly for a moment and then they broke the circle and went outside; Mercy moved swiftly to the bed. Perspiration was rolling off him now, down his forehead and oozing out of his neck just as the scum of the swamp oozed from the ground. As though his body fought to liberate some terrifying poison.

Mercy heard Simon calling outside and turned away and went out to him.

Joseph looked at her, comprehending how near her time was. " Save yourself in nursing your boy," he said. " Save yourself all you can. He'll be all right. And you know there's more than one that deserves your care."

" Thank you."

She did not look up at him for fear he would see the disappointment on her face. If Jarvie could have got up and walked, like the others folks told about.

" There is a remedy we've found effective," the Prophet went on, " and we're not among those who won't advise remedies when faith is lacking." She felt the rebuke and looked swiftly at Simon, knowing he would be cut to the heart.

"Take the bark of the wahoo, of the prickly ash and wafer ash, and of the wild cherry. Soak it all a time in water and let it cook on the fire. When the liquor is cool, strain it off and let him swallow it. And wash his body with it."

"Thank you," she said again, gratefully. She was conscious of his earnest eyes, so deep under his lashes, and thought, remembering Eliza: "It would be easy for a woman to love him very much."

When she returned to Jarvie, she found him unchanged. When faith is lacking. Who, then, lacked faith? Surely not Simon, who had crossed the river to fetch the Prophet. And not Jarvie, who believed everything good to believe, being still a boy, for all his unnatural tallness. Then who?

Mercy Baker, she was always one to wonder. One of the neighbors had even told that to Simon just before he married her. *Mercy Baker has always been one to wonder.*

When she heard the Prophet and Bishop Ripley saying good-by, she hurried out the back door to bring a bag and one of Simon's knives. When he came in she went to him, holding them in her hands. "Here," she said. "You'd better hurry before it's dark."

He stood still and looked at her, and on his face was an expression she had seen only once before, one time when he caught her telling a little but bald-faced lie to make a situation easier.

"Jarvie'll be all right," he said.

She felt as though her bones were cooling in her skin. But she spoke stubbornly. "You heard what he said, Simon—wahoo and ash and wild cherry. You heard him tell me, Simon!"

"And you heard what else he said. And you hear me, and I say Jarvie'll be all right."

Then he went out, quickly, as though he did not want to hear her answer. She stood without moving for a long time, hearing his footsteps down the bluff, his heels banging on the rocks he'd set in for steps on the steep places. Then she could not hear him any more. There was only the sound of Georgie digging outside the door. Little ground-hog Georgie, he'd rather dig than anything. You had to watch him the way you'd watch a puppy or he'd dig up everything you planted.

Betsy came to the door and stared in solemnly. Betsy had an extra sense that smelled trouble on the wind.

"Is Jarvie awful sick, Mamma?"

"Yes. Very sick."

For a moment Betsy stood staring at the bed, fascinated, and than she disappeared again. Mercy turned to the boy on the bed. He lay in a welter of sweat with his eyes blank as a statue's and his mouth sagging. A little sound came out of his throat at perfectly even intervals; not a word, but a sound. A descending sound forever on the same note. Mercy went outside and wet a cloth in the cool water Simon had brought from the spring, and returned and wiped the boy's body. The air was cool today, but a heat sprang from his body that was like summer heat.

"Jarvie!"

The little sound, not an answer.

Mercy Baker was always one to wonder. She felt frightened tears in her eyes and brushed at them fiercely and got up on her feet. Then she wiped his face again, went deliberately to pick up the sack and the knife, and went out.

"Betsy, Daddy and the boys will be home soon. You're big enough to watch out for Georgie a little while, aren't you? Don't let him go down the bluff, but just play here together, the two of you. If anything comes, if you see a snake or anything, go in the house and shut the door."

"We want to go with you, Mamma."

"I want to hurry, Betsy—if I go alone I can hurry. I'm going for something to make Jarvie better."

She went back into the house and brought out another spoon and two kettles. "Here, you can dig with Georgie. You can play cooking. You pretend mixing and there's water in the bucket there."

Instantly they were absorbed, and she left them.

The woods were mad now. The wild, the terrible prodigality of autumn surged through her senses as she walked. First down the gulch, watching carefully where her feet caught hold. Her unnatural belly made descent difficult, made her breath come sharply. She remembered she had seen wahoo down Stony Hollow, just below the spring. The first she had seen in this place—today it should be crying out with autumn. Her eyes were alert for scarlet berries trembling on their little stems.

Already one walked deeply, crisply, feet pushing ahead with a great whisper. It came to her: "Jarvie loves autumn-wading—he loves to run through leaves and push them into piles and jump into them."

A sudden burning assailed her ankles and she lifted her skirts to see beggar lice clinging in brown knots to her stockings, every bur ripe and seeking sharp hold. She leaned a little, but to reach was agony now, so she straightened and went on. There would be more, anyhow, no use pulling them now. As she walked, her skirts were peppered with burs, pointed ones and round ones, all wicked and clinging, tenaciously concerned for a far-flung posterity. She saw a squirrel running along the bough of a tree with an acorn in his mouth, also involved in an eternity of summers and winters. She wanted to call out to him: "If I could come up there with you, these burs couldn't get at me." And she thought of Jarvie again, Jarvie who loved to climb the trees, a little one until it leaned and yielded a pathway into the next, and on in the trees, one day nearly to the spring, he said.

She saw that the fruit of the pawpaw had fallen, that strange fruit yet clinging together in twos and threes and looking like feet caught together at the heels. Pigeon berries were white on the boughs and the rich red plush on the sumac was falling.

Then she saw wild cherry stones on the ground, a million bone-white beads dropped at a thousand bird-feasts, and she took that bark into her bag first, working at the tree with feverish intensity. Then she went on. There it was, burning bush, just where she had remembered. Maybe Moses saw wahoo, just at dusk. She broke off little boughs with her fingers and stripped them. Then she cut some bigger ones and stripped them also.

Ash. She went on, over the rocks in the gulley bed, stepping with care where the ground was damp below the spring. At the pool she knelt and dipped up water with her hands. She knew she would find ash where the ground was low and damp; no use climbing on up the hollow. She remembered her father singing one of those little songs he made for her to remember by. "Comes last of all, early to fall!" By now it would be almost bereft of leaf.

She walked back a little, searching, watchful for ivy, bright now with warning. She could hear father once more: "Leaves three, quickly flee!"

Dear and familiar, everywhere woods were the same. Variously populated in different places, but usually these few old friends. And this common enemy.

She saw at last what she was searching for, a bush of prickly ash up the gulley where a smaller spring seeped down into the greater one. She lay the sack over her shoulder where it would distress her progress least and crept past the spring.

There was a place where water had washed the earth down and left a deep wound in the ground under a great oak. Almost indecent to gaze at the vitals of that tree so intimately, all the swarming roots that were usually so secretive and so protected, slim festoons of root, great branches and crotchets of root. " Underneath, everywhere, it is like that," she thought, " roots white as bone, meshed and crossed and pushing and searching." She straightened a moment to rest and suddenly her eyes widened, she caught her breath, every muscle intent.

Swiftly then she moved on, her eyes held unshakably on the tree she sought. Abruptly she stopped again, and this time she leaned forward and supported herself. No, no. Very still, she waited, and it came again. Slow pulse of pain, familiar as breath. Down the abdomen like a pressure, opening the spine and pressing forward and down into the thigh. She knelt and leaned her face forward upon her arms until it was over. Then she rose. Once she glanced back, and then on at the ash. That she would get too. There ought to be time – it was just beginning. She walked slowly and when pain came she knelt and waited until it subsided. Every movement deliberate until she came to the bush, and then she worked swiftly at the boughs, oblivious of thorns. Her fingers were strong and quick, tearing at the bark. Her mouth grew firm and determined, but presently she leaned forward, moaning.

" You Mercy Baker," she thought. " It's a good bit home! " Twisting the bag over its contents, she hoisted it gently to her shoulder again and started back, but even before she reached the spring she had stood waiting many times. It kept coming to her what old Hetty Bryan had told the neighbors back home after Betsy came – " Never a woman so little as Mercy Baker and yet could drop babies like an Injun – one, two, three, there you are! " Now she remembered in a panic, remembered her own assurance that the waiting hours other women spent walking their floors and well attended would be sweet beside the sudden rending she always knew, the urgent plunging heads that split her apart like an apple.

" Let me go home. Wafer ash – look for the seeds on the ground now. Round wings. Let me get home."

And it was home and all home could be, up there on the bluff so close she could almost see it. It was home and she bent to it with all her strength. There were walls around and a place in it for pain where you could call out and somebody would answer. You could shut the door and lie down on the tick and peel off the burs with your stockings.

She rose to her feet once more, but before she could move any farther her legs wavered beneath a fresh onslaught of pain. Determinedly she stood straight and found her face among crisp-voiced leaves. There was a cool motion in them and a brittle voice. Like a bright rapier, pain entered and descended and left a trembling waiting wound.

No use. She sat down and put her fingers to her mouth and called. " Simon! Simon! " And then unreasonably, strangely: " Father! "

" I don't belong here in this place, I don't belong here. I belong in another world. Indians and animals belong here, bearing their young against the ground. But I don't belong here. I belong on a bearing bed in a room with a door shutting the world away and a woman waiting with her hands cool and firm."

" Simon! "

And then it was another kind of pain, charging and urgent, and she knew it well, answering from her throat as an animal would answer. Pain was a fierce hand upon her now, and she ceased to struggle against it but loosened her mouth and breathed deep. She tried to call again but could not, only making with her mouth strange noises she could not control, a terrible pushing and grunting she had heard before. She looked up at the flame-colored branch that swooped over her. Oak and blood-colored, oak and the color of blood. She thought: "You have heard these sounds before."

She reached down and lifted her dress and smoothed her white petticoat beneath her, dragging at the burs with insensible fingers. She made wide deliberate motions and then lay back and the sound came again from her throat, from depth of throat. It came to her, without words really: "Perhaps I belong here after all with the leaves and the squirrels and the brittle bark. So they come to their time alone, the animals, and pain wraps them, plays over them, leaps over them and plunges down. Feeling and no words, feeling like the earth must feel, water trembling and seeking with water strength for the light and struggling through stone for the light. Stirring the mere size of a seed and wound the mere width of a root. Lie still, lie still, and let there be no sound but a soft rending."

Sudden liquid drenched her thighs. "For a hand, oh God – Try, my blessed, help me. You are not alone, I am here. For a hand."

At last she sat upward a little and moved the child apart. When the quiet patient pain had ceased entirely and she could move through vast weariness, she ripped a thread from the ragged bag that held her precious bark. "It's a good thing I brought this knife," she thought, and smiled at her unreason. The baby's voice was like the descending wail of a cat-voice. She took him close and felt the swelling stomach, hard with screaming. "You hush, Joseph," she said. "You great big boy, you hush."

She wrapped him in her apron and laid him down for a little, while she sought her wafer ash.

❧ ❧ ❧

It was early candlelight when she came to the house again. Always dusk lent peculiar clarity to sound and for a long way as she came she heard the voices of her children, sharp and clear. She could even hear their spoons against their bowls and she knew Simon had poured the milk and had broken bread. They were incredibly warm and intimate, she thought, in their widening circle. And the house was beautiful, set so high and candles warming the windows.

She heard Simon come from the house and saw that he held a bucket in his hand, empty from the easy way it swung. He started down the hill and then he saw her, saw her to know her in the dusk and yet he saw nothing but that she was there.

She waited and he laid the bucket on the ground and came to her.

"Mercy," he said, and his voice was vibrant with wonder, "Jarvie's been wanting you. I was just going for more milk down to Turner's. Mercy, that Jarvie got right up out of bed and nearly emptied the bucket!"

Even that was not strange.

"Mercy – for Christ's sake! *Mercy* –"

Suddenly she sat down upon the ground, sat on her haunches like a child, and he leaned to her. She remembered that she had not yet shed a tear, but now that he was here she felt the tears breaking like a storm. There was a horrible jerking of the muscles at her mouth as he lifted her and she turned her face to his breast, weeping weak and easy tears.

Chapter III

SIMON went down the hill, stumbling. Past the old barracks, they had told him, and then the first cabin. He was relieved when he saw a candle burning there; Mother Turner was at home, then. His fist rumbled on the door, and he thought: "This door is used to folks being in a hurry."

Mother Turner came to the door, already pulling her cape over her shoulders. When she saw Simon she said: "I was thinkin' she was due!"

"It's here," Simon said. "It came before I could come for you. But she's not well, there's too much bleeding – "

They started up the hill, and Simon tried not to hurry her, but he kept finding himself ahead, his anxiety pulling her along.

"If it's here," she said once, panting, "I'm sure there's not so much use for the hurry. Did you wrap it?"

"Him," Simon said. "It's a boy. He's in the cradle already."

Mother's body was wide and short and competent, and her hands were strong with long service. Her hair was black save for a straight line from the forehead, nearly an inch wide, that had turned white as wool. "I'm marked," she always said, "marked like a skunk, and I can't fool nobody."

Nor did she try. Her laugh was honest and you could trust her words if you allowed for the natural exaggerations of good talk. Her strength was a legend through Mormon settlements.

" Once I brought twins to Sister Lucham," she liked to tell folks, " and when it was safe over I walked two mile home and laid down and had twins of my own. Seemed like I was inspired."

When she came into the house it was as though the very walls sighed with relief at her coming. Mercy sighed, looking up at her.

Mother took off her cape, frowning and laughing at once. " You're a reflection on my profession, you are," she said. " Your husband was tellin' me – goin' out in the woods and havin' a baby like a rabbit." Her voice grew tender while she looked at Mercy's white face and turned down the covers. " You're too little to go gaddin' by yourself in this country, anyway. You ought to stay home in your house. But if it ever happens again, you pull your skirts front and hold tight till you get help for yourself. I knew a woman kept her baby back two hours, sittin' firm on a chair. And her boy had a flat-topped head all his life, but good brains in spite of it."

George crawled onto the foot of the bed and she thrust him away with a swoop of her arm. " Outside with you," she said. " And I'll get me a switch if you don't stay off'n her! "

George ran off, sniffling, and Mercy started to speak; but Mother interrupted. " I won't break his nose," she said, " but it might as well start a-bendin'."

Mercy took a deep breath and turned her face to the wall.

Some of the neighbors thought it was a good long time for Mercy Baker to stay in her bed for a childbirth. Yet even when she went to the christening, two weeks after, her knees were not so brave as she'd have them and she was glad to sink down on the bench in the grove. She saw the look of Simon's face, smug as he sat down with his new son in the circle of his arm.

Well, wasn't it a thing to be smug about, the row of his own there beside him? Jarvie and Amenzo and Albert and George in their good black suits, and Betsy prim in her pinafore with her braids tied like a little lady's, her hands clutching her Sunday handkerchief?

Twenty-seven babies to be christened this day. And the mothers tipping and rocking and nursing, waiting their turns to look proud and set out from the others.

When Simon's name was called from the rostrum, he stood up and carried his son forward, and Mercy stirred in her seat with a faint apprehension she always felt when one of the family rose in company.

Brother Joseph took the child from Simon, inquiring: "The name, Brother Baker?"

"Joseph. Joseph Benjamin Baker."

The shadow of a smile passed over Brother Joseph's face. Today there were a preponderant number of little Josephs, even little Josephines.

Simon himself made part of the circle. And it was a rich blessing the Prophet sealed on the head of Joseph Benjamin. Long life, virtuous life, a life of preaching the Gospel among far-flung nations. And it promised: "Thou, Joseph Baker, shall be a judge of men."

"A judge!" Mercy thought, thinking of her father. He would study law, then, this little Joseph, now as far below the complications of law as the first human creatures in the Garden, even wetting his clothes for the blessing and wailing up into the voice of Brother Joseph himself.

Simon tiptoed to his place again and handed Joseph Benjamin to his mother; she opened her dress at once and filled his mouth with nipple to stop the noise he was making. Other babies were carried forward and back to the benches again.

Suddenly all eyes were on the rostrum, for right in the middle of a prayer something had happened to Brother Joseph. He stumbled to a bench, his hands over his eyes, and sank down, leaning forward on his knees. Mercy heard the furious flurry of concern, the people crowding forward and being pushed back. Presently Brother Joseph shook his head and rose, lifting his hand for silence. The room waited, tense, only the babies clucked and crowed and wept.

Joseph walked forward unsteadily and leaned on the rostrum. Then he said: " I am all right now. While I was blessing your children, I saw clearly that Lucifer would exert his influence to destroy them and I strove with all the faith and spirit I had to seal upon them blessings that would secure their lives upon this earth. In so doing, such a great virtue went out of me into the children that I became weak."

The people were still, absorbed in his white face, and Mercy heard a man behind her whisper: " Almighty God! "

" Remember," Joseph said, " the woman in the eighth chapter of Luke who touched the hem of Jesus' garment and took virtue from him. The virtue here referred to is the spirit of life; and the man who exercises great faith in administering to the sick, blessing little children, or confirming, is liable to become weakened."

He smiled. " Bring the little ones; I am strong again."

For a moment, as he stood there, his figure merged with another figure that he had called up by his words, and a wave of feeling passed along the benches.

Mercy heard the man behind her scraping his boot-heels on the ground, heard him distinctly as he whispered to somebody beside him: " The God-damned Christer, him! "

She glanced quickly at Simon, but he had not heard; he was completely absorbed in another blessing that Joseph was speaking over the head of another child.

Chapter IV

THE THINGS folks can do together is a wonder. Simon, giving his tenth day of labor to the building of the Temple, marveled as he worked. " Just figger it out," he said to the man working next to him, " in five years, giving one working day out of ten for a tithe of labor, I'll have worked one hundred eighty-two and a half days, and that's a half-year of solid work. You do the same, and every Brother, through the whole Church. You see what we'll have when we're through."

Any Saint would tell you, besides, that work given was superior work if it was given ungrudgingly. They would tell you, as Simon told Mercy, that stone came from the river-quarry more easily when it was meant for the Temple, and it was easier to lift, stone for stone and hundredweight for hundredweight. What was it the Prophet had said to the workers to begin with? " If one man may build, what may two men build? A hundred men, a thousand, a thousand thousand men? "

Mercy sat among the women at Susie Yeaman's quilting and thought of what Simon had said, because here it came to her: " If one woman may build, what may a dozen women build? " How would Susie have done this long work alone, with what effort and weariness? But here were a dozen bright needles going in and out, steadily, digging through the fabric swiftly in long lines. Gradually the frames rolled inward; you could hardly believe how fast.

Talk was free at the quilting, and there was as much pricking with tongues as pricking with needles.

"It'll serve her right if her baby comes hard. I for one don't care how sick she is."

"Oh, Portia, that's not even Christian."

"Neither's sin Christian and Christians shouldn't tolerate it."

"And did you hear – "

Whenever Polly Yeaman or one of her sisters came in with biscuits and cake, the conversation flagged noticeably. Susie Yeaman shooed them like chickens, shaking her apron after them.

"It's a wicked shame – a woman can't walk out with her children but she meets that crazy man with his hands busy in his pockets."

"He does no harm to a soul. But the way he wears clothes out is a wonder. I took him a pair of Asehel's old pants – just a year worn – and in three days they weren't fit for a man to walk the street with. But there he walked by our house, spry as if his bottom didn't show behind him."

"Brother Joseph says he's a son of God, with brains or without, and nobody's to hinder him."

Lettie Smith worried to get her say in. Her husband was a true cousin of the Prophet, and President of this Stake of Zion. They had all heard her story before and sat stoically through it. After all, there were plenty such stories, and a body got sick of talking about Missouri.

"There I sat, in the seat of the wagon with my three little ones, and my china on my lap while the mob chased us out. Not a piece was broke, not so much as a chip – "

"I know some – oh, not you, Lettie! – that worries more about their china than their daughters." Portia Glazier spoke self-righteously. Mercy looked quickly at the long stern face that refused to compromise with joy. "Upon that face," she thought, "has been set the signet of sorrow, and wherever it goes it will press the whole air and stamp it with misery." "If I'd a daughter," Portia was saying, " she'd not tramp the woods with a boy the way Naomi Fordham does. They go for stones to line the walks with! "

" When the walk's lined, they'll border the flower-beds."

" Anything to get to the woods."

" And did you hear – "

It seemed they wanted to talk of little else, these round-shouldered weary women, these sag-breasted women who had nursed many babies and raised them or lost them. Was it ever really over then? Mercy wondered. Was it an ache that persisted in them, even after bearing was past? Their fingers flew faster with the spice of suggestion, the sugar of scandal, curiously quickened eyes following their needles. As though it were forever new, strange and charming and blood-stirring. She looked at them, the sharp lines of their faces, the lines cut with weariness and years and emotion. She looked at their hands with the knuckles hard and protruding. She looked at their breasts, swooping in unlovely lines where once had risen soft hills that lifted with breathing. She looked at Melissa Vermazon, who had lost four children in the Missouri purge and had left half her mind behind her in Missouri. Melissa's face was a sunless gray and in her eyes was the suspicious yellow of anemia. And again at Portia.

Black-clad, a gaunt crow in perpetual sorrow, resenting the world's joys because her own were lost, her croaking theme was *If Charles had lived*. But Charles had not lived; he had died a martyr to the Church, and what thanks did Portia owe that Church for a rotting house and a little food and firewood? It was whispered that she never so much as offered the Brothers a thank-you, but only said always: " If Charles had lived, I'd be requirin' help of nobody."

But Charles was dead. She had lifted his riddled body herself and carried him to the barn when the house had burned, and in the night she woke from sleep of exhaustion to find the barn afire and was barely out of it before it was a pillar of fire and she could smell Charles burning. What thanks to the Church for that, I ask you!

Mrs. Fordham came late, when her family scandal had been long exhausted. She spread in her chair, her flesh drooping over the sides in great cushions and her words coming shallowly from her chest, perpetually panting.

" I was just like Naomi before I married Lije – he could span my waist with his hands."

" Well," Portia said, " I'd not tell it aloud till Naomi's safe married off."

Mercy looked at all of them. Here they were, the end of desire denied now, to most of them, and yet the desire still stirring in them, still shining from their fagged faces, their full-throated laughter still responsive. It was in them then, and remained anxious if not passionate, like the tongues in their mouths.

Next to Mercy sat Peter Cuddeback's soft wife (Peter would be teacher at the stone school when it was finished), and Mercy noticed that she wore gray as though she had created it expressly for herself.

" What you thinking so sober, M's Baker? "

" Oh – I was just thinking – " Mercy spoke in a low voice, impulsively. " I was just wondering if people ever grow too old – "

She hesitated, but, to her surprise, Mrs. Cuddeback began to laugh and her dimples came running out, more like wrinkles now and so much like Peter's own you'd think she'd caught them from him during long and intimate living together. " M's Baker wants to know," she said loudly to the others through her laughter, " M's Baker wants to know how long it lasts! "

Mercy turned scarlet, but Mrs. Cuddeback patted her hand reassuringly. " I used to wonder, too," she said, and laughed again. " Well, I'm glad to tell you it lasts as long's you want it."

Mrs. Peck, she who came from one of the farthest farms out on the rich bottom lands, jabbed her needle fervently into the thick fabric. Mercy had always thought her a lewd and common woman. "Oh, yes, M's Baker," she said, delightedly, "they say the older the ram, the harder the horn!"

Polly Yeaman came in just then with a plate of refreshments and the laughter abruptly subsided. But behind their backs Polly showed her teeth, grinning as she moved around the circle with honey and biscuits. She thought: "They think I don't know what they're talking about."

Mercy was shocked that she had precipitated so much, and said hastily: "I want to tell you about a quilt I made when I was engaged to Simon. Every time I work on calico like this, I think of it. The pattern was clusters of tiny stars, you know the one. It seemed then as though nothing but poetry would do to write to Simon. And I wrote a verse about that quilt. It keeps coming back to me when I work like this, just the way it did when I wrote it, to the rhythm of the needle."

Mrs. Cuddeback patted her hand. "Can you remember it, deary?"

"I think so." Mercy looked around again at their faces. They were ready for soft things, too, these women, they knew life every way. But not enough was soft for them; sometimes they forgot there was anything soft and tender left in the difficult world. Long days of body-work and short nights of body-pleasure, but their minds little nourished. She began softly and gently, mindful of each word as one of her teachers had been at school, the one teacher she remembered vividly because he had read poetry like slow singing. She sighed as she spoke the simple verses, in the places a girl might sigh.

"Stitch and stitch and one and one,
My darling comes when this is done—"

She looked around at their listening faces, and sometimes she leaned a little and slipped her needle in and out with the words:

> "Prick and prick and prosy, prosy,
> My darling will be warm and cozy."

She saw Melissa Vermazon looking at her strainedly, Portia looking down embarrassed. When she finished they were all quiet for a moment and then Mrs. Cuddeback pressed her hand, fervently. "It was just sweet," she said. And Polly Yeaman lingered to listen, unreproved.

Chapter V

THE HOUSE was closed and chinked and winter settled down.

Simon went to the first Nauvoo election, riding Ginger because she gave him a sense of youth and spirit, a sense of importance. Ginger danced under him, responding. You would think, Mercy always said to herself when she saw him riding off, that Simon would be prouder of a bit of flesh he begot himself.

He did not generally seem to be. And yet today, just as he was ready to leave, he turned abruptly to Jarvis and asked if he would like to go along. As though he had suddenly remembered how close to manhood Jarvie was getting to be.

It was as great a day for Jarvie as that day when everything was ready to move west and Simon had handed him the reins for the second wagon. "It'll be a long old haul," he had said, looking steadily into his son's face.

It hurt Simon that, living in Iowa, he could not vote in Illinois, because what concerned Nauvoo deeply concerned him whether he lived there or not. But he could have his say, nevertheless, and guard at the polls all day with the Brothers.

Men were pouring into Nauvoo, in carriages and on horseback and afoot, to lay their power in one place for certain men to take in their own hands and use as they saw fit. They stood in knots on the street corners, their boots mired, and when Simon dismounted and joined some of them, Jarvis was close to him, listening. They talked of elections and governments and city charters and habeas corpus and courts and constables. They spoke of these things intimately as men do who make them with their own power. These were, after all, the men who had broken from the clots of good Yankee blood coagulating in Eastern cities, with an eye to putting new and better cities where none had ever been before. Not many months since, these corners where they stood had been unmarked, like all the rest of this country of swamp and willow. And they were proud of themselves. The city of Nauvoo was theirs and they looked at it, stroking it with their eyes as they might a horse of quality. Nauvoo, crawling over the flat and up the hill like a live thing; steamboats unloading immigrants with knapsacks over their shoulders and wide eyes in their faces asking advice of men who owned land already; wagons rolling in from the east and south loaded with furniture and children and banging skillets and sides of bacon.

"There's a little place up north has a good site, too – Chicago, they're calling it; and Springfield has the state government, that mud-spot on the road that folks pass on their way to Nauvoo! But this will be the City of Cities. Isn't there already a charter, signed by the Governor, that makes Nauvoo pretty near a city-state? What do they have, those Eastern cities, that won't be right here on the frontier when we've voted and set our power in motion? We've brought the whole danged world here on our wagons!"

It was all satisfaction, a song of self-praise, until Brother Joseph came riding along on Old Charley, and beside him was riding that new man, Dr. John Bennett, who had just come with Brother Joseph from Springfield.

"Why's he so important? Who is he, anyhow?"

"Quartermaster-General of the State of Illinois. He's got Connections at Springfield, took a lot of trouble lobbying for the charter. They say Brother Joseph promised him if it went through, he'd be Mayor of Nauvoo. First Mayor of Nauvoo."

They twisted their heavy heels in the mud on the corners. Brother Joseph didn't go around making promises in Nauvoo or offering benefits and offices. For the work of God, he always said, and he who asks rewards and benefits isn't worthy of being in God's hire.

Sidney Rigdon's ring of whiskers twitched at the sight of John Bennett. He, too, had been an elegant gentleman in his day. But a man didn't wear white stocks and good hats and carry gold-headed canes while he built in a swamp. And now this John Bennett walked carefully where the Brothers had laid timbers for his benefit.

Sidney understood more than these men did, standing on the corners. He knew that Brother Joseph was not going to depend upon land titles alone this time, as he had done when the Mormons were in Kirtland and Far West; this time Joseph was after power and prestige, he was going to use some of his charm and power over his people where it would do Nauvoo the most good. He had been to Washington, but when he came back he said frankly that he had been lost in the huge pool of people in that place, governing and seeking favors; he had been put off by committees and insulted by the President and deeply annoyed by the good Southern manners that held a man at arm's length and never permitted him to get to the bottom of anything. But he had learned something of suavity and something of the ways of politics; he had learned that out in the world, wheels move faster when they are oiled with rewards; he had learned that the stick is not wielded by the imposing thing called Organization at all, but by single men who manage in strange and devious ways to control other men and so amass majorities.

"Maybe when I have fifty thousand votes to show them, they can talk my language," he had said bitterly. And so he was building his kingdom. He had his plans.

He began with Springfield. A new man, Dr. Bennett, wielded some influence, and he was not yet beyond benefits. He was a glib and precise talker and to the still rough West had brought an Eastern smartness that abashed certain frontier senators into regarding him with admiration. When he came out for the charter of a new city, Nauvoo, being built by the Mormons who had come from Missouri and were still dependent on the bounty of Illinois, they were amenable. If it was a liberal charter, all right, a struggling new city needed a liberal charter.

When it was over, John Bennett rode beside Joseph Smith back to Nauvoo. And he got himself baptized in the river, one sunny day, when Joseph said that would help in the elections. An important conversion, surely, that folks spoke about with pride.

Sidney had spoken to Joseph, much troubled. " I don't like mixing religion and politics," he said. " It's not godly."

But Brother Joseph said, as always: " Religion mixes well with politics if the good of the Church is involved. Why not? Religion mixes with anything, and should. If there was religion in politics and government, would we be likely to have dishonest men at the head of our country? Would President Van Buren refuse the plea of an innocent people for redress from Missouri if he had some God in his politics? Would Christ have wavered for the vote of Missouri? Put your religion in everything, Brother Sidney, put it in every hour of every day. There is no place where religion does not belong."

Yet there were troubled eyes watching from street corners when Brother Joseph passed with Dr. John Bennett.

" I don't like it." Robert Foster, lean and sneering, dared so much.

But one of the heftier Brothers looked keenly into his face. " I've no call to say Brother Joseph hasn't picked us a good Mayor," he said slowly. " Maybe a real medical doctor will do Nauvoo some good, and maybe the state Quartermaster will get our militia right well supplied, so's traitors can be tended to."

Foster flushed. He himself practiced medicine. "It seems like one of the men who's worked hard on a city and knows it from the beginning would be a better mayor," he said. "That is, if Brother Joseph wants to give mayorships away to somebody. Strangers coming in, fancy and high-talkin', don't set well with me."

The first Brother touched his arm. "With the Prophet Vice-Mayor, there won't be much high talkin' on the part of the Mayor," he said.

They all laughed, but harshly as though even such a comment as this might be illegitimate.

Jarvis listened, fascinated, standing close beside his father, and in meeting he looked at John Bennett with a boy's frank curiosity and judged him with a boy's keen judgment. He saw that the feeling of the men was justified, that Bennett did not belong. He was shifty-eyed and quick-talking; you even hated him a little when he spoke to the solid mud-booted men before him. He was amiable and soft-voiced, but he was too careful with his words, too polite and pretending. Jarvis glanced up at his father and saw that he was frowning. But when Brother Joseph talked, charming and rich-voiced and beloved, it was different. With Simon and all the others, or almost all.

Jarvis sat very still and straight and heard the Prophet counting Nauvoo's official eggs, nearly hatched with the warmth of the new charter protecting them. There will be in Nauvoo a mayor, a vice-mayor, four aldermen, and nine councilors. Now Nauvoo will be protected by three judges, two clerks and a police force. Now Nauvoo will have her own schools and a university to teach the arts, sciences, and learned professions and having a board of trustees and a chancellor, a registrar, and twenty-three regents. Now there will be a Nauvoo Legion, to which every able-bodied Saint will belong, and Brother Joseph himself has obtained a commission as Lieutenant-General of that Legion. Mayor Bennett will also be a General of the Invincible Dragoons, and there will be aides-de-camp for Brother Joseph and cavalry and long swords and shining pistols (provided by the State of Illinois) and, if the Sisters will co-operate, a silk flag before Independence Day. And a band of musicians to march before the Legion, called the Nauvoo Legion Band.

A city of cities, stretching like a youngster and uncertain of her voice, yet grasping eagerly at all the refinements of any city. Jarvis sat with his eyes proudly on Brother Joseph. There would be all this, and still the firm thing under it all that had made Simon work so hard to get his outfit together and turn farther west. A city, a whole kingdom at last, without idle hands and crumbling houses. A city where no man would be cheated or subdued. A haven for every man with a dream and a faith and a will to use the power in his hands.

There was much for an orator to say about Nauvoo on election day. There was a world of things to say.

BROTHER JOSEPH was riding Old Charley with passion, with vindictiveness almost, out on the road north, anywhere, anywhere to be moving and riding.

He had left on the streets of Nauvoo the men who had just done his will at the polls and made John C. Bennett Mayor of Nauvoo, and him, Joseph Smith, the Vice-Mayor. He had left the fine talk of Nauvoo and her future and her greatness and her charter and her dream. He had passed the hill where lumber and stone were being gathered together for his Temple. If he closed his eyes he could see how the Temple would look, high over the river and the prairie.

But a man cannot keep his eyes closed forever. However long he might dream of the hill, he must come down to the swamp again. A man had to open his eyes then to guide his horse through the mud and the slime where mosquitoes bred by millions in summertime and willow bugs rose out of the very water like a pestilence. And a man could not look at these city lots, staked out precariously, and say *Nauvoo* with pride. Yet it was Nauvoo. It was not fit land for inhabitants – and yet inhabitants were here, living more closely together than the inhabitants on the dry flat or on the hill or back on the prairies.

He himself had just gone to the doors of some of the shacks, with Charley looking dainty and outraged under him, to collect overdue money for Horace Hotchkiss and Company, land brokers, New York City. Even a man of God must have land to build up a city, and be concerned over profits.

He clenched his legs against Old Charley's sides, revolted and ashamed. In his elegant Eastern office, what did Hotchkiss know about opening a city in the wilderness? What did he know about immigrants who came from England, fresh from the midlands and the potteries and the coal mines, with nothing but their knapsacks and their hope and their yellow-faced children? He could see Hotchkiss, smug and fat, going to those shacks day or night to pray over children that smothered with fever and died before you could say Amen – Hotchkiss getting up from his gouty knees and mentioning the matter of the mortgage.

And it was on a Prophet of God's word they had come, glad to sign their names for any land and listening to advice as a child listens.

Like that new Brother Moon – only a few minutes ago he had stood up on the leg that was crooked as a snapped stick, part of the wages secured during a colliers' strike at Newport, he said, when the troops came in. And he had said: "My father lived on the land, I remember, before we went into the town, though I was a tad then. Always we wanted the land again."

Well, now he had land, if you could call it that, and his only boy was dead of the swamp fever.

Brother Joseph rode swiftly, because he needed the wind to cool a heat in him.

Brother Moon was one of those who had come along after dark one night, in Newport, and had heard the Elders preaching on a corner. "*Five pounds to New Orleans and up the river to a new city*." He had stood there, tired as death, and listened, and presently he forgot he was tired.

All over England people were stopping to listen. Before this they had stopped to hear the Chartist Gospel, but now the Chartist cause was mentioned in whispers. It seemed a good thing to hear of God, for a change, in place of government, it was good to hear of people who spun and wove in their cottages from their own flax and wool, it was good to hear of land stretching for endless miles, unused and rich, and of planting and harvesting.

Five pounds. Half for a child. To gather that much together, a family could eat hope for a while! They had eaten hope before, during sacred holidays when work stopped to force up the wages. But every time another leader went to jail or overseas to save his own skin, every time the troops came marching, hope was less digestible and finally they voided it entirely and crawled back into the factories for a wage that had dropped to punish them.

Now, this hope the Elders fed them had the taste of bread. They began to crowd into Liverpool with their knapsacks. And they had begun to arrive, gaunt and wide-eyed, in Nauvoo.

Frightened, Joseph had written to the Elders in England: "When I consider the magnitude of this great work and the relationship I sustain to it, I need your faith and your prayers. You must keep the poor back awhile – let men of means come first and start manufactories for the poor to come to."

But Brother Brigham Young had answered: "Almost without exception it is the poor who listen to the Gospel."

And why should the poor not come to Zion? Did Christ say:

"The poor cannot come"? Why should men of means stand on the wet streets of England to listen to the Elders talk of hope? They had warm beds to hurry home to. But the poor stopped in warm crowds and heard words like *equality*, *land*, *freedom*, *brotherhood*, *love*. And then — unbelievably — *five pounds*. It was hard to believe that freedom could cost so little.

Listening to the Elders, something was restored to the laborers that had been lost for a long time: a sense of dignity and fruitfulness. A sense of importance and of power came alive and began to ache again in their muscles. Did not God intend for every man to be a God? You could find it in the Bible.

Listen —

For thou hast made him a little lower than the angels, and hast crowned him with glory and honour. Thou madest him to have dominion over the works of thy hands; thou hast put all things under his feet.

A fury rose in them as they listened, a fury that bolstered hope. Had God intended, then, that they should be cheated forever?

Over and over the Elders said: "You are God's children and He loves you. He has destined you to become gods and possessors of glory. His kingdom is waiting."

WHEN Joseph came back along the road, it was getting dark and he could see candles coming alive gently along the river. He had told the people to come to him if they were in want, he had told them he would divide all he had with them. What more could a man do? There was the land to be paid for.

He came to his new store, square and well built by the Brothers, with a solid stone foundation and good red brick. When he went in, he stood by the counter and wrote a list on a slip of paper. Then he handed it to his clerk and said: "Take these yourself. And write a bill for it; don't say anything about the money now. You can ride Charley."

Upstairs in his office he sat down heavily and took his quill in nervous fingers.

To Horace Hotchkiss and Company
Sirs:

I presume you are no stranger to the part of the city plat we bought of you being a deathly sickly hole, and that we have not been able in consequence to realize any valuable consideration from it, although we have been keeping up appearances, and holding out inducements to encourage immigration, that we scarcely think justifiable in consequence of the mortality that almost invariably awaits those who come from far distant parts (and that with a view to enable us to meet our engagements) and now to be goaded by you, for a breach of good faith and neglect and dishonorable conduct, seems to me to be almost beyond endurance. . . .

When the letter was finished and sealed, he went to the window and looked out at his Nauvoo. He looked at her sweeping flat and her gentle hill and the rows of houses looming in the dusk in straight lines. It would be beautiful, his Nauvoo. Gradually the swamp would be drained away and the land built up. He would keep the Brothers working; men had a way of living until they had finished the thing they worked upon, and by that time the swamp would be gone and the worst would be over. Keep them working, then, and keep the dream before them like a beacon.

A slender lady picked her way along the darkening street, and he leaned from the window, recognizing her dimly. She lifted her skirts daintily as she stepped by the muddy places, in that charming way women have, their toes out and their petticoats rustling.

Eliza Snow.

Joseph took his hat and his stick and his letter and went hurriedly down the stairs. Eliza was always one to understand a man's troubles.

She greeted him gladly, and he was conscious of the swelling manly feeling her look always gave to him. Sometimes when he looked up in meeting, he would find her eyes on him, like a child's eyes, worshipping. And whenever she was asked to perform a service, she was eager the way a child is eager to run a little errand, and whatever it might be, it was done instantly and well. If all the Saints were as ready to serve as Eliza Snow, Nauvoo would grow overnight, like a mushroom.

" I was just thinking," she said, " the day of the first election is a day to remember, even for us women, who cast no ballots. You'll be writing it in your journal when you get home. And so will I."

" A great day," he said. He tried to look into her face, but it was too dusky now, and besides she kept her face down, watchful of mud and stones.

" Now that we are prospering ourselves," he said soberly, " we must begin to think of those not so fortunate. Nauvoo has its poor already, Eliza."

" I know. This afternoon Emma and I were out. We dressed a baby for burial – they had nothing, even for that."

" We haven't had much time to think of the poor before this," he said; " we were too poor ourselves, I guess. But now – It's part of the Gospel, you know, Sister Eliza, that the man with means must share with the man without means. No one must suffer in Nauvoo – or in all of Zion."

" We talked of it. We thought the Sisters might do something. After all, we are the ones who know what a family needs, aren't we? "

She wondered why he seemed so excited, so relieved. " An organization in the Church," he said, " part of the Church itself. An organization of Sisters, for that one purpose! "

"Don't think of it yourself before we have a chance to ask you! "

"A Benevolent Society of Sisters— "

"Not benevolent," she objected. "Not something that seems to stoop, but only to reach out, to *help*. We were thinking about that."

When he left her he took her hands and pressed them until the knuckles whitened. He was comforted. A Female Relief Society. And he had sent food to Moon's, and he had written the sharp letter to Hotchkiss; it was here in his hand, ready for stamping. When he went into the house, he was whistling.

MAYOR JOHN BENNETT emerged jauntily from the door of his rooming house and moved up the street, swinging his gold-headed cane. The city lay dimly before him, over the flat, and he was possessed of a certain satisfaction in it already. Ten thousand—fifteen easily in a few months, the way they were coming in—thirty—fifty thousand. With some speculation and some capital and a dam to convert the rapids into power, it would be a city to give a man what he wanted.

A girl hurried along the path from one of the houses, and he recognized her as the postmaster's daughter, Nancy Rigdon. She passed him without a glance, decorously, and he lifted his hat. Then he turned and looked after her, his eyes narrowed, entertained. A city to give a man a few things he wanted—

When she had disappeared, he entered the gate of Rigdon's place. The postmaster was a man the Mayor should know. She'd be back before dark, girls didn't walk the streets nights out here.

Chapter VI

MERCY shivered, looking out into the early spring morning. There would be wind for conference and maybe rain. It was getting to be a joke about how you could rely on plenty of rain for Church Conference. But for baptism, for going right into the river yourself, all over, you didn't want wind or rain, either. After all, and she smiled, thinking: "There is something besides the spirit to think about."

It was thinking so much about baptism, and working late on the white ceremonial clothes, that had made her dream last night. And even when she was awake, to lie and think about things that had happened years and years ago. Father had been such a rebellious one about baptisms and sacraments and everything to do with the Church that it had always been a heavy cross for Mother to bear. Mercy had decided very early that whatever her husband believed, she would also believe. There was no use doing anything else when it seemed to matter so much.

She could hear Father saying sternly when the pianoforte came from Boston: "But don't play hymns on it forever; play *music!*"

And Mother calling from the bedroom in a fury: "And what, Ab Young, do *you* call music?"

Poor Mother! She had been watchful as a cat, but when her

illness took her, there was nothing she could do. After she had seen that Mercy was spotlessly clean for Sunday school, then she had to turn her over to Father and trust to whatever mood he happened to be in; though he was sweet enough about everything, he just had a way of ignoring certain things he wanted to ignore and no amount of stewing could convince him they were important.

Very likely he would stop at the church gate – as a truant boy might, fiddling with his collection nickel – and look critically at the sky.

" You go on in, Mercy, and look around."

" Aren't you coming with me, Father? "

" Maybe I will. We'll see." He leaned to her ingratiatingly, smiling. " Now, you and I came here to see God and Jesus, and all I want is to be sure They're here all right. See? You go in and look around. If They aren't there, you come right back out and we'll go see if we can find Them. I really doubt if They'll be in there on such a good day."

So, Mercy remembered, smiling, she went in.

" How primly, through the wide doors and slipping behind the back pews to look around! I knew everybody there and not one of them was either God or His beloved Son. So I slipped out again and told Father They weren't there.

" ' All right. I don't think Mother would mind if we went out to find Them, do you? I think she'd decide it was just the right thing for us to do.'

" We passed folks hurrying to the church and I thought they looked at us tiltedly. When we got out of the town, Father took off my dress and let me walk in my petticoats and folded my dress so the fluting wouldn't be spoiled. After a while, we walked in tall grass and climbed fences, and Father took off everything but my little shirt and I swam in sunlight. But he *was* right, after all. We saw God and Jesus in the corner of John Graham's meadow, but when we got right close They had gone on to another corner, leaving white violets to show where They had been standing. We kept seeing Them ahead of us. And we kept seeing things They had done to show us we were going the right way. They left Dutchmen's-breeches once, clean as pins and filled with bees. And they changed white violets to purple every little way, so we knew nobody else could have been responsible. And once They changed them to yellow. Father was amazed and we kept on following and he said he'd never taken much stock in the miracles, but he guessed there might be a great deal to them, after all.

" We never did quite catch up with Them. But one Sunday when Mother was right bad and there was a nurse with her, we followed Them until sunset and saw Them going home. We could see Them plainly, two great columns, with robes just the color of French lilacs in April and trimmed with the color of an oak tree when the promise of frost has sent down all the sap; They were moving off together, arm in arm, toward the west.

" Then the next day Deech died, and he was the first dead thing that mattered to me. Father couldn't tell me what had happened to him, but Mother could. He said he didn't know, but she said she knew and told me all about it. People died, too, and birds and every other living thing. She herself would probably die very soon, she said, and I must know that she was in heaven looking down, watching everything I did and listening to every word I said, helping me to do and say the right thing, always and always.

" But Father said nothing, except that nobody knew. He said Mother didn't know either, not really, and there was a sharp argument and the nurse came back and Father was ashamed, crushed the way Deech had always been when we caught him at the hams. And the controversy was in me, especially in the night."

Mercy stood still by the window; she could almost hear him coming.

"But you do believe it, Father, you really do?"

"I believe all I can, Mercy girl, all I can. Everywhere I go I'm looking for more good things to believe. Even if it's the be-all and end-all here, then we'd better keep busy believing good things. Hadn't we?"

Then after Mother died he hadn't wanted to talk about it any more. A long death, lingering and inevitable, and visions at the last, even conversations with her own mother on the other side, staring up widely, seeing.

And then school, and then the full routine of teaching, and then suddenly Simon, and what to believe was settled, quietly and securely settled. It was to Simon she had leaned when he told of seeing the White Dove when he came up from the waters af baptism and Father had murmured, with his lips twitching: "Somebody's pigeon!"

She shivered, looking out into the early April morning. It wasn't just the sort of day one wanted to be ducked in the river. But Amenzo and Albert would love it, both of them. Like a good swim out of season.

THE WIND was searching for leaves to make a noise in, and was disappointed at all the empty boughs, whining around them like a lonely puppy in the night. Then, out of revenge, he broke the sunshine into bits and prevented it from warming anything. It tried, looking squarely into the river whenever it could, but the wind was too much.

Mercy lifted her hands to keep her hair from flying into her eyes, because the wind persisted in sudden changes of direction, failing in one attack, trying another. Other women held their hands flat against their brows for the same reason. They stood in a white knot, white dresses and white stockings against the cold sand. Over there, south a little, the men, also in white, and Menzo's and Albert's tow heads among them. They couldn't be quiet long, even for a baptism, those two, but chicken-fought with their elbows and played beans-porridge-hot with their hands together and even squatted down to dig in the sand and once got to skipping stones till Simon put a stop to it.

The wind clung in the sleeves of the men and stirred in the skirts of the women, and nobody else seemed to mind the cold, nobody but Mercy Baker. They all watched the river, silently, intently, watching a man who stood waist-deep in the water. Constantly there was one broken from the group of men and then one from the group of women standing at the waterside, and one wading in and one wading back, dragging knees forward against sodden clothes. The one coming out and the one going in always passed each other, smiling and shivering, the one looking determined and the other looking chiefly disheveled.

Mercy shivered.

" There's no need to be a-scared," one of the women said. " It's over in a minute."

" Oh, I'm not scared. But cold, a little."

She kept thinking: " What is this I am doing? " There was a ludicrousness in it, something ridiculous, now that it was the thing she was going to do after this next breath; after this next woman wading in, maybe she would have her turn wading out. A kind of unbelief swept over her, and her father kept smiling back in her head, as he had done all the morning, and he kept saying: " If it's the be-all and end-all here, we'd better keep busy believing. . . ." A paradox, she could see that now.

She looked at the men, their rough red faces over their white collars, great calloused hands hanging from their white sleeves. And when they passed, coming out, she smelled strong yellow soap on them. And the women, holding their wisping hair, bent their toes into sand unfamiliarly, toes lovingly enclosed in stockings knit from their best bleached wool especially for the baptizing. They belonged home roasting beef or standing over their soap-kettles, but here by the water in white clothes, sober as judges, and worried over the wind in their skirts while they sought the breath of divinity – Mercy wanted suddenly to laugh and put her hand helplessly to her mouth. The men, too, with their legs bent from the bodies of their horses, and their hands hard from the handles of their plows – they stood watching Brother Joseph out in the muddy water, believing that his words would presently forgive them their sins of nature and clothe them with the austerity of membership in the Church of Jesus Christ of Latter-Day Saints.

A girl brought a wailing baby to one of the women who waited, and she took it and opened her dress and laid the breast in its mouth, moving her body back and forth, back and forth, as mothers do holding babies. The child relaxed, there was a half-sob or two, aftermath of despair, and then contented suckling. Could it be, perhaps, that this little one was a sin to be here expiated? One heard of it often enough. Or, if the mother came, as Mercy had, to receive the badge of belief, what was it that could add an iota of divinity to her as she stood here comforting her child in the wind?

Then it was Amenzo's turn and he went out, grinning at her and Albert and at the family among the trees, floundering back after the ceremony with his fists in his eyes and gasping a little. Then grinning again, and into the blanket Simon held for him.

Albert almost leaped for the first few yards, looking down at the water with self-consciousness, she knew, before so many eyes. There was no way to make Bert's hair stay firm against his head, no way at all, Mercy thought. But when he came back to the shore, streaming, his hair lay flat with water running out of it onto his shoulders and she saw that his lips were the color of ripe plums. Maybe a baptism every day would flat Bert's hair for him!

"Mercy French Young Baker."

She turned and saw Simon and he smiled at her and they all smiled. Jarvie lifted his hand to wave, and even Joey smiled, or seemed to. Eliza stood holding Joey in her arms; she came often to see him now and he was always good as gold with her.

For a moment Mercy stood uncertainly, looking at the water, and her father's face was in it, his lips twitching. But she turned her head, and Simon was there, a look on his face that she knew. All this was not ludicrous to Simon, nor even unimportant; it was beyond the body and above it. To Simon, her soul stood with her, hovering over the water. She smiled at him and moved from the shore.

The water was very cold. It came to her flesh through her stockings and moved up slowly as she walked. To the hem of her dress, and the dress rose and stood wide on the water until she pressed it down with her hand. Then she put her foot into depth of mud and it sank. She brought forward her other foot and it sank too, sickeningly, until the water stood over her knees, eddying and brown, mud churning up from the bottom. She looked out. Brother Joseph stood far away, smiling and beckoning.

"It's all right," he called. "Come on out a little and you'll find a firm place."

She floundered on, lifting her feet quickly, one after the other, and spreading her legs wildly, like a duck in the mud, to seek firmer hold. She saw that the carefully whitened clothes were muddied and ugly, and she felt ridiculous, floundering through the water. She could hear Father laughing over that old story – "And they went out on the river because this boy came running into town to tell how there were a flock of ghosts out behind the dam, and when they got there, it was a bunch of Mormons baptizing each other in their night-shirts!"

She tried to catch hold of the idea, the depth of idea that declared a man was purified and dedicated by the holy water upon his flesh. But this muddy water with a fish-smell in it sullied the idea and it escaped her while she struggled to hold it.

When she came up to Joseph she found the footing firm where he stood, she could feel the ridges of hard sand through her stockings. " If you don't keep moving," he said, " you sink clear in."

She was shivering and her teeth knocked crazily together. " I must look like a witch," she thought. A path of sunshine reaching out from her to the sun, over the water, appeared suddenly when the sun managed to lose the pursuing clouds. Perhaps a symbol, after all; she faced it, blinking. Then, as Joseph raised his arm to the square and began to speak, the cloud raced over and the river darkened. She felt the breadth of Joseph's hand on her back.

" Having authority given me of Jesus Christ, I baptize you, Mercy French Young Baker, in the name of the Father and of the Son and of the . . ."

The Holy Ghost. She knew it, but she did not hear it, because the water closed over. It entered her mouth and her throat and her nose, and a furious bubbling came out of her. Then she was up, it was unbelievable how quickly, and he held her while she gasped and sputtered and rubbed her nose with her hands and sought her tumbled streaming hair.

He released her and she turned and went from him blindly toward the shore. She felt the sodden mass of fabric on her body, bearing her down. The shore then, and she stood shivering and Simon brought the quilt. They prayed over her, and she thought of Jesus the Christ under the hands of John. But maybe the Jordan wasn't so muddy, maybe it was one of those clean sparkling rivers –

She looked down as they prayed, stooping under their hands, and saw that her dress clung to the shape of her legs. She drew it apart, ashamed. And when she looked up, she saw how mottled the sky was, unchanged, full of disgruntled wind. But there was not a white dove – not even a pigeon – not a bird of any kind in all the sky.

Chapter VII

THEY had thought " Spring," and then there had been rain, so cold one day that it froze as it dripped from the trees, and the whole world was brittle and glistening when the sun came out. And then spring really came. Shining and beckoning and pushing and listening and shouting. You wanted to throw yourself down and hug the world and throw your arms wide and take it close and open your mouth wide and swallow it all.

Mercy wrapped Joey carefully and tied on Betsy's bonnet and put a muffler on Georgie because that sore throat persisted, and they went out into the world and down the hollow. There were mystical things happening all the year round in Stony Hollow. Now arbor-Judas was pink in it and every little while dogwood beckoned mistily and you saw the blossoms exotic and sensuous, flowers that should bloom in a hot and passionate and sultry land. But willows belonged here, fur-coated and winsome on the boughs. Arbor-Judas belonged here, too, bright and startled and young. And jack-in-the-pulpits, short and stately as diminutive kings. The sycamores stood white, sparsely budded yet, and the blossoming trees around them were like pink and white girls moving gaily and unwittingly among ghosts and memories.

Jarvie saw them from the field and Mercy called to him. She saw him speak to Simon and then come running. A shame if

Simon'd not let him go awhile on such a day. When he came up to them he said: " Father says I can go along for a ways."

Dapper leaped up and licked Jarvie's face and then ran ahead and in circles like a creature gone wild. And after a time Jarvie got into his trees, showing off for the children. When they were tired and wanted to go home again, he stayed where he was, luxurious and contented. The tree in which he remained longest was an oak tree, wide-armed and just suggesting the camouflage to come later. Now it was all oak and no softness except the too pointed primness of budding. He climbed high, using his knees pressed together like vises, his arms around the trunk until he reached the height. From here the hollow was his and the river, too. For a long time he sat looking. And then he got up and reached for a wild grapevine and rode on it – oooout – and then his hands loosened – and slipped – down – and he swung in a half-circle – and oooover – the high ground – and let go! Almost soundlessly he dropped into the grass and sat grinning and breathless.

Then he was aware of somebody talking, just over the ridge in the hollow. Of course it didn't matter to him what anybody was saying, but nevertheless he could hear it and it arrested him.

" Don't let me say anything to change your mind. After all, if the prettiest is spoken for, a man has to take the next best. When I first rode into Nauvoo with Brother Joseph, I saw you there at the store with your mother, you remember, and I said: 'Are all your Mormon women so beautiful? ' And he said: ' No,' that I'd happened to see the most beautiful first. But, as I said, if a man comes too late and the prettiest is already spoken for, it's really natural enough – "

" There's nothing settled between Jake and me, nothing at all."

Jarvie knew her voice now and wanted to go away quietly and not be seen. It'd be a big surprise to Jake Hardman that nothing was settled between him and Naomi Fordham if anybody should happen to tell him. Jarvie didn't want it in him, because he wasn't one to tell things. He lifted himself and moved one foot; the leaves from fall were packed on the ground and still wet beyond crisping, and so he could move as silently as an Indian. Menzo had shown him; you put the ball first, tentatively, without weight, and then give it the burden, slowly from the toe back, and at last the heel. He took one step and then another.

"Really, Naomi, on a day like this, to resist –"

He saw, wishing not to see, the slim and elegant figure of John Bennett, dressed in the uniform he loved to parade in, Brigadier-General of the Invincible Dragoons, saw him draw the girl toward him with an upward motion of his arms until she stood tiptoe, and his head lowered with his mouth against her face.

The man looked up then and laughed with a kind of joyous triumph. "You have heard my motto," he said. "*Suaviter in modo, fortiter in re!*"

Jarvie sat down again; he must not be seen now. Especially now. Because it was not a thing to see the Mayor of Nauvoo doing with a young girl like Naomi Fordham. It somehow fortified a distrust you had felt all along, but even so there was the thing it did to your limbs, just to see it, weakening you and sending a sweet aching through every part of you. The swift upward motion of the arms and the way she curved to the uniform with her flounces crushed back and all her skirts behind her in a great circle, and her face lifted – It was the same feeling the day gave you, but stronger, as though you had climbed higher than you had realized and stood on the air, suddenly, trembling like a kite. The same things that happened to you when you read in books about lovers, but sharper, with it here in your eyes. It must be the way Mother said, to see lovers in the theater, real on the stage, and to feel as though you were one of them and really participated in all that happened to them. That same night she was telling it, Father had said, disgruntled, distrustfully: " Your father shouldn't have taken you to the theater, Mercy, you were too young. There's no good in it. There's enough wicked love and enough death in the world without any pretending."

Mercy had protested: " It was not *wicked* love — "

But here was love that seemed somehow wicked, that filled him with a vague revulsion, and yet flushed him with a sweet sickness. He stood up carefully once more and looked frankly, and then he turned and ran, as swiftly as a rabbit.

Naomi was laughing, her laughter too high and arid and shaken. And Mayor Bennett was kissing her hungrily and seeking her neck with his mouth.

This was a new thing. Far down the hollow, Jarvie climbed again, swinging up, this time a beech with gray limbs moving out forever and ever. But he wasn't thinking about spring, he was mostly not thinking at all, but full of a dim thing without words, a new thing, and it touched him with a vague reality, like water when it is warm in summer and you enter it gradually.

Chapter VIII

There is something good about fabric in high suds on a day in spring. When Mercy straightened from the wooden tub and felt the white fluff of suds breaking on her arms, that was good, too. And the air going in and out, smelling of grass, and the river down below like a glazed blue dish, and Betsy and Georgie digging under the sloes where the leaves were starting to curl. And once in a while the sound of Simon from the south field, speaking abruptly to the horses. Plowing these fresh stump-faced fields was difficult for horse and man, but she knew Simon was happy this day and contented with his world as she was with hers. You could break happiness off the world today and eat it like biscuit, chewing it full-flavored.

She wiped off her arms impetuously and swooped down over Joey, sitting solemnly in the clothes-basket.

When she stood up, holding Joey, someone was coming around the house. It was Mayor Bennett, dressed to kill, with a cane in his hand, stepping with care over the holes old Dapper had dug in the dooryard for his bones. But even so the Mayor stepped jauntily. She remembered, smiling, what Jarvie had said of him when he had first come to Nauvoo. He looked as though he had stepped right spang out of a book and didn't belong here at all. He was Pamela's dear master before Innocence had worked the great reform, he was Mr. Darcy being too stiff and too polite.

"It is a picture for springtime, Sister Baker!" John Bennett cried. "You and your beautiful child. A Madonna for a frame, believe me."

"I'll call Simon – he's out in the south field." She returned Joey to the basket.

"No, no, no!" he cried gaily. "Let the good husbandman remain at his task, by all means."

He found a place on the wash-bench, wiped it with his handkerchief, and sat down.

"I thought it would be a good plan," he explained, aware that she was flustered, "to speak with the people themselves. And to the women at their work. A mayor, you know, scarcely ever gets the ideas of the women."

Mercy leaned over and touched Joey's head, running his soft hair through her fingers. She did not dare look up for fear the thoughts in her mind would come clean out in her face. "Like Portia has been saying, Mayor Bennett is *mighty* interested in the ideas of the women, so interested he doesn't bother about the men at all. Or the city, either. Or anything else." It was getting to be a popular conjecture which of the young girls would be the first mayoress of Nauvoo. Naomi Fordham had forgotten all about walking in the woods with poor Jake Hardman, and even Polly Yeaman was all decked out last Sunday in a fancy bonnet, after meeting fluttering around the Mayor with her mamma.

"It's a good day to be out," she said finally. "I was just thinking how much I'd like to take my littlest three and go on up the hollow again. We went a few days ago. But," she continued cheerfully, "there's usually a better reason for staying home."

"A man in my position hardly goes walking for pleasure, either," said Mayor Bennett with soberness. And Mercy dropped her eyes, thinking of a thing Jarvie had mentioned.

Even in Bennett's voice was something that did not belong here. As carefully greased as his boots, strange against Simon's good honest ground. Simon had felt it, too, and lots of other folks had felt it – Mayor Bennett looked the part of a sham, a make-up, in spite of the charter, in spite of his titles and his fancy prose and foreign quotations, in spite of his connections in Springfield – maybe because of all these. Folks were whispering hopefully that he wasn't getting on well with Brother Joseph, either, for Brother Joseph liked a plain-spoken man and always had. Even in City Council there'd been a word or two between them.

"I was just thinking," he said, tapping the ground with his cane, "what a shame for all you good people to put improvements like this on land that, in all probability, you will never really possess."

She stared at him, uncomprehending, and he said hastily: "Certainly you know, Sister Baker, that a warrantee deed like you got from Dr. Galland is not very final, to say the least. How can there be titles for land that's not legally divided? There's bound to be a settlement, some time."

"I didn't know there was any difficulty." She hesitated. "Of course – Simon likely knows."

He smiled with that air of superiority some men always assume with women in matters of business. "When the government gave the Indians the right to dispose of their holdings, there were no names on the act at all, and so the land-grabbers came in. They always do, you know. It's really very doubtful whether Isaac Galland owned your land at all."

"It seems to me," she said heatedly, "that if it's true, the Prophet ought to be told about it."

He laughed. "Yes," he said, "the Prophet really ought to be told."

She did not like the tone of his voice, looked at him sharply. But he was gazing raptly down at the river.

"He could tell us what to do," she said. "We traded our land in New York for our farm out here."

"Dr. Galland likes New York land," he said. "And after all, Sister Baker —" He looked at her. "After all, since land speculation is in the air out here and the Prophet needs land, it's natural to expect him to go into it in rather a large way, isn't it? He's a man with a deal of customers handy."

She heard her voice growing unsteady. "It's a grand thing for him to stand behind us. Lots of us couldn't have land at all if the Church wasn't willing to stand responsible."

"Naturally. And besides, a church can take risks — you follow me — that a man can't afford to take. Especially a man with a family he's responsible for. After all, a church can't be sent to jail."

"A Prophet can," she said, "and has been."

"So I've heard," remarked Mayor Bennett. "Ohio and Missouri had some tempting slices of land, they say."

She felt a curious tightening of the throat, a familiar feeling to her when she was forced to speak around emotion. She had never been able to talk business or even to tell a doctor where a pain was because of this happening to her throat. And a ghastly feeling at the knees as though they were turning gradually to water. Simon always said it was a thing to conquer — to be bereft of power just when power was needed was ridiculous. What if she should have to manage her own affairs one day?

"If I were in your shoes," Mayor Bennett was saying, "I'd insist on a sworn deed, just to see if General Smith is able to supply one."

She swallowed slowly. "I don't know about such things," she said. "But if it's something my husband ought to know —"

He waved his hand carelessly. "It's going the rounds," he

said. He frowned then and looked at her curiously. "How did this get started, anyway? Merely a remark about the improvements. Wasn't it?"

"Before you finished, it was more than just a remark." She felt brave to say so much, but her knees were weak.

He rose, smiling, his silky beard shiny on his face. "You must forgive me, Sister Baker. I am one of those impetuous men who lets his tongue go too far, sometimes, without thinking. When I see a wrong being done, I'm right in the fight, right in the middle of it before I realize it myself."

She turned to the tub and put her arms into the suds, hoping the Mayor would feel dismissed by her return to her work. But he only moved closer and leaned familiarly on her white sycamore.

"I understand, Sister Baker," he said gently, "that you are not yet baptized into the Church of Jesus Christ."

She looked up, surprised. "Oh, yes! I was baptized just at conference time. I would've been sooner, but I was so long getting well after Joey."

He raised his brows quizzically. "I understood that baptism was supposed to cure any weakness of the flesh. Sister Emma, I heard, was baptized three times during her last sickness before the flesh finally yielded to the spirit."

"It depends on the sickness," she said, aware of the unsteadiness of her argument. "You're a doctor and you ought to know; there are certain times you can't dump a woman in the river."

He laughed with great pleasure. "That's what I say. Now we're getting somewhere, you and I — "

"I didn't know that you and I were going anywhere in particular," she thought, but said nothing.

He looked at her, still smiling. "We're going to be friends, you and I, I can see that," he said.

She began to rub at the clothes, up and down, up and down.

" It's a pity, though, you didn't keep on thinking about being dumped into that river; once you're in, as you've likely found out, God's holy counsel becomes rather forceful."

She lifted her hands from the water abruptly and began wiping them once more. " If you don't mind, Mayor Bennett, I'll go call my husband. He's there in the south field, he could come in a minute."

" Oh, don't trouble, don't trouble! "

" I suppose you know you've said things about Brother Joseph that Simon wouldn't stand for."

" Men seldom know their friends," he said. " Or their enemies." He bowed, exaggerating the stiffness of his spine. " If there's anything I can do for you, just let me know. At my office in Nauvoo. I'm as human as the next man – I've a little land for sale myself! "

She stood there when he had gone. Joey began to howl dismally. Georgie and Betsy had begun to quarrel over something and she heard them running, screaming after each other. And inside of her all the harmony of the day was gone, and whether she wished it or not, or whether she believed it or not, really, what he had said remained in her and she knew she was unsure, wondering. She turned and looked toward Nauvoo, lazy and lovely in the sunshine, the houses plain because the trees were still bare. It did not look like a city for speculation; in the whole dream there was no room for it.

She was standing there when Eliza Snow came, hot and flustered and disturbed. " That Bennett! I met him on the hill and he stopped me – "

" He was just here."

" Mercy, I hate a man who looks at a woman like that. If one of the Brothers did it, they'd excommunicate him in five minutes. His eyes come out and wrap around and around – Well, that's the way he makes me feel! "

Mercy stood, considering. " I wonder what made him think I hadn't been baptized."

" Did he? " Eliza's question was sharp. " He's been at the records, he gets at everything. Wherever I go I find he's been talking to folks about this or that. Always looking for some little thing to be dissatisfied with. Everywhere I go, some little thing – I can't understand Brother Joseph bringing him here at all, a man like that. But then – " and she spoke quickly to cover over her criticism – " but then, we had to have the charter. And Brother Joseph never forgets a promise."

Betsy and Georgie forgot their quarrel when they discovered Eliza, and there were stormy affectionate greetings. Presently, with one of them on each side of her, she said: " Let's not waste time talking about Bennett on such a day." She hugged Betsy against her. " I'm going to sit here and pretend these two belong to me."

Mercy laughed. " I wish you could have this new one that's coming. I'd let anybody have it that wanted it, just now – "

" You'd let them *have* it – but not keep it. I know how it is, you're all alike."

They spoke lightly but Mercy saw the shadow pass over Eliza's face that she was beginning to know. It was a pity, a real pity, a woman like Eliza, living alone in a little room at Stephen Markham's. And around thirty, she must be, with no husband and no babies, none of the things that make women happy. She remembered a thing her father had said one time about people who wrote poetry – " It's not always the things they have and the things they know that go into their poems, but the things they want to have and the things they wish they knew."

" Eliza," she asked suddenly, careful to keep her voice light and easy, " why in the world don't you get married? There's not a man in Nauvoo that doesn't love you."

" Oh, it's not that I've never been asked! " Eliza's face flushed. " There's always been something more important to do, that's all."

" Then it's your own fault and you ought to be ashamed of yourself." Mercy hoped Eliza would relax again and they could go on talking about everything and everybody the way they had been doing lately. The two of them seemed to belong together, as Mother Turner had told her in the beginning, " just like two pawpaws on a stem." And that first day Eliza had said: " You and I will be friends." As certainly as she had said: " A boy, Joseph." And the two of them had been friends and here was Joey, real in Eliza's lap.

" And after all, Eliza, if it gets to be important enough, you can get married any time. Like Portia says, as long as there are men getting older, too, there's no law against it."

Eliza looked up. " Maybe you get your heart set on one particular man."

" Well, Portia could give you some ideas there, too, I'd reckon. She was saying just the other day that if you keep looking at somebody long enough, they finally look at you. They can't help it."

" Suppose you've been looking for ten years already? And suppose – " Eliza paused as though wondering just how much to say. Then she plunged on. " And suppose you had no right to be looking there at all? "

Mercy stood still.

" Suppose," Eliza went on almost sharply, " he was a very great man whom everybody looked at and he couldn't possibly know when there was another little look, no matter how long it kept looking. I'd like to know what Portia would do in a case like that! "

" She'd look all the harder," Mercy said abruptly. " But you wouldn't. You and Portia are two different people."

She went to the tub and began to empty the water into the

bucket. " Simon made a little spigot for me," she said, " so there's not much lifting. He thinks of more little things like that."

Eliza sat rubbing her nose through Betsy's hair and looking straight ahead of her, blankly. After a while she stood up and came over to Mercy and stood there, tying on her bonnet, wearily. " And suppose, Mercy, just suppose you liked his wife very much and she read his letters to you whenever he went away, and suppose you took care of his children and loved them, too."

Mercy stood up and looked into her face. " I'm so sorry, Eliza," she said.

There was nothing else to say.

After Eliza had gone, waving back, she finished the emptying and there was much to think about. " I knew it before she told me; it shows all over her every time she mentions his name."

AFTER Simon went to see Joseph Smith about his title, he said nothing to Mercy. When she asked, he said it was all right. That was all. Everybody on the Half-Breed Lands had been to Brother Joseph about his claim; Bennett had caused a nasty stir. But all Brother Joseph could say was that he had acted in good faith as Galland's agent, that he did not know more than he had told them in the beginning, that he was guided by God and they must trust God in this as in everything. So they waited.

And that worrisome thing Brother Joseph said in the Grove, at the Priesthood meeting – Simon didn't tell Mercy about that, either, because women leap to scared conclusions about such things. Alarmed into comment by the troubled stir, Brother Joseph had spoken of the Iowa lands: " In relation to this Half-Breed land, it is best described by the name – it is half-breed land; and every wise and judicious person as soon as he can dispose of his effects, if he is not a half-breed, will come away. I wish we could dispose of some half-breeds in Nauvoo and let them go over the river. There is a chance in that place for every abomination to be practiced on the innocent, and I ask forgiveness of all whom I advised to go there. The men who have possession have the best title; all the rest are forms for swindling."

He had spoken briefly of his troubles concerning titles there, and then said: " I am not so much a Christian as many suppose I am. In matters of business and in other matters, when a man undertakes to ride me for a horse, I feel disposed to kick up and throw him off, and ride him. David did so, and so did Joshua. But my only weapon is my tongue. All I can say now is that I would not buy property in Iowa territory; I would consider it stooping to accept it as a gift."

But this was small comfort to a man who had traded all his capital for his land; even an apology from the Prophet gave no title and was not worth money before a harvest. But there was that about possession being the best title, and if a man had built a good house and barn and fences, all he could do was to sit tight and work his land and say nothing to anybody. Simon talked with Bishop Ripley, but Ripley had land in Nauvoo and reckoned on moving over; he talked with Peck and the rest, and they reckoned they'd sit tight, too, having no other choice. But some of them were sharp with Brother Joseph, and a man could hardly blame them, though he kept a shut mouth himself.

After all, whose fault was it? If the Indians had been cheated and misguided, not understanding what paper could have to do with land, not seeing how land could be put on paper, whose fault was it, after all?

Chapter IX

THE QUESTION of the Indians was one to concern a man these days, for with summer the Indians began drifting through the settlements that lay on land where they had lived and hunted. They camped for days in Montrose and some of them crossed the river on the ferry and on flatboats and even in their own canoes to visit the man they called Great White Chief Joseph. When he did not appear at the landing, Chief Keokuk and Kiskukosh and Appenoose refused to step on the shore, outraged at the dishonor done them. So Joseph was hastily notified and came flying to the river-bank on Old Charley and outdid himself with graceful salutations when he got there.

Menzo Baker was a shadow among the Indians, unafraid. Their bronze hairless bodies were beautiful to him, their voices were music, their high feathers stirred him with a response keen and strange. He had been warned to stay away from their camps, but he could not; there was no fear of them in him, but only a sense of brotherhood deeper than he had felt for any creature before.

When Brother Joseph spoke to the Indians in the Grove, he listened anxiously, as if he, too, were touched by this message. And when Keokuk stood up to reply, his spine like an arrow, Menzo saw that Brother Joseph was very pale and stooped a little. Brother Joseph, who had always seemed the most beautiful of men. Keokuk's voice was full and touched the very limits of the Grove, full from his throat. "I believe you are a great and good man; I also am a son of the Great Spirit. I have heard your advice – we intend to stop fighting. We will follow the good talk you have given us."

After that, Keokuk sat aloof and saw his braves and his brothers treated to meat and cakes and melons by the white people. He ate very little, but afterward he graciously offered to dance for their hosts, and he himself rose from the ground with a simultaneous motion of every muscle of his body; and when one of the Indians began to beat upon the great tomtom, gently at first with a weird and baffling rhythm, he danced with the others.

Menzo heard the tomtom with his nerves like liquor in him. The great and beautiful figure of Keokuk remained in the center of his eyes, a blaze of color on the pupils. It was a long dance and there seemed little change in it, little variety, so that many of the people wearied of it and went away, but Menzo did not grow weary and he saw small and subtle changes that some did not see, heard small and subtle increases in the tempo of the drum, recognized diminuendo and crescendo, was aware of the arms lifted higher, the balls of the feet touching the ground with gradually changing accents. And never for a moment did he lose the figure of Keokuk.

When they had ceased dancing, he went to the brave who beat the drum and pointed to it with his finger inquiringly. The brave spoke with a guttural sharpness, turning the drum over and moving it slowly around. Menzo touched it reverently with his fingers, for out of this did not the spirit come? And then he saw that Keokuk was standing close, watching him. The Chief moved to him and said: "Tomtom is from my wigwam. It is yours."

Never again in Menzo's life was there to be a greater moment. Never afterward could he explain it, and he was to love the

Indians all his days and was to be a scout among them and was to learn to speak with them in their own tongue. It was not that he received a wonderful gift from a great Chief, not even that every boy on the grounds envied him fiercely. It was something else, a tangible motion between himself and Keokuk that was almost a movement of air with a sound in it, a swift and enveloping sympathy.

The Indians remained another day and night in Montrose, and Menzo haunted their camp and even went with them out on the river. Mercy was frightened, but Simon laughed at her and said: " He is safe; they wouldn't do anything now to forfeit our friendship."

And Menzo forgot he was only a boy. Had he not smoked with a Chief the bark of red willow? And had not the Chief said beautiful words to him when he told the story of the land? Keokuk was not bitter, but puzzled; not angry, but sorrowful. And Menzo, young as he was, could see that this story was angry and bitter and sad.

" Many white cities have been built where our villages lay. Their names are new, their names are no longer of the Indian. Nauvoo, before Commerce, was Quashquema, our village. The river was ours, and the land."

Quashquema. Menzo took the bitterness and sorrow home to his family.

Mercy listened with sympathy, as Simon did, remembering the feeling her father had for Roger Williams, great founder of beloved Providence. It had been Williams's idea, too, that the Indians were unfairly disinherited, and he paid them money for the land he took, or goods when they desired goods. But he was laughed at by many as a sentimental idealist, losing for himself the influence of his Church and his King to stand for a Principle, as he called it. What Indian could show you a title? And land without title on paper was land without owners, as all white men knew, and when you found such land you were simply glad of it and took what you could and got your papers quickly and sealed them.

"I had always heard about that," Mercy told Menzo, "but I never really understood until you told me what this Keokuk said. Father felt the same way as you do about it, and a few other men have felt it. But while they quibbled with their consciences, men like that, the others got all the land."

Her own experience with these Sac and Fox Indians was different and very amusing. She had been gathering eggs when Betsy came to her, wide-eyed and breathless. They had come knocking, two of them, Indian squaws, and Betsy had been afraid and hid behind the table, pretending not to be at home. So, without ceremony, they walked in, the two gigantic women, one bearing her child on her back. Then Betsy ran out the back way and refused to go in again, even with her mother.

When Mercy came in, they were seated calmly on the benches, their hands folded in their laps, and their knees spread apart, stretching the buckskin of their skirts taut and level. They looked at her directly but without curiosity. She was carrying the eggs she had gathered and, on an impulse, she laid them in the laps of the squaws, dividing them equally. They made no sound, watching her, and she sat down opposite them and told them something of the way her son felt about their people. They seemed to listen, regarding her with their sharp brown eyes, but apparently without comprehension. Presently Mercy began to feel foolish, talking into their round empty faces, and went to the back room and took a side of bacon down and gave it to them. Still they said nothing, but looked at her imperturbably.

"Would you like milk?" she asked.

They said nothing. She thought: "I wonder if they were ever slim the way we learn Pocahontas was."

She brought them a jar of cool milk from the cellar, and spoke to the baby that peered bright-eyed at her. The baby at least could smile, giving her a toothless response. The mother nodded and grunted, and the two rose and moved to the door, without looking around, carrying the gifts she had given them.

Menzo frowned when she told him. " I hope it was all right to give them things," he said. " They didn't come begging, you know. Keokuk said they would come, to honor you."

" I am honored, Menzo, but if they'd have talked! "

" Some folks talk and some don't," Menzo said. He was thinking of his good friend Keokuk, whose stature itself could speak, whose grandeur was a thing beyond words.

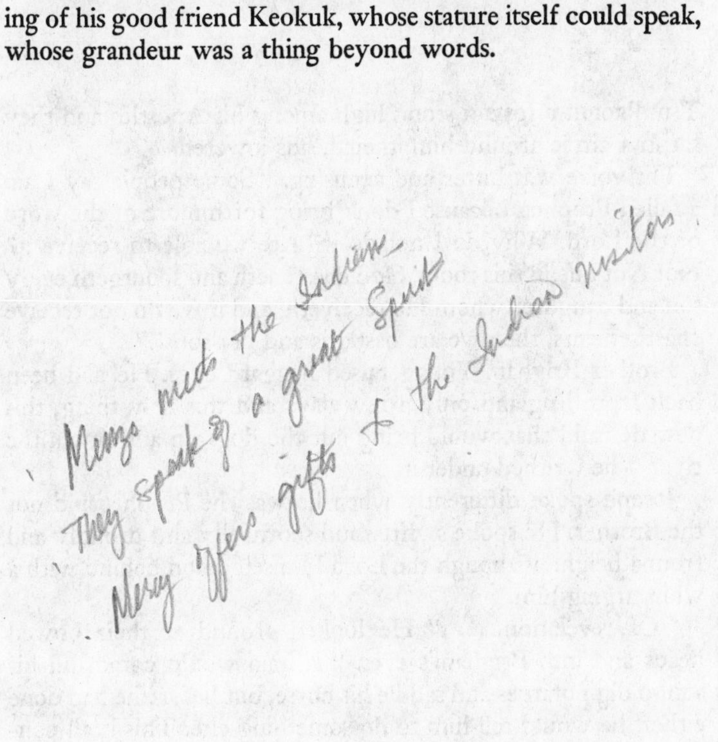

Chapter X

THE PROPHET JOSEPH stood high among his Apostles and they sat in a circle around him, their heads lowered.

His voice was bitter and accusing. "Some people say I am a fallen Prophet, because I don't bring forth more of the word of the Lord. Why do I not do it? Are we able to receive it? No! Not one in this room. God chasteneth and scourgeth every son and daughter whom He receiveth, and if we do not receive chastisements, then we are bastards and not sons!"

Brother Brigham Young raised haggard eyes. He had been back from England only a few days and this new thing, this new demand that would bring out the dogs up and down the river – he writhed under it.

Joseph spoke differently when he was the Prophet and not the Brother. He spoke swiftly and scornfully and proudly and from a height as though the Lord Himself stood behind with a whip urging him.

"Of revelation. . . ." He looked around at their bowed heads and into Brigham's eyes. "A man would command his son to dig potatoes and saddle his horse, but before he had done either, he would tell him to do something else. This is all considered right; but as soon as the Lord gives a commandment and revokes that decree and commands something else, then His Prophet is considered fallen."

He was very straight, very strong, and the blood came and went furiously in his cheeks. "That's the way he looks when he talks to them," Brigham thought, "and they listen and he carries them out with him like a rip-tide."

Joseph's voice softened, ever so little, and they knew he loved them in spite of the bitter things he had said to them. As God loved them, in spite of all He was obliged to send to chasten them.

"Did not God say: Thou shalt not kill? And then did He not say: Thou shalt utterly destroy?"

Brigham's head, too, went down, a great abrupt nod with sorrow in it.

"And He said: Thou shalt have one wife and cleave unto her and none else. And then He said: Thou shalt take many wives to thy bosom—"

He prayed then, and they knew they were dismissed. They filed out, not looking at one another. Were they, then, as rotten-hearted as John Bennett because they couldn't accept this as the word of God? They shook hands all round at the door and then parted, going their ways in silence and meditation as the Prophet had advised they should.

Joseph watched them go, from his window, and as he stood there he noticed that his heart was beating rapidly, so rapidly it dizzied him and made him soft-boned with a weakness. He pulled his chair to the window and watched until they were all gone. He saw that they followed counsel, not speaking with one another. Prayer and meditation, that's what they needed, every one of them. He had gone through it after the Word came, had gone through it alone. Then let them go through it as he had until they saw how it was. Let them walk as he had on the streets of Nauvoo late at night and have women crawling after them in the darkness, like animals, calling them. Let them stand by the river when the steamships came, as he had, and look at the women and the women who were following God into Nauvoo; for always more women than men would hearken to the missionaries. Let them. And then let them ask for an answer.

He pressed his hand to his breast, counting his heartbeats. Then he took out his handkerchief and wiped his forehead, where perspiration lay in great beads. "I need to go out and chop wood," he thought, "or maybe I could hoe in the garden. Or if there were someone to pitch quoits with — "

Then he saw Eliza Snow, just as he had seen her that other day, going briskly toward the ferry landing. She was half-running, and he saw that Dan Jones was holding the boat for her. He got up, still trembling, and went to his desk and straightened his papers. He laid his books in a neat little row, deliberately. Then he looked at his watch. Half an hour at least till the boat came back again — but a ride over the river with the wind on him, it would be a good thing.

When he boarded the boat, he asked Dan if he had noticed where Sister Eliza was bound, and Dan said he reckoned she went on up the bluff, like she usually did, to visit Sister Baker. She was so fond of the little ones.

HALF-WAY to the Baker's, Eliza stopped to look down through the trees at the river. She saw the ferry going back, looking little and fragile from here, the horses walking and walking like toys wound with a spring. Sometimes, she had seen, when they did not want to start, Dan would beat them with his whip or they would fall back and strike the nails pointed menacingly through a board behind them, and whinny and go forward again, and the wheels turned. Cruel. But the men said no harder than walking in the hot fields all day.

Across the river she saw a figure on the landing, waving its arms. A little toy man, wound up and waving.

When she came to the Baker's, the children were digging as usual, making a town, they said, and Mercy was busy as usual, this time making bread. Eliza helped get the bread into loaves, something she loved to do, and then she went out and squatted down to look at Georgie's town. All the Baker children had a certain knack about making things, Jarvie his poetry and Amenzo anything you cared to name that could be made of wood; and Betsy could sew a seam as well as a woman, little as she was, and had started a sampler. Now Georgie was making hills and valleys and marking streets and making little cabins out of broken twigs.

"Brother Brigham is building a house out of red bricks," Eliza said. "Did you know that? Out of real red bricks. We could try to make a rock house, maybe, with pebbles and some of that clay at the spring."

Joey pointed with a dirty forefinger along the path, and Eliza turned and stood up abruptly. Then she moved swiftly to the open window and said: "Mercy, there's Brother Joseph!" She was standing by the children, very calmly, when he came up. He leaned down and examined Georgie's work with great interest.

"Maybe you're going to help us," Georgie said hopefully. "Eliza and me, we're going to get clay and make some houses like Brother Brigham's."

"He ought to be able to help," Eliza said, laughing. "He's built some real towns himself."

Mercy came out and took Joey, and Eliza noticed that a fresh knot of lace wavered at her chin. "Won't you come in?" she asked. "I'll just wash Joey's face and hands and dry his clothes – "

Joseph said: "Your boy Georgie remembered me, and I even think Joseph did. He started waving before I got to the top of the hill."

"Their father doesn't let them forget you. But I think he has confused them a little. When he asked Georgie where God was, he insisted God lived just across the river. We can see your house."

Joseph threw back his head and laughed. "Maybe that's the way to make good Saints out of them!" he said. Then he knelt down on the ground and helped line up the long twigs that would be rail fences, zigzagging along the border of Georgie's town.

"If you had some of that clay, they'd stick," Eliza said.

"That's right," Brother Joseph said. "Just a little where the corners come together. Do you have some clay, young man?"

"There's some at the spring," Eliza said. "As sticky as anything. He'll have to have his brothers bring him some."

She could see that Joseph was enjoying himself, there on the warm ground. He looked up at her and said: "It's going to be partly my town, so I'll furnish the clay myself. I wanted to walk today, anyway."

He stood up and brushed sand from his knees.

"You'll need a bucket."

"And somebody to help me carry it."

"I'll get the bucket from Mercy."

He touched her arm as she turned to leave him. "And help me carry it, too?" he asked.

He smiled at her primness. "Certainly, if you need me. Georgie can go, too, if it isn't too far."

"It's a long way to the spring," Brother Joseph said. "And Georgie could be getting the rocks in a pile, all ready. Couldn't you, Georgie?"

She saw that he was laughing at her, and went into the house, flustered. While Mercy found an old pail, she tied on her bonnet, trying to seem very casual. But her fingers were unsteady.

" I always said," Mercy murmured, " that if Eve had only *nibbled* a little – "

" We'll be right back," Eliza said.

ELIZA walked swiftly ahead of him, aware of her hot cheeks and of her confused hands. He laughed and called: " Eliza, wait a minute! " And when he came up to her: " After all, a poet ought to stop and look at something, whether other folks do or not."

She stopped abruptly and looked along the bluff and down at the river. Obediently she said: " It's beautiful," and then flushed at the inanity of her words. " I don't like people to call me a poet," she said hastily; " because they're all like Mother Turner, they expect me to go around spilling poetry and I can't. Poetic things don't just come to me when I'm talking."

" I know how it is. They're always expecting me to say beautiful things, too. And I can't. Prophecies don't always just come to me when I'm talking, either."

She protested that every time he spoke he said a beautiful thing, but he shook his head. " It's hard, Eliza, to be either a poet or a prophet; some people even think they are the same."

" Oh, no, they aren't. Poets say what they feel whether it's true or not, but prophets always say what's true."

" Always, Eliza? Are you sure? "

Her eyes widened. " Of course I'm sure! "

He moved ahead. " Let's sit on that rock up there for a minute and see if we can think of some poetry and prophecy about the day and the sky and the river." He jumped up and then turned and reached for her hand. A great surge of feeling responded to his touch, and she did not dare look into his face, but as soon as she could she withdrew her fingers and sat down. Joseph looked at her and smiled and sat down too, very close because it was not a great rock. They sat looking down where the river was so bright it hurt their eyes and over it shimmered Nauvoo in her green and the low walls of the Temple showed white upon the hill.

"I'd like to say something poetic about that."

"And I something true of it." He turned and looked at her face, steadily, and she tried to think only of the river and of Nauvoo, but presently she looked down, lowering her head so that all he could see was her forehead and her rich coiled hair.

"You are beautiful, too, Eliza."

She looked up, startled.

"And the best part of you is that you never seem to know it. Most beautiful women are always trying to make pictures of themselves, when, if they only knew it, modesty would make them even more beautiful."

"You say that to be good to me." She spoke with difficulty, bitterly self-conscious. "Mother always called me her sparrow because I was the skinny homely one. And I've never cared – I've always been afraid that if I were beautiful myself, it would – well, it would sort of interrupt me, looking out."

She raised her eyes, laughing a little. "That was awkward, but maybe you see what I mean."

"It wasn't awkward at all – it was pretty, I thought. Rather like a poem, even."

He sat quietly, looking at the river and at his city. Then he spoke gently. "The body, Eliza, is the most beautiful thing God ever made. It is more beautiful than that river out there or any city any man could build. It is so beautiful God will never let it be lost – it will always be just as it is, but made perfect, without pain."

She scarcely breathed. She, too, Eliza Snow, would be among those who had heard him speak like this, as The Mouthpiece.

He went on, slowly. "In heaven, Eliza, there will be lips and hands. And men and women will love one another there."

Then he turned to her and took her hands in his and held them with a strength that hurt. "I will love you there, Eliza! God tells me I will! I love you here in this world, I've always loved you — "

She tried to draw her hands away, panic-stricken, but he held them.

"Ever since that first day when I saw you sitting in a corner, back in Kirtland, remember, in a dun dress like a little mouse — "

Something in his eyes drew her wide gaze to his face. "No, no, no," she heard her own hesitant monotone.

"Since before time began I've loved you, Eliza. We were spirits together — remember, if you try you can remember — I loved you and told you so and we were meant for each other. I held your hands before we were born into this world, and they were as real as this."

He leaned down and kissed every finger on her hands, slowly, and she watched, appalled.

Slowly it came to her and she seemed to remember. It had happened before, all of it, and she had known it always. Forever there had been this moment on the bluff, the very sky and the very shining river, and the man beside her and the hard grip of his fingers and the light touch of his mouth on her hands. It was familiar, every shrub and every tree and these very clouds in these very places. Her face came alive, remembering, and she whispered, awed: "Oh, yes, Joseph, I *do* remember — "

Then he took her and kissed her mouth with a passion that flowed into her and she knew for the first time the exquisite merging of herself with another. Nothing remained in her brain except the memory of all this and a tortured awareness of herself and of all the beauty in the world, rushing upon her in one terrible beautiful wave. Stiffness left her and she began flowing like water, a movement in time.

His voice was vibrant and joyous. "You love me, Eliza."

"Yes. I love you." And then in a burst of self-abnegation, she said: "Everybody loves you, Joseph."

"We'll be married. Soon. As soon as I can arrange it."

She drew back, shaking, and looked at him. And he told her as he had told his Apostles, explained painstakingly. He must be the first, and she, Eliza Snow, would be the instrument of God to show the world a new way of life and a better way, a way that would give the world to women who had never had the world and would teach men the divinity and the impartiality of God. A way that would provide earthly bodies for the spirits clamoring for them, up there in heaven, and would pour love through all the empty women, the desiring women, and bring life out of them as it was intended to be brought from the beginning of the world.

He saw that she was shaken, uncomprehending, and spoke to her like a supplicating boy. "You mustn't think I'm confusing lust and love, Eliza! There'll be long waiting until the people understand and move with us, you must see that. But in time, when there are enough who understand as we do, when they see that we can live beautifully and unselfishly – oh, it's the way I told you, Eliza, God's masterpiece is the man He made. We two are His masterpieces, Eliza. It's all His plan, how we should live and create bodies in His own likeness, bodies to work for Him and worship Him."

She nodded, but her cheeks were hot and her mouth uncertain.

"You remembered, Eliza. You told me you remembered."

"Yes." She looked into his face, grieved. "I remembered for a little while, I thought – "

He took her again and kissed her, passionately. When he drew back from her, he whispered: "Revelation, memory –

it's like that, Eliza. Like a flash of light out of nowhere and that's how we know a thing is from God. While we have it, the moment it comes, we aren't just ourselves, but Him too. And when we have to come back from it, it's like falling down from heaven into the world again, down into the everyday, into streets and mud and trouble. I've lived through it so many times, Eliza. A great time of understanding, and I write it as though my fingers were mad, or I speak it like a river of words and somebody writes it down for me, to hold it still so it won't be lost again. Then – " He swallowed, sighing. " It's like – well, you're writing a revelation, see, Eliza, and somebody comes and calls you to supper! "

A great understanding came over her. After all, it was the same with a poem, just the same. And this moment with him, with him and being part of him, it was like that, too. She reached out and touched his hair and then drew her fingers sharply away as though they had ventured into flame. He smiled at her and she reached out again more firmly, and then moved her fingers against the silk of his head with an ecstatic motion. He bowed his head, stirred by the movement of her hand.

" It won't be easy for you, Eliza," he said. " Not in this world."

She smiled. " Living in this world has never been easy."

It was a long time before she thought about his wife and her friend, Emma. Such a long time that she was appalled when Emma came to her mind, beckoning furiously for attention.

" Does Emma understand? " She asked it softly, half afraid.

His voice was impatient. " Emma isn't either a prophet or a poet."

" I should think being mother of your sons would be as good." It was a gentle rebuke.

" That's it. She's a mother, born a mother, I think. Sometimes I think she's nothing else, she's completed in her children and satisfied."

"She's a good mother." Eliza hesitated.

But he spoke bitterly. "All right, a good mother. But must a man marry a mother and never a poet, Eliza? I think God wants me to marry a poet! Remember when He said to David: And I gave thee thy master's wives into thy bosom . . . and if that had been too little I would moreover have given unto thee such and such things. I love you, Eliza, and God knows it and because He loves me He's giving you to me. As He gave David His best gifts."

She sat very still, listening.

"There was a great poet, Eliza, over in England. A very great poet, I think. His name was Shelley. A little while ago I found something he wrote and I copied it and put it in my pocket. It seemed to me he was inspired to write this poem, just the way I'm inspired to write my revelations. That's why I said what I did about the prophet and the poet. They get at truth, I think, in the same ways."

He fumbled in the pocket of his waistcoat. She waited while he unfolded the paper, smoothed it over his knee.

> I never was attached to that great sect
> Whose doctrine is, that each one should select
> Out of the crowd, a mistress or a friend,
> And all the rest, though fair and wise, commend
> To cold oblivion, though it is the code
> Of modern morals and the beaten road. . . .

He looked up at her.

> Love is like understanding, that grows bright
> Gazing on many truths. . . .

She sat with her lips parted. He folded the paper and put it away, painstakingly. Then he took her hand with great gentleness and said: " You remembered, Eliza. If you say you didn't now, you won't tell the truth, even to yourself. You'll have lied, one time or the other."

She was very quiet, looking at him.

" And if my love doesn't mean anything to you, Eliza, then I'll keep it and treasure it, as a gift of God. It means everything to me. All my life I'll keep it with me and when I die I'll die possessing it."

She did not turn her eyes from his face, and he was disconcerted with them, abashed as one is by the steady look of a child.

" I didn't lie, Joseph," she said at last. " I'm sure I remembered."

He took her face in his two hands and kissed her serious mouth and then he closed her eyes with kisses.

When they came back to Baker's cabin, Georgie had piled a great pile of pebbles, enough for many little houses, as Brother Joseph said.

Joseph talks to Eliza
Say he loves her
Kisses her passionately

How would it be to trust God, believe in the prophets words? Would it be hard? Take a leap of faith?

Chapter XI

MERCY's seventh child was born when a great scandal was rocketing through the settlements — the excommunication and expeditious departure of Mayor John C. Bennett.

Mayor Bennett left Nauvoo with as much fanfare as he had entered it. It was whispered that he left three girls with child, and several others with grave misgivings for a time to come. But in spite of all this, in spite of all the bitter scandal he had broadcast against Brother Joseph from the first moment Joseph chided him for his loose living, he held his head at an insolent angle and swung his gold-headed cane as jauntily as ever. Some even thought the unanimity of opinion concerning his departure was somehow an honor, giving him more importance than ordinary men. He was officially excommunicated from the Church of Jesus Christ of Latter-Day Saints with the whole of the Twelve Apostles in solemn conclave. He was invited by the whole body of Nauvoo officials to tender his resignation as Mayor of the City of Nauvoo, and at once Vice-Mayor Joseph Smith assumed his discarded robes. He was cashiered from the Nauvoo Legion and stripped of all military grandeur at a ceremony which he politely declined to attend. And, as a last gesture, he was expelled in disgrace from the Nauvoo Chapter of the Order of Masonry.

When he was safely out of sight, the whole city breathed

again, deeply. Brother Joseph had made a serious mistake, but he had rectified it in good time, save for the unlucky girls whose heads had been turned by offices and uniforms and smooth talk. And Bennett left behind him the one good thing he had brought, the city charter.

A few days after Bennett's departure, the New York *Sun* reported: "Bennett now has blasted the spiritual and temporal Joseph Smith with a charge of horrid crimes; and Joe, in return . . . will attempt to blast the temporal and mortal John C. Bennett with . . . gunpowder. Up to this time, however, the only murder committed is that of the King's English."

The morning the scandal broke, Mercy was up and down with gnawing suggestions of first pains that refused to define themselves and get down to serious working. She drank hot tea and wrapped her feet and lay down when she could. Jarvie went for Mother Turner and she came bustling and officious, crying out: "Well, praise God, on a bed like a Christian!"

It was a girl, a beautiful little girl with a shock of hair like a puppy. When Eliza came, Mercy gave her the naming to do, and Eliza said: "Every time I look at her I think: *And the damsel was very fair to look upon.*"

So the child was Rebeccah. And to the family, so fond of diminutives that seemed to make them belong more intimately together, she was simply Beck.

ELDER William Weeks, the architect of the Temple, came into Joseph's house for instruction. After he had gone, Joseph wrote in his journal.

"He said that round windows in the broad side of a building were a violation of all the known rules of architecture, that the building was too low for round windows. I told him I would have the circles if he had to make the Temple ten feet higher than it was originally calculated; I wish to carry out *my* designs. I have seen in vision the splendid appearance of that building illuminated, and I will have it built according to the pattern shown me."

Is not God the Father of Architects?

Mercy has another baby, Rebekah
Bennett is excommunicated
Prophet Joseph Smith talks of architect

Chapter XII

Vic Moon stood on the ferry-boat and looked at nothing at all. She stood on the place she had stood when the boat lay at the wharf, never moving or lifting her eyes. Everyone else on the boat watched the big wheels turning and watched the horses forever walking or watched the water foaming in long lines behind the boat or even watched one another with an endless curiosity. But Vic watched nothing and nobody. Once she looked briefly at the paper in her hand.

> Mrs. Moon – Madam – There is a place for your niece, Vic, helping some folks across the river. They are nice folks, the Bakers, and live on the bluff. They will give her board and room and clothing, also fifty cents a week if she suits. Mrs. Baker has not been very well lately and needs help, but is up and will tell her what is expected. I hope this arrangement will benefit you and your family.
>
> Joseph Smith
> By William Clayton

In Vic there was bitterness as well as fear. Somebody else, back there in that old shack sinking in the muck – somebody else needed her. And here she was.

She did not know that the river was very lovely this day, the water choppy and sunstruck and a cool wind on it. She did not know that the trees were very wild, shaken by wind, and the air sharp with a promised thunderstorm. There was something hard in her, something that would not let her answer a civil question, even if somebody should happen to put one to her. But nobody did.

When the boat landed she carried her bundles onto the shore. For a while she stood there, and then timidly asked the pilot the way to the Bakers'. He pointed it out carefully and she gathered her bundles into her arms and walked very slowly, looking ahead and up a little as the path bade her look.

"JARVIE! She's coming – there she is. You go and help her with her bundles."

Jarvie met Vic awkwardly, somehow abashed by her own awkwardness. "Here, Mother said for me to help carry your bundles." She relinquished them without saying anything and he let her go ahead up the path and Betsy came running to hold the door.

"Hello!" said Betsy.

Vic looked at her, and then she half-smiled and said: "Hello."

"I'm Betsy. Who are you?"

"Vic."

Mercy came forward, smiling. "Betsy doesn't take much time to get acquainted," she said.

They all looked at Vic, even the big boy, and she felt smothered and ready to cry. Mercy took her to one of the doors leading out at the back. "This will be your own room. Simon just finished it – it's quite new. You see, he made a fireplace and a window so you can look down on the river when you want to."

She went out and closed the door, kindly.

Vic sat down on the edge of the bed.

That something hard in her, it wouldn't go away, but stayed, like a kernel in her. Maybe it was like the stone in a plum, it never would go away any more until she was broken in two for it. Maybe she would always feel like this. She was hot, and slipped out of her shapeless jacket. If there was one definite fact about her, it was this shapelessness, as though when she had been made some essential of form had been forgotten. It was chiefly a matter of clothing, one suspected, clothes that tried chastely to hide every essential of form in her. And an air of self-annihilation that seemed to lie over her as the poor fabrics did, making her a huddle of girlhood. When she looked up, one realized that her face was very small and sweet, but tense as though she waited for a blow. And her look was quick and then faltered and fell until nobody could be sure until he knew her well what color her eyes might be. Her skin had an uncertain pasty quality, denying care and substantial food and intimacy with sun.

Grandma'am had said: "Stand up to folks," and maybe if Grandma'am had lived to cross the water, it would have been easier. She *had* been brave in Liverpool, hadn't she, taking care of Grandma'am's bundles and her own too, and helping besides with Artie and Dottie? The Elders had said to be careful, there were so many rogues in Liverpool, and so she had and nothing at all had been lost. Grandma'am had been so terribly excited — her first journey and her being past seventy and just now crossing the water — and she had talked loudly; it was as though she had had too much hot ale in her. Folks had come closer to hear her talk and Grandma'am loved to talk to people when they gaped so and listened. Grandma'am had learned to stand up to folks herself, and that was why she wanted somebody else to learn it.

Vic could hear her, sitting on her bundles on the docks.

"In Nauvoo, now, they won't be peltin' us with mud on our way to church. We'll not listen to the Prophet hisself with gravel peltin' on the roof and the windows. . . . No, they didn't like to see the Devil cast out, he's a friend of theirn all over Burslem and Stoke, but I seen it done with these eyes. It was Mary Pitt and her never on her feet in eleven year. I can tell you it's true, knowin' her the whole time. But they carried her to the water and Elder Brigham told the Devil to get out and Mary Pitt got up and never used a staff even! Next day she walked through Burslem and folk followed along after her, but never a word to the glory of God, even for that."

She had chuckled and to see Grandma'am chuckle was a sight, her lips curled up so and no teeth behind them. "That Mr. Mathews, he was a preacher hisself, and he went out and baptized hisself all by hisself! An' what does he say to the Elders but if he has the authority to baptize other people, why not baptize hisself and save the Elders the trouble!

"And in Manchester, as I've heard tell, the Devil was in a mother and her babe till the babe writhed and spit in her arms. But out he came when Brother Brigham told him to come. And folk who saw it with their eyes shakin' their heads and sayin' it was the Devil cast hisself out."

"Stand up to folks." That's what she always said. But after the boat started on the ocean she was bad sick and stopped talking till you wouldn't know it was Grandma'am any more, her mouth drooling all day like a baby's, and four weeks out to sea she just turned over and died, without a word. She who had always taken such interest in folks' last words and called them holy and prophetic – not one word did she say herself. So they put her in a sack with her silence and let her down to the fishes.

Sitting on a strange bed in a strange house in a new country, Vic remembered all this without exactly remembering. It was inside of her like a twisted rope, a hard rope with tar on like those on the ship. Grandma'am had wanted to see the great river out the window there, the great shining river, so different as the Elders had said from Trent in Staffordshire. And the millions of acres of beautiful prairie where crops had never been planted and the soil was rich as Eden and the surface was as smooth, clear and ready for the plow as the park scenery of England . . . all this Grandma'am had read over and over from the *Millennial Star* until the paper was broken and worn with her reading and handling.

Some folks were full of doubts about the new country. Nauvoo, they insisted, was a barren waste on the seashore full of savages and snakes and beasts, and the Church leaders would sell every English Saint for a slave the minute he landed. But Grandma'am believed what the Elders wrote in their paper – Nauvoo was far inland, on a great river, with schools and colleges and temples and even factories starting. Folks were settling on their own land there, and work was to be had in plenty at excellent wages. And the cost of living – an eighth what it is in England! Can you think – beef and pork a penny a pound, flour from two to three shillings for forty pounds and Indian meal a shilling for sixty pounds. Real butter to be had for fourpence a pound and milch cows three pounds a head. A man could milk his own cows for his children.

But about England – what must the Elders write to Nauvoo, Grandma'am asked. "There is no confidence between master and man, men are afraid of each other, they are burning effigies of our great men in the streets. And people are hungry. Some work fifteen hours a day and others have no work at all – even those who work earn hardly enough to hold their spirits inside of their bodies."

So they were coming, following the Elders, pooling every resource they had and chartering vessels to go up the great river, straining their eyes for a glimpse of Zion. But Grandma'am – however young her spirit, her body had been too old and too weary for new things, and maybe there was something else, for all she was so brave starting out—the minute she saw the last of her England she had changed, the life had suddenly gone clean out of her.

MRS. BAKER came in and asked Vic if she would come to supper. She rose obediently and followed to the table, looking at nobody. She ate, fumbling with her spoon and seeming to examine everything with the greatest care from the way she stared at every spoonful. Simon and the boys were extra loud and gay, conscious of her, and Betsy and Georgie ate quickly and then stood far back of their chairs, looking at her. When supper was over, Mercy asked her to help clear the table and dry the dishes, and she did so, hesitantly. Then the boys tried to entertain her. Jarvis brought his books and told her she might read them when she pleased. "This one is by a countryman of yours—the greatest writer that ever lived." She sat very still, listening. Amenzo told her he and Albert could dance like Indians and offered to show her. She said: "Thank you, sir." They all went into gales of laughter then, until they saw she did not understand.

Amenzo got out his tomtom and Jarvie beat it—*tu, tu, tututu, tu, tu, tututu.* And Amenzo danced. She looked at him and never took her eyes from his lithe body while he danced. Mercy watched stilly, as always, seeing that his body was supple and sensuous, that he moved in a curving rhythm as beautiful as that of a squirrel's body moving across the ground. A flowing of muscle, an essential pattern of movement. When Bert joined him, she saw that although he was facile at imitating the steps, the spirit was different. It was a thing you could not touch or name, you could only realize it vaguely.

When they finished, panting, Vic stood up and for the first time spoke to them all. " There is a thing in my bundle – "

Eagerly Jarvie brought it from the lean-to. She squatted beside it and searched through her pile of choicest possessions until she found what she wanted.

" My Uncle Toby! " She said it worshipfully, shyly, and held the jug up for everybody to see. And in him was the charm of old England, of the Merrie England of tradition. His bright blue coat with immense pockets, his gay hat with its brave cockade, his mug of ale, his long-stem pipe, the jovial peace upon his face. He might have been sitting there regarding his great map of Namur, amiable, considering. The children shouted with pleasure, and Simon and Mercy sat smiling as Uncle Toby bade them.

Vic stood up and set him on the mantel. And when she came to her chair again, quickly, Betsy stood closer and Georgie ventured out from behind his chair to look up at the bright figure who seemed to laugh himself when the candle wavered.

When Vic went to bed, Mercy begged her to take Toby back into her bundle. " I'm afraid he'll be broken. Betsy or Georgie or Joey – they might climb up and get him and break him."

But Vic shook her head. " He was brought for children to laugh at," she said, and something in her had begun to soften, to melt and run away. " He was my Grandma'am's Toby and she said she would bring him to America for children to see. He belongs to them."

Often, during all the days after, she would stop and look up at him. He was all the best of England, none of the worst, all the best she had left behind. The skill and the color and the good things of life and the steady humor – the good things of life too many of the people had missed. He was so fat, this Toby, and his cheeks so red and firm. Not like the people in the potteries whom she had always known, yet like a dream they remembered, a something fine they had brought from their villages before the machinery came, a memory of gardens, sunny with color in them.

And those others she had known — they were proud of their Tobys because they had made them — they liked to say proudly: "My grandfather worked with Wedgwood," or with Spode, or with Whieldon.

EVERY day more missionaries left for England, and a few were going into France and Germany and Elder Orson Hyde went to Jerusalem, even so far, to dedicate the land to the return of the Jews, according to the commandment of God.

The Elders, congregating before their departure, were told how to conduct themselves:

"Don't fight with preachers of other sects, but convert them instead. Salt both sheep and shepherd too; get them up so that they will lick the salt out of your hands. Don't get sheep up to lick and when the old shepherd comes up don't hit him over the head with a cane. Their religion is as dear to them as ours is to us. But don't feed too much salt at once, give a little at a time, or they are cloyed. Elders of Israel, be wise! Give short discourses, or the hearers will say: 'A good discourse, but I got tired.'"

Elder Woodruff told of his own experiences in England. "The third of March I took coach and rode through Dudley, Stourbridge, Stourport, and Worcester, and then walked to Mr. John Benbow's, Hill Farm, Castle Frome, Ledbury, Herefordshire. I found over six hundred people had broken from the Wesleyan Methodists and had taken the name of the United Brethren. They had forty-five preachers. I converted all forty-five preachers and one hundred and sixty members the first day and baptized them and they put into my hands one chapel and forty-five houses, licensed according to law to preach in. A rector of the parish sent a constable to arrest me, but I converted him. Then the rector sent two clerks of the Church of England, and I baptized them. The rector did not dare send any more! "

Vic coming from England
leaving her heartland behind
Wilford Woodruff preaching & converting
100p.

Chapter XIII

MERCY sat still, staring into space. It was impossible, incredible, it couldn't be true. If you went to China or Turkey or Persia, there were exotic silken women and strange eyes and curious prattle and utterly new ways to go along with it. But here – the good steady farmers digging the ground in the good solid American manner, with their plain talk and their sober clothes and their stolid faith. It didn't come easy to you here; it jolted you and shocked you and turned you inside out with a kind of loathing. She shook herself, visibly, actually. It was another dream. Like the baptism, it was a thing wrenched out of the normal pattern of living. But she was hearing with these ears, one on either side of her head, these very ears.

Eliza's voice was hurried, excited. "He said I could tell you – I said there was nobody else I'd rather have at my marriage. Imagine, Mercy, my *marriage*."

"I can't, Eliza. I can't even imagine."

"I wish I could tell you just the way he told it to me. The most beautiful – " She spoke with unsteady lips and a shaking chin. There was the very real smell of cornbread baking and flies were swimming in the warm blue air of the open door. And the boys' voices were coming in, far away and blurred, and Beck's funny prattle was bobbing in and out through Eliza's voice. All very real.

Eliza looked at her, waiting hopefully, but Mercy only said: "Well, I guess you're like he said – you're not of this world."

"Yes I am, Mercy! Maybe I wasn't before, but I am now. I'm so alive I know I've never really been alive before. It's as though the air touches me all over, as though I breathe through every inch of my body, it's as though I'd just discovered the world and that I was in it."

Mercy fumbled with the sewing in her lap. There was nothing to say to an Eliza who had just been born into the world at thirty-two. But Eliza was waiting anxiously and something must be said, something not too much like the way she really felt.

"After all," she said, and she was sorry her voice was cool, "you're in love with him. It's better to marry him – like that, even – than to have him like a bad woman would."

"Mercy Baker!" Eliza turned scarlet until even her ears were bright. "If you think I'd ever – "

"Maybe *he* knows you never would."

Eliza stood up as tall as she could and she was so proud and sincere it was a sight to see, her chest uncertain with beating and her voice trying to stand up as tall as she did. "There's something in some of us that hears spiritual things. I don't know what it is, exactly, but I've always had it, and I can see what he means. I've never been happy like other women, and maybe there's been a reason – maybe God was saving me for something special and different, to teach a new and everlasting principle – "

Mercy stood up and took hold of her. It was as though she must seize her to bring her back into the room again. "Eliza," she said, "be sensible! He's a man and you're a woman and you're in love with him and he knows it and he must be in love with you."

Eliza looked at her as though she looked from a far height. "I don't know what you mean."

" Oh, yes you do! " Impaiently, Mercy took her seat again, and presently Eliza sank down beside her once more. Mercy spoke as she sewed, as women do when they are sewing, not looking up but accommodating fingers to words and the words pausing too when the thread must be cut or tied. " Eliza, I don't think about the Prophet the way most folks seem to. He's a man and a mighty handsome one. Everybody seems to expect him to be a Prophet every minute of his life, I've heard him object to that himself. I've heard folks marvel that he goes out and cuts wood for his family sometimes, as if they didn't need fire as well as the rest of us. One day his coat had some gravy right down the front, and you'd have thought it was blood from the sensation it caused. Portia said: ' Him with a dirty coat! ' as though that itself was a miracle."

Eliza laughed unsteadily. " I know. It'd be especially wonderful if anybody saw him kissing an old maid like me, now wouldn't it? "

Mercy saw that she had succeeded in pulling Eliza into this world again. She was not surprised at what Eliza was saying, either, it was what she'd been expecting, the human side of the whole thing, this side eternity. " How did you like it? " she asked, curiously.

Eliza studied her face, found it without guile. " Well – since I've started, I might as well tell you all about it. It was like – well, it wasn't like anything else in this world, Mercy. I didn't know there was anything – Well, it'll take me the rest of my life to write down how it was."

" When you get it done," Mercy suggested soberly, " you might hand it to the *Times and Seasons*."

Eliza gasped, and then they both giggled. But Eliza was too ecstatic for much laughter now. She laid her forehead on Mercy's knee.

" I wish everybody could be told, I wish they could all be told right now." She sighed. " But it's like Joseph says, no matter how faithful they are, some of them fly to pieces like glass when anything comes along that's contrary to their traditions."

"I'd as soon it didn't get around, myself," Mercy said, and Eliza started at the sound of her voice. Determinedly cheerful but with a cutting edge on it. "You give the men an idea like that and they'll all start looking around."

"Oh, Mercy!"

"I suppose it's never occurred to you about Sister Emma —"

"Of course it has, Mercy. I mentioned her the first thing, but he says she understands how it's got to be. It worried me quite a lot at first, but — he tells you how it is and you see it differently, you forget about this world, and all you think about is the spiritual thing — about heaven —"

Mercy wanted to laugh, but she could not. It would be like laughing when Bert told gently how he was in love, oh, desperately, with the little Peck girl whose golden hair curled like an angel's and whose face was utterly empty. To laugh would be shattering. Eliza's face was rapt. "Mercy, did — did you ever try to imagine God was so close you could touch Him with your hands?"

"Yes. I think I did. Sometimes I've thought I had Him right in my arms and He was Simon and Simon was Him. There wasn't any difference."

"Don't you think, Mercy, that I'm entitled to some of the good things, too?"

After Eliza had gone, Mercy saw that she had forgotten her bonnet, and she picked it up and stared at it as she might have stared at Eliza herself. The Eliza who first wore it was irretrievably gone — that Eliza who swung it gaily by the strings and was the good angel of the settlements. But after all — who knows? There were all the black-clad Sisters; some of them she had known well when she went to school, and their barren bodies testified to another love beyond the love most women know. What could you ask for Eliza but that she love a great man and love him deeply and believe in him in spite of everything? And Joseph, Mercy felt surely, was a great man. You knew that when you saw men like Simon lifting stone to build his Temple walls. You knew it when you saw the people in the Grove looking up at him, listening. You knew it when you heard him speak of equality, of a dream-kingdom where men are good enough to share everything with each other.

She hung Eliza's bonnet on a peg over the door, out of reach of the children. She was remembering a poem from Crashaw, a little piece of poem that had been written, perhaps, for some ancient Eliza –

> Happy proof! she shall discover
> What joy, what bliss,
> How many heavens at once it is
> To have her God become her lover.

SHE did not tell Simon exactly where she was going, only that she was going to Nauvoo to a meeting. It was getting to be an open secret now, this new idea about marriage; even the newspapers were getting some of it and *Times and Seasons* was filled with denials. Eliza had said it was intended to be a secret, and as far as Mercy was concerned, it could remain so. She said nothing when her neighbors whispered, and nothing to Simon – he would know soon enough. Joseph was afraid that open discussion and absolute knowledge, before the body of the people were ready, would breed rebellion among those already dissatisfied for one reason or another. And from outside he could expect nothing but bitter criticism.

Eliza had said: "It's going to be very casual, just as though it were only a little meeting in Brother Joseph's office. Drive up to Markham's for me, and we'll go over together."

As Mercy tied her bonnet on, it kept going through her head: "What a pity! What a pity! One must go to Eliza's marriage as one would go to something secret and shameful, with none of the joy and laughter and lace and flowers that belong with marriages."

She drove the carriage to the wharf and onto the ferry herself, as she had done many times before, going across the river to Relief Society. If Eliza wanted her so much, she would be there. But she kept seeing Sister Emma Smith's proud head and lean patrician features and unassailable dignity; what must it be for her to have her husband running off to his office for secret marriages, no matter how spiritual they were? And it wasn't any particular comfort that this marriage would last through this world and another one too!

Mercy sat high on the carriage seat until the ferry touched the other shore and then drove directly to Stephen Markham's. On the seat beside her lay a bunch of fragrant moss roses, their stems caught in a damp kerchief. If Eliza must marry like this, she could at least have something as traditional as a flower along with her while she did it.

Eliza's room was upstairs, a steep-ceilinged room that could bear a woman's height in only one place. Her narrow bed with its short spool posters had to stand out a little from the slope and almost filled the room; her chest, lovely in hand-wrought simplicity, stood by the little window. There was one chair, covered with Eliza's delicate petit-point. The room was Eliza, with Eliza's perfection, even to the cover on her bed, made from scraps of silk no bigger than a finger's breadth and put together with cat-stitch and feather-stitch. All simply Eliza.

She was breathless and pale, like any bride, and greeted Mercy with a fervent kiss.

"It's so good of you—"

"It's good of you to want me."

"I need somebody."

Mercy looked around the familiar little room. "You'll still live here?"

" Why, of course! Where else would I live? " Eliza laughed shakily.

" I thought maybe Brother Joseph – "

" Oh no, Mercy, not yet. You don't seem to understand that, Mercy – it's got to be a long, long time before that." She took her jacket up hurriedly and began to close the row of tiny buttons. Mercy picked up her bonnet when she was ready. It was new, a fancy straw trimmed with black lace and narrow rose ribbon, with a curtain of white satin and broad satin strings. At least, Eliza had taken pains to be prettily dressed for her marriage.

" I keep thinking, Mercy – in my father's house are many mansions – "

" One for Emma and one for you? "

" Oh, Mercy – well, perhaps – " It was strange to see Eliza Snow so flustered.

They went down the stairs and Eliza glanced back, as though she sensed that she was going to be different when she came back again. In the carriage Mercy took up the roses and pinned them to Eliza's shoulder. Her fingers were unsteady and she noticed that her voice was unsteady, too. " Here – you can have these, at least. They match the ribbons on your hat."

" Thank you. I'd never have thought of them."

" You're not accustomed to thinking about yourself."

Until they drew up at Joseph's store, closed now since it was dusk, Mercy hoped in a vague wild way that something would happen to prevent this marriage. But nothing did. Joseph met them at the door and led the way upstairs. Brigham Young was there and Dr. Willard Richards, and they both greeted her with drawn faces. She thought: " They feel the way I do about all this."

But Joseph was smiling and solicitous, a little anxious. He was evidently eager to have the ceremony over. He did not ask either of them to sit down, but beckoned to Brother Young and knelt with Eliza by a little makeshift altar near the table where his papers were littered. He had stopped his work for a moment to marry Eliza – Mercy felt a bitterness rise in her, and went to Eliza and took one cold little hand. Eliza's fingers never once stirred during the ceremony.

"You, separately and jointly, in the name of Jesus Christ, the Son of God, do solemnly covenant and agree that you will not disclose any matter relating to the sacred act now in progress of consummation, whereby any Gentile shall come to a knowledge of the secret purposes of this order, or whereby the Saints may suffer persecution; your lives being the forfeit."

Brother Young read the words from a paper, his voice uncertain over the new words.

Joseph nodded, and Eliza whispered: "I do."

"In the name of Jesus Christ and by the authority of the holy priesthood I now consecrate you and set you apart by the imposition of my hands, as husband and wife, according to the laws of Zion, and the will of God our Heavenly Father; for which especial favor you now agree to serve Him with a perfect heart and a willing mind, and to obey His Prophet in all things according to His divine will."

Joseph nodded, smiling, and Eliza, watching him, assented with a movement of her head. Brigham took a little bottle of oil from the table, like the oil the Elders used to touch the bodies of the sick sometimes, and opened it and touched his fingers with it, then touching the foreheads of the pair kneeling before him.

Joseph rose and took Eliza up on her feet. He lifted her chin with his hand and laid his lips upon her mouth.

Brigham spoke again, solemnly. "According to the prototype, I now pronounce you one flesh, in the name of the Father, and of the Son, and of the Holy Ghost. Amen."

"Amen." Joseph's voice was husky.

"Amen." Brother Richard's voice was like a small echo.

Mercy made no sound.

Joseph released Eliza and turned to Mercy. " Thank you for coming. Eliza wanted you so much."

" She needs somebody with her when she is married." Mercy tried to keep the rebuke from her voice, but he caught it.

" You don't congratulate us! " he said, smiling. " Surely we can have congratulations from our witnesses, at least."

Mercy said nothing, but turned toward the stairs. Brother Young hurried to help her, and Joseph called after them: " Sister Baker – would it be too much trouble for you to take Eliza home again? "

She heard him say abruptly to Eliza: " We're having Council in a few minutes; there's so much work to be done."

Presently Eliza came down the stairs, holding her skirts away from her feet, and climbed into the carriage. Mercy started the horse at once and they said nothing at all until they came to Markham's house again. Then Eliza pressed Mercy's hand.

" Thank you, Mercy. It was better to have you than my own sister, even if I had one here – "

" Thank you for allowing me to come."

To have something to say, she thought, something easy and comforting. But there was a blank wall between the two of them that had never been there before. It was impossible for Mercy to speak around it and say those things that must be said. They sat still for a few minutes and then Mercy blurted out what she least desired to say. " It's a pity he couldn't take time to bring you home himself! Not that I mind – "

" He had High Council meeting."

Eliza's voice was neither strained nor disappointed. Mercy looked quickly at her and saw that she was smiling tremulously as any bride might smile.

" Will he come here after Council, Eliza? "

" I think not. Why should he? "

They sat looking at each other.

" The ceremony said in *time*, Eliza. I heard it. It permitted everything."

Eliza turned and climbed down. " Won't you come up? " she asked. But Mercy knew that she wanted to be alone. So she said: " No, I must get along home."

She leaned down and kissed Eliza's forehead, that forehead where lived all the poetry, all the sweetness of the woman herself.

" Try to be happy, Eliza," she whispered. " This world is a place for joy."

" That's what Joseph says, you know, Mercy – *man is that he might have joy*."

" And women, too? " Mercy asked.

Eliza stood back quickly and turned away, and Mercy clucked to the horse. Once she looked back and saw Eliza disappearing in the doorway. She would go up to her austere little room and write a poem. That would be like Eliza.

" It isn't possible, it isn't true, it isn't possible."

She climbed down from the carriage when the boat started back across the river and stood watching the water streaming out behind the boat in two steady lines, deep rolling clefts of water. She realized that she was cold, but her face and hands were hot as though she had a fever. It was like being out of the world, out on a star maybe where nothing was the same and you marveled at nothing. Everything you had believed, the steady purpose of marriage, the faith and the certainty, it was all gone and you held out your hands and it eluded you. But you must think of it steadily. For Joseph, spiritual perhaps. Perhaps! But to these other men with their hard sunburned faces and their blunt manly desires, no longer enamored of the spreading bodies of their wives, how would it be for them? She faced it, flinching. Simon, suddenly in the night he could be different from what he was all day, an earth-colored man in an earth-colored field, clucking to his horses or urging his oxen.

But in the night a creature reaching and desiring. They were all like that, she knew it deeply. And it was something that belonged to you alone, knowing so much of one man and saying to yourself at meeting or during a polka or anywhere, looking at him: "He is mine and I know him as nobody else knows him."

She felt tears behind her face, a crowding in her nostrils. They would teach this doctrine, too, when it was safe to do it, and the women already involved would be held up as shining examples of dutiful unselfishness. Already it was beginning to seep down in the ranks, and already Joseph was saying things that the initiated caught:

"How many will be able to abide a celestial law, and go through and receive their exaltation, I cannot say."

And even so much: "Any person who is exalted to the highest mansion has to abide a celestial law, and the whole law, too. But there has been a great difficulty in getting anything into the heads of this generation. It has been like splitting hemlock knots with a corn-dodger for a wedge, and a pumpkin for a beetle."

Simon, now, good and faithful and ready for the word of the Prophet of God, Simon would be like plowed ground ready for the seed to fall. She had been so sure of Simon, sure as some women could never be, he had spoken his wedding vows as a man might speak a prayer. He was steady and sure and nothing could shake him from a settled law, she knew. But one law, as Joseph suggested again and again, may supplant another.

Joseph had even said: "A man and his wife must enter into that covenant in the world, or he will have no claim on her in the next world. But on account of the unbelief of the people I cannot reveal the fullness of these things at present."

Perhaps, as people thought, he meant only marriage in the Church, for eternity, but that the people already believed well enough. What was the fullness that remained to be revealed? The new gift, perhaps, sometime an injunction.

Mercy faced it squarely, staring out at the water. Joseph's own needs had changed, that he required a new law from God. And Simon's need—she knew certainly that she could make him happy, that she could shake him to wonder and give him glory that made him stare at her incredulously the next morning. If she could help it, Simon would never require the comfort of a new law. Never. And yet—face it—there was mystery and freshness that was never recaptured after a few years and long familiarity. Firmly, when the boat touched shore, she took the reins in her hands and drove onto the land and around the hill, lifting her hand to wave good-by to Dan.

She saw that Simon had set a candle in the window to light her way, and a great tenderness came over her and a great flood of recklessness. If any woman ever made a man happy, she would make Simon happy. And they two would be so close, so close there would never be room for anything else. For anybody else.

Chapter XIV

FROM the first, Vic liked Jarvie better than anybody else. When he read to Mercy as he loved to do, she began to come closer to listen, and he began to look up at her too, sometimes, and this inclusion pleased her. He always told her when he read from one of her countrymen and that, too, pleased her, although she said little about the things he read and he doubted whether she often understood much of it. These books he and Mercy had read together many times and there were few new ones to be had out here. So they read them again and again. Simon was uncertain whether novels and poetry were a good thing, especially for a boy just edging toward manhood and likely to think about such things too seriously. And that man Byron was notably wicked; and Shelley was a deserter of wife and children.

Once Vic heard Jarvie reading about the trials of poor Pamela and she was terribly disturbed, her mouth hanging and her eyes furious. "I heard tell of that," she said, "I heard tell of it. Grandma'am told me, and she told me to stand up to folks. Even gentlefolks."

"And did you, Vic?" Mercy asked.

"I never went to service, they took me on in the potteries right off. I'm quick with my fingers. But if I ever had, anybody tried using me I'd have killed 'im."

Mercy looked down, embarrassed, but Jarvie's eyes were on Vic's face.

"Once," Vic said solemnly, "Grandma'am stood up to a gentleman and spit on 'im an' they jailed her for it."

Jarvie stared at her, fascinated. She liked to have him look at her as though she were saying something important. She searched her mind for more about Grandma'am. Mercy herself had said Grandma'am must have been a wonderful old lady.

"Grandma'am knew beforehand she was going to go to the fishes," she said, studying Jarvie's face.

"Oh, Vic!"

"Yes, she did. She was always seeing things ahead of their time. She said there wasn't real religion in England – she said that a long time before the Elders ever come to say it – she said folks was too poor and too rich for real religion. Before ever she heard about going to America she said: 'When religion comes it'll be in a new place where folks' meanness hasn't got too big a start.'"

Another night, when Simon was at Priesthood (that was usually reading night for Jarvie and his mother) Jarvie read of Elizabeth's loud and hapless mother, so worshipful before gentility, and Vic began to fumble in her eagerness to talk. Mercy and Jarvie were coming to be familiar with that excitement now. Every once in a while she would begin motioning with her hand, and her mouth opened and closed frantically, and they knew she had thought of something she wanted to say and wanted to say quickly before it was lost again.

Mercy always said: "What's the matter, Vic? Did that make you think about something?"

"Of a woman I knew, over home. She was a funny woman, she'd stand on the street and bow and bow if anybody passed in a carriage that was important, but with her own folks she was – like you said one time, head chicken of the coop. I thought maybe you'd like hearing about her."

She paused politely to be invited. When Mercy had invited her, she rushed on, speaking anxiously.

" She was one to bow to some, and swear to some that was no better than she was. Her husband was Tom Cartwright, and she was mad because good old Tom, he listened to the Elders. Well, one night she came and asked Grandma'am where Tom was and Grandma'am said how could she know if his own wife didn't? Then after a while in they all come, Tom and the Elders and Tom singing at the top of his lungs every hymn he knew because what had he done but just gone and got himself baptized? Now, we called her Mrs. Tom mostly, and she yelled out: 'Damn ye, I'll dip ye! ' and she spit in his face, square. Then she said: 'If I'm ever such a fool as to go waterin' myself like an addlepate, I hope to God I drown! ' And she swore till Grandma'am pushed her right out of the place.

" Well, after a while she started to listen herself. And Tom was a better husband than he had been, not drinking as steady and stopping tobacco, so's she had money for something herself, and she got to listening to the Elders along with him. One night she went to be baptized, and they went to a place where Elder Pugmire had baptized eight or ten the night before. The creek had flowed over with a heavy rain that day, but Elder Pugmire looked up and down and said they wouldn't have to go in the regular bed of the creek at all. But just as he raised her up after the words were said, they both went under. The bank gave way and let 'em both down. I saw it all, and Grandma'am was with me."

Vic sat remembering until Jarvie asked impatiently: " Well, what happened to them, Vic? "

" Her husband grabbed her by the petticoats, but the water took her off and he went swimming off with her petticoat in his hand. And James Moore got hold of Elder Pugmire's hair and dragged him out, with Mrs. Pugmire a-helping. I ran on to the village for help, and then they pulled out Tom Cartwright, where he was a-hanging onto the stump of a tree. And the next day they found her, Mrs. Tom, dead, a-standing on her feet with her head above water."

Jarvie shook his head. "Vic Moon, you're making a story!"

"No, I'm not. The others'll tell you the same if you ask. They went to court for it and were in jail six weeks, the Elders. And just as the judge went to pass judgment, the Lord spoke in a voice of thunder that shook the walls of the courthouse, and so the judge listened a minute and then he said: 'It's an ordinance instituted by God, but be careful where you administer it in the future.' And they were let out."

Jarvie looked at his mother. "Do you think God drowned her for what she said, Mother?"

But Vic intervened. "Grandma'am said He did, for sure, and for meanness and swearing in His name."

Jarvie sighed. "That story was better than the one in the book." And Vic was starry-eyed for once.

"Vic is like one of those little wadded flowers," Mercy thought, "all shapeless and not meaning anything at all, and then you put it in water and it grows and spreads and all at once you see that it's something, after all." With Simon and most of the time with Mercy, too, Vic was abject and self-effacing, but with the children she was different. As though she were on her own level with them. And nothing was too good for Jarvie in Vic's eyes, Jarvie who was kind to everybody and anxious for everybody around him to feel pleasant and happy and comfortable. Anybody could see that Vic thought the world of Jarvie. But then everybody did. Something about Jarvie a person couldn't help liking.

To Simon it seemed as though the world were new. Even if the Prophet had to hide out whenever the posses came through town, he was able to give his influence to the building of Nauvoo, and he was usually at the Grove talking like an inspired angel on Sundays, even though the police guard must always be close around with their eyes canny at strangers. And sometimes, when everything was clear, the Prophet might come riding up on Old Charley to watch the men at work on the Temple. There'd be nothing like the Temple in the whole West, it'd be the biggest building most of the people had ever seen, and the finest. It was a good sight to see the Prophet and the Brothers being proud together.

For instance, the other day Brother Joseph came riding up where the workmen were busy at one of the big stone sun-faces that would surmount the columns. One of the men looked up and asked Brother Joseph: " General Smith, is this like the face you saw in the vision? "

With what careful connoisseurship Brother Joseph walked all around it! And then he said: " Very near it, but – " he paused, frowning a little – " except that the nose is just a *thought* too broad."

Is not God the Father of Sculptors?

And the Prophet's Mansion House was a-building, too, and the steamboats were bringing more and more of the niceties of life that Simon, as well as any other man, was fond of.

" You take a piece of wilderness," Simon thought with great content, " and it's like a piece of good wood in your hands, you make something out of it. You make a shape to it that folks can use, a shape that means something. And when it's done, it's the way you want it and it's yours. Like a house you build, it's yours and it's the way you thought it ought to be and you can go in and shut the door behind you, and stretch, and take your shoes off – and stretch – "

Simon stretched, contented.

And then if you had a wife like Mercy – there was that, too. You couldn't have made her any better if you had made *her*, yourself, because from the first she had been supple and sweet, bending how you would have her bend. Simon never laid abed long; he was not a lazy man and felt a great abhorrence for men who could lie and luxuriate when there was work to do. But sometimes, for just a little while, he would lie still, looking up into dawn, and feel comfort rich around him. Lately Mercy had been wonderful, more wonderful, even, than those first years when she had been a new world for a man to discover. He allowed himself, some of these mornings, to lie for a little while thinking about Mercy and about some of the times they had lived through together. That first night on the road coming to west New York, when she was so lovely and untouched it made a man ache to look at her. She had made supper over the fire and they had eaten and kissed and eaten and kissed and then she had cleared up, swiftly. Somehow he had been afraid then, afraid of himself so big and her so little, expecting maybe she would be shy and afraid too, that maybe she would retreat and he would have to follow her, waiting, and be very gentle and kind when he didn't want to wait or to be gentle or kind or anything but just to be himself and find what it was he had been dreaming of, find out quickly and then know forever.

But she had cleared supper away and then she stood in the firelight and undressed while he watched — undressed quickly, almost fiercely, and came to him. Had anything ever been so beautiful in this world as Mercy was before she had a child? Her breasts standing firm and round and the line of the hip sweet motion to the eye, like a river. She let her hair down, sometimes, until it came to her waist and it made her a legend and a fairy-tale. She delighted in everything she was, she was never cool and detached as he had feared a woman might be, but ready in his hands like clay he could mold to his wishes, quick to reach out and touch him and beckon him, quick to respond to him, moving and desiring with him. And not changing. All the years passed and she did not change, only sighed when a child was so big between them there was no coming together. It never ceased to be a wonder to him to wake after a dream of time and see her dressed demurely and busy about breakfast.

Sometimes he allowed himself a few minutes to lie still and watch her, remembering. When there had been a time that soared over the rest of life the way a peak soars over valleys around it, he wanted to linger over it, hold it in his hands awhile and look at it as he might look at a thing he had made.

❧ ❧ ❧

SIMON was praying, his family around him in a circle.

" We are Thy creatures and creatures of glory with a glorious destiny. Within us is Thy soul. May we keep these tabernacles of flesh and blood unsullied, that they may grow to match the glory of Thy soul, that they may carry us into godhood and grow more splendid until we are indeed gods like unto our Father in heaven.

" To this end, Father, guide our thoughts this night and our footsteps on the day to come. In the name of Thy beloved Son, Amen."

" Amen."

" Amen."

Mercy struggled up from her knees, pushing herself up with her hands on the seat of the chair. " When I kneel so long, my bones wrinkle," she said.

" Sort of sit back on your heels," Simon suggested, sympathetically.

Jarvie said: " Mr. Pratt was telling us about that same thing at school, Father – if a man believes he's a god it's easier for him to act like one, he said."

" It's hard enough, even then," Simon said, slapping his son's shoulder in the way all his sons liked because it made them feel like men.

" Shoo! " Mercy said, shaking her apron. " Into bed with you, Joey! Georgie, if you go out put your shoes on, you'll get slivers."

" Say *all* the Mother Bird, Mamma."

" All right, but wait for Georgie."

When Georgie came back, she stood in front of them, shaking her apron.

> " ' Shoo,' said the mother bird, shaking her feathers,
> ' Shoo, little birds, to the nest.
> The one that is first to cover his peepers,
> He is the one I love best.
>
> " ' Coo,' said the mother bird, shaking her feathers,
> ' Which little bird shall I name? '
> Together they crept in the nest and then slept —
> ' So I love them all just the same! ' "

When she finished, they were all in bed with their eyes closed, Beck and Joey and Georgie and Betsy. It had not been so long since Bert, too, she thought, had shooed himself into bed for the Mother Bird.

Betsy opened her eyes, curiously. " Were we all together, Mamma? "

" All togther. Except Betsy, now, she's peeping."

Betsy's eyes promptly closed again.

Simon and Bert sat at the table, working problems that Brother Pratt gave the boys. Bert was quick to catch onto such things, quicker than he should rightly be for his age, Simon thought. When Mercy came to the table to use the candle for mending, too, he glanced up at her. " We're going to have at least one merchant," he said.

" One rich man," she said, " can feed all the poets."

" A man has to work for what he gets," Simon said seriously, and she patted his hand.

" Bert will likely have to keep our Indian too," she said lightly, looking at Menzo. He was quilling now, embroidering quills that he had dyed himself. He looked up, grinning.

" Indians don't need money, Mother," he said. " The ground's money for Indians."

" The ground's money for farmers, too," Simon reminded him.

Mercy looked at Jarvie, because he grunted, hearing the conversation between the lines he was reading. Simon's look followed hers. " You'll pinch your nose off, Jarv, you close that book sudden," he said.

" You better get another candle, Jarvie. You're reading too close."

They were quiet then except for the murmur of Simon and Bert, at the problems. Once Betsy leaned up on her elbow and watched them from the trundle, but when Mercy shook her apron she dropped down, giggling.

It was pure peace, pure. It was a peace distilled from one blood. Nowhere else in the world was there a similar peace or a purer one. It had to be made of those who belonged together through the firm right of blood and bones. First the father and mother, brought together by love and the highest desire, and then the children, one by one taking their places, one by one as the years passed filling another and another chair, taking their places in the cradles and trundles and cots, taking their places one by one at the table. In every child the father and mother were together again, every child was a seal on them.

The Gospel was clear in its blessing upon the family. The First Family was God's, and it had grown like this, one by one, until it covered the world, and those who had gone home to God filled His world, Kolob, the Great Star. Each man, then, who achieved glory through this endless process of growing in his children was God over those children, and would chastise them and bless them worlds without end.

What was a nation or a race or a creed when you could know it so certainly – we are all sons of a Great Sire! We belong together, we are one blood, we should be tender and devoted and understanding with all men. Like one family sitting around one table, like one family under one roof.

Mercy sat with her sewing, thinking many strong thoughts.

Simon worked with Bert at his problems.

Jarvis read with his fingers unsteady, excited, on the margins.

Menzo embroidered, laying colors in symbolic patterns.

Betsy screwed her face carefully, feigning sleep, but peeped out sometimes through her fingers.

And Georgie and Joey slept in their trundle. And Beck in the cradle. And sometimes fire dropped from the log on the fire and sparks went spraying upward, crackling.

And the clock ticked in the little square place Simon had made for it, just the right-sized niche over the mantel.

Chapter XV

Eliza knelt by the little wooden chest and stared out of the window. It was like an altar, that chest, holding everything she loved most and symbolizing everything. She kept her quills and papers on it, always ready when a time should come. Whenever she came from speaking with Joseph, whenever she came from the Grove where he had been preaching, there was a feverish desire in her fingers, a medley of words in her brain that wanted putting on paper. Rhyme was easy; wasn't there an alphabet full of rhymes for every sound and all one had to do was go through them? Now, *lash* – ash, bash, cash, dash, ash again (for e), fash (no such word, silly, but it might mean something) gash, hash, ash again (for i), jash, kash, lash, mash, nash, pash, q – (nothing, impossible), rash, sash, tash, u – no, vash – no, wash (only half-rhyming, or it didn't make sense), x, y, z.

Not anything, not anything at all. Change *lash*, get something easy like *blow* instead. There now, bow, c, doe, owe, flow, foe. Flow – let's see, the idea, too, *and blood will flow*. Now, there was the idea and everything.

> Fear, O ye brethren, the assassins' blow?
> In God's dread time, their blood will flow –

Oh, no, not today, not today, anything today but blood and vengeance and Missouri, something today to smooth down the fear and drown the dream and make you forget the ways life is never full. Something with quiet in it and comfort. Something like what Joseph said this morning. Looking as though he were an angel put on earth by mistake; looking as though he spoke with his eyes on things the people could not see; looking as though he gazed straight into heaven through a shining gate and told them everything he saw there. And spent when he finished, as though he had come, running, a long way.

And what was it that had made her feel her spine soft against the bench – a lovely thing, lovely? "Our Father who art in heaven, and our families are in heaven, too, for how could there be a Father in heaven unless there is a Mother there, also? And must we not have brothers and sisters in the spirit land? For is not heaven our first and our last home? It is inconceivable to think of it as incomplete, that Home."

The idea; not his words, but the idea.

She tore away the sheet she had blotched and began at the top of a fresh one. There was little need for the alphabet now, the rhymes were ready at her fingertips, beckoning. Sometimes it was like that, and in the end it was always better, the poem. Poetry was not meant to agonize, then, it was not meant to walk sweating.

Oh, my Father, thou that dwellest
In the high and glorious place,
When shall I regain thy presence,
And again behold thy face?

She bit the quill and stared down into the street, unseeing. Even so early, heat quivered and rose in waves from the ground. A carriage passed and left streamers of dust behind it that settled quickly in windless air. Three birds scratched in the loose ground of Stephen's flower-bed.

In the heavens, are parents single?
No, the thought makes reason stare!

Truth is reason, Truth eternal
Tells me I've a mother there.

Her pen scratched and she lightened her grasp upon it. For a moment she felt strangely beyond the world, poised above it with her only support the tip of this moving pen. She wrote stanza after stanza.

When I leave this frail existence,
When I lay this mortal by,
Father, Mother, may I meet you
In your royal courts on high?

Reading it over, breathlessly, she knew that it carried with it the same quality of authoritative faith as that couplet she had always wished she might have written. Short and without rhyme, but carrying the indelible mark of a thing to keep in the mind and to repeat, already becoming an aphorism that leaped into the preaching, one of those verses beyond author:

As man now is, God once was,
As God now is, man may be.

All, in those few words. And her own brother Lorenzo had risen in a little meeting at Henry Sherwood's house to say it for the first time. It just came to him, he said, as though it had been whispered by an angel. And this – this had been sung into her fingers.

She looked at it. Hardly a scratch on it, hardly a scratch or a change. She read it aloud again, with emotion, holding the paper trembling in her hands. And because it wanted singing, she read it again with her voice making a simple tune for the words. This Joseph would like, he couldn't help liking this. It would help the people say over and over what he wanted them to believe. When they said it themselves, over and over, they would believe more deeply. And when they sang it, they would sing faith, for song denies arrogance and disbelief. For their funerals this would be, with a soft tune around it.

Painstakingly she copied it over and folded the original into a corner of her chest. Joseph had lost part of the Book of Mormon for not having a second copy – it had been a lesson to them all. She was terribly excited, and her body was blazing with something besides the heat of the day. I have made something, I have made something; if you make something from what you believe, then the blessing of belief can never leave you. I have something to show him that he will like –

She went downstairs and up the street toward Joseph's office. But the clerk in the store said he had gone home. She hesitated. He was home and she must go in, if she saw him, and tell him in front of everybody. If there could be a time when she could go in and say: "Joseph, I must see you alone!" Without anybody staring, only knowing that Sister Eliza would like to see her husband alone as any woman has a right to do.

She went to the homestead, passing the great house the Brothers were building for Brother Joseph. There would be no mansion like it this far west. Emma had showed her the pictures of chandeliers with prisms hanging like jewels, and had shown the samples of thick red carpet that would lie from wall to wall.

But Joseph was not at home, either. He had gone out with Emma and the children in the carriage.

She stood irresolute by the river. It would be better to read it to him first, while the shine of a new thing was on it. But there was Mercy – it would be good to read it to Mercy, too, and she wasn't one to take the shine off anything, but rather invested things with a shine of her very own. She wrote poetry, too, sometimes and understood a poem rightly – oh, she never wrote great poems that thousands of people could rise to their feet and sing together, but little poems that a woman could read by candlelight to her husband, or recite to her children. It would be something, Eliza thought, to read a poem by candle-light to one's husband —

She took the ferry and crossed the river. The river was never twice the same, never twice, nor ever the same sunset two nights running. Different colors, a different reach, a different depth. It was a wonder God had enough different sunsets to go around the years.

MERCY was not well today and was doing things that could be done in her chair. Nothing, only a touch of rheumatism that would pass off in a day or so. It was never very long, she said. Even this dampened Eliza's spirits; she had felt that since the poem was perfect, then the whole world must be perfect too.

She read the poem slowly, pleasure shining in the words. Mercy sat with her eyes intent and her lips parted in a way she had. When Eliza finished she said: "Beautiful, Eliza, beautiful."

Eliza took a deep breath, realized that she had read the whole scarcely breathing. "It wants singing," she said.

"It sings itself. So measured, so perfect. It's a hymn, Eliza."

"I know. It makes its own tune, almost. I took it right over to Joseph, but he wasn't home."

Mercy's face clouded. "You were thinking about him all the time, weren't you? You know, when you were reading I thought: 'Eliza always writes about heaven.' They say nobody writes about heaven unless he's unhappy in this world."

"I've always written about heaven," Eliza protested. "Even when I was little — "

"Maybe you never were happy, Liza."

"Of course I was! There never was a happier child than I was. I can remember how I used to play, pretending; I'd pretend I was everything in the picture books."

" Then you weren't ever happy except when you were pretending? "

" Mercy Baker! The way you catch a person up! "

" But the poem is beautiful, Eliza, just beautiful. Only I think about the poet, too."

Eliza folded the paper and put the poem in her bag. Her hands were unsteady. " Well," she said, " it's not his fault. He's always having to run to the Islands or hide out in somebody's house or run to Carthage and Springfield. I wish they'd leave him alone."

" I've watched you," Mercy said, " and I know nothing has happened to you, nothing like what happened the day you were on the bluff. When something really happens to a woman, it shows, especially if it's a woman like you. There's a look of coming alive, like you had for a while, something that shows in the skin, even, a warm-colored look."

" It's not his fault," Eliza said again. " They hound him to death, he can't live his own life. And it's the people's fault, too, because he can't trust them."

" Well, whoever's to blame, that's exactly the kind of poem I'd expect you to be writing."

" I'd rather talk about something else," Eliza said.

EMMA and Joseph Smith and their handsome young sons rode through Nauvoo in their new carriage. Brother Joseph removed his hat again and again and Sister Emma nodded to left and to right.

" Well – it's something to have a carriage again," Emma said.

Joseph handled the reins lovingly over his spirited horses.

" Daddy," little Frederick said, " do you know what I dreamed last night? I dreamed all the Missouri pukes had their heads chopped off! "

" Frederick! " Emma reproved.

" Well, I did. I dreamed that."

" It's a wicked dream. Don't think about it."

Brother Joseph twinkled. " Maybe you could dream them dead in a tidier way, son," he said. " It must be rather mussy chopping heads, mustn't it? "

" Yes," said Frederick positively. " It was."

The carriage passed Brother Brigham's new brick house and Bemen's cottage next door, where pretty Louise stood by the gate with her girl friends. Joseph removed his hat with dignity and Emma bowed. A storm of giggling burst from the group and they ran toward the house.

Emma flushed. " What were they laughing at? "

" Oh, just laughing," Joseph said, unperturbed. " Girls that age are always laughing over nothing, you know that."

But she frowned, glancing back.

" For goodness' sake, Emma, you don't think they were laughing at *us*? "

" No. Of course not."

But there was a sharp edge on Emma's voice and when they came home she was still frowning. Joseph went immediately to his desk, and she began to remove her bonnet, but changed her mind and went out again. Up the street to Stephen Markham's house.

Eliza was not at home, so Emma waited in her room, looking out of the window and drumming on the sill with nervous fingers.

❧ ❧ ❧ ❧

ELIZA picked her way carefully over the stones in the street and entered Markham's gate. It had not been much comfort talking to Mercy, after all. For quite a while it had not been much comfort. And perhaps it was natural enough that Mercy, a first wife, should champion the priority of first-wifehood. As though she thought, even when she tried to be comforting: "If you're a plural wife, take the leavings and welcome, but leave the home as it is, unbroken and sanctified. Stay in your little room and leave marriage the way it is."

Eliza climbed the narrow stairs and opened the door to her room. A woman was there, staring down into the street. She did not turn, but Eliza knew her at once, the straight back, the erect head with its high dusty-black hair. A dignity that never softened.

"Hello, Emma."

Eliza saw her lift her hand abruptly to her face, a hand carrying a wadded handkerchief to her eyes. She was crying, then, and didn't want it to be seen. Emma wouldn't want anybody to see her cry.

Eliza took her bonnet off and laid it carefully in the box. Then she sat down and waited. "Won't you sit down?" she asked.

"No. No, thank you." Emma turned and Eliza saw that she had not been able to obliterate the signs of her weeping. "I'd rather stand up; it's suffocating up here, I don't see how you stand it."

"It usually turns off cool at night," Eliza said.

She felt her heart thudding painfully in her side, and knew she had been dreading the time when Emma would come to her, dreading it without allowing herself to think of it clearly. She braced herself, holding her back firmly against the back of the chair.

Emma came across the little space with her two hands out to find Eliza's hands. "Eliza—I don't know how to tell you. I don't even know how to start." Her face was even paler than usual, and her eyes, always dark, were black in her white face.

Eliza held her hands firmly. Hadn't she always been dear Eliza, dear, dear Eliza, Eliza who was the only one to be trusted with the children, Eliza who must help select satin for a special dress, Eliza who should be consulted about the menu for those politicians from Springfield whom Joseph was so anxious to please?

"What's the matter, Emma? Has anything happened?"

"I don't know. That's the maddening thing, I don't even know. It doesn't seem as though I know anything any more, as though I couldn't think. And he doesn't tell me anything, either, just says I know him well enough to trust him. But I don't. Sometimes I think I know him too well to trust him, Eliza!"

Eliza was conscious of that painful slow beating of her heart, and took her hand from Emma's and laid it, pressing up, on her bodice.

"I've had a queer feeling that there wasn't anybody – not anybody in Nauvoo! – that I could trust. And then I thought of you, and I knew I could trust you if I could trust anybody."

"I hope I've never done anything to make you think you couldn't trust me." Eliza's voice was dry as a leaf.

"I couldn't stand not to do something; I thought if I were doing something maybe I wouldn't worry so much."

"Is there something I can do?" She wished she could put some warmth in that curt little voice, but she could not.

"Eliza –" Emma's voice pleaded. "You don't know what I'm talking about. Do you, Eliza?"

For a moment Eliza hesitated. Then she said, because she was not accustomed to lying: "Yes, I think I do."

"You do!"

Emma leaped up and faced her, furious. "Everybody knows, everybody knows, and they're looking at me when I go up and down the streets and whispering behind my back!"

Eliza tried to protest.

"Oh, I've seen them, Eliza! Whispering and talking and even laughing the way people do when they're laughing at you –

all at once *not* laughing when you look at them." Her voice sank, leveled. "What do you think, Eliza? Do you think it's true?"

The honest heart beat very slowly, Eliza could feel it under her fingers. She looked up and quickly down again, and said: "I – I don't know."

"Then you've got to help me. I can't stand not knowing, I can't stand it, Eliza. He's got his whittling deacons to spy out folks for him and I'll get me some deaconesses to spy him out for me. And you'll help me. Won't you?"

Eliza sat stunned.

"Won't you?"

"What do you want me to do?" Eliza wet her lips with the tip of her tongue.

Emma was not hysterical now, but calculating with the same mild calculation in her voice that planned a menu, planned what she would bring from St. Louis for the Mansion, planned what she would wear for an evening out.

"I've got to find out if it's true first, and then I want to know who they are. Sarah Pratt told me he was going around seeing different ones and having them at his office – that pretty empty-headed Louise Bemen, for one, she giggles when she sees me. And Lucy Walker."

She was too absorbed in herself to see Eliza's face. Louise Bemen, exquisite and small-boned, her feet pointed in the quadrilles and her flounces bouncing. Only a baby, really, and not a thought in her head. And Lucy Walker, with her high red heels showing, even on Sunday. Eliza felt a terrible silence where her heart should be beating, a terrible stillness where her blood should run. And Emma was standing in front of her, misty and yet real, and Eliza became deeply aware of this figure of Emma Smith that she had almost ceased to see because of accustomness. She saw that Emma's breasts were slumped from nursing her babies, her sleek hair turning gray over the temples, drawn black lines under her big eyes, and a pocket under each eye as though it might be meant to catch her tears. It was perfectly plain that she was going to have another child before many months, and Emma was never lovely carrying a child. Dark women with such white skin sometimes had liver-spots like that, and they showed their emotions without meaning to at these times. Eliza was surprised at her deliberate observation. Had not everybody always taken it for granted that Sister Emma was beautiful?

"What do you want me to do?"

"I was thinking – Well, everybody trusts you, Eliza, and you have so much to do with the Council, they'd never wonder about you. I want you to find out for me – go over to Bemen's when he starts that way and find out where Louise is – you can find out for me."

"Oh, Emma, I couldn't!"

"Of course you could. I know you aren't a spy or a gossip either, anybody knows that. That's why you've got to be the one. There's not another soul in Nauvoo I'd ask to do it."

Eliza sat as though she were turned to stone. If Emma would go, if she would only go! His face came to her; how many times had she seen his face, living over again that afternoon with the sun on the river, moving and not moving. A V of ducks moving over, and the soft sound of the river. Whenever she saw him, whenever he stood on the rostrum and spoke to the people, smiling at her sometimes in a way she knew was especially for her, meaning for her to remember, she had been on the bluff again. You would not dream how strong a man's arms could be, and how a mouth could make you think of heaven, as she had told Mercy. And now she thought: "If Emma would go! It's all I've ever had, I won't let her spoil it, it's not true."

But Emma was speaking rapidly, close to her.

"I've wondered. Hyrum comes and makes special little speeches about how chosen Joseph is, and how wonderful it is that Joseph married a strong-minded sensible woman like me. I've never heard anything from his family but how chosen he is. And I believe it, Eliza – didn't I choose him out of the whole world myself, and doesn't that mean anything? Haven't I been dragged with him, from pillar to post? Haven't I loved him in spite of his old mother and her tea-leaves and her crazy fits, in spite of William's meanness and that ghastly sister – I don't need to be told how chosen he is! "

Eliza fumbled for words. " Then you should be able to trust him, Emma. A Prophet of God – "

To her surprise, Emma laughed. " He's pretty much concerned with this world, for a Prophet of God. And I've never worried much about the next world, Eliza, I never have. There've been nights the past few years when I've wanted to die, but not to go to heaven, just to sleep and never wake up and face the world again. But it wasn't because I didn't love him, Eliza, it was because I did, and they'd not let him alone. Why – " and it was not the familiar austere Emma who was speaking – " why, Eliza, I've lived with him so long and loved him so much he's just like part of me. After fifteen years you get like that about a man. You couldn't understand that, of course, but that's the way it is."

Swiftly, unbidden, came the thought of Joseph's shining hair, his hands, the swift magic of his mouth. " Yes, I think I can understand it, Emma. I'm sure I can."

" Eliza – if this is true, I can't live. I can't."

" Don't think about it, Emma. He's a good man – there's not a man or a woman or a child in Zion that wouldn't tell you so."

" Oh, yes there is, Eliza. And I wish they'd leave us alone. We've been so happy sometimes, when they've left us alone. Back in Kirtland – one day he brought in a revelation and it was beautiful, like a poem. He made it for me, he said. You remember it – ' It is lawful that he should have one wife and they twain shall be one flesh and all this that the earth might answer the end of its creation.' And then: ' He shall cleave to his wife and none else.' How can people say these awful things about him, Eliza? "

A spasm went over Eliza's face, and she turned to the window. If Emma would only go!

But Emma talked on as though she must talk forever to ease herself. " After you've cooked and mended for a man for fifteen years, and you've nursed him when he was sick and picked off the lice he's got in the jailhouses, and taken tar and feathers off his body from his head to his heels, and hidden him and lied for him and carried things to him and kept his supper hot a thousand times – well, you get over thinking he's so very spiritual, Eliza. I guess I shouldn't say such things to you – you're so spiritual yourself – but I know how excitable he is and how passionate he is and how hot-headed, and how all of a sudden he'll get sick at his stomach – "

Eliza was rigid in every muscle; she wanted to cry out, to scream so loudly her voice would drown these confidences, but she could not. She gripped herself until her head rocked with the effort.

" When you've been married to a man for fifteen years, you know these things about him."

At last Emma rose to go. " You go to Bemen's tonight; he said there was council meeting at Brigham's and that's right next door. Don't say anything, but just see – I know I can trust you, Eliza; there's nobody else I can talk to."

" Thank you, Emma."

And they kissed.

Eliza heard Emma's footsteps going down the stairway; she heard the brief greeting to Stephen's wife, heard the door swing to. Then the ice broke and the sound of its breaking was clear. So spiritual – so spiritual! But she dropped her head upon the chest where she had made so many poems and wept as any woman weeps.

Chapter XVI

THERE was a skyful of rolling woolly clouds like lamb's wool and a moon in the west that looked like a cradle. A sky for babies. Eliza thought: "Not a night for spies."

Eliza was seldom afraid at night, but perhaps it was being so weary, perhaps being so guilty, that made every tree ominous. It wasn't fair to do this, she who knew intimately what was in his heart, she who should be beyond suspicion and not sneaking around behind him like an enemy.

But she walked on deliberately, toward Brother Brigham's. It wasn't for Emma, it wasn't for anybody but herself. She faced that, flinching.

A wind had come up with evening and was playing in the sky and making a great stir in the cottonwoods.

A man stepped abruptly from behind a tree and confronted her. A cry rose in her throat, a stilled cry that could not come out in sound but struggled to be heard like a cry in a dream.

He spoke huskily and she breathed again, shaken. "Jest Port, Sister. Gotta know everybody's business in this neighborhood, that's all."

Porter Rockwell. She should have known him at once — if the moon had been a little brighter she would have known him. Nobody else ever wore his hair long like that.

"You scared me, Port. You shouldn't jump at women from trees that way."

" Didn't know you was a woman till you got right close't. Women gener'ly don't walk streets nights. Where you bound? "

" If you won't scold me, I'll tell you."

" Tell me an' I'll take ye there. Got a lotta deacons along here mindin' after the Prophet. They'll be jumpin' at ye every other tree."

" Is Brother Joseph at Brigham's? That's where I was going."

" You on the Council? " Port's voice was jovial and easy.

" Me and Mary Ann'll have a special Council in the kitchen."

The shades were carefully drawn over the windows of Brigham's house and Port took her to the kitchen door. As he swaggered along beside her she could hear the clanking of his double brace of pistols.

" They say you can take a fence-post at a hundred yards," she said.

" I can take the eye in a weathercock at five hundred," he said mildly, " an' I can take a Missouri puke right in the bloody heart, clean acrost the river."

" Brother Joseph says you're the best bodyguard in the world."

" Did he say that? " Pleasure ran along his rugged voice. " Well, I reckon he was about right, at that. Nobody's gonna take better care o' Brother Joseph than Port is."

" I know it. And you've taken good care of me." She stopped at the kitchen door, rapped gently. When the door opened she turned to thank Port, but he was gone into the darkness.

It was pleasant sitting with Mary Ann and the children, but Eliza was sharp to hear the end of the flowing voices in the next room and the scraping of chairs.

" It was a little scary coming down," she said when she heard them at last. " If it hadn't been for Port, I'd really been scared, I think. I only wanted to walk under that little moon, but I guess moons aren't meant for single ladies."

Mary Ann laughed. " And I wouldn't say Port was too romantic."

" I'll just go and walk back home along with some of the Apostles."

She was feverishly anxious that it all sound very natural, and she was sure it did. She said good-night and went through the front way to join the Apostles who were shaking Brother Brigham's hand at the front door. Joseph looked at her with a pleasure and unbelief that restored something she had lost this morning, long ago this morning.

" Eliza Snow! " He took her hand strongly. " What you doing here? You spying on the High Council? "

She gasped, colored, but said lightly: " Can't the women have councils, too, Brother Joseph? "

Brigham stood by the gate, like the good host he always was, until they were well up the street. Then he went to the door, waved his hand once more, and went in.

Eliza walked smally among all the big men, and she saw the guardsmen move silently from their posts and come after, at a little distance. Joseph reached out and took her hand through his arm, holding her fingers among his fingers and she felt them curling warmly. Presently he released her and she saw that they were in front of Bemen's cottage and that a candle burned in a front window, shining faintly along the path.

" Wait a minute, Eliza. I've got something to tell Brother Bemen." And he went in the gate and knocked at the door. Louise herself opened it, standing against the candlelight, a trim silhouette. Joseph spoke rapidly and loudly. " Tell your father I can't stop tonight, Louise. I'll see him tomorrow. In the office, about sundown."

" All right." It was a sweet voice, very young.

Joseph came back, jauntily, to join Eliza at the gate, and they went on and once more he imprisoned her fingers. There was nothing, then, nothing at all. To be so suspicious – it was like the enemies of Christ, creeping and following. She'd tell Emma she wouldn't have any part in it.

One by one the Apostles came to their homes and fell away from the group, calling good-night, good-night. When they came to Markham's gate, there was only Hyrum.

" You go on, Hyrum," Joseph said, and she felt her heart begin that painful, suffocating beating. " I'll be along."

Hyrum teased pleasantly as was his way. " You be careful, you two. That's a lover's moon tonight."

" A lover's moon has to be fuller," Eliza said.

But when he had gone she was not sure. Even that baby moon made a great shining on the river, and sometimes the clouds raced over for a moment and then abandoned the chase to clear sky and then raced over again. Perhaps it was a lover's moon, hiding and retreating and then shining so that it lighted the whole world.

Joseph turned to her and gathered her up close against him and whispered: " Little Eliza-wife! Wife-Eliza."

For a moment she thought of Emma and stood stiff, struggling to be cool and detached, but Emma would not stay. " If there are any more spies," she thought wildly, " here's something to spy for."

" Oh, I've been lonely, I've been so lonely – " It was not what she meant to say and she did not say it with despair but with contentment, against him, meaning to tell him that it was all over and forgotten in this moment. She felt her body grow plastic and feminine and light. She knew that she would never move if she could help it, never as long as she lived.

Joseph moved, stood back looking at her. " I'll try to do better, Eliza. There's been so much; my life's not my own, you know; I can't do the things I'd like to do."

" After all," she said, " if you're a prophet and important and famous, you should be willing to pay for it." She wished he would come close again. He said: " When there's a new moon, a moon in the quarter like this, I'll come. Will you like that? "

She laughed shakily. " Full or quarter or anything," she said.

He came close once more. " Still love me, Eliza? "

" Yes – oh, yes." They both whispered. " The way I love God, Joseph! "

He drew back with mock surprise. " Eliza Snow – Eliza Snow *Smith* – I thought I'd taught you better! "

" I wrote a poem this morning, I wanted you to see it. It's about heaven, the other heaven. When I go in, I'll write one about *this* heaven." He was very quiet. " It *is* heaven, you know, Joseph. Right here, this way, standing like this."

He stood back, trying to see her face. " Not quite," he said.

She trembled. " I know. Not quite."

" Maybe by the time there's another quarter-moon, Eliza, they'll all know and then I'll teach you what heaven really is. When they all understand so you'll never have to suffer a scandal because of me. I couldn't stand that."

She stood very quiet.

" You can see how it is, can't you, Eliza? "

" I'm not afraid of what anybody could say."

" Maybe it won't be long." His voice was husky. " Maybe by the time that moon grows again."

Then he was gone and she saw the shadows melting out from the trees along the street moving along after him. He had taught his guard not to stand too close. It was hard to see him go; she stretched out her hand wanting to call him back. But he was gone. She stood by the fence, biting her mouth, and Emma came back to her. She was not welcome, poor Emma, but she came.

THERE was a meeting that night in Law's steam mill, too, and some folks were together in their back kitchens. Over the river by Pagett's blacksmith shop, men were sitting on bummer's logs in the moonlight. Some of them talked and some of them laughed and some neither laughed nor talked but listened with their mouths tight on their faces. " Old Joe! " some said, and some said: " Brother Joseph." Some smacked their lips and said: " He knows how to make his bread fall butter-side up, he does; he gets his bread buttered both sides, an' then he butters the crust, both ends."

It was late afternoon before Eliza screwed her courage to the point of going to Emma. She plunged at once into words.

" It wasn't anything, Emma. Just a council. And right home after. I'm sure there wasn't anything."

Emma stared at her as though she saw her obscurely, through a mist. Her eyes were haggard, but there were bright spots on either cheek, coming and going.

" It's good of you to come," she said deliberately, " but I don't think I'll need you any more, Eliza. This morning Hyrum came and brought me the Revelation and a very nice list of the favored ones. A neat list Brother Richards copied out especially for me."

She watched the dull red wash over Eliza's neck and over her face.

" I don't think Dr. Richards forgot any of them," Emma said. She spoke as one speaks who is through crying, who will not cry again.

The bantering irony left her voice then, and she came closer and seemed to blaze from within like a candle lantern.

" So I guess I won't need any more deaconesses! I won't need you any more! "

Eliza looked at her, but not steadily.

" I had no idea, Eliza, you could be so sly. Not one word out of you, not one word. I should have known you were deeper than you looked. I've heard it before – the narrower a woman and the colder, the deeper she's likely to be. I'll not forget it again."

" How could I tell you? I couldn't tell you, Emma."

Emma did not hear the misery in Eliza's voice; she was studying her list with dry eyes, her eyebrows lifted. " Good women, all," she said coolly. " Nothing short of marriage would make whores out of any of you."

She had no idea how it was cutting, she did not notice how Eliza flinched under it. She looked up, but did not seem to see Eliza, not really, her gaze was so bright and dismissing.

" Please don't expect me to recognize you, Eliza. Or – what would you think? I'm so used to asking you for advice! Maybe I could go around with a retinue behind me, like his Legion. A staff of aides-de-camp, in uniform. We could choose an appropriate uniform, don't you think? His favorite color – let's see – blue – "

Eliza escaped. She saw that it was nearly sunset and the west was coming alive. A blazing one, tonight. Deliberately she walked the block to Joseph's store and crossed the street to stand in the shadow of a tree. After a time, Louise Bemen came down the sidewalk, dressed in pale green with matching ribbons on her bonnet; she might be going to a party. Eliza's teeth set rigidly into her under lip, watching, and as Louise turned in to the stairs to the office, her heels clicking on the wooden steps, Eliza heard her humming gaily. *Duke Street*. Once Eliza had made hymn-words to that and they pleased Joseph very much.

Chapter XVII

"THIS is meant to be read aloud," Jarvie said to Vic, apologetically.

Quickly she said: "I like hearing it. Go on, it's all right."

He turned the pages. "Look here, I'll find something you *will* like – Wordsworth, a man who loved England."

He read to her slowly and when he looked up, he saw that she had stopped knitting, for once completely responsive to what he read.

"I'll find another one. Let's see – Keats. 'I stood tiptoe . . .'"

At the end he closed the book and sat looking at her. She began knitting again, very fast. "Did you love it terribly, Vic?" he asked. "Things like this – they make it all out to be may trees and nightingales."

"I don't know if I ever heard a nightingale," Vic said.

"You know, when I think about it, I feel sort of solemn and strange, like I was marching to an old tune and wore a bright coat and buckles. Maybe it's because of the poetry and Toby, together."

He was half laughing, but Vic looked at him soberly. "It's an awful green country," she said. "It's awful green when you get out in it like that. I didn't get out much, maybe once or twice in the summer of a holiday. It's so green you feel green all over. And early morning you get wet to the knees in it. It's a green wet, too, all grass."

She paused, reflecting.

"But it's awful black, too, England is. Green – and black."

"What do you mean, black?"

"Just black. In town, I mean. You get smudged and it's dark early."

She herself was puzzled, looking back into it. She saw that he was looking at her frankly and deeply, with sympathy on his face.

"My mother named me Victoria," she said suddenly. "I used to think it was too grand for me, but now I'd like it."

"You look more like Vic," Jarvie said.

"Do I?" She was disappointed; so he said:

"But I'll call you what you want, of course. If it matters to you, that's what we'll call you, all of us. Only you should have told us sooner; we'll forget."

"Once," she said gently, "I saw the Queen."

"Vic! Did you?"

"Yes, I did, riding along in her carriage."

"How'd she look?"

"Not very big, and young and laughing-like. Some of the people said a little bit shiny. That was silly, of course."

"Did she have a crown on?"

"No, just a big hat. Like anybody. But soldiers went first and last and I couldn't get close enough for real good looking."

Jarvie laughed, ashamed of his childish question. "You know, I used to think they always wore crowns," he said. "That's when I was little."

"I did, too. I sort of thought they were *attached* –"

Jarvie was delighted. "Me too, Vic! For years I thought that. Like the halo on Jesus."

They were silent for a time and he turned the pages of his book without seeing them.

" I'm sorry you didn't get close enough to see good, Vic. Victoria! "

She flushed. " Maybe you better not."

" What? "

" Call me that."

" Why? "

" I don't know. It makes me feel funny. For people to hear — "

" All right, just when nobody's around, then. Would you like that? "

She nodded, excited. Then he asked: " Vic, did you ever see any lords or ladies or people like that? "

" Oh, yes, lots of them. All the time. We've got lots of them folks in England."

" We don't. But it's better, not having them. Don't you think it's better? Then everybody's just the same."

" I don't know." She looked at him strangely, her eyes kindling. " If it was true, it would be all right," she said. " But it's not true, really. You say it, but it's not, and the Elders said it, but it's not."

" Why, Vic, of course it's true! "

" No, it's not." She shook her head stubbornly.

" But in Nauvoo it's true, Vic. That's the whole reason for having Nauvoo, you know, so everybody can be the same. Maybe it's not true every single place, but it's true in Nauvoo. Back in New York we had some land but it wasn't enough and Dad had to work a mill for a man. That wasn't being the same as the man that owned it; he was a nasty old man always making out he hadn't made enough to give Father any more. So we came out here."

" Do you think," Vic asked sagely, " that I'm the same as you? "

" Why, of course! We both work, don't we? And Father couldn't work longer unless the sun forgot to go down, and Mother wears herself out every day. It's like Brother Joseph says, a community of labor is a community of love – you work with somebody, he has his job and you have yours, and you're happy together and you have the same things, all you need, and then you're good citizens, and then a town full of good citizens like that is a good town."

He was breathless.

"It's loving a place together, Vic, and you don't love it together until you've worked on it together. That's what Brother Joseph says, and it's true."

She looked at him doubtfully.

"All the same," she said, "some gets the sugar and some gets the slops."

"Well, then, if a man's getting slops, all he has to do is work hard enough and he'll start getting himself some of the sugar."

"Maybe," Vic said enigmatically. "Maybe not."

Jarvie looked at her, worried. "Vic Moon," he said, "you talk like a gentile."

"Maybe I do."

"Didn't you come over here for the Gospel, Vic?"

"Sure. Sure I did. But some others did, too, and for some sugar they thought they'd get, besides. But some has mansions on dry ground and some has shacks in the swamp. That's what I mean."

He was still, hardly understanding what it was that made him so disturbed.

"Do many people feel like that about it, Vic? When you go over to your aunt's, do they talk like that?"

"They don't talk about much of anything," she said, scornfully. "They're too mixed-up and disappointed – and tired. But there's plenty of talking to hear if you listen, anywhere you go. Over at Nunn's store when I go buying for your ma, at Pagett's blacksmith shop, any place."

"What do they say?"

"Oh – things."

“ *What* things? ”

“ Well, about Brother Joseph mostly, and Brigham Young, and all the Apostles. Nunn can't see why Brother Joseph sells stuff cheaper and takes the trade out from under him. Schrench Sirine can't see why a Prophet should have a corner on the liquor business.”

“ Vic – he doesn't! ”

“ I don't know, I'm just telling you what they say.” Her voice was injured. “ You *asked* me – *I* didn't say it! ”

He was frowning. “ What else do they say? ”

“ Oh, about the wharf and the ferry; that meeting your folks went to tonight, it's about the wharf trouble.”

“ I hadn't paid much attention. I thought they were just voting whether to open Water Street or not. After all, the city's got to collect some wharfage, and Hiram Kimball won't collect it. So all the boats stop on his land.”

“ That's it,” Vic said, kindling. “ And why should he collect money and turn it right over to the city? It's his land, isn't it? ”

He looked at her, uncertain. “ Where do you get all this stuff? ” he asked.

“ I told you. I just keep my ears open.”

They heard the carriage coming up the bluff. Vic stood up and moved toward her door. “ It's just like I said, it's all a fight about sugar and slops. Everybody wants the sugar.”

“ I guess that's it.” He stared at her, impressed.

“ And then,” she said lightly, “ the only ones that want to share everything, they're the ones with the slops.”

They heard Mercy get out of the carriage; Simon drove around to the stable. Vic slipped away to her room.

When Mercy came in, she was already removing her bonnet.

“ Jarvie, you still up? You won't be worth a bag of beans tomorrow.”

“ I'm going.” He started up the ladder, stopped and looked at her. “ Mother, what was the meeting about tonight? ”

" Oh – there was a fight yesterday when they opened up Water Street, there had to be a vote on it." She loosened her skirt and it slipped down over her petticoats. " I'm glad to get that off," she said, " it's getting too tight, for some reason."

" Everybody *knew* it was Hi Kimball's land."

" I guess I must be getting fatter again," she murmured.

" Anyhow, why did there have to be a fight, why didn't they vote first? I heard that young Pagett kid got his cheek split."

" I know." She frowned. " I thought they should have been more serious about it tonight, it was made to seem sort of funny."

Simon came in wearily. He grunted as he sat down and began immediately to unbutton his shoes. " What's funny? " he asked.

Mercy smiled. " A woman always takes her corset off first," she said, " and a man his shoes."

" What's tight wants to come first," Simon said.

" I was just telling Jarv about the meeting."

" That was good, what the Patriarch said." He grinned, looking up at Jarvie. " He said the lawyers were like wigglers and toads, they'd all dry up in the fall! And then, when they'd let him for laughing, he said lawyers were made in gizzard-making time when it was cheaper to get gizzards than souls! He's good when he gets started, Brother Hyrum is."

" Brother Joseph was funnier when that fellow came up the aisle with the big book – "

" You could see he was right." He looked up at Jarvie. " He said the lawyers had never looked into a book on maritime law in their lives and here came this fellow with the big book – "

" Well, it's settled," Mercy said, and slipped over into the shadows of the bed to put on her nightgown.

" Good night, Jarv."

" Good night." But he hesitated a moment. " Father, hadn't Hiram Kimball paid for his land? "

Simon looked up sharply. " Sure he had," he said. " He'll get what it's worth if he don't make so much trouble the lawyers get it."

When Jarvis was in bed, he lay thinking. He knew Hiram Kimball, a jolly fellow who didn't seem likely to make anybody much trouble. When he woke up, it was still on his mind, and after breakfast, as he and Simon were walking along the bluff to the south field, he asked suddenly: " You think our river-land is worth anything, Father? "

Simon looked down at it, the narrow beach below the bluff that was his piece of the Mississippi. " Sure – maybe it'll be worth a lot some time. There's power in the rapids right along here."

" Brother Joseph's surveyed it," Jarvie said. " What'd you say if he opened a street on it? "

Simon stopped in the path abruptly and looked at his son. His words were slow and deliberate. " I'd say the city needed it and shut my mouth."

They moved on, but Jarvie kept looking down at the river. " It's a funny thing – " he began, but Simon interrupted him.

" If you're still thinking about Kimball – all he had to do was pay the city wharfage according to law. He's a trouble-maker, he talks too much."

" Anybody'd talk about his own land. It's like you said, maybe it'll be worth a lot some time. Maybe he didn't want to sell it for what it's worth right now."

" And maybe," Simon said, his feet heavy and deliberate on the path, " maybe it'd be better if young folks didn't worry too much about things that're not their concern. Getting so they chip in about everything."

Jarvie sensed a new and unfamiliar coolness in his father's voice, and in spite of it, maybe because of it, he wanted to say something more. It was almost an unspoken challenge.

" What I wonder – did Brother Joseph have a revelation about it? "

Simon's voice rattled. " He didn't say." But he controlled himself. " He likely did. A godly man goes to God with his troubles and problems." He spoke rapidly as they came closer to the field. " That's one thing I can't understand, why folks object to God Himself settling their affairs. The other day somebody was saying it's queer to have a revelation ordering the Brothers to build Joseph's big hotel. But what's queer about it? It's like he says himself, if strangers are accommodated well in Nauvoo, they'll think well of us. And if they stay in Brother Joseph's house, he can preach them the Gospel. . . ."

Jarvie was silent, kicking a stone along ahead of him, absorbed in kicking.

" It's like Brother George Smith said – God ordered Noah to build a boat and that seemed a funny thing for God to do. But it saved the world. Then He told the Children of Israel what kind of locusts they could eat – how big a thing was that for God to be concerned with? "

" I guess," Jarvie said uncertainly, " for a *prophet* to be in business seems like taking advantage – "

Simon's voice was cold. " Listen, Jarv, the other night one of the Apostles compared Zion to a threshing-floor. He said there were some green heads and they had to be pelted a little harder, so that if folks got a cudgeling they'd know it was because their heads were green."

Jarvie looked up at him.

" I hope, Jarv, you don't need a cudgeling. I don't want one of my sons among the green heads."

" No. I'm not. All I want is to know what folks are talking about."

" Who's talking? " Simon's voice was sharp.

" Oh – everybody. Joseph Nunn – "

" Joseph Nunn! He's a cheat and a shyster. Do you think he'd give a poor man any credit at his store? Not if he starved on the doorstep! He's mad because Brother Joseph gives credit, that's all that's giving him belly-ache." Simon walked with his heels banging on the path. " Who else is spouting off? " he asked.

" I don't know."

" You said everybody. Joseph Nunn's not everybody."

" I wasn't saying – "

" Who else? I asked you a question."

" Well – Schrench Sirine, and that Peterson fellow that started the new ferry – "

" Schrench Sirine – Lord Almighty, you can't say his *name* without hissing. I don't need to tell you what's his trouble, do I? Dram-drinking was a shame on the face of the city; how else could it be settled but stopping it by law? If a responsible man like Brother Joseph is the only one to sell liquor, we'll have no drunkards in Zion, thank God."

" It does give him a corner on – "

Simon's voice was slow and deliberate. " Listen, if anybody ought to have a corner on a business like liquor, it's a Prophet of God whose business is how people conduct themselves. Liquor can make a beast from an angel; I've seen it happen. If that's not the business of a Prophet, I don't know what his business might be."

They reached the field and began to work where they had dropped the tools yesterday. For a time they were separated, and Simon watched his son, puzzled. Presently he stopped working and came over. " There's not business enough for more than one ferry, Jarv," he said. " It was a case of having one or none, see? There's got to be the use to maintain it."

" Sure," Jarvie said.

" What else is on your mind? You must've been going around."

"I heard the fellows a little – and then last night me and Vic got talking about it."

"Well – " Simon sat down on the ground. "Come here and sit down; if you get the trouble straight from the beginning, there's no question to ask."

He waited until his son sat beside him.

"Every great man has his enemies, Jarvie. Christ had His, you know that, and it didn't mean anything was the matter with Christ, but only that Lucifer had a following, too. You remember that editorial I was reading the other night from *Times and Seasons* – it told all that was troubling the world, the trouble and war that's everywhere, and ended with this: 'It is not in man that walketh to direct his steps.' And I think it's true. Man is so imperfect he's always making a mess of everything. Now, the Gospel promises that some time God will take over the reins of government, and then, like that editorial said, 'Nations will learn war no more.' I liked that – '*Nations will learn war no more.*'"

Simon's voice was sober, intense with feeling. "Nauvoo is the beginning of the rule of God, Jarvis. It's a grand thing to be here, a privilege to be part of it. But Lucifer is here, too. And he doesn't want God to take over, he doesn't want God's rule to get started. He works through Brother Joseph's enemies, sometimes even through some of the Brothers. When you start wondering and being influenced by things like these we've been talking about, you can know Lucifer is working on you. It's an eternal watch, Jarvie, it's never over. Lucifer'll never give up till the millennium."

Jarvie stared at him.

"He works in little ways as well as big ways. Just now Brother Joseph is beset from every side and he needs every friend he has. John Bennett has written a book and published it in Boston, 'exposing' the Prophet, as he says. And he's trying to start a new move from Missouri. There are scandals in every

Warsaw and Carthage paper you pick up; they're even starting to have anti-Mormon meetings like they had in Missouri before the trouble there."

Jarvie's face was incredulous. Simon stood up. "And that's the trouble," he said. "Now you'll know where it comes from and you'll be able to tell for yourself who's God's man and who's Lucifer's. It's the same old battle, it goes on everywhere and inside every man."

"I see." There was a tension between them, as though a shadow had suddenly fallen and cut them apart.

"If I had a son that went out against Brother Joseph, I'd never lift my head again," Simon said. "Do you hear me? I'd rather put a son of mine in the ground and cover him over."

A startled necessity for defense thrust Jarvie's voice out of him. "You can't help thinking about things, and it's not hurting anybody to listen — "

"A man's mind is his own, he can think what he's wanting to — to school your thoughts is to come to be a man."

"It seems to me to think about everything there is and then choose — "

"You can choose when you're old enough. Till then let your elders choose for you."

"How old — "

But Simon lapsed into awkward humor. "Your head *is* green, Jarv," he said. "You'll be gettin' a headache, so much thinking — " Jarvie saw his lips set at once over the tail end of his laughter.

As he worked, Jarvie's thoughts turned in his head. He kept remembering what Brother Joseph had said only last Sunday at meeting. "Some folks whisper that I have silver and gold enough for ten men. But let me tell you the amount of my possessions on this earth: Old Charley, my horse, given me in Kirtland; two pet deer; two old turkeys and four young ones;

the old cow given me by a Brother in Missouri; old Major, my dog; my wife, my children, and a little household furniture. This is the sum total of my great estates, my splendid mansions. . . ."

At dinner he asked, deliberately casual: "Father, who does the new Mansion House belong to?"

Simon dropped his knife on his plate. He started to speak sharply, but steadied himself. Strainedly then he said: "It belongs to the Church."

"Oh. That's what I thought."

Now, what was it he'd heard after meeting, Jarvie thought. How funny it was that the Mansion should be secured to the Church and so exempt from any tax, city or county or state, and yet be secured to the heirs of the Prophet and to his use while he remained in the world!

He shook himself.

When he passed Sirine's closed shop that afternoon, he walked slowly. There were men sitting along a bench in the sun. One of them was talking loudly. "Joe listed his *wife* in his property – by God, even *there* he underestimated!" And there was deep and significant laughter.

Jarvie began noticing the court statistics in the papers. There was listed case after case of "Libel against Mayor Joseph Smith and the heads of the Church." Always the verdict was "Guilty." Then another report would appear. "William Foster, brought up for libel against the city court, swearing he did not receive fair trial." "Case dismissed."

Well, if God had the power, Simon said, let Him use it where He had to. Thank goodness there was *one* court in the land where Lucifer did not sit as judge and jury.

One day the paper announced that the Prophet Joseph Smith and his Apostles would henceforth handle the editorial columns of the newspaper, and advised succinctly between news items:

"Let every man mind his own business and then every man's business will be attended to."

THE PROPHET JOSEPH SMITH announced a new organization which would comprise the Youth of Zion. The young should study together, work together, play together, he said; they must learn to wield authority and understand power. They must be imbued with an unalterable and unshakable belief in the work they would be called upon to continue.

Brother Joseph himself spoke to them. "When I talk to the young people," he said, "I experience more embarrassment than I should before kings and nobles, for I know the crimes of which the latter are guilty . . . but my young friends are guilty of none of them. A prophet becomes accustomed to denunciation; it is a sublime experience to speak of the future in terms of hope and not in terms of fear and consequence."

Jarvie listened, impressed. And when Brother Spencer spoke, his words were also significant. "Those opposed to this great work will tell you that power is dangerous. But if power is subordinate to the power of God, it is good, and you can all secure it from the same source."

Before the speeches were over, the girls were stirring, and as soon as the prayer was said, their dresses rustled as they rose in clusters, and the young men looked sideways and moved quickly into dark rings around the curls and the ruffles.

Brother Joseph smiled and spoke to Spencer. "I don't have to search Scriptures to give the reason for some of their hope," he said.

Spencer smiled. "It's good ground to put seed in," he said. "There won't be a meeting in the Church better attended."

A few days later an item appeared in the *Nauvoo Neighbor*. "A pleasure party has been got up and our young citizens have had an opportunity to enjoy themselves in an excursion to Quincey on the Mayor's ferry. They left from the Nauvoo House site, returning later than expected, being delayed by a thunderstorm. But a good time was had by all who attended."

VIC climbed the hill. There was a hard core at the center of her throat, a turning aching bitter core that would be neither swallowed nor choked up and spat out like the foul thing it was. A pit in her, like she had that first day she came to Baker's. For hours she had been among the young girls she had longed to know, at the first Young Lady's Organization meeting. When she had come in, Eliza Snow had taken her arm and said: " Girls, this is Victoria Moon." And Sister Eliza had found her a chair, among the very nicest, the very prettiest.

Their bright glances still seared her, their taking-in glances, their glances saying How-plain-her-hair-is and Why-is-her-face-so-red. Especially Naomi Fordham, her head tipped sideways like a little bird's, her eyes glancing under her black lashes, and the color in her cheeks sharp to the observer as the first redbud in April. She had a way of talking around one who sat next to her at the table, her glance had a way of lifting over the head in beatific indifference, she could whisper secrets across a rigid body in the next chair.

Vic swallowed and swallowed. She cleared her throat and leaned beside the path and spat.

Then she stooped quickly and peered at the ground. Lying there just out of the grass was a bone hairpin. It lay with one end tipped up against root-tufts, and the closed end pointed almost due west. Vic followed with her eyes the direction it pointed, conjecturing. Between Baker's north field and Smith's south one. There wasn't a house she knew of in that direction. Still she stooped there, staring. She had heard them plainly, the girls in their mad brook-flowing talk: *See a hairpin pointing clearly, It points to him that loves you dearly.* Naomi herself had found a hairpin on the way to the meeting pointing across the river to Jake Hardman's house as sure as fate.

Vic touched the pin gently, turned it ever so little until it indicated Baker's field. Then a little more, a bare touch with the toe of her shoe this time, not looking. She glanced at it half in fear and saw that it was lying toward the house on the bluff, directly and surely. She leaned down and took it into her hand, closing her fingers over it. Maybe he was young, as the girls said, but he was bigger than Jake by half a head and in summer when his shirt was off in the field his muscles stood firm and high on his arms and golden hair grew in a plain V on his chest. Jake was nothing beside him. Jake was a stoop-shouldered ignoramus. Jake was a loud-mouthed smart aleck.

She carried the hairpin enclosed in her hand, and when she went into the house she moved to her bed and slipped it under her pillow.

MR. HIRAM KIMBALL, lately dispossessed of Water Street, was invited courteously to sit with the Council of Nauvoo. In the midst of the business he saw Mayor Joseph Smith send toward him a wad of paper, as a boy might send a spit-ball. For a moment he thought it was a pointed and childish joke, and then he saw that there was writing on the paper and took it up and looked at it. Written in Joseph's difficult script, it bore the underscored title, *Revelation.*

Hiram looked up at the Mayor, but encountered only cold unrecognition. His eyes dropped to the paper.

"Verily, thus saith the Lord unto you, my servant Joseph, by the voice of my spirit, Hiram Kimball has been insinuating evil and forming evil opinions against you with others; and if he continue in them, he and they shall be accursed, for I am the Lord thy God, and will stand by thee and bless thee. Amen."

Hiram stuffed the paper respectfully into the pocket of his waistcoat. He himself told what happened afterward; every time he took the paper from his pocket and tried to throw it away, some invisible power prevented him. And back into his waistcoat it would go again. He tried putting it in a hind pocket of his pantaloons, as though he could sit away its divinity, but in passing the new shop across from the Temple, he caught that very pocket on a squarehead nail and ripped it clean off. So, ruefully, he picked the Revelation from the dust of the street and placed it over his heart again.

Chapter XVIII

THE MONTHS passed and the last nail was driven into Joseph Smith's Mansion House. It was opened with a jubilee, on a night of gayety and grandeur. Everybody who was anybody was invited, and when the big white door opened, there had never been a more beautiful assemblage of party-goers on the old Mississippi. Those who had come from the East, whose eyes had seen gowns and broadcloth and jewelry and bonnets among the best people of the nation, swore that there had never been anything better anywhere – in the capital itself!

The Prophet had never been handsomer and the Elect Lady Emma had never been dressed more richly. For that night they all forgot Kirtland and Far West and Haun's Mill and all the troubles they had ever known. Tonight was jubilee. There were no guns in the world, but only fiddles. Feet were made to dance, there was no retreating but in the retreat that waited for a call to advance again. Advance and retreat to the fiddles. And there were cakes and pies and doughnuts and Brother Joseph's favorite drink, applejack sweetened with honey.

It was good to see Joseph this night, handing the Sisters around, in turn. He was as delighted as a child to take groups of his guests from room to room, he felt an almost sensuous joy when he exhibited the shining new furniture, solid cherry and mahogany, the great four-posters canopied with red silk and blue, the inlaid desk for his own use, the red carpets and the swinging chandeliers answering the candles with their prisms as a river answers the stars. Tonight was Joseph's night and he was surrounded by his friends. He saw them honestly rejoice with him – this they would all have, they would have everything good in this world if they worked faithfully. It had been promised.

Elder Taylor read a resolution, standing in the middle of the room expectantly until every last soul was listening:

" Resolved: to give a vote of thanks to Prophet and Lady; that General Joseph Smith, whether we view him as a Prophet at the head of the Church, a General at the head of the Legion, a Mayor at the head of the City, or a landlord at the head of his table, if he has equals he has no superiors! "

There was shouting, and the resolution was unanimously passed, and Brother Joseph bowed and laughed and took Emma by the hand to bow with him.

" A toast to Nauvoo, a toast to Nauvoo! "

" The great emporium of the West, the center of all centers, a city of three years' growth, a population of fifteen thousand souls congregated from the four quarters of the globe, embracing the intelligence of all nations, with industry, frugality, economy, virtue, and brotherly love, unsurpassed by any age in the world – a suitable home for the Saints! "

" A toast to Nauvoo! " And they lifted their glasses and swallowed their applejack together.

Eliza, in her turn, danced with Joseph. He spoke into her ear when they came briefly together, gay things, compliments. And he was whimsical and filled with a kind of young deviltry tonight. " You notice the old ones," he whispered; " they can't quite get over being scandalized at the dancing! But music and dancing, Eliza, were made to praise God with – I can give you Scripture for it! "

And there were those who, from a lifelong denial, were

awkward in the figures. Brother Parley Pratt, willing enough, could only stand miserably because by the time he achieved a half motion the others were on to something else. His brother laughed at him and shouted: " Why don't you move forward, Parley? " And when Parley came out of the figure, mopping his brow, he said: " I can't do it – when I think which way I'm going, I forget the step, and when I think of the step, I forget which way to go."

Everybody laughed and Joseph said to Eliza: " *You* teach Brother Parley; you dance like an angel." He pressed her hand briefly before he found his next partner. There was high color in Eliza's face tonight, and Mercy saw that she scarcely took her eyes from Joseph all evening. But then nobody could help watching Joseph tonight; he was everywhere at once, he was gay of talk and quick to laugh, he spoke to everybody and everybody spoke to him. It was as though he must take the part of both host and hostess because Emma was not well and could not move about as he did. She was only six weeks up from giving birth to a child, stillborn; it seemed that the child had taken something from her, a vital part of her, and carried it into the ground. Emma was gracious – it was not that! She was always gracious. But tired and appearing, wherever she stood and no matter among what people, as though she stood alone and was very, very tired.

From outside, nobody would ever have dreamed there was anybody in the Mansion either tired or sad, least of all the mistress of the house. From the flat and the hill folks came walking by to see the jubilee, and some said defensively: " They couldn't ask *every*body." In spite of knowing this, it was hard to stand on the street, especially now it had turned bitterly cold again; looking on at so much brilliance and hearing the fiddles so gay, your toes wouldn't behave out here on the sidewalk. A few took partners and danced on the street, and about midnight Sister Emma had cake and applejack sent out.

" After all, he couldn't ask *every*body." But some said: " I helped build his grand house, I helped build it."

❧ ❧

ACROSS the river Jarvie and Vic sat on the river-bank looking over the river where the Mansion House shone like a jewel.

" They must have a million candles! " Jarvie said.

Vic said: " Ssssh! If you're real quiet, you can hear the music, just faint. Can you hear it? "

They sat very still.

" I thought once I did."

Vic gathered her shawl around her shoulders, shivering.

" Mother won't like it, not being able to dance," Jarvie said wistfully. " She hasn't danced in a long time and she says her feet tickle till she can hardly sit in her chair. You know, she dances awfully well, Vic. When she's feeling good, some time, we'll get her to dance for you. Sometimes after a party she teaches us the steps and swings and holds her hand to her mouth and hollows in a deep voice: ' Circle, all! ' "

" When I first came, I used to think she sort of danced, even when she was just walking."

" I know – she's so light. Father says she's just like a feather and when he whirls her she goes right off her feet. Once the floor-man told him not to whirl her so high, and Father felt foolish for a week after."

He looked pensively across at the jubilee. " You know, her feet are all swelled up. That's what happens when women have babies – I guess it's pretty hard."

" I guess it is, all right." Her voice was self-conscious.

" Sometimes – and I guess it's not right to say things like this – but sometimes I wish she'd never have another one as long as she lives. She's so different when she's slim and light. You even love her more then, and that's not right either. Sometimes I wish God would send the babies somewhere else."

Vic shook her head scornfully. "I guess God don't have much to do with it," she said.

"Vic Moon!" He looked at her aghast. "You *do* talk like a gentile, Vic, every once in a while you do."

"I'm older'n you," she said unreasonably, and there was that wise searching look he had seen before and wondered at.

"You're not much. I'll be sixteen next birthday and I'm two heads taller."

"I'm a whole year older," Vic said imperturbably, as though all wisdom were thus explained.

"I'm going to tell Mother she needs to let you go to church oftener, Vic. You got some funny ideas in your head."

"If a girl don't know beans by the time she's my age, she's likely to learn 'em. She's likely to have 'em stuffed in her mouth till she swallows 'em."

Jarvie shook his head. "You're funny, Vic. I don't see what beans have got to do with religion."

"We weren't talking about religion."

"We were too."

"We weren't."

"Well, what were we talking about, then?"

She jumped up. "I don't know. But I'm cold, I know that much."

She went in, walking swiftly, not saying good-night. He puzzled for a while at what she had said and then forgot her and sat watching the jubilee. Mother had said they'd likely dance till four in the morning. Sometimes, and not very long away either, he could go to jubilees and dance with ladies in colored dresses. After all, sixteen was getting on. Father was only eighteen when he was married to Mother. And maybe some time poor Vic could go to a jubilee, too, and then maybe she'd get some of those funny ideas out of her head. Sugar and slops and all that stuff. Vic was a funny girl. But she was nice to talk to, and sometimes a warmth came out of her that made you forget she was thin and pinched and her face the color people had begun calling *English*. As long as he would read, she would listen, too, maybe not always understanding, but listening with a look on her face as though she enjoyed it whether she understood it or not.

"Funny, too," he thought, "her wanting me to call her Victoria. I'll try to remember."

❧ ❧ ❧

OLD John Smith bowed to left and right when he took the honored seat with his guitar. And the folks clapped for him till he was red-faced with pleasure.

"What you want?" he called, and they began to shout back at him. Jolly songs, they wanted all jolly songs at first. Later, Old John knew as well as they, they'd be calling for ballads to stir their hearts and wet their eyes. But now "*You've Got to Put on Airs*, John!" "Do *Grandma's Advice*, John!" "Do *Old Dan Tucker*!"

He struck a chord with his hard old fingers and the music that came out of his instrument was sharp and sweet and quick, tickling the instep and tapping at the toe. Folks joined hands and rocked to and fro with the rhythm that came out from under Old John's fingers.

Brother Joseph lifted some of the windows and the folks outside crowded close to listen, and some of them joined the singers until the whole Mansion, inside and out, was shaken with singing.

"Raccoon's Got a Bushy Tail!" Old John's fingers flew on the strings and his voice quavered.

> Raccoon's got a bushy tail;
> Possum's tail is bare;

Rabbit's got no tail at all —
Nothing but a little bunch of hair.
  Get along home, home, home,
  Get along home, home, home;
  Get along home, home, home,
  Down the riverside.

If I had a scolding wife,
As sure as you are born,
I'd take her down to New Orleans
And trade her off for corn.
  Get along home, home, home!

They grew louder and jollier, and the applejack went round and round. O'Hara, an Irish convert, startled them with a sweet tenor in *Kathleen*, and when they must have more, he made spirited *butter in the Old Man's Boots*.

Finally the sad songs, as Old John had predicted knowingly to himself. *The Frozen Girl*, *The Babes in the Woods*. Brother Joseph sang with his head thrown back, as folks always remembered who remembered this night, and he served doughnuts with his own hands and applejack, spilling it over his fingers and laughing.

Portia Glazier, sitting rustily among the widows, found her mouth open with singing, and Melissa looked at her, surprised. But Portia said, as though defending herself: "Well, it does folks good to get their fix-ups on and stretch their throats a little."

When Old John had subsided into a mere member of the company, she went to him deliberately, and with something of the bravado of older days she said: "Well, John, I must say the older you get, the better you play."

John's smile was empty of teeth now, but he did not believe in abandoning it, for all that. "If I play, I don't get any older," he said placidly.

" I wish," thought Portia, " I'd had sense enough to wear one of my good collars."

❧ ❧ ❧ ❧

It was long after midnight and the Mansion House was still bright. Sometimes the door would open for somebody going home, and those who still lingered outside could see into the hall where the bright throng milled together, even yet, and could hear the laughter and gay talk that came bursting out across the lawn.

" Good night! Good night! "

" You mean good morning! "

" Good morning, then. Good morning."

Eliza Snow slipped into the big bedroom upstairs and found her shawl in the heap on the bed. Then down the stairs quietly, pausing on the first landing until Joseph looked up and waved his hand at her. Then through the dining-room and out the side door. As she latched the gate after her, the door opened and she saw Joseph burst out and run down the path after her.

" Eliza! What do you mean, leaving like that, without saying good-night to anybody? "

She stood on the outside of the gate with her hands firm on the palings. " I didn't think anybody'd notice if I went; there're some who don't get as tired as I do."

He laid his hands on hers. " There's somebody who always misses you when you go, Eliza. Don't forget that."

" Thank you. I'm glad."

They stood looking at each other. " You'd better go back," she said, " you'll be cold without a coat on."

" It feels good. It's hot in there."

" You'll catch cold if you come out like that, sweating."

He opened the gate impulsively. " Give me a little piece of

your shawl, then, and I'll see you to your gate. After all, Eliza, you shouldn't go around at night by yourself the way you do."

Laughing, she gave him part of the shawl and he laid it around his shoulders. "I don't think anybody wants to steal me," she said. "There's nothing for me to be afraid of. If a bad man were going to steal a woman, he'd take a younger one."

"Of course, I'm not a bad man and so I don't know what sort of women they like, but if *I* were stealing a woman — " He pressed his arm about her waist. His voice deepened, grew tender. "You're the one I'd steal, Eliza."

Trying to sound very gay, she said: "I wouldn't have thought that at the jubilee. It was the young ones all of you were stealing."

He stopped and faced her closely, looking down into the shadow of her face. "Eliza Snow, you're jealous. I was thinking, back there at the party, how you looked standing by the mantel the way you were. Like an angel, I thought. And there you were, jealous as a little green-eyed cat."

"No, I wasn't! "

"After all, Eliza, a man has to dance with his guests, all of them, if he can get around to them. Now, doesn't he? "

She pushed at him. "I wasn't jealous."

"Now I recall, I can see that you didn't look like an angel at all. You were a ruffled little cat, a little cat all tucked and ruffled — "

She knew he was teasing her, but she could not bear it.

"Well, then, suppose I *was* jealous. Suppose I was. Suppose I stood there by the mantel and was jealous for hours and hours! " Her voice edged upon hysteria, and he sobered, looking down at her. He raised his hands to her shoulders and shook her a little.

"Then you're like all the rest of them, jealous and bitter

and selfish, and I don't want that from you. Do you hear me? I expect more than that from you."

She said nothing.

"Shouldn't I expect more? I've never had to say *Ye of little faith* to you yet, Eliza, and I hope I don't have to start, now."

She stood stiffly, quietly, staring up toward his face, and it infuriated him. He had seen too much of jealous women in his day, and jealous men too, for that matter.

"I didn't think I'd have this from you," he said. "I thought you were different. You always understood everything; you could grasp what I meant and put it in forty stanzas of rhymes before the others even got it. And now you're jealous. Like any other stupid ordinary woman!"

"Please — " She lifted her hand, touched his chest.

"You're jealous, and the next thing you'll come around crying for a house like the Mansion House, the next thing I know that's what you'll want."

He pushed her hand away and tore himself from the shawl. But she ran after him.

"Joseph!" She clung frantically to his coat.

He turned, fierce and impatient.

"Joseph — you said when the moon was in the quarter — "

"Well," he said brusquely, "it isn't."

Her voice was suddenly very sober, steely sober, and he was shocked into listening because he had never heard Eliza's voice so cold before. Not to him. To little Frederick, maybe, when he had not learned his lesson. But not to him.

"No, it isn't in the quarter now, but it has been. Three — *four* times — since that last night. And if I'm your wife, as I hope in the name of God I am, you owe me at least a quarter-moon. Not a whole one, I'm not asking that, but a quarter."

"Eliza, I was in Springfield — I thought of you — and then last time — "

She interrupted. "If you think it's a house I want, you're mistaken. I don't want a house – even a mansion – I have plenty of room where I am, thank you. But if there's any reason for this marriage, you know what it is I want."

She was weak, daring so much, more than she had ever dreamed of daring.

He came to her then and his head was bent and he spoke with emotion. "Eliza – I can't. It's like I told you before, when they all believe and you won't have to suffer. Then. You don't know what it's like to be pointed at and jeered at. But I do. Ever since I was a boy I've had that. And you'd have it, too, even from the Saints. You don't know what it'd be like and I don't want you to. It's something you have to fight, and a woman like you can't do it – it takes gall and it takes strength. You have to break through it, head first. And you couldn't."

"Oh yes I could. I think my head's as strong as anybody's. And I don't care what they think, the pig-headed things, them! The way they wrangle, it doesn't look as though they'll ever – Not all of them, Joseph."

He held her close. "But it's not only for you, Eliza dear. It's because of me, too. I didn't dream how long it was going to be, but it was too big for them to take all at once. It's like the United Order, sharing everything; they've got to grow into it. It isn't their fault – it's too much to take in one mouthful after they've always thought different. I see how it is with them, all right. And if it came out like that – whispering from house to house, Eliza Snow and the Prophet – they'd come out on me. The minute it goes out of Nauvoo, they'll come out on me. We've got to be careful now, Eliza. I know it and so do you."

He saw that she was weeping.

"Please, Eliza, please don't."

"I can't help it. I was planning what I was going to say to

you — all evening I was planning it. And I made pretty sure you saw me coming out — "

"Did you say it like you planned it, Eliza? "

She shook her head. "I was going to say I wasn't afraid of anything anybody could say as long as you were with me, but there was another thing, and I'd like to say that, too. Every time I look at you I think of it, and every time I look at your little boys, all dressed up in their black suits for Sunday school."

"What is it, Liza? "

She pulled herself up close to him until she could almost look over his shoulder. Her voice was low.

"I'd like — Joseph, I've written so many songs for them, and I've taken every song and held it out and said: 'Sing this; it will help you.' For *Oh, My Father*, I could say: 'Sing this, it will comfort you.' And now I'd like to be the first one, the very first to show them what can come from a life as empty as mine has been — out of a body that has never been really alive or of any use to anybody — I'd like to take a little boy, a little boy such as you must have been, big and strong and fair-haired, and say to them proudly: 'Now, *sing this!*' "

She realized that he was weeping, too. She drew back and wiped his face with her handkerchief, gently. "Now, you've got to go back to your guests," she said.

Chapter XIX

THE GRASS was drenched and the trees were damp to touch and when the sun came there was a shining on the land for a little while that defied the shining on the river. Now was a time for forgetting again that there had been winter, and mushrooms were delicate and pale among the grass of the woods and fields, testimony of the way spring is implicit in winter. These leaped into being suddenly, overnight, huge and flowering, saying: " It is possible, anything is possible now."

Jarvie had a bag to put them in, and when he got up, before daylight, he found Vic outside before him.

" I'm going to walk fast," he said, noticing her bonnet and her heavy shoes.

" I can walk," she said. " If I get a chance to, I can walk fast as anybody."

He did not wait for her, but moved ahead, thinking that it was not a thing for girls to do. He had never seen a girl out so early hunting mushrooms.

" Nobody's up but us," Vic said, and he heard the pleasure in her voice. It was a natural pleasure, for the world was alive with every creature in it but mankind, alive with damp enthusiastic buoyancy as though the air itself was leaping skyward. In the dampness, too, was rain-smell, that heady wet-dust fragrance that comes only from the ground and catches persistently in the nostrils, saying: " Breathe deep."

When they came to the top of the hollow and began to trace along the little hills rolling back into farmland and woodland, he waited for her and asked: " Can you whistle? "

She whistled, a sweet and piercing sound, using her fingers at her mouth.

" I didn't know you could do that."

" I learned when I was little."

" Well you go that way, see, and when you find some, you whistle. If it's just a few, cut them and go on, but if it's a lot, whistle. I'll do the same."

She looked disappointed. " Can't we go together? "

" It'll be faster this way. I've got to be back before Father goes to the field. We'll get more this way."

" All right."

She looked back at him, and he called: " Sometimes there are lots under the beech trees, and look around old snags that've fallen."

When he had disappeared, she turned and followed him slowly until she came to ground high enough to see him again. Then she walked along, watching him. Again and again she saw him stoop down on his haunches, absorbed. But he did not whistle. She allowed him to disappear once more, and then she looked at the ground for a time. Presently she put her fingers to her mouth and whistled. She saw him come running, and ran toward him.

" Where are they? " he asked.

" I can't find any," she said, looking flustered. " I haven't found *any*. You show me, and I'll help you gather them."

" You have to look sharp," he said.

She saw that his bag was already high with them. She leaned over them and touched them with her fingers. " Oh, that's what they're like," she said.

" Vic Moon! Don't you even know what you're looking for? "

He laughed and she laughed too.

"I'll help you now," she said childishly, and she walked along with him, looking sharply. He could not help noticing the pleasure with which she walked, the bright way her eyes searched, and she kept humming dimly in her throat. Once she saw a bunch of them first, and she was like Betsy over that surprising nest of eggs she had found in the elder bushes.

"Proud as if she made them," Jarvie thought, and praised her.

When he said: "That's plenty," she said: "A person hates to stop. You never know what you'll find in the next hollow."

"More of the same," he told her. "And you'd never find bigger than those you found."

She sat in the grass. "Let's rest a minute before we go back," she said. "We'll be straight walking, going back."

"All right, a minute." When he sat down, he probed around in the mushrooms and showed her the biggest ones again, separated the delicate layers of tissue, showing how they crumbled in his fingers.

"Naomi Fordham used to gather these with her beau," she said. "I'd see them go by, only I didn't know what they had in the bag."

She saw that his face flushed, and it amused her. "They didn't get married any too soon, did they?" she asked, watching his face.

"I don't know. I don't know anything about it."

"She married Jake Hardman after she was expecting."

Speaking of such a thing with a girl was new and distasteful to him and he stood up. Her saying the two of them went out after mushrooms –

"I guess it's like your mother says," Vic continued mildly. "It's harder for those that are so pretty. A lot harder. She even went walking with Mayor Bennett – that was *seen.*"

"It's none of my business," he said, but he remembered a

day, 'way back now, and it seemed to him that he had been very, very young. Because, since, he had been wise to so many things, and he had been conscious of a humid embarrassment whenever Naomi and her giggling friends came into church or into the young people's meetings or into the school parties, clustering and fluttering. And of a stir in his muscles, too, that made him half ashamed. Now Naomi was married to her Jake and had appeared last Sunday with her husband beside her, soberly and chastely dressed. She was not despised or ignored for her trespass, but everybody in Zarahemla – and everybody in Nauvoo, for that matter – mourned for her as though she had died. She was mentioned in family prayers and public ones, and every time Jarvie heard her name, she was in his mind, dressed in all her bright flounces and pressed against the uniform of the sleek officer of the Invincible Dragoons. The whole settlement and everybody over the river knew that this trouble of Naomi's was another aftermath of the influence of a wicked man, even though Bennett himself had been gone too long to have fathered Naomi's child and Jake Hardman had confessed to it in Priesthood, begging the forgiveness of the Elders, who sat in rows with their eyes on their boots and their hands fumbling on their knees. "One wicked man with a romantic tongue can pollute a generation," people said, shaking their heads.

But that day, that spring day of climbing and swinging, remained for Jarvie a day of awakening and revelation, when he had first felt the terrible and beautiful stirring of manhood in him. Naomi's throat had been long and white, and the man's mouth moving along her cheek and then finding the white –

"It's none of my business," Jarvie said again, suddenly, and picked up the bag from the ground and started home. Vic did not move to follow him, and when he saw that she was not beside him, he turned to look for her. She was stretched out on the ground, on her face, her head on her arms. He went back a little way and said: “ Come on, Vic. Mother’ll be needing you.”

“ All right.” She turned a little, and began to rise, so he leaned over and helped her, taking her arm. When he saw her face he was startled, because her cheeks were red from the exercise and her eyes bright. He saw that her hair was loosened around her face and had been crimped above the forehead – something he had never noticed before.

“ I don’t get outside much,” she apologized. “ It feels good.”

“ Gosh,” he said, “ it must be six. We’d better run.”

She trotted obediently after him, holding her skirts from the ground. Only once she stopped and called: “ Listen, Jarvie – there’s Jenny Pooter! ”

“ Over here she’s Jenny Wren,” he said, and they laughed together.

Chapter XX

"This, then, is Joy," thought Simon, watching Menzo.

Perspiration rolled down Menzo's face, dripped from his body. Keokuk had said: "Squaw do," but Menzo had no squaw to do, and wouldn't have given the joy of his work to her if he had. Into the pit the Chief had helped lift the white inner bark, life-stream of birches, into the hard-packed ground. For days the clay had been tamped and pounded until even the rain could not do more with it to destroy the form they had given it. And now the bark lay to its shape. The boy ironed with smooth stones, ironing the liquid away, pressing sap into the air. Where the stitches lay, stretched smooth, the pressing stone was obliterating them. He had not dared believe, but it was happening under his hands. Drier, drier, smoother, smoother, so white.

Ever since the Indians first came ("the *red* Indians," as Vic said, with a lilt of excitement in the adjective), Menzo had no other devotion. Now he had been over the river in Keokuk's own canoe, and had watched dancing all night long, and had come home in the morning when it was over as spirited as when he first climbed into the canoe, still wearing his feathers. For weeks, he had spoken for all the turkey feathers the neighbors had and had spent hours with Mercy at the dyeing kettle.

As Keokuk had said it, in the glory of the world he would

clothe himself, in secret color, and the great round wing upon his brow would lift his mind to the spirit as the goose-wing takes the goose toward the sun.

Yellow lives secretly in dried onion skin, glows abundantly there to be sought out. Green stains the woods, waiting. Pokeberry, royal weed bearing royal purple, waits on the stem, and falling, seems to bloom again. Walnut is brother to the Indian, his skin-color implicit in the bark. These Menzo learned.

The names gave Jarvie joy, Jarvie who was sensitive to words. Kiskukosh, Keokuk, Appenoose, Poweshiek, Eagle Heart, Oomaha. And it was Jarvie who beat the tomtom when Menzo danced, understanding the rhythm that must turn Menzo's body and pound from his heels. Simon said they'd bring the rafters down, but when folks came for an evening, he never failed to get the drum himself and say: " Put on your feathers, Menzo, and give us a round or two."

Out north of Zarahemla, Keokuk had showed Menzo where the Indians had buried their beloved Princess, Kolawequois, and it was Menzo who spoke to Josh Downing and got him to turn his fence in at that corner to leave the little heap plain at the side of the river road.

And now the canoe.

Jo Nunn, rolypoly son of the storekeeper, and little Lije Fordham, first son of Elijah, more quickness in his narrow bones than a person would think to look at him, and Jack Peck, only Peck like the rest of the family but true boy – these three came every day to stand watching. They did not trouble Menzo at his labor, but rather inspired him.

" What you doin'? "

" Told ye yesterday – ugh. See, that's why squaws grunt – I'm ironin' bark. Ugh." Back and forth. " Ugh."

" Think she'll float? "

Fiercely: " She better! "

" Who's gonna float her? "

" If I can make 'er I can float 'er. You gotta paddle, slow and even. She'll be tricky, she's so light."

" She don't look light."

" She is, though. Nothin' but thin bark, nothin' in her but bark."

" Kin we ride in her? "

" Sure – one at a time. With me, though." And Menzo grunted as he pushed and pushed.

Enviously they stood. Menzo looked disdainfully.

" Whyn't you make one, you want one so much? "

" You help us? "

" Sure, when I'm done with mine. I'll show you how it's done. It's pretty particular."

" Le' me do it awhile."

But this Menzo could not bear. It was his, his own. And Keokuk's perhaps. But ownership with Keokuk was grand to think of, that Indian of Indians, with light in his heels and his eyes, and a fever for creation in his two hands, desire in his eyes for creation. Between Menzo and Keokuk language had been no barrier. It had seemed rather that lack of complete physical communication forced them to understand each other. They must grope for feeling, delight over single words exchanged. Keokuk had seen the boy-hand stroking his own canoe, had seen the eyes longing, had seen the hands bent with desire. Already the boy wore what he had made, insignia of a race he instinctively loved. Forever he trailed the woods with his white feathers lolling down his back, a belt of rattler skin around his waist. Keokuk had offered moccasins, knowing that a boy could not master the intricacies of a tanning anxious white men could not master. How delicate for stones! What magic makes soft-strong together? Squaws knew, sitting wordless under questions, and braves shrugged, smiling eternal smiles.

Menzo pressed with blistered aching hands and feared there

would be sap forever. But the stitches faded down, dissolved in bark. Smoothness incredible stretched from bow to bow. And then the bows lifted proudly, facing east and west.

There was no more. It was a heavy fabric, wood-firm. It answered the thumbnail with a clicking. Menzo lifted it up and it came like a feather into his arms. He turned it over and balanced it on his head as he had seen Keokuk do and walked easily under it. And then he laid it down tenderly and trimmed the edges, designing with them, leaning to perfection. Usefulness was over, waiting. What remained was more significant. Simon came to see and understood without words. For the same reason he had turned the legs of the washstand, waxed them, arched the back and sides. It didn't make washing any easier, but the stand gave to the room out of itself. So Menzo's canoe would give to the air and the water and to every eye that looked upon it and to something in Menzo that required beauty in what he made. It never cut the water until the bows were intricate with color, color with the secret heart of the woods in it.

The time came. Menzo was busy with worry, looking every way at once to see it tight against invasion of water, but it was a citadel between water and sky and nothing could come in upon him but sunshine. And maybe rain when rain must come. He paddled in the backwaters first, and one calm day slipped easily over the river and back again, between the Islands. Then to the Islands, where persimmons were ripening red in the trees. Menzo stalked the bush, bearing his feathers, and brought down two squirrels with his arrows, and laughed aloud. But he never went far from the slim carrier of joy that lay waiting on the beach. All his games returned to it and he stroked it interminably.

"Mine. Mine. This I made with my hands."

In his games, even in his hunting, he was a boy playing. But in the canoe he was a chief conquering. Real and only a little shorter than the best of them. He sat by it on the Islands and repeated guttural words he had learned, smooth words, rippling words.

A few years before, Menzo had taught Simon a lesson of childhood. Must it be forever less, this long childhood, and unrespected in its longing? Instead of helping Simon in his shop, Menzo would slip away to Fred Devish and stay till suppertime. So Simon asked why: " Can't you stay home and work with me if you like wood and tools so much? " Jarvis had no care for man's work, but Menzo had; and now he must go off to Fred Devish as if his own father hadn't better tools and weren't a better carpenter, besides. But when the boy was asked, he answered: " Fred holds the board and lets me drive the nails; home, I have to hold the board while you drive the nails."

So Simon held the board and Menzo's nails went in straighter as the years passed. And now his hands were strong in a task and sensitive to perfection.

The Islands became his kingdom. He resented men who came there for timber because they infringed upon his own. And whenever he came back to land, there were the boys waiting for a chance to paddle, and he took them grudgingly, one by one, instructing them how to sit steadily. But he could not allow them to sit where he sat. Even Jarvie must sit quietly and not ride conqueror here. Simon said it was right, too, when Jarvie said Menzo was selfish: let a man earn his joy with his work. Simon understood no other pride.

The boys waited their turns, standing impotent upon the shore. Menzo made no secret of the fact that he would rather be alone, because then he was anything he wished to be, he was Chief Little-Strong-Eel, as Keokuk called him. Or, if he must have company, let it be Dapper, who could lie without moving a muscle and then leap to the shore and be after the squirrels like an arrow.

Young Lije started a canoe of his own, under Menzo's direction, but envy was not so strong or patient in him as a dream would have been, had he possessed one truly. And besides, Elijah Fordham had not been taught to hold the board.

ONE night they came just at dusk, Jo Nunn, rolypoly Jo, and Lije Fordham, quick and narrow and impatient, and Jack Peck, boy. They had it all planned – during supper – Menzo had his daily stint to do because he had gone off without chopping his share of wood that morning and they knew it. That would be after supper, then, and he would not be likely to notice. An hour for paddling. The canoe lent itself to treachery, so light to lift, so silent to slip through leaves.

They went into the water and Lije took the paddle in his hand excitedly. They laughed softly and Lije imitated the deft strokes he had seen Menzo make. Gently, soundlessly almost, the canoe slipped through the water.

"That ol' Menzo, he's a selfish son of a bitch."

Out of earshot from home, where their tongues were curbed with hickory withies, they were strong-tongued, and proud to use strong words, used them loudly before each other, repeated them as though manhood increased with repetition.

"He's a old selfish son-of-a-bitch."

"The bastard – the God-damn bastard, him! He said we couldn't paddle her!"

They vied with each other in strength and manhood.

"Now you le' me paddle her, Lije."

"Wait'll I beach 'er."

"Aw, naw, I can slip over easy."

"Be careful, ye crazy – !"

Jack took Lije's place. "That Menzo – that selfish son-of-a-bitch him – he says we can't run 'er!"

"Now let me paddle her, Jack."

" Easy, now – "

Dusk was coming down and sounds from the shore were lonely, distant. Dusk has a lonely way with her. There was only one shout, from which one could not be told, but it mingled with the lonely sounds of dusk. The water churned, fought against itself, but it might have been catfish leaping up. It might have been a turtle lunging down.

" Son-of-a – "

The canoe, so smooth with Menzo's labor, lay with its white back glittering on the water, but it eluded hands, slipping away, gliding treacherously.

And the river lay still, slipping down, seeming not to move. But the canoe moved gently south, face down, until it lodged downstream in a clump of willows.

❧ ❧ ❧

By midnight Fordhams and Pecks and Nunns were missing their boys and talking together. And before that, Menzo Baker was missing his canoe. It was near Nunn's store they came together, Simon Baker with a bellow of accusation in his voice, and Menzo just behind him trying to be beyond tears. " They'll split her," he said. " They don't know how to get by the rocks – by the islands you've got to know how to pilot her – "

They took lanterns and went out. Simon himself found the canoe, and near it a cap floating. They were all next day dragging the river. They found Lije first, bloated and terrible. And then Jo, rolypoly Jo Nunn, and that boy Jack Peck, very near together. So they were carried to their homes, their mothers wailing and their sisters sobbing and their little brothers curious. Jo's round face was fixed in terror, Jack's in a white peace that was not Jack and never could be.

Menzo sat still, stroking his canoe. He was there when Elijah Fordham and Joseph Nunn and John Peck came for justice.

He knew it was no use, but he said, standing up to them: "It wasn't the canoe's fault — they stole it."

"It wouldn't have happened," Joseph Nunn said brokenly.

"We don't want our boys a pack o' Injuns!" Elijah cried, and his ax came down.

And Joseph's ax came down and John Peck's. It lay riddled and sick, like white bones with gay colors where the flesh clung. Menzo turned the color of the ashes in the hopper.

Then they burned it.

But the next morning, and it was a great joy to Simon and a wonder to Mercy, Menzo was out on the ground again, his mouth set. Tamping, tamping, hardening the clay again to receive the bark.

Simon stood over him, watching. "You won't have Keokuk to help you this time, son," he said. "You like me to help?"

"Yes, sir," Menzo said. "When I get the bark out, if you'll just help me lift it in."

"It's going to be a lot of hard work," Simon said.

But Menzo shrugged. "This one'll be a lot bigger," he said. "A lot bigger." He measured the ground with his eyes.

Chapter XXI

THE RIVER was torn in pieces with shadow and sun. Once there was rain and sun at the same moment and Mercy said to Betsy: "The old man in the sky is beating his wife!"

Out of the willows on the shore, Menzo guided his new canoe. He had no wish to be seen, and made for the Islands with a swift paddle, his head bent. It was unbelievable how swiftly he could cut a long silent line over the water. He reached the Islands, moving to a place where foliage was heavy, and when he left the canoe he carried his bow and arrows and crept stealthily through the trees, making no sound. Presently he turned his head sidewards, his eyes narrow and his teeth set.

"We will attack from the trees, all together," he whispered, tensely. He fitted an arrow to the bow, slipped around a thick-set oak, and fell upon his belly and let the arrow go.

Suddenly he was upon his feet, his hand moving on his mouth, and his voice came out in a weird broken cry.

Then somebody laughed. And Menzo, with the skin rising on his bones, saw that he was not alone. A man sat leaning against a tree in the little clearing.

It was Brother Joseph. No other, alone and here and smiling.

"For a minute," Brother Joseph said, "I thought you were after *me*."

Menzo stood, chagrined.

"You know I have to watch out," Brother Joseph went on amiably. "I'm here hiding from my enemies – really, you know – and every time I hear somebody coming, I get my gun ready."

"I come here all the time, in my canoe."

"A canoe? Wonderful. You're the Baker boy, then?"

"I'm Menzo."

"Did Keokuk give you a name?"

"Little-Strong-Eel."

Brother Joseph sat very still, looking at him. "I'll call you that, too," he said presently. "I like it. Little-Strong-Eel, suppose you come and sit down and keep me company. I've been here nearly a week now, with callers only at night. You can imagine I get lonely."

Menzo sat down by the next tree, playing self-consciously with his bow, loosening the string and tightening it.

"Although," Brother Joseph went on cheerfully, "I can't think of a nicer place to be. Can you?"

Menzo had heard how the Prophet was in hiding again and how posses stalked the streets in Nauvoo and even entered the Mansion House forcibly to search for him. There was a new warrant out from Missouri, and some said John Bennett's work was responsible. Once already the Prophet had been acquitted at a trial in Springfield; you'd think they'd leave him alone.

"No," Menzo said, "you couldn't find a better place to be, I guess. I come here lots, to sort of get away from everybody and play like I want."

"I guess that's about my reason, too – to get away from everybody and play like I want." Joseph was very serious. "It really isn't very often folks can play like they want, or work, either. It isn't very often they can even *be* what they want."

"No," Menzo said, "it isn't."

They sat still, aware of the clearing and the river through the trees and the sound of light rain. A jay came briskly to a bough above them and spoke without fear. Then he threw himself into the air, extended, and marked an arc to another tree, almost faster than an eye could follow. There he spoke again.

"He's a scold-bird," Menzo said.

"What's the cardinal?"

"He's cheer-bird."

"Crow?"

"Steal-bird."

"Robin?"

"Spring-bird."

"Blue bird?"

"Joy-bird."

Joseph laughed. "You know any more?"

"Buzzard, death-bird. Eagle, strong-bird. Woodpecker, hammer-bird. Wren, sharp-eye bird." Then he stopped, looking self-conscious. "They're my names," he said. "I guess I've got a name for any bird you can mention."

They sat listening. As soon as the ear becomes conscious, it knows the woods are full of singing. Menzo marked chickadee song, shrike, sparrow, thrush. And the mournful descending note of the dove, repeated at intervals.

"That's love-bird," Menzo said. "You know that song Mr. Cuddeback sings with his fiddle –

> Dig my grave both wide and deep,
> A marble stone at the head and feet,
> And on my breast a turtle dove
> To let the world know I died for love.

That means the love-bird."

Joseph sat looking at him. "I almost wish they'd be after me more," he said, "so I could stay here and learn about things the way you do. Sometimes people lose track of what's outside, working so much under a roof."

"Now look there," Menzo said.

Beside him, strung from bough to bough, was a spider web, and the rain had fallen from the leaves and caught upon it in rhythmic patterns. When the sun came suddenly out it was a circlet of jewels.

Brother Joseph sat looking. "A glorious shining jeweled pin for the breast of the world," he said, and looked pleased with himself. "You know, Alexander Campbell was right about one thing – he said it takes three fine adjectives to adorn every good word as it deserves to be adorned. Now that – you can't even say it in three!"

"You don't say it at all," Menzo came back, with certainty. "You just look at it."

So much seriousness was almost ludicrous on his boyish face. Joseph wanted to smile but he did not, and after a moment he did not want to smile any more. He spoke seriously too. "I want you to remember something, Little-Strong-Eel. I want you to remember all your life to love the world the way you love it now. The world is yours, it was made for you, for your benefit. And it's not just the world, the way some think it is, but it's heaven too – right here."

Menzo was silent before his intensity.

"Just before you came, I was sitting here thinking. We're everything, you and I and all of us. Men are the beginning and the end and the center, because they are the children of God, and He gave us the world for our own."

"Sure," Menzo said. "Sure He did."

"Some don't believe it," Joseph said. "They think people are nothing, they think people are worms, and when they think that, they don't make the world a place to love the way you and I know it should be."

"Why don't they believe it?" Menzo asked, appalled.

"I don't know. I can't imagine. Sometimes I try to figure it out, and all the reason I can see is that if they believe men are important, then they have to believe *all* men are important, and they don't want to believe that. They've always figured that some people are better than other people."

"Gosh," Menzo said frankly, "how could they think that?"

Joseph shook his head. "I've been sitting here trying to figure it all out. It's like I've told the people so many times, if men are not equal in earthly things how can they be equal in obtaining heavenly things?"

Menzo sat deeply perturbed and moved by something he did not completely grasp. Joseph hitched himself closer and laid his hand on the boy's head. Instantly Menzo's neck was strained with self-consciousness, and his eyes moved from side to side, absorbed in his position.

"How do I know what is here under my hand?" Joseph said. "How do I know? But it is something wonderful, I know that much, something more wonderful and complicated than I can understand. And it will gradually grow more and more complicated and more and more wonderful; it will develop from a boy into a man."

He moved his hand and sat back, looking at Menzo steadily. "Jesus said: Be ye therefore perfect, even as your Father in heaven is perfect. What do you suppose he meant by that, Little-Strong-Eel?"

"He meant – well, to get more and more good."

"Exactly. To get more and more good. And to whom was He talking?"

"I don't know. I don't remember." Menzo was beginning to feel that this was an uncomfortable catechism, like question-time in Sunday school.

"To you or to me or to all of us?"

"To all of us."

"To all of us, of course. Did He mean the body or the soul?"

Menzo plunged. "He meant the body *and* the soul."

He was flustered at Joseph's pleasure. "The body and the soul! And when He spoke of the abundant life, He couldn't have meant that some should have it and some shouldn't have it. He didn't mean only the rich, because He was always speaking to the poor."

Presently Brother Joseph apologized. " I always think about things like this when I'm by myself. There's so much to be happy for and so few people are happy – even when I was your age, I used to think about things like that, and every time I see something the matter with people, I want to do something to fix it. It's so easy when you think about it, really; all you have to do is think about people and what's good for them. If something that's being done hurts people, then it shouldn't be done – something else should be done that doesn't hurt anybody. Every little thing that comes up you can figure out like that, always thinking of the *most* people. And nothing should be done that makes the world less a place to love, and nothing should be done that makes a man less than he was before he did it. Because there's one big job to do, and that's to grow. You're doing it, and it's not hard, is it? It's fun and happy and natural. When you get to be a man, it'll be a different kind of growing, but it'll be as important and as easy and as natural and as much fun."

Menzo said nothing. But his head was full of ideas, touched with Brother Joseph's feeling.

" Do you see what I mean when I say you can go on growing after your body is as big as it can be? "

" You mean learning things. Father says that."

" Your father's a good man. Learning things. Then, is there something besides your body or not? "

" Yes, there's something."

" Then when your body dies, it doesn't mean that everything is dead, does it? "

" No – "

" Then what's to keep it from going *on* growing, even after the body is dead? That's the way I have it figured out. It's all a long process of growing. It starts before you're born, you know that, and goes on and on. If that's the way it is, then that must be the way God planned it to be. And we look at all the world around us and know God planned it, too."

Menzo nodded. "He planned it all right," he said positively.

"Then we don't have any right to do anything to stop anybody from growing, do we? It takes food to grow one way and ideas to grow the other way; then it isn't fair to keep either food or ideas away from people that need them to grow with."

Menzo could see that Brother Joseph was trying to make it all very simple, that he was anxious to make it clear. "No," he said, "it isn't fair."

"I want you to remember that idea and give it to everybody you ever talk to in your whole life, Little-Strong-Eel. Because it's one of the ideas that will help them grow. We're going to make a place where people can come and get all the food and ideas they want. We're going to have schools and universities and churches and factories and gardens and fields for everybody."

He took a little stick from the ground and with one hand swept the leaves aside and made a clear place on the ground. He traced a little square. "Here's Nauvoo," he said, "and the whole country spreads around it, north and south and east and west. It goes south over another continent, South America, because what I said in the Grove last Sunday is true – Zion is the whole of America from north to south, and the two continents belong together or God wouldn't have made them as He did. *The Book of Mormon* tells the history of both continents, and says it is the promised land. Well – every seven miles we will build a city like Nauvoo – and then other cities." Rapidly he traced other squares around the central one. "Everybody will live in the cities and have his house and plenty of space for his garden, and outside everybody who loves the soil will have his land to work. It will grow and grow and become mightier and mightier, the Kingdom of God."

He looked at Menzo curiously and saw that he was putting a vision into the boy's eyes. "Everybody will believe the same things," he said, "so nobody will have to hide the way I'm hiding. And everybody will be working all the time to make food and all the things people need."

"Food and ideas," Menzo said.

"That's right, food and ideas, clothes and books. You remember what Daniel said about the kingdom of the last days? When I was in Liberty, Missouri, on trial – isn't it funny I should be six months in jail in *Liberty* jail? – the court asked me if I believed that prophecy: 'In the days of these kings shall the God of Heaven set up a kingdom, which shall break in pieces all other kingdoms, and shall stand forever. And the kingdom and the greatness of the kingdom shall be given to the Saints of the Most High.' They said if I believed that prophecy, it was a strong point against me for treason."

"Oh, that wasn't true," Menzo cried, aghast.

Joseph spoke quietly. "In a way it was true, because I want a kingdom created in this land that will sweep away all the kingdoms of the world – but not by war. When you believe every man is a child of God you can't believe in war. But kingdoms can be swept away with ideas when ideas get big enough and are believed fervently enough. It will begin in Zion – and I told you that Zion was both Americas – and grow and spread the way the Gospel spread from Jerusalem. Isaiah said the *word* of the Lord would go out from Jerusalem, and it has. He said the *law* would go out from Zion, and it will."

He went on brushing away the leaves and making more and more little squares at even intervals.

"The way cities are now," he said, "folks just come from

different places and live wherever there is something to do. It's all accidental what people happen to live together. All those in one section, then, decide to have a government and they have one. But they believe a thousand different things and want a thousand different things, so their strength is divided. Now, these cities of ours will be different. Everybody will come because he believes what the others believe and because he wants to lend a hand at what the others are doing. Like your father when he came to live here. Their strength will be all together and so it will be a greater strength than any separate people have had before. And as the numbers increase there will be more and more to go out and preach as well as more and more to stay and work."

Menzo's face was rapt.

"You see?"

"And more and more towns and more and more people," Menzo cried, "all thinking the same things and doing the same things."

Joseph leaned back against his tree, sighing. "I thought you'd like it," he said contentedly. "Anybody who loves the world would like it. I've been thinking about it ever since I was a boy, not much older than you are now. I don't want to make just another religion, Little-Strong-Eel. I want to make another society, because a religion that won't take care of the people in this world isn't very likely to take care of them in the next."

When Menzo went back to the shore, Brother Joseph went with him and admired his canoe with three long adjectives.

"Your Indians, Little-Strong-Eel," he said, "they'll be right with us in our fine new world. The same blood runs in the veins of the Lamanites, remember, as *The Book of Mormon* says; and they've forgotten more about building up great cities out of stone than white men are likely to learn in a long time."

Then he stood among the trees and waved his hand and Menzo turned and smiled over the water.

Before Joseph went back to his tree, he looked back at Nauvoo, thoughtfully. It was a great city but already it was a beleaguered one, and already he, the builder and the leader, was not safe in it. He turned his face and watched Menzo's canoe diminishing toward the west and an old idea stirred again in him, an idea that had been stirring in troubled men for years already and would move them for many more until the West ceased to be an invitation and a refuge.

Presently he had the idea formulated into a plan for action, as his way was. If there was no peace here in Nauvoo or in Illinois or Iowa, then the Church must go where there could be peace – peace to grow and time to grow according to its destiny. He got out paper and pencil and wrote very slowly, upon his knee: "Twenty-five men – at once – exploring expedition – look out for a site – "

Then he wrote swiftly:

> "Let that man go that can raise five hundred dollars, a good horse and mule, a double-barrel gun, one one-barrel rifle and the other smooth bore, a saddle and bridle, a pair of revolving pistols, bowie-knife, and a good saber. Appoint a leader, and let them beat up for volunteers. I want every man that goes to be a king and a priest. When he gets on the mountain, he may want to talk with his God; when among the savage nations, have power to govern them."

Pray God peace would come and they would not have to go. The people had already sent deep roots into this good land by the river, they would not want to tear them out again.

BRIGHAM YOUNG, grim with a knowledge of men and their ways, wrote letters in his new brick house, glancing at the list he had brought from Brother Joseph on the Islands. The most important was to Reuben Hedlock in England, the new head of the Latter-Day-Saint Shipping Office in Liverpool.

My dear Brother,

You are at liberty to print as many *Stars*, pamphlets, hymn books, tracts, etc. as you can sell; and make all the money you can in righteousness. Don't reprint what you get from Nauvoo. Many things are printed here not best to circulate in England.

We also wish you to unfurl your flag on your shipping office and send all the Saints you can to New York, or Boston, or Philadelphia or any other port of the U. S. Ship everybody to America you can get the money for — Saint or sinner — a general shipping office. And we would like to have our shipping agent in Liverpool sleep in as good a bed, eat at as respectable a house, keep as genteel an office, and have his boots shine as bright and blacked as often as any other office-keeper. Yes sir; make you money enough to wear a good broadcloth and show the world that you represent gentlemen of worth, character and respectability.

Start some capitalists if you can. Could five, six, or seven thousand dollars be raised to commence a dam and erect a building, any machinery might be propelled by water. 'Tis the greatest speculation in the world; a world of cotton and woolen goods are wanted here.

The Laws and Fosters and Higbees and Father Cowles have organized a new church. 'Tis the same old story over again – the doctrine is right but Joseph is a fallen prophet.

Your brother in the new covenant,

Brigham Young

And surely the Elders in England were doing great things; it was written to Nauvoo that they had formally presented to the Queen of England a copy of *The Book of Mormon*, with Joseph Smith's own signature on the fly-leaf.

Chapter XXII

SIMON was going to Warsaw to look over a team of oxen offered for trade there, as advertised in the Warsaw *Signal*. He planned to leave long before daylight, and Mercy was always up most of a night when morning meant a special thing. She kept getting up and into bed again, huddling against Simon's back, although the night was warm.

"What's the matter, Mercy? You hurting?"

"No. Just thinking."

It wasn't exactly true. There was that trouble at the joints again; Portia always said if they swelled extra it meant a storm coming. And Mercy had noticed that the storm generally came.

"I was just thinking you might have a bad storm before you get back. And then Warsaw's that rough town – I don't want to be a Missouri widow, Simon."

He laughed. "You get the funniest ideas in the night, Mercy."

"Anybody does. Besides, it's not so funny about Warsaw. They don't like Mormons up there."

"Or anywhere else, seems like. Fact is, there's an anti meeting up there tomorrow night. Thought maybe I'd stay, see what they've got on their minds."

"Oh, Simon! You do and you'll say something!"

"I hope I'll have better sense in a crowd like that."

She stared up into the dark. " I'll bet that's part of the reason you're going, you like excitement like that. You want to go to that meeting – "

He put his arm over her. " You know all about it, don't you? "

" Well, I *suspect* – "

" There was a placard on that barge yesterday when I took the lumber aboard. It said John Bennett was going to be up there."

" Simon! "

" Just made me curious."

" Can you imagine, Simon, somebody getting baptized just to do what he did? "

" I guess there are lots that do," he said dispiritedly. " There was Galland, too, you know, sold this land we're sitting on. They say he got baptized just so's he could pull better deals with the Church. I expect there's plenty that do it."

She lay very still and the thought came over her unwillingly: " In a way, that's how it was with me. Thinking how this was Simon's chance to come west and get some land and be doing something for himself. I was thinking of advantages all the time."

She tried to tell him. " It makes me a little ashamed to hear it said just the way you said it. You know – I always did think about this world more than about the next one, Simon. I guess that's because of Father – he always said if God wasn't right here He wasn't any place."

" Well, Brother Joseph says that. The two are connected, they belong right together. Being here is only part of your whole life, not all of it, and everything we do here has something to do with what we'll do in heaven, later on. That's the first thing I liked about Mormonism. You remember, I used to say: If this world is all of it, then you work and work and get a lot of things together and then you die, and that's the end, like a cow all of a sudden stepping in a slough. You can moo and beller all you want, but you'll sink right down. I don't think like that any more."

She was very quiet, close against him, thinking: " These times in the dark when Simon talks to me, they're the best times we ever have."

He went on quietly. " But it's like the Prophet says – every good thing you do, every good thing you get or think, it's yours and you keep it. Everything you learn is like an inch of growing on top of your head, and you've got some use to live and some use to get ready to die."

" Simon, you're talking poetry! "

" I'm not; I'm talking horse-sense. Even after a man dies, why shouldn't there be land and a place to go? "

" Why shouldn't there be? " she murmured. " Stars of land."

In the night, it was not strange. When she went on, there was laughter in her voice, but sweet laughter full of understanding and hope too. " And when we die and get our star of land, Simon, we can get Joseph to sign a deed for it (and not just a warrantee deed, either!), and then, if it's late in the season when we get there, all the neighbors on all the other stars will turn to and help us clear the dust off it and put in a crop of whatever grows on stars – "

He turned to her and took her close. " There's nobody like you, Mercy. Nobody on earth. Or on the stars either, as far as I know."

They talked then of Nauvoo, as Simon loved to do – Nauvoo that would survive when others faded out because she was founded on an elastic belief that could embrace all good. She was beleaguered now but she would survive.

She would not fail like Shakertown, over in Indiana, where the women tilled the fields and denied their bodies the joys of motherhood and wifehood; where men worshipped Christ and Mother-Christ, neither resisted nor participated in earthly government, and looked aside when the body of a woman came between them and the sun. Nauvoo would emulate her simplicity, she would dance and court the ecstasies of true believers, but her women would remain women, and her men would remain men.

She would not fail as New Harmony was failing, where there was too much free government and not enough religion. Blessed be the name of Robert Owen, who preached so vehemently of the dignity of man. But how can a man succeed at Utopias if he exalts man and denies God? Nauvoo would exalt man and God together.

At last Simon went deep into sleep, but Mercy could not. She got up and rubbed her legs and stirred up the fire to heat water. While she was waiting for it to boil, rubbing her joints tenderly, she thought of her own little verse, one she had made to remind her not to worry in the night:

> Dark and daylight make, I find,
> Dark and daylight states of mind.

She told herself that in the morning when it was light and Simon rode off on Ginger, she would not be so worried. And when she got moving around at the work, she wouldn't worry about the soft swelling on her limbs, either, because they never ached so much in the daytime. "It seems like having babies gets both harder and easier," she thought; "they come easier at the last as though the path were all laid out for them, but they *grow* harder, seems like, as though each time I have less to give."

When she crawled back into bed with the warm bottle to lay against her legs, she looked at Simon with tenderness. "We're funny," she thought, "just funny. For all he talks about the little spirits waiting on the other side for bodies, he never thinks about them, really, when he and I are getting them. There's no thinking at all, then, but we're just conscious of being alive, terribly conscious. And the consciousness narrows down and narrows down until there isn't anything in the world but two people and they aren't even two. It's as though the world closed in on us and then the walls until we're in the only space left and fill it all; just a little point, he and I, and yet everything."

She lay thinking and trying to forget the way her joints seemed to grow on her, spreading out and subsiding, spreading and subsiding. "I don't even remember there is Jarvie and Menzo and Albert and Betsy and George and Joey and Beck. It never stops being the way it was before I ever thought of babies at all – Simon and I are alone in it. The children come after, not part of it, really, but new things to share, quite new things."

When she fell asleep at last, she was thinking of the meeting at Warsaw. "He doesn't have anything to do with that part of things – it's all peace and growing and building for Simon. I hope he won't let the things they say make him mad –"

SIMON hitched his new oxen outside the town hall beside Ginger. He was deeply disturbed. Among the men gathering at Warsaw from settlements along the river and from prairie Illinois and from prairie Iowa and even from Missouri, there seemed to be a striding conviction that something desperate must be done about the "Mormon menace," as he heard them call it. All afternoon he had heard them, talking in knots on the corners, and on the benches in front of the grog-shops.

Their hate filled him with unbelief, and their numbers. As he listened to the talk on the streets, it was as though his mind swelled with a question: "Why do they hate us?"

"I heard 'em myself! He says right in meeting', if any nigger wants to come to Nauvoo, he's a free man! Ain't no difference, he says, white skin er black, it's all the same to God Almighty an' Joe Smith."

"He says there ain't any man's got a right to any more land

'n he kin work hisself! All the extry gets conseecrated – he says *conseecrated!* – to God an' Joe Smith."

Listening, Simon found part of his answer. "They're growin' too fast to set well with me – folks comin' in ev'ry direction, last month three hundred seventy from steamboats an' God knows how many by land. More'n twenty thousand in there, some says, an' Holy Joe, him sellin' lots like a batch o' griddlecakes an' buyin' hisself a house big as the White House at Washington!"

"You know what he says? He says God told 'im *ever' church was wrong but his 'n.* Ever' church, the whole kit 'n' bilin', Cath'lic, Methody, 'n' all. But Joe's got all the good from all of 'em an' none o' the bad. He's gathered all that together, an' out the winda with the bad an' in the winda with the good. He says that!"

"Now me, I don't give a God-damn as long as it's a church. But by God, when it gets to be a militia –"

"An' when it gets to be a block o' votes that Joe Smith can put any place he wants, I don't like it. He sends his representative to state Congress – pretty soon he'll be sendin' his gov'ner to Springfield!"

"Joe says: 'Votes talk!' Back in Washington, he says, nobody listened to him when he asked 'em to make Missouri pay for the land she took. So, he says, he'll take a hundred thousand votes back with him next time he goes, an' then, by God, they'll listen! That's what he says he'll do, right in meetin'. An' Rob Foster told me hisself an' he heard it."

Simon knew then that these men were afraid of the Mormons, and jealous, too, without knowing it. They didn't trust a community that could grow as Nauvoo was growing, they were afraid of her. But it was more than that – it was the same thing that had happened everywhere, in Ohio and wherever they went in Missouri. Folks didn't like their neighbors to be different. And the Mormons deliberately set themselves apart. They gathered themselves together around Joseph like chicks around the mother hen and they didn't welcome outsiders; they boasted that their way of life was not the same as other men's ways of life. And they worked together and boasted of what they built together.

They could forgive anything, Simon thought, but being different.

The doors of the town hall opened and great crowds of men pushed in. Simon moved in among the others, among strangers.

When the leaders came in and filed toward the stand, John Bennett was not among them. But Simon started when he saw the others, because it might have been a meeting in Nauvoo. The Law brothers, William one of Joseph's constant companions — one of his guardsmen, even, when his turn came. And Dr. Foster and his brother Francis, who'd just had land trouble with Joseph. They had sold land on the hill that they themselves hadn't paid for, and when Joseph issued an ejectment to the people living on that land, there had been a big stew. But Joseph said he had to pay for the land himself, and until Foster or somebody paid him, the land was still for sale.

Then Chauncey Higbee, who had caused the Prophet so much trouble spreading scandals and had shamed his father, Judge Higbee, until he was likely to go into his grave over it. A man, Simon thought, thinking of Jarvie, should keep his son in hand from the beginning.

Peck and Downing, too, Simon's own neighbors. Sore over the Half-Breed tract affair. At the sight of them, Simon's throat constricted. And there was Joseph Nunn, big as life and amiable as butter. And Schrench Sirine, talking at the top of his voice to anybody who'd listen.

Simon leaned sideways so that his face was behind the man ahead of him. It'd be better if he got out of here without them seeing him. No use to go now —

The meeting began. A Warsaw man whom Simon did not

know but suspected of being the Mayor stood up and took over. He had difficulty in making himself heard for a long time. The crowd was a motley one, not many good solid farmers that Simon could see, but men who looked as though they might fight for the sake of a fight oftener than for the sake of a principle. Yet they were speaking of principles.

"What we need to do," the chairman shouted, "is get up a strong vote against the Nauvoo Charter. Like Law here says, we wanta hit Joe Smith in the belly, 'n' that's his charter. Why can't we take a prisoner in Nauvoo, even the Prophet, 'n' try 'im at Carthage at circuit court like a regular prisoner of the state? Because he's got habeas corpus on his charter! An' what does the court do at Nauvoo? Any Mormon is let out after a few questions, any gentile is fined or sent to jail without the trouble of questions. What do they do with horse-thieves in Nauvoo? Give us the horse, they say, an' out you go! An' what does Mayor Joe Smith do with his city charter? He gets himself a personal guard, he does, that hangs onto his heels day an' night so's he can't be legally arrested. An' he has a militia, besides, to guard the city of Nauvoo, an' our taxes pay for their guns an' their uniforms!"

He called on William Law.

"There's a good many down in Nauvoo," William said, "that feels the way you do. Only we feel it stronger because we're right in it and have to stand for it, day after day. Live in Nauvoo and you're not a free man. You're told when to work and how to vote and when to mind your own business. You've got to spend one day out of ten working on a mansion for Joe Smith." He drew his hand suggestively across his throat. "Or else!" he said, and the room buzzed for a moment.

"Now, our idea," William said, "is that Joe Smith needs to be relieved of his big city."

Some laughed. All leaned forward with interest.

"It seems to us that if we come on him both at once, us from the inside and you from the outside, he hasn't got a chance. We can tell you how and when and where to hit, because us that's inside know. We even know a good many of his militia that's not so satisfied with what they're getting out of this deal, and it'll help to have them cross over the lines at the right time."

Simon's heart beat in his throat; he could scarcely breathe. With difficulty he stayed in his seat and listened.

When Law had finished, Foster spoke. And then Chauncey, bitterly and brightly as a young man will whose real devotion is to the rebellion itself and not to the reasons for the rebellion.

Then the chairman stood up again. "It was advertised," he shouted, "that John Bennett hisself would be here tonight, an' I see by the commotion at the door he's arrived on schedule."

His voice rose, imitating a barker. "Gentlemen! I give you John Bennett, the first Mayor of the city of Nauvoo!"

They shouted and beat the floor with their feet, and Simon half rose. John Bennett himself, as suave and assured as ever, coming in the door and bowing and waving his hand to a roomful of hoodlums. He came to the stand, held out his hand to make them subside, and when they were quiet he said dramatically: "Friends, Romans, countrymen! I come not to praise Joe Smith, but to bury him!"

There was a bedlam of mirth.

Then John Bennett removed his elegant hat, deposited his cane on the bench beside him, blew his nose on a clean handkerchief, and leaned his elbows familiarly on the rostrum.

"You have been hearing from the Brethren from Nauvoo some of the reasons why we are here. I won't go over the same reasons, although God knows I know them well enough. I'll just quote one line from that eminent divine, Holy Joe Smith, and that tells the whole story better than I could in an hour. I've heard him say: '*I want all the power I can get!*'"

He waited. "We all know in a democratic country a growing minority group like the Mormons is a menace and ought to be dissolved. I was foresighted enough to see danger. I went to Nauvoo to find out what I could about their purposes, because I was afraid of what they meant to do to a country I love and cherish and would protect at the risk of my own poor life, if necessary. Well – I found out. I was, as you know, put in a position to find out. I wanted them to have the charter to see what they would do with enough rope. I knew that if an unscrupulous man like Joe Smith was given enough rope, he'd hang himself and his city, too. Now he's done everything I knew he'd do, and all you and I've got to do is officiate at the hanging."

He was an emotional and forceful speaker, John Bennett. He had the advantage of education and superior language, of a presence that these men envied without realizing it.

"All we want," he said, "is to be sure that when these gentlemen give the signal from Nauvoo, you'll be ready to go in and mop up. They can't do it alone – Holy Joe's militia is too strong. All they want to know is that you'll be ready when you're needed." He looked down over the listening men. Then he raised his voice, asking: "Will you be ready?"

They replied, shouting and stamping their assurance.

"The first thing we want," John Bennett continued, "is to work on the folks in Nauvoo and get as many on our side as we can get. All we have to do is show them the truth. There are plenty of people in Nauvoo who'd like a change, but they're afraid to do anything about it. Every man that's got a cause to complain is another man for us to work on. We work quiet, we keep our mouths shut, and when the time comes we take over."

He could see by their faces that they were ready for all he had to say.

"You've heard rumors of pretty bad things going on in the city of Nauvoo. Well, let me tell you, and I've lived there and I know, that Nauvoo is a sink of iniquity the like of which exists nowhere in our country, if in the world. Women aren't safe on the streets, girls are sacrificed to the lust of the men in power. Joe Smith has a mansion where he keeps his harem of women – it's not only gossip you've been getting out of Nauvoo, it's God's truth and I can prove it."

He took a paper from his pocket. "It's got as far as the east coast, this Illinois scandal. This is the kind of thing they're writing in the New York papers about your fair state of Illinois! This is from the New York *Sun*, an admirable and conservative organ of the people of that great city." He paused, straightening the paper on the rostrum, and began to read:

"There is an almost inconceivable moral courage in a man of our age, who uneducated in political sciences, could call together a mighty host of uncivilized human beings and finally adopt the holy privileges of the ancient prophetic race. The rule of our male Cassandra, our modern Jacob, – a combined prophet and patriarch – cannot last forever. He has degenerated from the religious moralist and priest into the lowest grade of chicanery and vice; he stands before us a swindler of his community, an impious dictator over free will, and now a Giovanni of some dozens of mistresses, and these acquired under the garb of prophetic zeal! "

John Bennett looked up, his eyes kindling. "Let this doctrine spread," he said with great emotion, " and our wives and daughters are not safe. Our most holy system of monogamous marriage will be sacrificed to the lust of a so-called Prophet of God! "

There was a murmur along the benches as the men spoke among themselves.

" And what does he preach but that outsiders and even some of the men within his Church are not good enough to be husbands for the women! I've heard him myself, I've heard him say: ' It's better for a woman to have part of a good man than all of a bad one.' As though he and the men he selects for his Holy Order are the only decent men in the world! He announces from his harem that you foster harlotry and beat and misuse your wives."

The murmur rose in intensity until it was almost a roar, but John Bennett held out his hand.

"I have talked with tender girls," he went on, and took out his handkerchief to wipe his eyes, "girls who have lost their purity and innocence for this monstrous religion and have realized their mistake too late to mend their broken lives. Once they have fallen, there is no return. The loss of their virtue is their initiation into Joseph Smith's Veiled Sisters, and after that they are legitimate prey to the Prophet and his Holy Apostles in the name of Matrimony."

They began to rise when he paused, but he begged them to listen. "I've hardly begun," he said. "And besides, the time for rescue has not come. We must be strong first so that when the time comes we won't fail to accomplish what we must do. Let me go on."

He waited until he could speak into silence. "This man preaches that the goods of this world, and the land, belong by right to no man. No man can own any part of it. He takes over tracts himself when he achieves his Utopia and gives it out as stewardships to those men who please him with obedience. He contends, furthermore, that since a man can only eat and wear so much, he should have no more and must put all the rest into a general storehouse. His purpose is clear – the community works to amass the Prophet of God a fortune! And he sits at his big desk with his hands lily-white and writes his orders out – or has them written for him! – and robs the general storehouse for whatever luxuries he or his family need, or desire. He is the center, the manager, he never asks or explains, he says: 'Do this in the name of God!' and 'Do that in the name of God!' But who is God, in his conception? Who is God – but Joe Smith, Holy Joe Smith? His Honor, God, the Mayor of Nauvoo; His

Honor, God, Lieutenant-General of a militia *your* taxes are arming; His Honor, God, Chief Justice of Nauvoo; His Honor, God, editor of *Times and Seasons*, a paper that prints shameless libels against your city and against your sister cities in Illinois; His Honor, God, Regent of Nauvoo University; His Honor, God, President of the Church of Jesus Christ of Latter-Day Saints; His Honor, God, organizer and head of all industries on his part of the river, ferry-owner, storekeeper, land broker, hotel-keeper!

"I've seen and heard his plans for empire. I've listened to them for hours, I've seen him draw his plans on paper. Nauvoo, the center, and she *is* growing with the spread of this pernicious Gospel, growing faster than Warsaw here, or Carthage, or Keokuk or Fort Madison or any other town in forty counties. He's already starting other towns and settlements, east and west and up and down the river — towns calculated for an inter-commerce that will rob you of your commerce, towns planned to steal your enterprises. He's already taken over Montrose, across the river from Nauvoo, His Honor Joe Smith, the surveyor with his instruments, striding over old lawns and gardens to mark his streets and renaming the place Zarahemla, after the big city in his Golden Bible, without a please or a thank-you. Downing here can tell you it's God's truth, and he was there when it happened. When Joe Smith is big enough, he'll take over Warsaw and Carthage and whatever he pleases — by force if he has to; why else does he have a growing armed militia?"

Somebody shouted: "The law don't allow it!"

But Bennett smiled. "Joseph Smith is beyond law," he said. "He *is* the law. He *makes* it. He goaded the legislature into giving him more power than any city ever had before, pleading the misery of his people. He has his own court and sits as his own justice."

Excitedly a man rose and stumbled up the aisle, holding something before him in his hands. Simon could see that he was full of frontier whisky. " Here's a silver bullet," he cried, " bullet for Holy Joe! "

He reached up and laid the bullet in Bennett's outstretched hand.

" We don't even want his ghost back! " he shouted, and the room roared its approval.

Bennett held the bullet high above him, between his fingers. " A silver bullet," he shouted, " for a black heart! "

Simon sat still. There was no use, no use at all. But he wanted desperately to get up and fight them with his fists, fight the whole crazy lying roomful of them; he wanted to put his fist right in the face of that sham showpiece standing there smirking behind the rostrum. But it was no use, no use at all.

If they wanted to hear a good speech, a speech to touch the heart, let them go to Nauvoo and hear a speech like the one Brother Joseph made to the people last Sunday. Foreseeing this trouble, wasn't it, as he foresaw everything? " As I grow older, my heart grows tenderer for you. I am at all times willing to give up everything that is wrong, for I wish this people to have a virtuous leader. I have set your minds at liberty by letting you know the things of Christ Jesus. When I shrink not from your defense will you throw me away for a new man who slanders you? . . . I never told you I was perfect; but there is no error in the revelations which I have taught. Must I, then, be thrown away as a thing of nought? "

Of course, there was what Brother Joseph said right after; some would look down their noses at that, not understanding as the people understood, knowing how his patience was tried from day in till day out by those that sought to discredit him. " I testify that no man has power to reveal it but myself – things in heaven, in earth and hell; and all shut your mouths for the future."

Some would not understand that, not comprehending the

necessity for Authority as the chosen did. But they could understand, maybe, that Brother Joseph's store had closed its doors only last week because he gave too much credit to the poor; they could understand prophecies that had come true, word for word, act for act, if they'd listen. Even these blunt, stupid faces could understand, if they were told. Perhaps.

But it was no use. He sat still on the bench, clenching his hands.

Bennett's voice was rising. "Within a country of free men there is no room for dictators. Only consider some of the ordinances of the city of Nauvoo, passed by a weighted Council, and see where the heavy thumb is lying. There's an ordinance that prohibits any man from running a ferry at Nauvoo but Joseph Smith – I've got it right here, I could read it word for word from the *Nauvoo Neighbor* if I'd the time for it. Now, there's your free American competition! On your own river, in your own fair Illinois!"

Again along the benches the strange stir of outraged voices, but Bennett raised his hand once more.

"A man's belly is his own in this country," he said dramatically. "But not in Nauvoo. This angelic City Council takes over the liquor business in the name of Almighty God."

Simon saw a hairy arm suddenly lifted ahead of him and saw Schrench Sirine rising to his feet. "I can tell you about it," he shouted, "an' I was sellin' liquor on the Mississip before Joe Smith ever sailed it."

He half-turned to his audience and his voice shook with rage. "It used to be a service to humanity to be ready for a man's natural thirst with a dram of good liquor. But it's a sorry business in Nauvoo when decent thirsty men have got to sneak in all hours of the night or send their boys the back way of a Sunday!"

There was a murmur of laughter. "I'm movin' down to St. Louis, where good liquor is appreciated; they can kiss Joe's ass for their snifters and welcome. But there's plenty in Nauvoo will fight for their liquor – I can promise you that. They come in late at night and say their say, lots of 'em, and carry their bottles home under their jackets, whistling like they was out huntin' cottontails! "

He sat down, and the room roared its approval. When Bennett could speak again, he leaned on the rostrum and put his words in their faces. " There are some more good ordinances in Nauvoo," he said. " A stranger can't walk the streets after nine at night, and the city pays forty policemen to guard and protect the person of its Mayor. There's an ordinance called by the fancy title, ' An Extra Ordinance for the Extra Case of Joseph Smith '! It holds the honorable Mayor exempt from arrest on requisitions from Missouri, and allows to be arrested, without process, any person trying to take him. There's another ordinance that gives the municipal court of Nauvoo the right to arrest any process issued by the state's circuit courts and even the courts of the United States itself; this wonderful municipal court can go behind all such writs and try the cases on their merits! Here is your kingdom within a democracy! Here's a dictator that can overrule the duly elected President of a people. Here's a man that forbids free speech, free press, free trade, in a free country. Here's a man that has the gall to say he doesn't speak for himself but only for God Almighty. It's *God* that wants a corner on the liquor business, *God* that is throwing aside the judicial writs and decisions of the courts of these United States. Joe Smith's got nothing to do with it – you can blame it all on God! "

Simon was breathing deeply, fiercely; he felt his muscles taut upon the hard bench.

" Thank God," Bennett said piously, lowering his voice, " and I am thanking the true God in heaven and not that self-constituted monarch down the river at Nauvoo – thank God, there are other prophets besides Holy Joe. There are men like you and me who can see ahead of us a little, if not into the millennium as Joe can, and we can see enough to know when a thing goes too far, enough to stop it before it gets its head. We can see past our noses, even with a stink like the Mormon stink in Illinois, and we can recognize a villain when we see one, even when he masquerades with titles and uniforms and wears a halo as broad as his backside. I look into your faces and know that there are other and true prophets, and I say: 'Thank God.'"

Quietly, bowing his head, he sat down. William Law took his place instantly at the rostrum. He was a deliberate talker, William, but with a quality of importance in his talk that made people wait for his words, even when they came slowly.

"You remember," he said, "the celebrated case of Elijah Lovejoy. Folks thought they could keep Elijah Lovejoy quiet by burnin' his paper and piein' his type. An' they burned the paper and pied the type, all right, but when they did that they started somethin' that's not over yet. They got the whole country comin' out on 'em — there's not a newspaper in the country didn't shout: 'Freedom of the press!' An' they're shoutin' yet. It's just got a good start."

He stopped and looked at them, gathering them together with his waiting.

"That's where we come in. The whole country's wonderin' about Joe Smith, like the New York *Sun* is, an' Bennett here has done his share to make 'em wonder. Now we'll show 'em what they're waitin' to be shown, we'll let 'em see for themselves. An' whatever we do after that is all right, see? The whole blame country is on our side."

He knew they did not yet understand. Let them wait once more while they wondered.

"We start a paper, see, right in Nauvoo, right under the Prophet's long nose. There's a man that'll edit it for us, an' he knows what to say an' he knows sharp ways to say it. Sylvester

Emmons is his name an' he's a councilor, one member of the City Council of Nauvoo that has a mind of his own – only he can't use it on the Council. Well, we make that paper bad, see, as bad as it can be made. We put everything in it we've said here tonight, everything we've said at Carthage an' at Keokuk, see, an' more too. Well, His Honor the Mayor of Nauvoo, he don't stand for things like that! "

They began to see what he meant and murmured along the benches.

" He can easy break it up. We won't fight much – just enough. But when he breaks up our press, we yell an' we yell loud so's every paper in the country hears us yell. An' that's the only signal we're goin' to need, because from then on things are movin' fast. We're fixin' it so's Holy Joe himself gives us the go-ahead."

The meeting was over. Simon rose abruptly, half-turning from the rostrum with his face down, and walked toward the door. He sensed rather than heard the rush of footsteps behind him and felt no surprise when a hand clapped him on the shoulder.

" Well, Brother Baker! Who'd have thought – "

It was Bennett, smiling and offering his hand. But Chauncey Higbee came up behind him.

" He's not with us," Chauncey said excitedly. " He's as Holy Joe as they come! He'll spill everything he knows in Nauvoo."

There was a tense silence. Simon used it, thinking swiftly and evenly. When he spoke, he directed his words at Chauncey's wild young face. " Mayor Bennett knows whether I have any reason to go out against Joe Smith or not," he said. " I've as much reason to be here as Peck or Downing has, and Bennett knows it."

Bennett smiled, perhaps remembering Mercy at her washtub. " Sure, I know he has," he said. " He bought on the Half-Breed tract! " He laughed infectiously.

" A man," Simon said softly, " don't want to pay for his land twice."

Peck and Downing crowded up, offering their hands. William Law offered his, and Robert Foster pressed Simon's big firm hand with his bony knuckles. " Almost like a Priesthood meeting, eh, Baker? " he sparkled.

" We're takin' subscriptions for the *Expositor*," William Law said gaily. " Five dollars, Brother Baker, for the one and only issue! "

" What if he doesn't do anything about the paper? " Simon asked.

" We'll print two issues, then," Law said. " But I don't think we'll need more than one; I know Joe's well as my grandfather."

Simon rode home with them, clear to Nauvoo, curbing himself more strictly than he curbed Ginger, who was going home to her stable and was impatient with the slow oxen. It was hard for Simon, when the party came into Nauvoo at dawn, to turn over the river instead of going directly to find Brother Joseph, but he knew he had better go on to Zarahemla with Peck and Downing. Because he knew that he was going to be watched; from now on, he was a watched man.

Chapter XXIII

WHEN Simon went over the river the next day, he surrounded himself with reasons for going. He had wheat to sell and he had a cow to buy. And Jarvie went with him, carrying with care a cake Mercy had made for a Relief Society social. But the news he had for Brother Joseph seemed small today, compared with what had happened the night before at a meeting in Nauvoo itself. It had been a political meeting concerned with the coming election for the President of the United States. Men were talking of it on the streets, in the stores, everywhere.

" And we asked Brother Joseph who was going to be our man, and he goes through 'em and reads us the letters they wrote when he asked what they'd do for us if they got in. Well, Calhoun, Brother Joseph said, wrote pages of fine words on very white paper – he showed us the letter. But Calhoun says our case don't come under the jurisdiction of the Federal government – that disputes between states must be settled in the courts of the states themselves and we got to take our case to the courts of Missouri! "

" To the courts of Missouri! For God's sake, to Missouri! "

" And Clay – he's a brave man, Clay is. He says go to Oregon! When you get there, you can make your own laws! "

" And Van Buren – he don't even answer Brother Joseph's letter, but his secretary writes to remind us of what Van Buren said when the Prophet was in Washington – he can't come out for us or he'd lose the vote of Missouri. Now, there's another brave man for you! "

" So then we just stand, wondering who's our man. And then Brother Brigham jumps up and says: ' We'll put a name on the ballot we can vote for with a clear conscience! '

" So we put up Joseph Smith for President of the United States! "

Simon listened and his heart was dull in his side. They were excited, even full of confidence, some of them.

" We're not very big – "

" We're big enough."

" We'll grow bigger – "

" We've got a thousand Elders volunteering to go out stumping through the country. You heard what Brother Joseph said – ' There's enough oratory in the Church to put me in the Presidential chair the first slide! ' "

Simon tried to remember how important the meeting at Warsaw had seemed last night, the way the hate there had weighed on him, smothered him. Today, in Nauvoo, with friends everywhere and hands ready for shaking and everybody shining-eyed over a new distinction for Brother Joseph, the meeting seemed to diminish; and the men at Warsaw, motivated by unreasonable hate and jealousy, seemed small compared with these men in Nauvoo, full of zest and love and a sense of growing power.

Joseph's eyes were strange, absent, when Simon finally stood in front of his desk. What Simon had to say sounded almost silly before that removed look. The Prophet had been working all morning on a document that would be distributed all over the United States of America, a document called *Some Views on the Powers and Policy of the Government of the United States.* A document that expressed new ideas about economy, about slavery, about public officers.

"A newspaper, you say?" Joseph smiled obscurely. "And they expect me to be criticized for suppressing a sheet of deliberate scandal!"

Simon nodded dully. But Joseph reassured him. "It seems to me," he said, "that they may expect a little criticism themselves, starting a sheet designed to defame a candidate for the office of President of the United States."

"Your candidacy won't make them feel any better about you," Simon said anxiously.

"Nothing would. But it's not what they think I care about. We've always had enemies, Brother Baker – we're getting used to them. In fact, the Mormon landscape wouldn't be the same without the shadow of the enemy, and sometimes I even think we work better under it."

At the door Simon turned to him and said: "I'll be glad to do anything I can to help in the campaign. Just let me know anything I can do."

Joseph rose and came to him, holding out his hand, strong in a handclasp.

"You know, of course, the people decided to name a candidate for the good of the Church. Every election both the Whigs and the Democrats have come toadying. They're all for us before election, they love us like brothers. But whichever one the vote takes over the top, the other one is immediately a sworn enemy. Every election our quota of enemies has increased by the exact number of unsuccessful candidates and their supporters. This time we vote for ourselves, and nobody will be led to expect anything else."

"It's throwing our votes away, then?"

"No. Because there isn't a man in the ring that we could vote for now, with a clear conscience. As a people. This way we can at least get our own ideas of government before the people – and our ideas of religion, too, Brother Baker – and among those that hear there will be many humble and true-hearted who will come to us and add their strength to ours. My candidacy, Brother Baker, is another Mission."

He went back to his desk when Simon had gone, and became instantly absorbed in the flow of his ideas. Always he had wished to write something like this, a document for the nation. He felt a sure pride in his power and in his ability to express himself adequately. This morning he was filled with a solemn knowledge that he was destined to exert an influence on the thought of his country, not as President necessarily, but as a man who has a right to publish his ideas concerning the Presidency because he has been mentioned for that office by a convention of citizens, a man who bases his right to be heard on the influence he exerts over thousands of free people. The whole country would know about an enterprising new religion that had as its basis a whole new concept of society, and converts would flow into Nauvoo. Then perhaps, after many growing years, he could be heard again and conquer. As he wrote, he frequently referred to a book by his side containing the inaugural addresses of the Presidents of the United States.

It was after dark when he went home, and Emma had kept his supper warm in the big oven. Before he had finished eating, he heard the band coming, and stood up by the table with his fork still in his hand, straight, as though he stood at attention. The music came closer, martial and wonderful through the darkness, and he laid down his fork and went to the door and flung it wide to watch his people coming. The street was already filled with them, and when they saw him they threw up their hats and cheered and called his name. Suddenly a torch flared and he saw that they were burning a barrel of tar in his honor. "Brother Joseph, Brother Joseph, Joseph Smith for President of the United States!"

He stood there against the light and they came and took him on their shoulders and marched around the fire, singing. He laughed and waved his hands, and when they put him down he stood there in the glare of the tar-barrel and spoke to them.

"Once before I was carried out and there was a barrel of tar—"

They roared, remembering Kirtland, remembering Brother Joseph crawling half dead into the house, grotesque with the tar and the feathers.

"But that day is over and, praise God, will never come again!"

He told them what he had written that day and read aloud to them from the paper in his hand, turning the writing to the fire. *Views on the Powers and Policy of the Government of the United States.*

They listened, appalled by the grandeur of what he had written. Was there any wonderful thing Brother Joseph couldn't do?

He spoke of the equality of man, of the power of unity, of the fomented discord in the government, declaring that it was his desire to bring peace and unity to all the citizens. He spoke of the great men at the head of the country, and quoted copiously from their inaugural addresses. When he spoke of Van Buren as "poor little Marty" there was shouted approval, and he swallowed the rich tonic of applause avidly, for it was a tonic that he loved. Then he spoke with increased emotion, advocating an abolishment of political division among the people. "Democracy, Whiggery and cliquery will attract their elements and foment divisions . . . to accumulate power," he cried, "while poverty, driven to despair, like hunger forcing its way through a wall, will break through the statutes of men to save life, and mend the breach in prison glooms." He advocated the release of all prisoners, asking that they be allowed to pay for their crimes with honest labor on public works rather than with the horrors of iron bars and isolation. "Rigor and seclusion will never do as much to reform the propensities of men as reason and friendship," he said.

He asked that slavery be abolished at once and that slave-holders be paid adequately for freeing human beings, saying: " An hour of virtuous liberty on earth is worth a whole eternity of bondage.

" Wherefore, were I the President of the United States . . . God should be supplicated by me for the good of all people."

He bowed his head and prayed, loudly and earnestly. And they sang and the band played and in Zion there was great rejoicing.

Eliza watched and listened, smiling, and even Emma smiled with pride plain on her face. Across the river Simon Baker pointed to the glare of the tar-barrel and said to his wife: " I'm afraid for Brother Joseph – he's not scared enough."

Chapter XXIV

SIMON looked at it. Then he took it in to Mercy and said: " Well, there it is."

" The *Nauvoo Expositor*."

Mercy watched his face as he sat reading it, saw the lines of his jaw tighten.

" Listen here, Mercy, they start by declaring that the Gospel is true! Then this — ' We most solemnly and sincerely declare, God being our witness, that happy will it be with those who examine Joseph Smith's pretensions to righteousness. Do not yield up tranquilly to a man whose designs are pernicious and diabolical. . . . We are seeking earnestly to explode the vicious principles of Joseph Smith and those who practice the same abominations and whoredoms. . . . We are aware, however, that we are hazarding every earthly blessing, particularly property and probably life itself, in striking this blow at tyranny and oppression, but we have abundant assurance, in case of emergency, that *we shall all be there*.' "

Simon looked at Mercy. " They say it right out. And here they've got a bunch of resolutions — " He read silently for a moment. " Good God, ' we discountenance every attempt to unite church and state,' ' we consider religious influence exercised in financial concerns by Joseph Smith unjust and unwarranted,' ' the " gathering in haste " has been taught to enable Joseph Smith to sell property at exorbitant prices.' "

Mercy picked up her sewing. "There's nothing new in it, is there?" she asked. "It's all been said before."

"But not *printed*, Mercy! Some folks are funny – anything black and white looks like the truth to some folks."

Simon's face burned. "When they call him 'Old Hat Joe,' my fingernails nearly go through my hands," he said. "Listen to this editorial – this is Emmons – 'the departure from moral rectitude and the abuse of power have become intolerable.' And here he talks about Joe Smith and the Presidency. 'One of the candidate's recommendations which will no doubt be very congenial to his nervous system is to open all the prison doors and set the captive free. . . . Joseph Smith, the candidate of another *powerful party*, has two indictments against him at the moment, one for fornication and adultery, another for perjury.'"

Simon rose deliberately and went to the hearth and laid the *Expositor* on the flames. "Then I'll stir the ashes," he said, "to be sure it all goes up the chimney."

THE *Nauvoo Neighbor* came out next day, its pages seething with scandals against the proprietors of the new paper. "We have not wished to be scandalmongers," an editorial said, "but forbearance is no longer a virtue. To blast the character of the most chaste, pure, virtuous and philanthropic man on earth, this *Expositor* . . ."

In the afternoon Joseph Smith faced a special session of his City Council.

The first business of the day was to rid the Council of member Emmons, editor of the *Nauvoo Expositor*. The City Recorder was instructed to notify him of his suspension.

Councilor Taylor reported how Emmons had come to Nauvoo without two shirts to his back or anything else, and Brother

Joseph himself told how he had been blackguarded out of Philadelphia and dubbed with the title of Judge, out of humor. "He was so poor," the Mayor said, "I had to help him to a coat before he went away last fall."

Councilor Peter Hawes told of an English girl in his own house who had been seduced by Wilson Law, and she an orphan with a younger sister to take care of.

"Dr. Foster came in the Mansion House and threatened the Mayor with a gun – but he wouldn't discuss the issues between them before witnesses. Then he made a public dinner to give food out to the poor, and when the poor came, there was no food to be had."

"During the scarcity of grain the Law brothers cheated at their mill till the poor had nothing but themselves to grind!"

The City Council of Nauvoo spent over an hour relegating all the proprietors of the *Expositor* to the dung-heap, and then they got down to the *Expositor* itself, handling it as they would handle chicken-droppings on the back stoop.

Mayor Smith sat drumming his fingers on the arm of his chair. "You've all read it," he said. "All I ask is whether or not this paper is treasonable against our chartered rights and privileges, whether or not it is against the happiness and peace of this city. What it does to me is no matter; what it does to Nauvoo is what we want to consider."

Councilor Taylor rose to his feet. "No city on earth could bear such slander!" he said. "William Law and Emmons were members of this Council, and Emmons never objected to any ordinance while he sat here, but to my personal knowledge was nothing but a cipher. Now he edits a libelous paper, out after all the ordinances and the charter, too!"

He read, very solemnly, from the Constitution of the United States on freedom of the press. "We are all willing for the truth to be published," he said, "but it's unlawful to publish libels.

The *Expositor* is nothing but a nuisance and stinks in the nose of every honest man."

Councilor Stiles said a nuisance was anything that disturbs the peace of a community, and read Blackstone on private wrongs, volume two, page four. "If we can prevent the issuing of any more slanderous communications, I'll go in for it. This community should show a proper resentment."

Mayor Joseph Smith gave Councilor Warrington the floor.

"My situation," Warrington said, "is a peculiar one, because I don't belong to any church or any party. But I give it as my opinion that to declare the paper a nuisance is too harsh a measure."

"What," the Mayor asked, "would you suggest as an appropriate measure?" He looked keenly at Warrington.

"I'd give a few days limitation, and assess a fine of three thousand dollars for every libel. Then if they don't stop publishing libels, I'd declare it a nuisance."

There was a murmur of voices. Mayor Smith sat very straight, drumming his fingers. "I'm sorry," he said, slowly, "that we have a dissenting voice in declaring the *Expositor* a nuisance."

Hands came up, all over the room. Councilors rose in their seats, among them Councilor Warrington.

"Councilor Warrington, take the floor."

"I don't want to be understood as going against the proposition," Warrington said, "only that I'd not be in *haste* —"

Hyrum Smith rose. "The proprietors of the *Expositor*," he said, "have so many mortgages on their property, there wouldn't be a chance of collecting damages for libels. All of you know that as well as I know it."

Alderman Elias Smith leaped into words at the Mayor's nod. "There's one course to pursue," he cried, and his old voice was high and shaken, "because these men are out of the reach of the law. We've got to put an end to it! I've heard plenty this morning, and yesterday, and if we don't attend to the matter ourselves, the citizens will do it without us."

Councilor Hunter believed it to be a nuisance.

Alderman Orson Spencer accorded with the views expressed.

Councilor Levi Richards said: "I feel deeply on this subject, and I concur fully in the view expressed of it this day."

Councilor Phineas Richards trembled as he stood in his place. "Maybe some have forgotten the transaction at Haun's Mill," he said, "but I've not forgotten it. My son, George Spencer, is lying in a well without a winding-sheet, shroud, or coffin, and I can't sit still when I see the same spirit raging in this place that raged in Missouri. The publication of this paper is as murderous at heart as David before the death of Uriah!" His bright little eyes spilled over. "The quicker it's stopped," he said, "the better for all of us."

Councilor Phelps had investigated the Constitution, charter, and laws. "The power to declare a nuisance is granted to us in the Springfield charter," he said, "and a resolution declaring it is all that's required."

John Birney was sworn. "Francis Higbee and William Law declared in my hearing that they'd commenced their operations and they'd carry them out, law or no law."

Stephen Markham was sworn. "I've been told," he said slowly, "and by good authority, that the publishers say the interest of this city is done the minute a hand is laid on their press."

A swift murmur of voices filled the Council chamber. Alderman Harris rose and shouted: "The whole thing ought to be demolished!"

Mayor Smith leaned to his Council. "One thing more," he said, "before there is any definite and unchangeable action – I can't at a time like this, bear the responsibility for this thing on my shoulders alone. You must share it with me – it is your opinion we have been considering. With the exception of Councilor Warrington, you have spoken of this paper as a nuisance, and I only bow to the will of the Council. Personally, it distresses me deeply to be forced to soil my fingers with it."

Some of them realized the game he must play and played with him, stood up instantly against his last-minute waiver.

"You'd rather have your name smeared than your fingers!"

"You're letting them scare you, a handful of hoodlums and bogus-makers."

He dropped his eyes. "Not just a handful. I have many enemies, I am afraid."

They came around him. "And many friends. You can count your enemies, but you could never count your friends. No more than you can count the hairs of your head. No more than you could count the people around the tar-barrel who sang for you and carried you on their shoulders."

In his eyes was the peculiar brightness they knew well.

"If I destroy the press, the country will say I'm afraid of it."

"They'll say you're afraid if you don't!"

"They might say it's the truth that hurt me —"

"They'll say there's at least one place in this country where slander gets punished and lies aren't tolerated!"

"Of course," he said gently, "we promised that this Council would keep Nauvoo clean. That meant something besides boarding the sidewalks and removing trash. It meant getting rid of grog-shops and whore-houses. It meant —" He paused and they took it up.

"It meant cleaning out slander and lies and filthy sheets that go right into our houses. What did we do with that grog-shop across from the Temple Block?"

"We got rid of it."

"That fence around Marshal's field where somebody kept writing such obscene slander?"

"Got rid of it, got rid of it."

"And a sheet of filthy words and lying insinuations — is slander on a paper any different from slander on a fence-post?"

They were all together, except Councilor Warrington.

"Read the resolution."

"Resolved, by the City Council of the City of Nauvoo, that the printing office from whence issues the *Nauvoo Expositor* is a public nuisance and also all of said *Nauvoo Expositors* which may be or exist in said establishment; and the Mayor is instructed to cause said printing establishment and papers to be removed without delay, in such manner as he shall direct."

It was unanimously passed.

Immediately the Mayor issued an order to the Marshal of the city.

"You are here commanded to destroy the printing press from whence issues the *Nauvoo Expositor*, and pie the type of said printing establishment in the street and burn all the *Expositors* and libelous handbills found in said establishment; and if resistance is offered to your execution of this order by the owners or others, demolish the house; and if anyone threatens you or the Mayor or the officers of the city, arrest those who threaten you, and fail not to execute this order without delay, and make due return hereon. By order of the City Council. Joseph Smith, Mayor."

IT was John Peck who told Simon, and told him jubilantly, slapping his shoulder. "Joe took it, Baker, took it hook, line, and sinker!"

Simon writhed under his hand. He hardly knew what he was saying, but all the fear he had known on the ride home from Warsaw came back to him, and the whole matter loomed again with a terrifying importance.

"They've not done it yet!" And he shook Peck off and went after Ginger, running. Peck did not move after him, but stood grinning, because there were already torches running along the river over at Nauvoo. Simon hardly seemed to see him, standing there, when he rode by on Ginger.

"When it comes right down to it," John Peck thought, "I don't know if Baker's our man. Better let Law know about that."

He could see Ginger dancing, waiting for the boat; he still stood until he lost sight of personalities, beyond the Islands. He did not see Ginger stumbling up the other bank, or that Simon was beating her fiercely, or how she reared up, whinnying. Nor how she took the hill, understanding the urgency of Simon's voice, nor how, when she came to a stop, Simon did not slide to the ground as Ginger had expected him to do, but only sat there with her sides heaving under his legs, as though all the hurry had been for nothing. As indeed it had. Simon sat there looking at the little frame building that had housed the *Expositor*, crumbling beneath the flames. And somebody at Ginger's side was telling him excitedly how they had dumped the press into twelve feet of water, over near the quarry.

"By God, she's burned an' drowned!"

Sylvester Emmons was there and he kept yelling: "You can't do this in a free country!"

And Old Port, "Seems like folks do what they damn well please in this here country –"

"You'll get paid for it!" Simon saw Emmons's face, triumphant as his building burned, and his stomach sickened. After a while Emmons got on his horse and went as fast as it could run for Law's steam mill on the river, where a crowd of men waited.

Some of the Brothers brought a bag of potatoes and threw them into the fire to roast and there was great sport over the *Expositor* burning in hell with the rest of the sinners.

"You think it'll spile those potaters?"

But Simon could not laugh. He rode around by the mill and in less than half an hour he saw the Law brothers and Sylvester Emmons start out for Carthage as fast as their horses could trot.

William Richards, City Recorder, wrote in the City Record that night:

"Marshal's return – The within-named press and type is destroyed and pied according to order, on this 10th day of June, 1844, at about 8 o'clock p.m."

Chapter XXV

"SSSSH! Don't even say it out loud, Jarvie! Don't even say it! "

Jarvie looked at his mother strangely. It was an exciting thing to have Brother Joseph himself hiding in the barn, but it wasn't any use unless you could have something to do with it. He had seen Joseph for a moment at dawn, had seen his father carrying bed-quilts and later a hot breakfast out through the back door, and tiptoeing. Silent messengers kept coming and going, not using the road but the paths kids and hunters and Indians and animals had broken through the trees up over the bluff itself.

Even Port Rockwell came, trying to walk quietly in his big boots. Bert kept right at Port's heels, listening to the clank of his pistols, until Port threatened amiably to step right-square-smack on top o' him.

With all the trouble and the rumors and the bitterness and the street-fights and even the Governor afraid of civil war, no Brother was surprised to see Brother Joseph at his back door. It was let out that he might go from place to place, ahead or behind the posses, and to be always ready. Gang after gang and posse after posse had invaded Nauvoo and now they were searching systematically with their fingers on the triggers of their guns. Amazed and silent, the people opened their houses and let the searchers come in. With pride they whispered that Brother Joseph was always just one jump ahead of everybody.

Just in time to keep a mob out, he had appeared in person and declared martial law in Nauvoo. Then, under protection of his Legion guns, he had disappeared again, hoping, as he said, to avoid a battle for his own person, a battle that would endanger the lives of the people.

Now the Prophet looked around at the faces of the few who were still with him, all anxious faces and faces to be trusted. They looked at him with unbelief that pained him, but his voice went on, soft through the silence.

" When Port comes back with the supplies, we'll start west. I don't know where, exactly, but I do know west. I guess it's true that if we want to be a law unto ourselves, we'll have to be alone in our own country."

He looked at them wearily. " A clean new world for the Kingdom of God on earth. Maybe Clay was right, after all; maybe we'll have to go clear to Oregon."

He saw his brother looking at him, in his eyes an unwonted touch of bitterness.

" I've Orson Hyde's advice," Joseph said defensively, " right from Washington."

" I didn't know you were accustomed to taking advice," Hyrum said. " And I don't notice that the government's going to help us any."

" No, but it's like Orson says, Oregon is getting to be a popular question; there's beginning to be a fever of immigration, and if we're the early majority, others won't come – if others are the early majority, they won't let us come."

He walked back and forth like a caged animal. " It seems to me maybe the government isn't acting in this matter because God won't let it act – maybe He intends Oregon for us. Anyhow, Judge Douglas says we'd as well go to that country without an act of Congress as with it. We could form a noble state in five years."

Hyrum put his face in his hands.

" Then," Joseph went on, " if they wouldn't have us in the Union, we could have a government of our own."

His eyes were bright in the old way for a moment. " I'd been thinking of the West, anyway. A government of our own, an unhampered government, growing as the people grow. God's government, unafraid, moving with one purpose to one goal."

But Hyrum said coolly: " You seem to think the people will follow you forever! "

Joseph looked at him, startled. Then he looked at the others. " Yes," he said, " I expect I do." His voice gathered confidence as he spoke. " I've always said that, haven't I? I've always said they'd follow me forever."

They heard Port coming then, and Joseph moved to the door quickly. He was nervous and quick-fingered, they noticed; he kept rubbing the knuckles of his left hand with the thumb of his right hand. The days of watching and keeping out of sight were beginning to tell on him. When the door opened, only enough to permit Port to move through, he went to his friend quickly, looking with anxiety into the eyes he had always trusted more than any other eyes and that had never failed him from the beginning.

" Cahoon brought a letter from the Governor – and Emma put one in with it." Port handed the paper to the Prophet and stood back respectfully while he opened it. They all noticed that Joseph's fingers were not steady as he read it. And when he looked up, there was great pain in his face. For a moment he did not speak, as though he could not. Then, very slowly: " I am promised protection if I give myself up for trial at Carthage."

" God Almighty! " It was Port who spoke. " At Carthage! "

" Many of my good friends," Joseph said, " have been giving my wife their opinions." He looked at Hyrum. " I think they're wondering, as you did, Hyrum, if the people will follow me forever. They seem to think I'll be going west alone."

Port grunted. "I calculated to go right along," he said. "You make your bed an' I'll lie alongside, here or there."

"I know, Port." Joseph looked around at all of them. "They think the whole affair will blow over, that I'm taking it too seriously – and the Governor has militia to protect me." He smiled whimsically at Port, who had heretofore done all the necessary protecting, and Port stood waiting tensely, as a dog waits for his master to throw a stick that he has retrieved before many times and brought back, panting, to be petted and praised and to wait again.

"They say it's not the time to turn tail and run." Joseph turned once more to his brother. "What do you think now, Hyrum? You're the oldest. What do you think?"

"I'd say," Hyrum said, steadily, "that it's not the time to desert your friends. I'd say go back and face them like a man and a Prophet of God."

Joseph nodded simply. "Then we go back," he said. And looking at them once more, he said what they always remembered with pain, reading it over in their journals with a new understanding: "After all, *if my life is of no value to my friends, it is of no value to me.*"

They went down the bluff together, in broad daylight, and Albert clung unreproved to Port's shadow. Jarvie went too, and even Menzo, because it didn't seem to matter how many went now. There were no more secrets. People gathered from the houses as they went until a crowd stood on the shore to see Brother Joseph push off for Nauvoo. Once he touched Menzo's shoulder, coming down the hill, and said: "Remember what I told you, Little-Strong-Eel. You'll have a long life to preach it in."

Nobody knew what Joseph was thinking after that; they only knew he was very still. Some have said he knew all the time and must have thought, deliberately: "Martyrdom is a last refuge, after all. A last refuge that men seek when there is nowhere else to go honorably. From that refuge blows a great wind that carries their voices back into the world again, and behind them there stands a great sun that is theirs alone, a sun that makes their shadows grow longer and longer upon the world, as the years pass."

QUITE openly, Joseph said good-by to his family. He kissed Sister Emma, and for many other women and brethren along the streets he had messages, leaning down from his saddle to speak to them.

To Eliza Snow he said, smiling: "This life is a small thing, Eliza. At best, it is a small part of Life."

He looked back many times at his Nauvoo, he kept looking back. There had been troubles and worries enough, surely, but Nauvoo had been the home of more happiness than any other place in his memory. It had held more hope and realized more ambitions, it had been the scene of more trial and triumph, of more suffering and joy; it had been the realization of his own dream and of the dreams of other men. He tried to tell himself: "Even now it is only a beginning."

When his party was a few miles from Nauvoo and he could look back no longer, he saw troops moving toward them on the road, and stiffened in his saddle. But the troops came on an errand of peace, as they said. They were detailed to go to Nauvoo and remove the guns and ammunition belonging to the Nauvoo Legion as a condition of peaceful settlement. They bore an order signed by Governor Ford and sealed with the seal of the State of Illinois.

Joseph turned back with them. And when he left Nauvoo again, followed by the Governor's troops loaded with his Legion's guns, his mouth was set and all softness was gone from him. Because he knew he was alone, and there is no room for softness in a man alone. Once he almost turned his head, as though he would have liked to look back yet again, but deliberately he held his face forward. With great effort he kept his back toward Nauvoo, because Nauvoo could make him soft and make him remember days that were better forgotten. Nauvoo had given him the power and the glory, she had almost given him the Kingdom.

His eyes memorized the width, the length, the contours of the pommel of his saddle, and he did not look back again.

Chapter XXVI

ELIZA came down the stairs, stumbling over her petticoats. She knew without being told. There had not been anything but the rush of the horse down the hill and the sound of its feet on the hard road. That was all she had heard. But she knew that Joseph was coming home.

She saw at once that the whole city knew. People were coming from their houses, stumbling as she had stumbled. They whispered to one another as though they dared not raise their voices. Eliza looked up at the sky, appalled, and saw the sun go under a cloud and come out again. You had to see the sun to be sure night had not fallen at noonday.

So it is like that with a city, even, if it is a city men have loved. If it is a city like Nauvoo that has been bright and growing like a child, with so much hope in her she lifted your belief and you believed you were meant from the beginning to be a conqueror of land and a builder of cities. Maybe it was because so many of the people had dreamed of Nauvoo long before she had been laid out by the river. She had been a symbol, a portent. And if she failed – then how could anything be great enough to escape failure in the end? Stirring out of swamp by the river, stretching and stirring, and the white badge on her brow growing.

You can strike such a city, you can strike her in the face and she will go stiff, she will groan even.

Eliza went with the people and the whisper ran along rows of them as they walked together: "Dr. Richards is bringing him home."

Once they were hysterical, but only once. Someone cried out: "Why did he let them take our guns?"

Someone else said: "It was a condition of peace — they took *all* the guns, not only *our* guns, but all of them."

"Then how did they kill him? What did they kill him with?"

They made a strange sound as they walked together, walking east on the Carthage road. And then they saw the wagons coming, behind eight guards, mounted. They went on silently, their feet moving without sound in the deep dust. They dragged their feet a little as they walked and the dust rose around them and they choked as though they were weeping. When the first of them met the wagon with Dr. Richards driving it, hunched on the seat, and behind him in the box a figure covered with bushes to keep the hot sun away and the bluebottles, they parted ranks and stood still by the side of the road to let the wagon pass. And then the other wagon, where Hyrum lay. They stood still, watching the procession pass; then they turned and followed it home again. When the ruts were bad and the two still figures rolled in the wagons, they shuddered in long lines.

Eliza saw Simon Baker, riding after the wagons with the other Brethren who had gone to Carthage when the first news came. She saw with great clarity that tears were running down his face as rain runs down a window-pane.

She wanted to say to him: "Why should you cry like that? He gave you all he had for you, but I was still waiting."

Then she saw Emma. Emma, walking with the others, her features like features pressed into a stone. Emma, expecting again in a little while, expecting a little boy, maybe. Eliza thought: "This is the last you'll ever bring him, there'll never be any more." And she was glad. It came to her unbidden, even on this last march, even marching in this last parade. "If I should die first, if I should go on before any of them, then I would be the only one for a little while. I'd be the only one until she came, and the others."

She remembered what he had said, many times: "It is folly for men to weep for death. If they knew what I know, they would realize that save for birth itself, there is no happier circumstance than death."

There was this to tell them from his mouth, then, and many, many other things that would comfort them. She must still make songs for them to sing. There would be years of songs and years of needing songs. This he had left for her to do, and he would be waiting to hear how she had fared with it.

She looked at them and raised her hands and began to sing. Presently they began to sing with her, slowly and hesitantly at first, but after a time swelling out as they sang in the Grove when Brother Joseph leaped to his feet and cried: "Make *God* hear it!" Eliza looked at all of them, walking together and singing together, and saw that they had forgotten they were walking in the dust.

Chapter XXVII

THE DAY Joseph and Hyrum Smith were brought back to Nauvoo and their long celebration as martyrs was begun, a miracle happened across the river. Some would say a natural miracle, if indeed such a thing can be said, but all would say miracle. It happened very suddenly, out of the normal time of its happening. Vic went like lightning down the bluff for Mother Turner and then, after, to the field to tell the boys, and they came and sat in a row on the step, waiting.

There was not much pain, only the great sense of miracle that followed.

They were exactly alike, two of them. An intentional emphasis on the part of God, surely, because He had never made anything so beautiful before as either of them. Both girls, and exactly alike, so exactly you did not believe in *two* without catching both together on the retina. The damp hair, eyes tight shut, doubled fists with nailless tips buried in soft palms. Fragility and littleness beyond anything but a carving in ivory — beyond anything but an old ivory carving done with the patient skill of devotion.

Mercy looked at them. She looked at each of them. She uncurled their fingers and let them go to curl again. She looked at them both together. Venus, then, had two pearls for her ears, two identical pearls, and while she was flying over to look at herself in the river, she dropped them, quite by accident –

Not one, not one, but two, as though one perfection were not enough to come from the dear offices of love but two must come, repeating perfection in a refrain of perfection. A poet finding at last the word soft enough, fluid enough, must use it again. The ground must repeat the pattern of one daisy through a field of daisies. The sky repeats blue stars.

That they did not cry like ordinary babies was a part of the miracle, and she did not worry, but only prayed for Simon to come soon. He would come grief-stricken, she knew, and then she would show him how the world goes on, and how there are lovelier things this now-moment standing on the very edge of happening than we ever dreamed of.

Lying very still, she saw there was a vast space to stare into through her weakness. Nothing on this earth has a quality so complete, so deep as that first rest of the mother when the child has come. She did not sense that her rest was different. When Jarvie and Menzo came in, and Bert, intolerably shy and afraid as he always was of climactic moments, she spoke to them from such depths of comfort, such white depths as she had never known. It was part of the miracle, only part, because there was no quality of strangeness to match the miracle itself.

"Look at them, Jarvie," she said, and heard herself as from far away. "There are two of them." And she said again: "Two."

He looked at her with terror, the color of her face indistinguishable from the pillow. He turned to Mother Turner, seeming to reach out for her, and she said soberly: "She goes out. It'd be as well to fetch a doctor."

He headed down the bluff, forgetting the flat rocks intended for his feet, forgetting everything but descent. The town was empty and the ferry lay white and inert across the river. He waved frantically, but the ferry did not move. He thought of the fishing boats, moored all together about a mile up the river, too far now. It'd have to be the canoe. He put his fingers to his mouth and whistled his signal to Menzo.

"Why 'nt you think of it?" Menzo said. "I could have been there."

"Go easy over the channel," Jarvie said. "And find father first, he'll find Dr. Richards."

Even at such a moment Menzo sent his craft through the water with tremendous joy, and part of his joy was in the adequacy of what he had done with his hands. Skill and care come back and reward the craftsman. The current took her far downstream, but he gained near the other shore and landed just below the place where the Nauvoo House was building. For once he beached her in plain sight and ran along the road. There was a dense crowd, he saw, around the Mansion House; he pushed through, asking his question. And people stared at him. His little news, his necessity, was like the extra flutter of one stone tossed into the water when a storm is alive in it.

He saw Dr. Richards himself coming out of the Mansion House, his face on his chest. Menzo used his elbows, thrusting himself through the crowd.

"My mother, she's bad sick, Dr. Richards," he said.

It was as though the doctor came alive, out of sleep. "You go get Dan Jones," he said, "he's there in the hall. Tell him the boat can't stop running."

When the doctor and Dan and Menzo came to the ferry, Simon was there, waiting to cross over. Menzo heard him say to the doctor: "I'm sorry – at such a time –"

But the doctor was brusque. "All there is for Brother Joseph now is to be remembered. And hide his body away. Our duty is still in this world."

The ferry was anchored across the river before Menzo started back. He found himself weak at the paddles for the first time in his experience; going over today he had been very strong.

THERE was not much Dr. Richards could do for Mercy, after all – only revive her with sharp draughts of whisky. She was not to be disturbed – about that he was emphatic – move her into the back room where the girl sleeps. Above all, quiet, and no concern over anything.

"Apparently the heart," he said.

Jarvie heard him plainly from the doorway. Casually, as doctors say such things. And he turned and went out.

"Apparently the heart." Not that it was too hard having babies, having two babies, but that central thing that beat in the middle of you, day and night, and that you held your breath to listen to, pressing your hand flat to the chest and thinking: "What will it be like when it stops beating?" The absolute center of everything.

For hours he walked in the woods with that center thing in him beating and beating.

THAT night Simon sat by Mercy's bed and she tried to tell him what the twins really were. So alike, so exact, you thought your eyes were playing tricks and making doubles. A miracle prepared in heaven, she said, with careful attention to detail, because it must startle, a double perfection. Not made by accident, she had decided that; accident never made even two leaves so alike. Made with purpose and laid down here in the world with purpose.

Her excitement was lost on him. He sat looking at her heavily, thinking of other things.

FOR one at least, the news of Mercy Baker's twins weighed more heavily than the news that Joseph had come home for the last time and lay waiting for burial over in the Mansion House.

It was Melissa Vermazon. "Two baby girls, tiny as kittens, not much more than four pound apiece — "

Portia sat glumly in Melissa's doorway. "Seems like," she said, "there might be something in that old idea of souls coming alive in another shape. One's for Brother Joseph and one's for Brother Hyrum — "

"Brother Joseph's soul was a big one," Melissa said. "What did you say, not *four pound apiece*? "

"Souls are always the same size," Portia said, impatiently. "They don't grow and shrink like bodies. When a baby dies, the soul that comes out of it is full grown like it always was."

Melissa stood up quickly. "They didn't say they might die, did they, Portia? "

"Who? The babies? " She shook her head. "No, they're all right. Mother Turner says they're doin' right well for such little ones that should've been carried longer. Now, me, I don't see how a little pale woman like Sister Baker can take care of two at once — seems sort of an imposition to me."

Melissa's face was sharp. "No, a blessing," she said. "If anything, a pure blessing."

It was getting dark when Portia went away, and Melissa sat alone in her doorway. The dusk came slowly as it does on the river in July, and she sat in it and was dissolved in it until one passing by would not have seen her in her black dress, sitting there. The sounds of the settlement came to her with the sharp clarity of sounds at dusk, and when dark had been everywhere for a long time, she listened still. She saw Portia snuff her candle, heard her roll across the tick, even heard the ropes give under her, stretched at the pegs with her weight. She saw Yeaman's candles, now and then obliterated briefly by figures passing before them. Eight daughters at Yeaman's. "Maybe if I'd had eight instead of four," she thought, "I'd have four left." For a moment the thought cheered her, then her chin dropped. "Then maybe all eight would have had pox, and eight dying would be worse than four dying."

The thought of eight dying appalled her.

One by one, Zarahemla snuffed its candles, doused the bitches in the saucers. Every hand belonged to one who thought of Brother Joseph, whose candle would burn no more. But Melissa sat alone, remembering her own dead and thinking of twin girls, little ones, not more than four pound each, folks said. She saw that Nauvoo was very dark tonight, the people could not bear to burn candles when the Mansion House was black save for two tall candles burning in one room.

It must have been eleven o'clock when Melissa heard the baby crying up the bluff. Very plain in the night she heard it, though small with distance and another height. She sat listening and it cried on. Once the sound stopped for a few moments and she thought: "They have taken her up now," but then it began again. At last she rose and left the dark barracks, moving toward the hill road. Her dress made a noise like that of the trees. She leaned forward, taking the hill.

Dapper met her, growling in his throat, but he knew her and went back to the step and lay down, his ears pointed and alert. She stood still and listened. It was not a baby born this day; it must be little Beck. She went to a window, standing open to the night, and stood there, her mouth twitching with sympathy. "For the first time not with her mamma this night," she thought. She put her face close to the window and said in a soft voice: "Darling! Darling!"

There was sudden silence. Then somebody moved across the floor swiftly and there was the sound of a bed being entered carefully. And silence. Melissa waited for a moment, and then she said clearly: "Darling, don't cry any more. Don't cry, darling."

The child cried no more. Melissa stood for a long time there by the window, and then she slipped quietly away and down the hill.

In the big bed where that night she slept for the first time, Vic Moon cowered with her legs drawn up to her chest. After long ages she heard somebody climbing down the loft steps and looked out and saw that it was Jarvis and that he carried a stump of burning candle.

"Who was it?" he whispered.

"I don't know. I got right in bed."

"Prob'ly somebody heard Beck crying." She saw that he was smiling shakily. "Anyway, it got her stopped all right."

"I was just leaning over her, trying to pat her quiet – when it came."

"Don't say *it*, Vic; it was *somebody!*"

He stayed and whispered to her, hoping to comfort her, and when he went up to the loft again, he left the candle on the mantel. She was still shaken when it guttered and went out. But Beck, as if silenced by magic, lay still all the rest of the night and the visitor came no more. Next morning Jarvie told the whole family about the Darling Lady who would be sure to come if they ever cried in the night.

It would have seemed imagination if other folks had not begun to tell of the Darling Lady after that, a lady who spoke out of the night to crying babies anywhere in the settlement. Mothers scurried into bed when they heard her, to lie shivering against the great warm backs of their husbands, and never a woman would get up any more in the night without a candle to light the way. But it was said that even children with earache or stomach-sick would be instantly quiet at the sound of the Darling Lady's voice.

Some said it was the spirit of Brother Joseph come to watch

over the settlements. But the men, who had learned to sleep whether babies cried or not, thought the whole tale was a woman-thing, a fabrication, and simply let it pass.

Chapter XXVIII

MERCY's weakness seemed to lift a little, and by the next night there was even regret that she could not have gone to Brother Joseph's funeral. She had no wish to see his body, it was better to remember him another way, unleveled, but there would be words worth remembering from his friends. Ah, well, Simon would have them – Simon had reported speeches before, and when they came out in *Times and Seasons* afterward, it was as though she had heard them, word for word.

Simon was gone all day, and after supper he was still away. She heard the children talking in the other room, Jarvie and Vic superintending the bed-going. The children never really believed Vic had any authority over them; it took Jarvie, too, and his bigness.

Poor Vic – she must be very tired. She got up so early – Simon said he'd seen her taking paper crimpers from her hair before dawn. Vic was a queer one, shy until she felt herself familiar, and then suddenly rebellious. The personal dissatisfaction so many people felt inside themselves, ashamed of it, came out on Vic like a boil and she exhibited it in her words, flaunting it the way a honey-locust flaunts its thorns. Something sweet about her, like a honey-locust all right, and then defiance when your hand came out.

Only a bit ago, doing the dishes, she had been singing a strange little song in her thin voice, thin and monotonous as a flute and plaintive in its very smallness. A song about love.

When the children were quiet, she heard Vic say as though she were complaining of a personal affront: "I don't see why they *killed* him."

And Jarvie: "I don't know, I can't figger it out. They say he had more enemies than friends, and it must have been true. But then – " His voice was very serious. "But then, so did Jesus."

"Well, they killed Him too."

"Already," Mercy thought, appalled by the idea, "he died for our sins and our salvation. *He sealed his testimony with his blood;* everybody that comes in says it. From now on, it will be one of The Things to say."

Presently Vic tiptoed across the big room and closed the door between; after that, the voices were subdued and Mercy slept.

Vic, finishing up those final things always to be done after children are abed, went on singing her little song, plaintively, noticing that sometimes Jarvie looked up from his book to listen. It was a good song, one that Grandma'am had sung always, ever since Vic could remember, in that same monotonous and simple tune –

Now what is love, I pray thee tell. . . .

When Jarvie dropped his eyes, she was sharply disappointed, but gave no sign. Presently he began to hum with her, however, and then he said, looking up: "I know all of it now, Vic; you've sung it so much I know it myself."

"I've always known it," she said. "I don't even think about it, it sort of sings itself. Sometimes it bothers me the way it goes right on singing inside of me whether I do it out loud or not. The tune, you know."

He went back to the page, but he was humming.

MORE than twenty thousand people filed through the Mansion House that day to look for the last time upon Brother Joseph.

How could this be Brother Joseph, this quiet, shattered thing here in a wooden box? How could this be Brother Joseph, with the holes in his flesh stuffed with cotton and his hands inert and his mouth without words? But the coffin was real – covered with black velvet fastened with bright brass nails. And the shroud was real, and the face – not really, no, not really, but yes, the face they knew so well, only pasty above the white neckerchief, and like nothing alive, not like Brother Joseph, really.

They came out into the sunshine after they saw him and looked at one another, dazed. How many nights ago was it when he came out of the Mansion, out of this very door, and we burned a barrel of tar in the street, right there, and carried him around the fire, and the band played? He stood right there in the doorway, big against the light, and then we lifted him – You remember, he laughed and waved his hands and then stood in the red glare and read us that grand wise thing he had written.

How long since the straw votes on the steamboats named this name with the other big names? On the *Osprey* the vote stood for General Smith twenty gents and five ladies; for Henry Clay, sixteen gents and four ladies; for Van Buren, seven gents and no ladies. There were rumors now that it would not be Van Buren at all, but a Tennessee man – Polk, the name was. Brother Joseph would have been interested in hearing that. It wasn't so long ago we saw him riding – That was a Monday, and on Friday –

This man was the one who pleaded only last spring – *this* spring, really – against those who fought him on every hand, and said: "I never told you I was perfect, but there is no error in the revelations which I have taught. Must I, then, be thrown away as a thing of nought? "

"He knew," they whispered. "He *knew*."

Is it Brother Joseph, then, and are they closing the box and screwing it shut on top of him?

They followed the box to the cemetery with their carriages draped in black, and watched it lowered into the ground. Only a few knew that Brother Joseph still lay at the Mansion House, because the Missourians could not even let him sleep in peace. There were ugly rumors, perhaps only hysterical rumors although some believed them, that his grave would be rifled for the reward still standing for his head. Those who had unknowingly watched the sham burial turned home again and went into their houses and shut the doors. Those who knew when the true burial would be sat and waited for night, and the whole city lay still under a smothering heat that waited for a storm.

With dark there was thunder and a heavy driving rain.

The coffins were carried out into the streaming dark and to the unfinished Nauvoo House, that house Joseph had prayed so earnestly for them to build, the house that had made many enemies before ever a shovelful of ground had been disturbed for it. There in the basement story, finished only to the joists, they buried him and his brother, and the sound of the river was loud as he had heard it many times.

"A good place for a hotel," he had said. "Guests who sleep here will like to lie and listen to the river."

So here he slept.

The boots of the Brothers were caked in mud as they worked over the graves of the Prophet and the Patriarch.

Edward Hunter said brokenly: "Even the sky is crying."

Simon always remembered that. An epitaph for an angel.

They worked together, silent and flint-faced. They knew it would be in them to stay, the memory of this night. Their shadows, broken on the broken ground, scrambled briefly into the long narrow holes. One of the Brothers groaned when the coffins were lowered, and Simon was deeply aware of the rope slipping through his hands and then of lightning showing briefly, with a brightness beyond the dim lanterns, what they were doing. They shoveled together then with a painful rhythm, and the wet mud fell heavily on the heat and fire and dream that had been Brother Joseph. He had done nothing, said nothing without passion, Brother Joseph. And now the wet mud.

Dimick Huntington's voice was limp and wrung. " God, lift him up again! "

They flattened the graves, and William Marks said: " It's a good storm; nobody could trace it by morning."

They shook hands all around, pressing hands as Brother Joseph had always done; their lips were set over words they could not say or bear to listen to had they been said. Just before they parted, Dimick said one little thing and it happened to be the right thing to say. " If you think he's gone, it's not true."

" It's not true. Good night."

" God bless you."

" Good night."

Over the river, Simon went quietly up the bluff, tiptoeing even far from the house, aware of a heaviness in his body and on his mind, heaviness in the sky and over all time to come. Quiet – it would be a shame to wake the family up so late.

❧ ❧ ❧

JARVIE had to close the south and west windows, because the wind brought the rain right in. After the hot day the rain smelled sweet and fresh and it was a comfort to lie on the rug and listen to it drumming on the windows.

Beck lay wide-eyed for a long time and watched Big Brother

and listened to him reading, and then she fell asleep and he lowered his voice. Vic moved closer, listening in the profound way she had. When he paused, she nodded quickly, and sometimes she made a soft little cluck of sympathy.

He read from *The Book of Mormon* tonight.

"The soul shall be restored to the body and the body to the soul. Every limb and joint shall be restored to its body. Even a hair of the head shall not be lost. But all things shall be restored to their proper and perfect frame."

"So you see," Jarvie said, looking up. "He's not different, he's just in a different place."

"Your father's over there," Vic said dryly, "and they're putting him in the ground."

"Yes, but, Vic, it doesn't matter about the ground or anything. It's like it says here, *Even a hair of the head shall not be lost.*"

"But he's gone now, he's dead. He's not happy and enjoying things."

He looked at her quickly, because she spoke with a kind of excitement.

"I know. It's hard thinking about Brother Joseph dead."

"Well – all I say is – *we* aren't dead."

"Of course we aren't!" It seemed a silly thing for her to say until he saw her face again. She was intensely sober, looking at him.

"I was thinking today while I was stirring the soap-kettle – it'd be a lot better to be dead in the ground than to be like I've been in my life. Not having anything particular you cared about. Used to be there wasn't any *particular* thing, unless it was the parish picnic and that was too long coming and too quick over. You worked and you ate what you could get, and slept, and worked again."

She looked at him. "Till now," she said, "there wasn't so much I was glad to be alive for. But now there's getting mushrooms and riding in Menzo's canoe and listening to books – and – "

He turned over on his stomach and put his chin on his hands. "I like more things than I can name," he said. "All my life I've liked doing lots of things."

"Do you like doing this?" she asked. "Sitting up when everybody else goes to bed, like this, talking?"

"And hearing the rain," he said. "Sure I like it. I like it a lot."

They were silent for a long time. Then Jarvie said pensively: "One good thing Brother Joseph always said – Mother thinks it's the best thing he ever did say – and that was: *Man is that he might have joy*."

"That *is* good. That's just what I was saying. Isn't it?"

"Yes, but you were talking about yourself, and Brother Joseph was talking about everybody."

She nodded. "But I meant everybody too. I don't want to feel happy like this all by myself, Jarvie."

She leaned close to him and he smelled her hair, remembered he had seen her washing it last night in a basin of rainwater from the barrel. There was the same sweet blowsy smell in it that was outside tonight.

"Mmmm, your hair smells good, Vic."

She shook it under his face. "It feels good too," she said.

They were pensive and quiet for a long time. Then she said: "You know, Jarvie, about that being happy, I know what makes it. And everybody could have it, maybe, if they tried. Grandma'am used to tell me about it, but I didn't know what she meant, hardly. Now I think I know."

He looked at her with great interest. "What is it? You mean, for everybody?"

"Yes, for everybody."

"Religion. Isn't it?"

"Maybe. One kind of religion. A kind that belongs to you and nobody else, though, only everybody can have it if they get it for themselves."

"It's sort of mixy, Vic. How do you mean? Do you mean having everything the same, like you said before?"

"No. It's even easier than that. It's not even everybody having everything – it's just – well, everybody having *somebody*. That's all it is. Like me, for instance. After Grandma'am I didn't have anybody at all. Then, after you and me got talking, I had you. That's all the difference."

He did not look at her because her fervent voice embarrassed him.

"There's your mother, too, I can talk to her. And you."

He found her hand close to his, felt the quick brush of her fingers. He had a strange feeling that she was seeking him, groping to find him in the half-dark, fearing him unaware. He was shaken, and so he turned over and looked up at the ceiling; then she wouldn't see he didn't dare look at her. Every once in a while lately, she'd acted queer like that, talking about things and reaching out, touching.

Her voice was bright. "It's nice on the floor, isn't it? It's cool."

Then, knowing that she was waiting for him to look, he looked at her. She was closer than he had thought, and he dropped his eyes, confused.

"There's something else Brother Joseph said." Her voice was low and close. "He said if you wanted anything right bad, all you had to do was pray for it, pray all the time, while you work and while you eat and while you sleep, even. That's the way I've been praying."

"What you been praying for, Vic?" he asked, but he knew.

"I want to be happy more of the time. I guess that's it. I wish –" He looked at her again. "I pray Beck'll cry every night. Then you'd come down every night – if she did, I mean, wouldn't you? Then I'd be happy every night."

She moved close to him, huddling like a soft animal. He knew deeply, intimately, where she was closest. Then she drew far back and all touch was lost to him. He was surprised that loss was suddenly exquisite, and was confused by his emotion. He wanted to shake his head like a dog, to get the grogginess out of it and the confusion.

The thought came to him: " This is what the fellows mean. It happens to you, you feel weak and sweet together and strong and all in a thousand pieces, waving. It happens to you. Girls think of you like that, too, and want you in secret. And a time comes."

He heard his own voice strangely through air that was heavy between them. " I don't know how to love anybody."

He was surprised again, because she laughed. And dipped her head before him until her hair fell forward and the rain-smell lifted into his nostrils. She whispered then: " I know, Jarvie. But I'll show you if you want."

When she laid her mouth on his, it was soft and wet. He felt his mouth answering, and then a kind of shame rushed over him and he drew away. But loss was more overwhelming than shame or anything, and he reached for her.

" I don't know – I don't know," he said, excited and confused together.

" Look, Jarvie, I'll show you, Jarvie." She was ecstatic, eager, as though she could not be quick enough at giving him pleasure. She reached among her skirts wildly, excitedly, as one who must live her time, and lifted them over her thighs. He saw that her legs were very long and slender and white. Surprise and stupid fascination held his eyes and a roaring emotion began to tear at him.

" Please don't, Vic. You oughtn't to – "

Her fingers moved in his, but his hand was inert and inadequate. After a time she laughed again in that soft strange way, and laid his hand on the sweet white crest where the flesh went sweeping up to the hip.

"It's all right, Jarvie," she whispered. "I love you, Jarvie."

Inert, his hand, incapable. It was so new, so sudden, so incredible. But she stirred, stirred in a long motion that begged him, and feeling flooded through him like a tide. With unbelievable slowness he moved his wakening hand, found the swift dip of waistline. Presently he thought of nothing but the strange new ecstasy of exploration, and the sweetness, the softness, the warmth of touching a live thing that answered and beckoned and was eager and loving like this. He sensed this corner in time, complete and adequate. And he gloried in his response, trusting it. You were completed in someone else, then; there was no other way to tell it all to another one as you desired always to do, you must experience great joy together and it was all told without telling. You forgot what you were and what another one was and time narrowed and space until you understood and reached it all.

She whispered, almost gaily: "See, it comes to you, Jarvie—"

But words did not exist for him. Only awareness, stretched to breaking. Being a man. Not Vic, somehow, but woman. Oh, lovely, lovely. Now he would know, he would be wise with the others, maybe wiser than all of them. He thought: "You have it with a poem, sometimes, you have it, but even then you need to read it to somebody."

SIMON's voice was horrible, shattering night, breaking the candlelight into blazing fragments on the eyeballs. For the flash of a second there was Vic, white-faced, her dresses falling around her feet, Vic running to the bed and plunging out of sight. Without the terror it might even have been funny. But now there was Simon.

He stood in the shadow by the door, shuddering with rage.

" For God's sake! Jarvie! "

Stunned, Jarvie saw Simon move to him, looking out at him steadily in a new way, a terrible level way. " Your mother would rather see you in your grave! " he said.

Jarvie had heard that expression before, but never for him, never involving him. He turned to the ladder and began to climb, blindly. He heard Simon climbing behind him and braced himself. But when Simon sat beside him, shielding a candle in his hand, Jarvie saw that his father's face was long with pain and that anger was not there.

" I thought you were still a baby," Simon said brokenly.

And after a time he asked: " When did you first go to her? "

Jarvie's chin shook when he spoke and through a curious numbness poured hot shame and he was aware of it, tumbling through him like lava. He shook his head. " No. There was just tonight. I was going to read awhile, I didn't feel sleepy – "

Simon clenched his fists. " God pity her," he said. He moved close so that he would not wake the other boys. " They're not like us, Jarvie, these foreigners, they're different. Even if they talk the same language, it's not the same with them, honor's different in different places. Brother Brigham told us how it is with them; they work too hard and live too close together."

Jarvie said stumblingly: " It wasn't Vic, Father. Not all. I – " He stopped, knowing that he hardly understood, himself.

Simon stood up and spoke in a thin voice, bitterly self-conscious. " There's something you save for a good woman you'll be wanting to marry one of these days. And it's not yours, because it's hers too. It's hard to say – you'll know when the time comes. All you need to know now – it's not beautiful. It's like – well, I've seen men – and women too – rotting from the inside like apples. It's not beautiful, Jarvie, it's like that. You're old enough to know."

He went to the ladder and started down. When his head alone remained in the room, he said briefly: "Don't go thinking I'm ashamed. But now you know, and if it ever happens again, I'll break your head for you. Now you get some sleep."

Jarvie heard him speaking briefly to Vic, his voice from above like far thunder. Terrible for Vic, he knew. Then he heard the door close and knew that Simon had gone outside again.

The rain had stopped but for a soundless mist that touched the face gently. Simon stood and stared across the river where the last candle was gone now, and there was nothing but blackness, the land and the river inseparable. Nauvoo was as black as Brother Joseph's new grave. Simon felt his legs weak under him; he was spent with feeling.

Of all the children, Jarvie was the least animal, Jarvie and his books and his thoughts and his lean serious face. Yet there he was, not sixteen, in that place –

But it wasn't Jarvie's fault, it wasn't, it couldn't be. It was like Brother Brigham said when he came back from England and told about all those folks flocking over. Crowded, and seldom looking up unless it was a look abashed with inferiority; crowded and slow to be wakened to the fact of their humanity and the fact of the Godhood innate in them. Teaching them a doctrine of pure hearts and unsullied bodies, of men equal in Godhood, you bucked a barrier as old as their island. Thick sprawling crowds of them, living in foggy rooms with penny heat, and no other pleasure – families of them in a room, Brigham said, sleeping together.

Brother Joseph had said at last, when he understood: "Let them come to Zion." And they came, but it was a slow thing, helping a man to live the Gospel. Ignorance, weakness, another standard, they could cross the water and strike at a man's own boy, 'way out here on the frontier. That was the reason, then, why the Gospel must go to them all, to every kindred and every people, as Joseph had said. Nothing less than a World Gospel would do, else it would fail and the poison of ignorance and misery would fester in far places and come back and strike at the innocent.

There must not be men who knew nothing but labor and poverty and pleasures that leaned nowhere, least of all to eternity; every man must become aware of the growing spirit within him that struggled to become a God – in poor Hyrum's words, that struggled to stride the planets. Joseph had said "Every Man," and Every Man it must be.

The idea stupefied Simon with its greatness; it entered him and he stood shaken with the terrible necessity for equality in all the world. Poverty of soul and body and intellect – it could reach across the water, even to the farthest frontier. Joseph had never said it just that way, but that was surely what he meant. Certainly it was what he had meant. Simon felt that Brother Joseph had been summoned when he was needed; he, Simon Baker, he too had had a revelation.

AT dawn, half-wakened by the wild slamming of a door, Jarvie heard footsteps. Stumbling toward the river, down the hill. He raised himself until he looked from the narrow window. Poor Vic – Vic and her bundles. But he knew there was no use calling to her now. He crept to the loft-hole and looked down at the mantel, half afraid, but Toby was still there, smiling the way he had always smiled.

Chapter XXIX

Brother Wilford Woodruff stood before the little ones in Sunday school and spoke to them with the disarming simplicity that had won for him thousands of converts in England.

"Now suppose there are one hundred thousand millions of fallen spirits sent down from heaven to earth – that makes one hundred evil spirits to every one of us. The whole mission and labor of these spirits is to lead all the children of men to do evil and effect their destruction. Now, I want all our boys and girls to reflect on this and see what danger they're in. The spirit of the Lord tries to preserve us, and the angels do all they can. Yet we must be the ones to choose whether the bad or the good gets the best of us. It is not the Lord that tempts us to do evil, but the power of the Devil in these thousands of evil spirits hovering over us night and day."

Betsy sat still, looking neither to the right nor to the left, her eyes fastened unswervingly on the face of Brother Woodruff. She could think of the number *one hundred*, because she could count so far, using both hands full of fingers surreptitiously among her dresses. The other numbers he said had no meaning except a terrible vista of endless black wings, beating and suffocating, but the hundred – for *her*, Betsy Baker, one hundred black-winged things against the tall whiteness of being good. She trembled, counting along her fingers.

"When I was a boy," Brother Wilford went on, "I was raised in a place called Connecticut where they had laws they called the Blue Laws. Nobody could work or play from sunset Saturday night to sunset Sunday night. I had to sit right still in my chair for hours and hours, and my legs ached, I remember, until I rubbed them with my fists to relieve them. And all that time I had to recite the Catechism and the Bible. Now, you are not taught to sit still and not to use your muscles and be happy, but you must remember to be watchful at all times while you are free lest evil spirits catch you unaware."

Betsy's fingers moved in her dresses, and she was flooded with a feeling of terrible helplessness. Of course, if God were caring – but how could He watch so many? One little girl and one hundred – *If it only weren't so many*.

As soon as the children became used to Vic's absence, they took it as a matter of course. Mother was up sometimes now, and Betsy was proud as a cock pheasant to be helping with things. Georgie managed Joey, and Beck was such a clucking fat little contented one she did not need managing by anybody. Jarvie did the heavy things, moving with an odd abstraction that hurt Mercy because she knew where it came from.

He even helped her pommel that vast dough-pile on Saturday morning. She was aware of his face, of a curious misery.

"You know," she said, speaking as lightly as she could, "sometimes it's just as well not to expect folks to be everything we'd like them to be. Because somebody's always failing you and it's such a hurt when that happens. I remember when I first found out that people lied, lied deliberately and with malice. It took some faith out of me that I've never got back again."

"I guess that's so." Jarvie's voice was bleak.

" After all, Jarvie, Vic couldn't know things weren't the same with us as they were with her, and with her people. Even when her grandma'am talked about – such things – it wasn't just the *things* she cared about, but about high-up folks mistreating folks not quite so high-up. You know, Vic was always frank about saying things right out, things that we wouldn't say even if we thought them."

She was surprised at his response. For a moment it leveled her. " I don't see why people shouldn't say what they think. Let 'em say it and then maybe it'll be out of 'em and won't be bothering 'em any more."

Flurried, she said: " But then there's *doing*, Jarvie – you don't *do* what you think about! "

It was a new subject. They had spoken of these things idealistically, but never as part of reality before. Like Simon, she was hesitant, walking on ground too soft for her to trust.

He was sober, kneading the dough the way she had taught him, using only the palms and quickly, so that there was never sticking.

" I don't know," he said. " I don't know, maybe I'm wrong, but – Well, things are good, see, and you're happy and you feel light and like you're part of the world and you're glad. Then something that was good isn't good any more and you start wondering if it's all like that. Then, as soon as you start wondering, you don't feel light any more."

He was puzzled even at himself, at inarticulateness, at how nothing would be said, even.

" It's growing up," Mercy said gently. " Things are bound to change. I guess our eyes change and we see things differently."

She knew what it was that changed, and she knew that it changed for everybody. Jarvie, for all she worried over him, was only having growing-pains.

But Simon was quiet, too, and even a little hostile with the children, for another reason. It was Brother Joseph's going that worried Simon and the thought that maybe somehow, somehow he should have made Brother Joseph scared enough. As if anything could have made him scared those last months when he rode like a king on the crest of his wave.

There was another thing, too. In the check-up when the Half-Breed lands were divided, nearly the whole north half was found without legitimate title. About this, at least, Bennett had been right; whether Joseph had known or not could never be certain now, and hardly mattered. The important thing was scraping together new payments to secure the most important fields on the property.

For Mercy herself to worry over, there were the twins, Mary and Sarah, named after the two most beautiful ladies, mothers of the greatest of men. Sarah was stretching out a little, though little enough certainly, but Mary was uninterested in what this world had to offer. When Mercy took her into the bed to nurse, she lay looking up and the nipple had to be laid in her mouth and shaken against her lips before she began to make the soft motions of sucking. Then she did not suckle for long, but stopped every moment until the breast was moved against her mouth again to remind her.

Mercy knew them apart now, knew them in many ways. The way they looked up was different, their sounds were different, the hair at Mary's temples grew in a soft circle and on Sarah's forehead there was an abrupt point in the center, promising a widow's peak. Then, the way they suckled was different, Sarah absorbed in the breast and falling asleep with her mouth still moving, and Mary somehow beyond breasts and milk. Mercy gave one breast to each of them, alternating, and always Mary came to her first. Once, fearing that the milk was inadequate, Mercy had Susie Yeaman come up the hill, Mrs. Yeaman, whose own baby was growing like a calf and whose milk ran in buckets, according to her own proud estimate. But Mary lay quiet, without interest, and Mrs. Yeaman put her great black-tipped breast back into her dress, still heavy with milk.

So there was Jarvie to worry about – though, goodness, he'd get over that if you gave him time enough! Young folks have got to wake up, haven't they, and see how things aren't all rosy-easy and romantic, and that you've got to forget even things that have shamed you? And there was Simon to worry about, but surely they'd give him time enough to pay off the land now he'd improved it and put up his fences? And there wasn't any use pining after Brother Joseph's going, but do like Brother Brigham Young said and build for him better than they had ever done while he lived, because if anybody was in heaven watching out for the people, he was. He was in the other world, it was preached every Sunday and folks liked to hear it; he was there planning for his Brethren with nobody to stop him any more. And now he was gone, there was less trouble, although the surrounding counties were alert lest the Mormons seek revenge; a certain terrible tension had been broken, temporarily at least, and there were some who were glad of it.

Menzo was happy enough, paddling again to the Islands, and Bert was just as always – meeting life with his arms out as though it were a big show, all for him. And the children, happy as birds in the morning. But Mary –

One day Mercy tried giving warm cow's milk to Mary with a spoon. But it ran down her mouth, out of the corners. Once she choked and it was terrifying for a moment; she did not struggle, only lay coughing and strangling, until Mercy swooped her up and patted her back and made the milky saliva run forward onto the floor.

There were enough things to worry about to fill more hours than the day held. But, strangely enough, if you think about *other* folk's worries, it helps a little. "Think about Eliza trying to believe there is something ahead but remembering; think about Melissa, who has lost her four children; think of poor Portia; and of Vic, who is so hard-pressed in a new world.

Then maybe you won't think you are so bad off! You with a good husband and one of the best houses on the river and such good children to help on the days you don't feel good – "

IT was not much past dawn and there was that half-awake feeling of depth and comfort, a half-dreaming depth filled with familiar people and unfamiliar pleasure. And then, through it, the little sound from Mary's cradle, like the one the day she choked. Mercy's bare feet touched the floor, two steps, dazed. And when she lifted the baby, she saw that something was terribly wrong. She lifted her, face forward, and patted her back as she had done before. But the body was limp in her hands. Then down upon the bed and the clothes up, rubbing the limbs, fiercely. Simon woke and sat watching, his face incredulous.

She was dead. There was no gainsaying it, no pushing it back. She was dead; a little choking and she was not here any more. It was incredible. Mercy rubbed until she knew it was no use trying to move the blood again. Nothing moved except the body under her hands, like a doll.

She was hysterical, and Simon put the little doll-body back into the cradle and made her get under the covers to stop her shaking. But it would not enter her, for hours it did not really enter her.

God had not intended to make two, then, He had only meant to show what two could be. He showed two, briefly, and you knew He could do anything at all, and then, like one showing his most precious possessions and then withdrawing them jealously from hungry eyes, He broke two apart, and it was over.

There had never been anything so cruel as destroying two. To take all, both, could not have been so terrible. But taking one of two that belonged together – When she talked of it like that, Simon shook her, though gently, and said: " Mercy – think of the others like you told me to think. Think about Melissa losing four, some of them have lost five or six. You've only lost one out of nine."

But she said: " I've lost one out of two."

He went to Kimball's shop to make the coffin, so she wouldn't have to hear it being made. He had the Sisters come to dress Mary and they washed her and put on the christening clothes that every Baker baby had worn to church on his naming day, Jarvie first and then all the others as they came. But Mercy got out of bed and took all the clothes off again, herself, right before them.

" Sarah'll need these to go to church in," she said. And she put on Mary the little flannel gown she had worn when she died. The women stood around helplessly and she said: " You know, she never got big enough to wear dresses – she never wore anything but her nightgowns. She's used to them."

Then she had a spell of coughing and sat down in a chair with her breath hard in her throat. Mother Turner made her a drink of vinegar and honey and it helped her. After that she seemed to be herself again.

At the funeral she carried herself right well, and at the graveyard she did not make a sound, though after it was over, she fell into her bed as one falls who has no strength left for standing.

Chapter XXX

SIMON brushed his shoes again when he came around from the barn with the buggy. Mercy stood in the doorway, leaning on the frame.

" You go back to bed, now," Simon told her. " There's no use killing yourself with work on a Sunday."

" Somebody older," Mercy said. " Somebody who can take hold, somebody more serious – " Jarvie heard it as he leaped to the seat of the buggy, and his face flushed.

The children pressed around Mercy, waving. " Good-by, good-by," a hundred times, and waving frantically. Every time anybody left the house, it was the same, all the waving and calling, over and over. Then, when the departing ones were out of sight, good-by was a little tune to be remembered.

" Dapper – you stay home! "

She got them all settled at play and lay down to feed Sarah. When the suckling stopped, she was terrified. It wasn't right for the body to bring a child and then stop short of its true work, withholding the milk. She had heard of such a thing happening, hardly believing it, and now it was happening to her. She could hear Mother Turner whispering over Mary's body: " Poor mite – plumb starved to death."

Now, Sarah – she had to be different. There were both breasts for her now. There was everything a body could give.

When Sarah slept, Mercy put meat in the kettle and lifted it onto the fire. Then she leaned over for a log, and it was suddenly blackness where the log should be, and she groped blindly, and then forgot the log and the fire and everything.

BECK laid her hand confidingly in Betsy's hand and they picked their way down the hill.

" If you won't say you get tired, Beck, then I'll take you. I can't pick you up; you're too big."

Beck shook her head and her plump legs made two steps to Betsy's one.

" There are *six* kittens, Beck, that's as many as all my fingers on this hand and then one more, like if I put my other thumb here, see? That many. And they're all black and white but this one, and he's got yellow, too, just like Posey did."

Beck gave an extra skip.

They reached the gate to Yeaman's place and went to the porch, but the house was deserted, everybody was at conference. Some of Susie's hens were pecking around the door and Snarl Yeaman's old dog, who had come with him through thick and thin, yawned by the door. He did not bark at the children, only raised his head for a moment and then laid it down on his paws again and closed his eyes. But with Snarl's new dog it was different. He came furiously around the corner of the house when he heard steps upon the porch boards, and seeing Betsy, he flew upon her with rapture, his tongue anxious to caress her, his body twisting with the unmatched ecstasy of a young dog.

Beck stood chuckling, and Betsy cried: " Down, you! " fearing for her good dress. The dog sat back, alert, panting, his tail drumming on the boards.

Betsy stood irresolute. " Maybe they wouldn't care " she

said. " Charity wouldn't care a bit. I've been to see these kittens every day. You wouldn't think *every*body would be gone, would you? "

But she knew she should have expected everybody in the Yeaman family to be gone to conference. She glanced back at the hill; it was a long way to come to see kittens; and then to go back without seeing kittens at all, that made it seem longer still. She took Beck's hand and led her around the house to the granary, just to show her where Charity kept her kittens. It was closed and a wire loop held by a twig made it fast, just above a little girl's hands.

She had known that, too, but stood regarding it with disappointed eyes.

" With a good stick I could poke it up out of there," she said, and glanced around her on the ground. She could hear the kittens on the other side of the door mewing.

There was a bit of broken picket in a bucket Snarl used to stir his feed; it was there close at hand, invitingly, thick and strong and just long enough – to – poke – up – . Betsy pushed it up against the improvised lock and it took no poking at all, really, but parted immediately and the door swung open. The young dog stood quivering, watching, and when the mother cat and her little ones came tumbling from the door, rolling and scampering and climbing over one another, he was among them, belly dropped, swelled with excited barking.

Betsy shrieked at him and turned to him with the stick, flailing his back. Startled, he fled from her, his tail suddenly diminished and tucked behind him, crying around the corner of the house.

But even so it was too late. The kittens were scattered in all directions, terrified, and the mother had fled up a tree, her loyalty submerged temporarily in an instinct as old and as active.

" Beck, we've got to find 'em," Betsy wailed. " They've never been like that, they've always stayed in that box, they've *always* — "

She stood engulfed in an overwhelming knowledge of her own guilt. Charity had left the kittens safe, and she, Betsy, had broken in like a thief, and now this had happened — like a thief she had broken a lock on another's door. She shook violently, and inside of her was a swelling horror that grew and subsided like a stomach-pain. She looked up briefly in terror, thinking of the black-winged spirits.

" Yeamans won't like it," she thought, " and Father won't like it. Especially Father won't like it. There's never been a stealer at our house. I wasn't going to be a stealer, I was just going to look, but how will Charity know I wasn't going to be a stealer, how will Father know? I have opened a locked door."

She saw one of the kittens peering tentatively around some of the corn shocks Snarl had piled against his barn. She ran and pounced upon it anxiously, and then she took it back to Beck, who was sitting placidly on the steps to the granary. " Here, Beck, you hold this while I go a-looking for the others."

Presently she brought one other, and disappeared again. Beck sat still with the two kittens wriggling happily in her lap. One tried to escape over her knee and she grasped him firmly. Still he struggled and she took her skirt and folded it tight around him to hold him. She managed with both hands to keep the other safe. For a moment there was a mighty struggle among her skirts, but she pressed her knees together and then the hidden kitten grew quiet. Betsy brought two more, and Beck rolled these also in her petticoats, clucking and scolding. After a long time Betsy brought the last two, one her blessed tortoise-shell. She went into the granary and put them down in the box.

" Now you bring those, Beck, and we'll close the door quick," she said, and Beck came in, holding her skirts high around her legs. When she had set down the one she held, she allowed her skirt to unroll slowly to release the other three, but they dropped to the floor soft and boneless, like crumpled rags. The mother entered, arching her back and mewing softly. She moved to the kittens and stood waving her tail. But Betsy was staring at the three quiet ones.

"Something's the matter with them," she said, appalled. "Something's the matter."

She leaned down over them, touching them, and when she looked up, her face was terrible, anguished.

"They're not alive, Beck," she said.

Beck reached up and patted her arm reassuringly, but Betsy drew sharply back. "You hurt them, Beck!" she cried. And her tears began to run.

The other kittens showed a disposition to leave the granary once more, and Betsy seized her sister's hand and they rushed outside and pushed the big door to. Then, with her tears running, she stood stricken against the door. Above her the wire rattled, uncaught, and she realized for the first time that the twig the big stick had pushed out could not be pushed in again.

"Don't cry, Betsy," Beck said, perturbed and frowning. "Let's go home now."

Through her tears Betsy looked at her sister with utter scorn. "We can't get away from this old door," she said coldly. "We've got to hold this door till Yeamans come home again. Then – " A terrible fear choked her. "Then we – then they'll see what we've done to their kittens."

Beck was not big enough or learned enough to share the hideous burden of guilt, but she stood pleasantly close, lending her weight to the door.

"If you hadn't wanted to see these kittens – " Betsy tried to alleviate her burden. "I'd never have opened it just for myself – I opened it for you. Then that dog, that *bad* dog – "

It was a slab door and heavy, wanting to move outward. Beck began to complain and then to cry, and said: "I'm tired, Betsy."

"You promised not to say that!"

"I'm tired now," Beck said, and Betsy stood silent and statuesque against the door, bracing her back and letting her nose run on her upper lip in a thin white dribble, not even caring.

"If we get spanked and spanked and shut up in the dark, Beck, it'll jest be our needings."

Beck sat down and presently, in a solid plump way she had, she was asleep on the step. Nappy time was nappy time, sin and evil notwithstanding. But Betsy stood holding the big door, like Peter at the dike. Her back ached and her legs ached and her arms ached and, worst of all, her heart ached, too. The three kittens, suddenly muffled and not alive or wriggling or mewing, suddenly nothing kitten about them because kitten was alive and wriggling and mewing, kitten was not just a soft heap but an inexplicable motion like the curlicues in the air when you stared up without trying to see. And Betsy thought: "This is how wrong things are done." First something little, not wrong at all, then something a little wronger that doesn't seem really wrong, and then out of a little wrongness a great *big* wrongness, and you don't know hardly how the big one happened out of the little one. Just to see the kittens, and now half of them were dead. It was impossible, but it was true. This was Sin. She, Betsy Baker, had become involved in it, personally, irrevocably. The hundred spirits had conquered her.

Earnestly she prayed for forgiveness. She prayed aloud for forgiveness and for sustenance. She mentioned the way her legs ached and her arms and her whole body and was glad for the aching because already, before her true inevitable punishment had begun, she was doing a penance of her own. In a pool of fall sunshine on the step, Beck slept peacefully while her sister did penance against the heavy door.

"Never, never again will I do even a little wrong thing, even the very littlest wrong thing, even the littlest beginning of a thing that's wrong to do."

CONFERENCE was in the Temple, in the big room, and folks were proud with a fierce pride over the tall windows and the great stones and the woodwork, finished with loving hands. Even though the whole was far from finished, this room was a promise and a fulfillment.

"That's the way with men," Simon thought; "they make something, they lift big stones up and put great faces on the stones, and then when it is all done, they stand, awed and little, looking up."

When meeting was over, he told the boys to wait in the buggy and went up front to talk to Brother Brigham Young.

"Brother Baker – how are you? And how's the little one?"

You never expected him to remember everybody or what happened to everybody, but he always did. In that he had torn a leaf from Brother Joseph's closed book. Every man was one man and a complete man, and what happened to that man was a world in itself, worth attentive looking and listening.

"Not so well as we'd have her, thank you. That's why I came up, in fact – we need help over at our house. Mercy don't seem to get any stronger."

"A mighty little woman and a brave one," Brother Brigham said, and fingered the side of his nose, frowning. Then he spoke briskly: "Can you come with me to dinner? We'll think of somebody –"

"It's too bad to bother you," Simon apologized.

"Not at all! Just what you ought to do."

Simon knew that in what Brigham said lay implicit the things he himself had been thinking. Brother Brigham knew everybody, placed the immigrants, was acquainted with the needy all over Zion. He had made it his business, even before Brother Joseph died, maybe knowing how much he would be needed. And was not the President of the people their servant too? Part of the failure of free government was the failure of those in office to realize always that they are the servants of the people.

Simon told the boys to drive on home; he would be there when he had tended to his business with Brother Brigham.

"And see that your mother stays down – everything she starts doing, you up and do yourselves, and keep her down."

Jarvie nodded, thinking: "Apparently the heart."

They had fun on the ferry and fun driving Ginger up the hill and fun unharnessing her, too, with her stamping and impatient for fodder.

When Jarvie came into the house, he saw at once that it had happened again. She was sitting up this time, but she was white in the same terrifying way, a whiteness beyond any color skin should ever have. She looked at him, and her voice was short on the syllables, as though there was little breath to sustain it. "That log, Jarvie, I was just going to lift it on, and I – "

"You shouldn't have tried." He noticed that he scolded her as a grown-up scolds a child, but it seemed to do her good because when he lifted her she relaxed against him. She even laughed, shakily.

"Imagine you lifting me," she said. "It isn't – any time – since I – lifted – you."

Apparently the heart. He felt his own heart pounding in his side.

He took her to the back bed again. "Now you stay quiet," he said.

She knew what she must do now. If she would live, she knew what she must do. It would pass, of course, in time, but now there must not be anything deliberate to bring about this hot unreasonable weakness. A thing that had been growing, she could see that, and suddenly that day Mary and Sarah came, it had taken charge of her, urgently, and she belonged to it, had belonged to it, really, ever since. It took decision from her and she was possessed of no power to do as she willed to do, that was certain after this morning. It must be thrust off with a slow and deliberate care until she had grown strong enough to grapple with it and master it.

She lay very still. Once she had to cough and sat abruptly up, but, frightened into submission, she lay down again and controlled the coughing with great effort, breathing rapidly.

Now then – now then. She grew quiet, and Jarvie closed the door so she could sleep.

❧ ❧ ❧ ❧

To Betsy it was forever until she heard Jarvie calling to her, and she answered, and when he came she dissolved in tears against the door, hardly as much a little girl as a terrible storm of tears and self-crimination. Quietly and magnificently Jarvie fixed the lock and took his sisters home. When he knew Snarl would be home for the milking, he went with Betsy to the foot of the hill and sent her on to make her confession. She did not protest; there was nothing else to be done.

She stood close to Snarl while she told him, stumbling. He listened with interest, but kept his eyes on his working fingers and the two hissing streams of white that shot like magic from black teats and rose into a ring of mounting foam whiter than sea-foam. She did not see him grinning, but spoke with agonized self-reproach. When she had finished, he stopped milking and stood up from his stool and looked down at her.

"You get that piece of broke crock over there," he said, "an' we'll take some milk in the granary an' have a look for ourselves."

She brought the crock and he filled it from the bucket. Then he went with her into the granary. To look at the three silent ones, there on the floor, was almost more than she could bear. Once more the full horror of what she had done confronted her and it was a black wall she could never hope to scale, her life long.

Snarl gathered them up, stiffened and unreal. "Now, to tell you a secret, Betsy Baker, I told Charity this mornin' she could have two kits and no more. I was fixin' to drown 'em before she came home. But she said you wanted this here spotted one, is that right?"

Betsy nodded miserably.

"You an' Beck saved me the trouble of drownin' 'em," Snarl said. "Now, this one you can just take along with you –"

She saw that he was smiling, handing out the adorable one.

She recoiled. The remorse that struck out at her from his kindness was infinitely more bitter than all the guilt she had suffered. And obscurely, strangely, a sense of justice, or fitness, was outraged, although this she did not comprehend.

"I couldn't," she said. "Oh, no, Mr. Yeaman, I couldn't."

Snarl set the kitten down and it was beautifully alive, tonguing the milk rapidly from the bit of crock. Snarl stood there watching with her. Then he gathered the kitten up, very small in one big hand, and laid him in Betsy's arms. Her shame was a gathering storm in her, she could not look up at him or speak, but he patted her shoulder and they came out of the granary and he returned to his milking, saying only: "Don't you worry, you run on home with that cat."

"What'd he say?" Jarvie asked anxiously when she joined him.

She only lifted the kitten for him to see, and he saw, too, the profound question on her face, but could not answer it.

Chapter XXXI

Brother Brigham looked at Simon quizzically, listening.

"That Vic Moon," he said when Simon had finished speaking, "she's a good girl, really, but she needs to get married." He sat thinking, removed. "Now, Ellis Mayhem – he'd make a good husband for a girl like Vic Moon."

"Ellis got married last year, didn't he? What's happened to his wife?"

"A cool stiff piece," Brigham said seriously. "Ellis is a strong man."

Simon stared at him with the stark beginnings of understanding.

"And you, Brother Baker, you're a strong man, too, and there's Gospel for every trouble a man can have."

When full understanding came to Simon, he tried to quench the excitement that came out in his voice and even in his face. What Brother Joseph had dreamed about and what he had only dared accomplish in secret was to Brother Brigham a thing to announce in a normal voice to his friends and Brethren and begin to make useful wherever he could. Brother Joseph had said that in time the new marriage would be a cure for many evils – well, the time for curing evils for Brother Brigham was now and not tomorrow. Let other men dream of what should be done, what would be ideal, and then hand it to Brother

Brigham to make it real and watch it function in the hands of men. For him the Gospel was Service and Now; it dealt with the future only as a continuation of the present. If Brother Joseph had been too wary of public opinion, what use to be wary now when the worst had happened and was over with?

Simon's face was flushed.

" Now, you're doing right well, getting your farm over there and a good bit of stock. A fine family, too, but a sick wife. A sick wife."

" She'll get better," Simon said huskily.

" Taking care of eight children? " It all seemed very simple to Brigham; like two and two it added up to a simple total.

" I'd say it was a mighty foolish thing for a man like you to pay the right sort of woman to keep his house. Too many women who'd like to do it for nothing."

Simon shook his head. " I don't imagine many women are around hankering to marry me."

" There," said Brigham, leaning forward, " you're too modest, Brother Baker. And fundamentally wrong. Look at our women; there'll always be more women accepting the Gospel than there'll be men – it's in the nature of things and always has been. Maybe part of it's because the Elders are men, in the first place, and women are women. But they're quicker, somehow, to listen to spiritual things than the men are."

Simon nodded.

" And it's easy for men to fall by the way out here; life's too open and too free. Well, if every woman deserves a good man, it's like Brother Joseph said – the good men have got to spread themselves around."

" I hope I'm a good man," Simon said steadily, " but I never expect to be as good as that! "

" You'll be that good if you can see your duty and do it. Brother Joseph preached it to us, and it was hard for us to take; he got impatient with all of us. But we kept seeing a case that made it seem right, and first thing we knew, we were teaching it to other men. That's the way Gospel principles do – they grow on you. First they seem revolutionary and they scare you; then, when you get used to them, they start looking wise, and after a while they look indispensable."

"I've got a wife," Simon said, "that wouldn't like it."

"So have I."

They looked at each other and Simon liked the frank sympathy on Brigham's face. When he spoke he spoke slowly and deliberately in a way that made a man feel ungrateful for not believing him.

"Suppose you find a woman who's known the length and breadth of Zion for her fine house, a woman who takes care of other folks' children because she loves every child she sees, a woman with power and strength in her to take care of a sick woman and maybe make her well again. A woman who can make a house move like a skein of silk. No girl can do that, Simon. You should have learned that already. They're too busy wanting to get married themselves."

Simon nodded. "I know. She'd get up mornings and instead of starting the mush she'd sit curling her hair by the fire."

"It seems to me," Brigham said, "that a sick woman ought to like it. She'd be apt to think it was pretty nice."

Brigham opened the drawer of his desk and searched through it. Presently he handed a paper to Simon.

"Now, that's what Brother Joseph said about it. He was thinking of men like you when he wrote that, and of women like your wife. And he was thinking of women who love children and houses and don't have any of their own to take care of. And he planned it for men who were strong-minded, not for men who wanted a thing that's the least part of a woman."

Simon held the revelation gingerly; then he looked down at it and sat still and his eyes moved slowly along the lines.

" Read it out loud," Brigham said. " You get it straighter in your head when you hear it."

Simon's voice was harsh and he cleared his throat. " Abraham received promises concerning his seed, and of the fruit of his loins – from whose loins ye are, namely, my servant Joseph. . . . This promise is yours also, because ye are of Abraham, and the promise was made unto Abraham. . . . Go ye, therefore, and do the works of Abraham; enter ye into my law, and ye shall be saved. But if ye enter not into my law ye cannot receive the promise of my Father. . . ."

For a moment Simon was silent, and Brigham said: " Go on."

Swallowing, Simon continued. " Abraham received concubines, and they bear him children, and it was accounted unto him for righteousness, because they were given unto him, and he abode in my law, as Isaac also, and Jacob. . . ."

Brigham stood up and went to the window and stood looking out into the street.

" Let no one, therefore, set on my servant Joseph; for I will justify him. . . . And if he have ten virgins given unto him by this law, he cannot commit adultery, for they belong to him, therefore is he justified. . . . And now, as pertaining to this, verily, verily, I say unto you, I will reveal more unto you, hereafter; therefore, let this suffice for the present. Behold, I am Alpha and Omega. Amen."

Brigham came back to his desk, smiling a little. " It sufficed for the present," he said. " You probably heard Brother Joseph speak of it, but you didn't know exactly what he meant. We did, because we learned these principles along with him. Remember when he said: ' A man must live the principle, the whole principle, if he would inherit the highest degree of glory in God's kingdom '? I've come to see how right he was – because if a man lives this principle as it should be lived, he learns to be impartial, like God. And women learn to be unselfish, they learn what's the best and the most important part of marriage, giving and sharing. That's the best part of any life, Brother Baker."

When Simon handed the paper back, his hand trembled.

"I was shocked when I first learned this principle, and so were the other Apostles, shocked until we were sick at heart and sick of body. But we started to look at things with different eyes, knowing what we knew, and we saw that the one-wife system isn't so perfect. We saw that it didn't answer the demands of society, it permits debaucheries and whoredoms, it exalts some women and lowers others to the dust. Wherever you may have lived or traveled, you'll know that what I tell you is true. And according to history, heathen nations previous to getting Christianity were comparatively free of abominable lusts – remember how awfully the sons of Jacob avenged the abuse of their sister Dinah. And yet their father, a mighty prophet, had taught them the rightfulness of having many wives."

Simon felt a weakness, an excitement that was like something he remembered from the years when he was very young.

"I couldn't ask such a woman to marry me," he said presently. "Such a woman as you told me about – if there is one – till I knew her and she knew me."

Brigham stood up and put on his hat. "We'll get you acquainted," he said lightly. "She can go over with you if she wants to and see what she thinks of your family – and you. Maybe I'll be wrong the first one." He shrugged. "I've been known to be wrong, you know."

When they were on the walk outside, he laughed and added: "But I haven't been wrong very often."

They walked along Parley Street for a long way. "Maybe you've seen this woman," Brigham said. "She does a good bit of work with the Relief Society – her name's Charlot Leavitt. Good Yankee folks from Pennsylvania – had a deal of property there. She and her mother came out to Nauvoo alone; lots of courage, Charlot has. Since her mother's passed on, she's been alone."

Of course it was unthinkable. Simon felt strange and light and unreal, but Brigham noticed, smiling, that he straightened his cravat.

CHARLOT LEAVITT's cottage was prim and neat, with a box hedge and a path of stones with moss planted carefully between. There was a wild-flower garden in a corner of the lot by the fence, and trumpet flowers leaping along the chimney and spreading green and gold over the roof.

Simon paused by the gate and Brigham laughed and clapped his shoulder playfully.

"I know just how you feel, but I tell you, you're lucky. Charlot's a mighty handsome woman; I'd been thinking some about Charlot, myself."

As Simon watched Charlot coming and going between her sitting-room and kitchen, he saw that Brigham was right. She insisted on serving a dessert to Brother Brigham and his friend, so Brigham placed Simon carefully where he could watch her. She *was* a handsome woman, there was no denying it, with the sleek bloom of perfect health on her and the story of lifelong prosperity told in her bearing and her manner. She was wide-hipped and big-busted, a deep cleft at the neck of her Sunday dress showing where the breasts were lifted and bound in her corset. A row of precise ringlets bobbed when she walked, and she had a way of regarding a man brightly, as though she asked a perpetual admiring question.

When they had finished eating, Brother Brigham came directly to the point. Charlot sat very straight, listening, and she began to look at Simon with quick little breathless looks.

"It seems very sudden," she said.

"Take all the time you want," Brigham said jovially. "But there's a place you're needed. You asked me for a place, and there it is. Go outside on your porch and you can almost see it across the river."

"I didn't ask —" Charlot began, flustered, but Brother Brigham motioned her out and told Simon to follow. He stayed in the house, relaxed in one of Charlot's excellent armchairs.

"It's there on the bluff," Simon said, pointing.

Charlot squinted, following his finger with her eyes. "It must be beautiful there," she said.

"Very beautiful."

"I'm sure I'm going to like it fine."

He started.

"You said eight children, now? I think that's wonderful!"

The two men waited while she got her things together in her traveling case. Simon asked if she did not want to wait for the night session of conference, but she shook her head. "Duty first with a good Saint, Brother Baker!" she said vehemently.

Simon stood awkwardly at her side on the ferry-boat, her things piled at his feet.

"Of course," he said hesitantly, "there's nothing definite — It's for you to decide, you know, anything you want to do —"

"Aren't you quite converted, Brother Baker?" She asked it archly, looking up into his face, and thinking: "There's something handsome about him — oh, not *handsome*, but then so nearly, so nice and *smooth*-looking, and his eyes —"

He flushed at her question, knowing her words criticized his reception of the Gospel. "Oh, yes," he said, "I'm converted. But then, I feel like you, it's sudden, and then Mercy sick and things sort of not going right —"

She laid her hand over his on the railing of the boat. "Poor man," she said warmly, "it must have been very hard on you. Her sick and losing the baby and everything."

"It was harder on her than on anybody."

She withdrew her hand, but her voice was still warm and rich. " Of course. And even that girl disappointing her so! "

" Vic was too young. And I guess Jarvie's more a man than I thought."

" When we get older, we get wise, don't we? It wouldn't be natural if we didn't."

They stood silent. Then she looked up at him again in her particular inquiring way and the curls bobbed under her bonnet. " How long would you imagine it takes people to decide such things, Brother Baker? "

When she smiled he saw that she had good white teeth.

" Oh – what would you say? How long should a thing like that take, anyhow? "

They both laughed around their discomfiture. " We're not used to doing these things, are we? " he asked. " It isn't something you do every day and have rules for! "

" No. But it's – very interesting."

They both looked at the water.

" It's always been a theory of mine," Charlot said, " that if you're going to like somebody, you know it at once. You either do or you don't. If you like a person, it can grow; if you don't, that can grow, too. But it's always one way or the other."

Simon hesitated and she gave him the look that waited.

" Well – " He tried to make his voice light. " I guess I've been one to like almost everybody. That's a theory of mine – there's something to like about anybody if you've a mind to find it."

She was silent and he thought she looked disappointed and he was flustered because of the way she looked.

" How did *your* theory work out with *me*? " Her voice was soft and hopeful.

" Oh, it isn't hard to find things to like about you! " Simon said quickly, and saw the quick color on her cheekbones. She stood half turned from him and he noticed that although her bonnet tied with soft lavender ribbons, it was vaguely competent.

She waited.

" And how did *your* theory work out with *me*? " he asked at last.

" It's a strange thing," she said, " but the minute Brother Brigham brought you in, it seemed to me I'd known you for a long time. Even before he said a word, I knew you meant something important. Women can tell things like that; at least, I always could."

" Then — people like that — it shouldn't take them long to decide."

" No."

Simon felt smothered and his words came with difficulty. " You'll want to know Mercy and the children. She's sweet, Mercy is, but she doesn't believe everything she hears." He hesitated. " It's hard to tell you about Mercy, she's been sick quite a while now. Half-sick before the babies, and then this — "

" It's a shame! " Charlot's voice was gentle and concerned. " She shouldn't be worried with all this trouble, should she? She should stay right in bed till she's better — we'll see what we can do."

Simon saw that they were nearing the Iowa shore. Charlot spoke hurriedly. " It's another theory of mine," she said, " that when a thing's already done, people accept it. If they're intelligent, they make the best of it, and then it's not so hard on anybody."

" I guess that's so."

He felt rushed and shabby all at once, and a little slow beside this woman whose thoughts were so ordered and so definite.

" I hope it won't appear to the people in the neighborhood," Charlot said, " that I'm a servant in your house. You know, I'm not accustomed — "

The boat touched the boards of the Iowa landing, turned,

straightened. Simon saw that the sky was beginning to turn pink and the sun was very low. He leaned down and picked up Charlot's things.

"I suppose –" She looked at him hopefully. "I really wish I had a little more time to collect myself. Maybe we could go back and come over again; I've always wanted to see the sun set out on the river."

"As long as you don't get off," he said, "it costs just the same."

She raised her brows. "That's fine," she said.

They stood and watched the sun lower, watched it slowly brighten on the river. The sun was a red ring, cut clean through the center with a white cloud, a slim knife of cloud that seemed to sever it. As they watched, the horizon clipped it entirely, and it disappeared and color came up over it and spread and touched the water in a long line.

"From my house I look at the sunset every night. There never was such a city for sunsets as Nauvoo," Charlot said.

"I guess I haven't taken time to look at sunsets much, lately."

"Oh, I hope I'm not being selfish, keeping you out like this when you ought to be home with your family!" Her face was haunted, distressed. "I'm ashamed, really I am. You ought to have reminded me. You know, I haven't had a soul since Mother died, and I've done just what I pleased, eaten odd hours, anything. You forget what it's like to have people depending on you."

"I'm afraid you'll find it hard over there."

"I'll love it," she said. "I like work and I like seeing things after they're done." She looked pleadingly at him. "You'll have to forgive me for thinking so much about myself tonight."

"A woman's got a right to think of herself when it's a matter of getting married," Simon said, and started at the knowledge that he had said it himself, right out. "A woman's got to get acquainted and have some quiet time to get used to a man; she can't do something like that, right off. Like I told Brother Brigham – "

Her face stopped him, excited and flushed. " I don't see why not. That's the way I've always done things – right off. I know what I want when I see it, I always have."

" I can tell," he said unsteadily, " I can tell that's the kind of woman you are."

" Besides," she said, " I *am* a woman, you know. Not a girl, but a woman who knows her own mind and doesn't take forever to make it up."

The boat waited for a time at Nauvoo and then moved back over the water. Charlot held her breath for a moment. " It seems to me," she said softly, " that I'd like to be married on the river, at sunset. Sunset is my favorite hour. And if you're married on the river, you don't have to go to Carthage for a license."

It came to him what she meant. He stammered uselessly. But she was thorough and competent and pretty, too, like her bonnet.

" I keep thinking," she said, " of the song we sang this morning – ' God Moves in a Mysterious Way.' It seems like everything was ordained to happen. And Dan Jones is an Elder as well as a pilot."

It was Charlot who called Dan Jones from the pilot-house.

MERCY leaned up on her elbows to look out of the window at the river. The color reached east desperately tonight, clear to the east as though it couldn't wait until morning but meant, at once, to make another dawn. She heard somebody coming up the bluff, walking slowly, and Simon's voice, but she could not hear what he was saying. Because his voice was weak, really.

" There's no use telling anybody – there's not any use telling the family yet, I should think – "

Chapter XXXII

THE LITTLE children called her Aunt Charlot and liked her at once. And for Mercy, it was as though God had made Charlot Leavitt to order and then opened the sky and sent her down.

That night she came, it was pitiful what she walked into. The house with just boy-care for a long time except for the day of the funeral, when Mother Turner had come for a few hours. Jarvie had been feeding the children, and the dishes were on the table and the benches and even lying on the hearth, with the spoons still in them. Beck had spilled her milk as she usually did, and Jarvie had Sarah over his arm to keep her from crying, and Beck had gone to bed in the trundle, storming because she must go "wisout Edy." Now, Edy was a mutt pig and couldn't be allowed to go to bed with anybody.

Simon picked up some of the dishes, set them down again, conscious of the turbulence of his household, vaguely ashamed of it. Then he took Charlot in to Mercy. And Mercy thought she looked to be a very nice woman. So competent. God bless Brother Brigham.

She *was* competent, Charlot. And what was more, she saw that everybody else was. There was not a wrinkle in the household that she did not tackle and smooth out. The first few days she had Simon get two of the Yeaman girls to come in and the three of them cleaned house from the loft to the cellar. And everything washable went into the washtub. " Not many more days of sun for these quilts! " Charlot said, and when they were dry brought them in, smelling as though all autumn was in them.

Mercy lay small and inadequate before this avalanche of energy.

" Don't do too much, Miss Leavitt! " she pleaded. " You'll wear yourself out with what I should have done long ago."

But Charlot protested, laughing: " How could you do all this with twins to carry around and your trouble coming? "

" Your trouble. I wonder what it is," Mercy thought. " I wonder what my trouble really is." It was a question, sharp and unyielding, that was beginning to absorb her.

Jarvie thought miserably: " Apparently the heart."

In a few weeks the house shone. Charlot had even emptied the pillows and washed the covers and filled them again, coming into the house triumphantly with the full pillows in her arms and sneezing with the down in her nose. With the back room, meant for Vic and now set aside for Simon and Mercy until she should be well again, Charlot took special care. She boiled the linen shams that had been in Mercy's hope chest until all the fade came out of them and they were white as new. She mended the rug, even, where the chest had worn it through, and made the curtains frilly with starch. Then, when it was all finished, she said firmly: " Now you're to forget everything about the house and just think of yourself for a change! You're the only one in the house that's sick."

And she closed Mercy's door.

Mercy relaxed in the pillows and the days passed. Sometimes Charlot brought Sarah in, but she never left her long. She brought Beck in, like a lady coming for a visit, and saw that she sat quietly in her little high-backed chair. " Now you remember," Charlot said, shaking her finger, " you're a big lady, Beck, visiting a sick lady! "

Betsy came, too, and Georgie and Joey, but in turn and fidgeting under their intention to be quiet.

"You take too much trouble for me." Mercy looked up when Charlot brought the tray with rich soup and vegetables bright with good slow cooking, and bread baked crusty and thickly buttered.

"My sister was sick for years, and then my mother," Charlot said. "I know about caring for sick people. Mother used to say she wouldn't have anybody on earth take care of her but me."

And Mercy could understand that. Calm and efficiency and order and good food, these were wonderful things. She began to rest deeply, sinking into sleep in mid-afternoon, even, and early at night. When she heard Simon coming to bed some nights, she would waken and whisper:

"I'm so much better, Simon. She's wonderful – Miss Leavitt. How ever did you happen to find her?"

"Brother Brigham, I told you. I said a good Yankee this time, and a woman, no silly girl."

"Have you noticed Sarah, Simon? She's different. She's getting brighter and there's a different look in her skin. Yesterday she tried lifting herself off the pillow."

"I guess we just didn't know how to take care of her."

"Oh, we knew *how*," she protested, hurt.

"We didn't, me and Jarvie."

"And I'm better, too. You notice, Simon? Before, when I got up and walked, even a little, I wanted to die of weakness. And now it's different. Today I walked to the chest and back and then sat up by the window. I'll be able to do most things myself again, before you know it."

Simon flinched. "That's good," he said.

ELIZA came the first real autumn day. Mercy heard the children fairly smothering her with greetings. Then she came in, and she had brought her sewing, meaning to stay awhile for once. It was not long before she was talking of what was uppermost in her mind. New troubles, as though troubles had never really ended as folks hoped. Like wars, one trouble bears seed for another one.

" Brigham's worried since Green Plains. The gentiles framed it, he says — they fired on their own meeting so they could blame the Mormons and have an excuse to come on, an excuse to start chasing Mormon farmers into Nauvoo. And now they've published a story about how some of the Brothers buried a keg of gunpowder in the road and blew it up just when some gentiles were passing over."

" I thought it'd be over when — when they did what they did."

" Why should it be? " Eliza cut her thread carefully, controlling her voice; she wondered if ever her life long she could speak that name with composure. " Brother Joseph was only the head, not the body, and the Mormon body is a fairy animal — it produces instantly twelve more heads when one is cut off. That's the way God planned it — He knew what was needed. The leader won't be dead until the whole Church is dead."

Eliza smiled, thinking of Brother Brigham, sober and substantial man that he was. He had said to the people when he came home after Joseph's death: " I don't care who leads the Church, even though it's Ann Lee, but I'll go out and baptize new people faster than mobs can kill the old ones off! "

He was a great leader, Brother Brigham, with no patience for folks who let themselves get discouraged. Once the Temple workers had come to him to tell him that they weren't getting paid and hadn't enough to eat. He stood before them like a rock and told a story. "Once before, all the food and money was gone, and suddenly Brother Toronto opened my door and brought me twenty-five hundred dollars in gold. The Temple committee said it was the law to lay it at the Apostle's feet, and I said: 'Yes, and I'll lay it at the Bishop's feet.' So I opened the mouth of the bag and took hold at the bottom and gave it a jerk and strewed gold clear across the room. 'Now go and buy flour for the workmen,' I said, 'and don't distrust the Lord any more; we'll have what we need.'"

And from somewhere, heaven knew where, he was still getting what people needed. Not only goods and food and money, but strength as well.

"Now," Eliza told Mercy, "he's starting to wonder if maybe we'll have to start over, somewhere else, after all. Maybe not, but we've got to be prepared for anything, he says. The gentiles are beginning to see that we can't be stopped – maybe they even see that something a man has died for can't be easily discarded."

Her eyes were too bright, Mercy noticed. "After all," Eliza went on, "the best thing he could have done for the Church was to die for it. I can see that now; he knew it all along."

She was pinched in a way new to her and there were fine lines around her eyes and a darkness under them as though she had not slept for many nights.

"I hope you're taking care of yourself, Eliza. Don't spend your life thinking about everybody but yourself or you'll have a lot less to spend."

Eliza shook her head, dismissing the idea. Presently she looked up and said: "I guess you heard about Emma's baby. Another boy."

"Yes, I heard."

"It's hurt everybody," Eliza said, "that Emma's turned against the Church like she has. I guess you know what she says about Brother Brigham."

" Simon said something — "

" She says polygamy is Brigham's idea — that's what she's given out to the big papers. She says Joseph didn't have anything to do with it and that she was the only wife he ever had."

" I don't see what difference it makes, now," Mercy said gently. " I don't see what possible difference it could make."

" The only difference it makes is that he won't like it," Eliza said. " He always hoped she'd come to understand it his way."

" I never blamed her. It's this world she's got to think of. Legally, besides, she'd have to divide his property, wouldn't she? And there are her children to think of."

" She's not the only one who thinks of her children, Mercy. I've been with them so much I almost think they're mine, too. But I never get to see them any more — not once since the funeral."

Mercy shook her head sympathetically. " I'm sorry, Eliza, but I never thought there was any good in it, and you know it. I never told you any different. Even when I knew it meant so much to you, I couldn't help thinking of Emma. I guess it all depends on which side of the fence you're standing on."

" No, it doesn't. If you're big enough, you can climb up in the middle of the fence, and look at both sides. You don't have to sit and growl over what's on your side, like the old dog in the manger! "

Mercy was surprised at her vehemence, her anxiety. It was over now; what did it matter? She took Eliza's good-by kiss silently, and only nodded when the poetess paused in the doorway and said: " The word of God has never been easy to accept with patience, Mercy. Even when He said *Love one another* — and that ought to be easy enough, goodness knows."

THE DAYS grew shorter and there was heavy frost before school started. The younger boys slipped down from the loft in the morning and dressed by the fire, their backs decorously to Miss Leavitt.

"For gosh sakes," Menzo cried one morning. "Lookit on Bert!"

Bert backed away, his face livid.

"You leave me alone," he said. "You keep still about me."

But Charlot had heard. She came briskly over and said: "Well, what is it? You got measles or something, Bert?"

"Naw. I haven't got anything."

"Turn around."

"There's nothin' on me. Menzo was just bein' smart."

"I wasn't. It's sores, big as my hand."

They turned Bert around, protesting, and Charlot leaned over and looked at the festered skin above the buttocks. "For heaven's sake, boy, what've you done to yourself?"

"Nothin'. They don't hurt."

Charlot turned him by the shoulders and looked into his face. He kept his eyes from hers, stubbornly.

"I can smell what's the matter with you," Charlot said. "I've been meaning to say something. I thought maybe you'd peed your pants at school."

Mercy, hearing, got out of bed and came to the door, walking slowly. She leaned there, troubled, listening. Then she said: "I should've told you, Miss Leavitt. Ever since Bert was a baby, he's had that trouble, wetting nights. Nothing will stop it. He's tried not drinking water afternoons and everything."

"Well, something's *got* to stop it," Charlot said decisively. "He's too big to pee a bed. When I washed his bed, I knew; now I guess it's ruined again already. But that back—" She turned him around again, and Mercy saw that his face was drawn, ashamed. " I don't see what's making the sores on that back."

" Since frost," Menzo said helpfully, " his bed don't dry."

Charlot gasped. And then they got it out of Bert, how he had been doing. He would roll up his bed in the morning and by night it would be stiff, and he would get into it and lie on his heels and his head till the ice melted, and then he could lie down.

Mercy listened and wept and slipped back into bed again.

But Charlot did not weep. She stood up and looked down upon Bert with troubled eyes. " Well," she said, " poultices for the sores. But it was always my way to see that a boy cleaned up his own messes. A woman can't clean up the messes after a whole family, especially after boys as big as you. You get dressed, Bert, and bring your bed down."

He brought it down, and Charlot sniffed at it, wrinkling her nose. " I'll get some water warm," she said, " and you can wash it in the shed. It can dry here when it's washed, I guess – dry it like this it'd drive us out of house and home."

Bert was silent, crushed. After a time Mercy heard him using the washboard out in the shed.

" Miss Leavitt – "

" Yes? "

" There's something *wrong* with Bert, something he can't help. He always used to bring his bed down and spread it to dry – he was ashamed to let you know, that's all."

" I should think he would be – that nice clean bed. But you can't just dry it with the pee in it, it's got to be washed."

" I'm afraid it won't get dry before bedtime."

" If it's not, then it's not. It'll be as dry as the way he's *been* sleeping in it! And a good sight more healthy."

That night, at bedtime, the quilts were not dry.

" Well, well," Charlot said evenly. " Doesn't look like Bert's got any bed."

He did not look at her, he did not look at anybody.

" Just keep your clothes on, Bert," Charlot said. " Anybody'd pee a bed at your age shouldn't go to bed, anyway."

Jarvie looked at Simon hopefully, but Simon did not look up from the paper he was reading. He seemed to be oblivious of the whole affair, he didn't seem to notice Bert sleeping on the hearth, rolled up in one blanket Charlot gave him.

" He can't help it," Mercy protested to Simon.

" Miss Leavitt can't stand a filthy thing like that," Simon said. " She's clean as a pin. You ought to be glad she can't. The Lord knows I've smelt Bert's bed all I want to! "

Mercy lay still, crushed.

Curled up on the hearth, Bert was almost asleep when Charlot crept quietly over to him and laid an old crock close by. " You want to pee in the night," she whispered, " you can use this."

Her voice was kind, and when he saw her face in the firelight, he saw that she did not look angry or scornful or anything. She reached into her apron pocket. " Here are some currants left from the pudding," she said. " You chew on these before you go to sleep."

At first he left them on the bench in a little heap and did not touch them. But after a time, when Charlot had gone to bed, he reached up and brought down a few in his fist and chewed them slowly, one by one. You did not get currants often. Again his hand went up, and after a while his hand, exploring along the bench, found not a currant left. By that time he felt a strong desire to urinate and got out of the blanket, stooping over the crock. The night passed and he was dry and clean.

The next night his bed was dry, and as he carried it to the loft, Charlot came to him and, smiling, reached up her hand to him and put something in his pocket. Unbelievingly, he saw her wink her eye and she put a finger over her mouth. It was a secret, then, from the others. More currants. After the boys were asleep, Bert was still slowly chewing; Charlot crept up the ladder and pushed the crock over near him. " It won't take any time at all," she said.

At breakfast next morning she looked at him inquiringly. He nodded, and she smiled. Menzo said, right out: " Bert's bed's dry as a bone."

Even Mercy could not help noticing how Bert followed Charlot around, doing things for her. She heard Charlot say to him: " Something you're ashamed of, Bert, you don't hide it inside of you. You bring it out, especially a thing with a stink to it, and wash it clean. Things on your conscience work the same way — you bring them out for an airing, and then they don't bother you any more."

Every night for weeks there were the currants in Bert's pocket, and every morning commendation, spoken or unspoken. And Bert began to call her Aunt Charlot, as the little ones did.

" I like it," Charlot said amply to Mercy. " I was always Aunt Charlot to my sister's boys, and it makes it seem like home to me to hear it."

Chapter XXXIII

MERCY had started on the pile of stockings, but Charlot came and gathered them into a bundle for the boys to take to the Stocking Lady in Nauvoo.

"Do your own stockings," Charlot said briskly, "and you're the same as stealing the bread and butter from Unity Jones."

Mercy knew that it was true enough. Poor Unity, another Missouri widow, had a misery in her feet that kept her from walking anywhere at all, and so, perhaps taking inspiration from her own suffering members, she had begun darning socks for other folks. She could darn socks that had holes as big around as your fist, and the darn would outlast any stocking, two to one. She would take a bundle of socks, tied in a careless bundle, and when the Sisters called for them again they would be finished and folded in a particular way Unity had – each pair in a plump square, and all of them piled like blocks in her basket. There was a stench from her suffering feet that went even into these stockings, and the Sisters generally dumped them into strong suds before putting them on the family feet again.

"I ought to be doing *something*," Mercy said.

"You get yourself better and then there's a plenty to do."

So Mercy read all her books again, and sometimes she knitted, but she was not so very good at knitting, not quick at it like some women she knew. Like Charlot, for instance, who could sit knitting and tend to the children and see that Betsy did the dishes and have the boys bring in the wood, and scare Betsy's cat Purrmiew away from the churn, and entertain a visitor, all at once, and never drop a stitch.

SARAH was crying, and lustily. Jarvie lay and listened and it jarred on him. Maybe because of Mary, maybe that made Sarah's crying so important, and maybe because he himself had had to keep her quiet so much of the time and the responsibility was still with him. She really had been his baby, Sarah. After a while he started down the ladder, quietly, but paused half-way down. Miss Leavitt was sitting by the fire, her lap full of fabric as it always was when she sat quiet.

She looked up at him. "What's the matter, Jarvie?"

"Just wondered what's wrong with Sarah."

"She's all right. She's just spoiled, that's all. She thinks all she's got to do is open her mouth and somebody rushes to take her up."

He stiffened, conscious of the vague dislike he had felt for her from the beginning. But Charlot smiled. "Babies learn things quicker than we know," she said. "They're like apples, they're never too little for spoiling."

Jarvie told her dubiously: "Mary never cried much. But when she did, you knew something was wrong with her."

"Maybe so. Maybe not. If she'd cried more, she'd likely still be here. I know there's nothing wrong with Sarah. She's dry and she's warm and she's full to the chest. Like I was telling your father, it makes a baby stronger to cry sometimes."

Jarvie climbed back up the ladder and lay down. Well, maybe she was right. She had a way of being right about things. No matter how much you wanted her to be wrong or how much you didn't like what she said, it was likely to turn out right.

Funny, the way he felt about her, from that first night when she just came in and started doing things, took things right out of your hands and started doing them until you just stood there, and when you started doing something yourself, you stumbled at it and then she did it, calmly and well, before you could blink. That bright busyness about her – it was right in front of her and you couldn't get around it. She made everything clean and comfortable and she saw behind everything and she made good meals and took good care of Mother – you had to see that – but something about her was so sure of everything it made you not a bit sure yourself, and you couldn't look straight at her when you said something, sort of afraid it might not be right, what you said. If you did look at her, she was looking straight at you, as though she were weighing every word you said, and if you said something wrong then because you were flustered, she corrected you very sweetly, and then your words fumbled more than ever. You didn't exactly *like* somebody to be so right about everything. It was a funny way to feel about somebody. It was a hard thing to understand.

He put his hands under his head and stared up at the rafters. Of course, maybe it was because she came right after Vic, and Vic was easy to talk to, listening the way she did as though everything you said was a good thing to say. Even when Vic had another idea, she was likely to nod first and *then* say it. There was a big difference, he could see that. Of course, there was that other thing about Vic – that cloudy moody thing you never understood. But it didn't make you fumble and feel little, it made you want to come closer and find just what it was. And you knew perfectly well Vic admired you and liked you – with Miss Leavitt you didn't know. You had a feeling that she thought you were pretty young to be saying anything.

He did not allow himself to think about Vic very often, because there was that thing that made him ashamed. And lonely. Ashamed and lonely together. He was sure she had wanted nothing but to be happy, like she said; and there had been happiness. That few minutes – there had been more happiness in it than had ever crowded into that much time before. Of course, there was shame and a reluctance about remembering, afterward shame tried to cover it all over, and you saw that it was something you would not want everybody to know about, the beautiful terrifying lifting and waving in you, a different happiness from any other. But it was a secret thing you wanted to keep in secret. He wondered if it would be in Vic's face when he saw her again. Looking up at the ceiling, Jarvie thought: "I guess that was some of the sugar, all right. And it wouldn't take much of it to make the whole dish mighty sweet."

He heard Simon come in from Mother's room, heard him talking quietly to Miss Leavitt. And then Miss Leavitt laughed; she laughed in a curious silly way that was vaguely familiar. Coming up through the loft door, it sounded right silly. He noticed that Sarah had stopped crying – guessed Miss Leavitt was right again and she'd gone off to sleep.

He heard their voices clearly, pushing and pulling at each other the way voices do in a conversation you get the sound of and not the sense. Miss Leavitt laughed again, and then Simon laughed. It sounded queer, hearing them laugh like that together.

Then he heard his own name, he heard Miss Leavitt saying his name, laughing around it. He sat up, almost ready to answer, and then realized she had not called, but was talking still. It seemed as though they had moved across the room now, because he could hear them plainly. "I don't think Jarvis likes me very much – he looks like he doesn't trust me. I guess he's too old not to suspect something. Now, Bert – I've won him over."

"I can see," Simon said plainly, "you've got to have some authority to manage the big boys; they aren't easy to manage,

I know that. I'll tell them, myself, if they don't do as you say you've my leave to beat them."

"I hope I won't need it," she said, "but sometimes a little crack helps, you know. It's always been a theory of mine—"

They laughed again. "Spare the rod," Simon said.

Jarvie felt himself sagging against the bed, a slow unbelief edging over him. Their voices were a mumble again and he strained to hear. Miss Leavitt laughed again, that giggly laugh. He slipped out of the covers and edged over the pallet to the floor. Then, braving slivers, he dragged himself carefully to the loft door, propped half open as always. He could see part of the room downstairs and could hear everything. He heard Simon say: "Mercy seems to be a lot better. It shouldn't be long now, I think you're right about that."

Something else she was right about. Jarvie edged closer to the door and saw them, standing by the fire. Miss Leavitt reached up and snuffed the candles on the mantel, but the firelight was still bright.

"It hasn't been so easy, you know," she said.

"I'm sorry." Simon's voice was contrite. "You're not used to working so hard, I know that."

He reached out and put his arm around her waist. Jarvie blinked, but there it was, plain against the light of the fire.

"You must be tired—I feel like I'm imposing on you."

She turned toward him. "I wouldn't say imposing exactly," she said. Her voice was coquettish, trying to be young, and Jarvie suddenly knew that he despised it, with all the fierceness of his being. It was the put-on voice like the put-on laugh, it was the voice women save for men; even the girls had it for the boys, sometimes.

"Well, maybe I can help you a little—" Simon's voice was trying to be young and light too, and Jarvie hated it with that same fierceness bursting in him.

Then Simon leaned down and kissed her mouth, and his hands

began to fumble behind her back and he untied the ribbons of her apron. It fell to the floor around her feet. Then – unbelievingly, unbelievingly – Simon brought his hands around her waist and upward to her neck and began to unbutton the long precise row of buttons under her chin and her dress began falling apart, falling apart, little by little. She protested, giggling in that silly, silly way, but not a sincere protest, just a teasing one. It was horrible, horrible, it was unbearable, more than a human being could bear in his ears or in his eyes or in his brain or in this world, hearing her laugh and talk like that to Father.

The dress opened to the full breasts and there was white lace over them with two white mounds of skin pressed together in the center. An agony so overpowering rushed over the watching boy that he clutched at his mouth with his fingers, but it escaped from him, came out of him fiercely.

Almost at once he felt Simon's hands on him, an annihilating power in them. He said, pleadingly: "Don't, Father, don't."

Simon felt him limp and shuddering under his hands, and so he flung him down on the bed. Then he sat down, trembling uncontrollably. He waited for what seemed to be a long time, his breath heavy and rhythmic, but Jarvie went on sobbing, turning on his face to stifle his voice in the pillow.

"Well," Simon said at last, clearing his throat, "well, I guess there's something you'd better know. It seems like I'd better tell you."

Jarvie tried to stop crying. He was a man, after all. He swallowed deeply and turned over. He could not see his father clearly, but knew exactly where he was from that heavy breathing.

"I guess –" he choked. "I guess, even when you're old, you don't – I guess even then it's the same."

Simon's breath caught. "What do you mean, Jarvie, what do you mean's the same?"

Jarvie whispered hoarsely: " I didn't know about Vic, because I didn't know – about things like that. But I knew about *her*, I knew about her all along."

Simon's breath stopped altogether. Then he said: " What'd you know about who? Miss Leavitt? "

" Yes." Jarvie's voice was hoarse and sharp, whispering. " *I knew she wasn't any good.*"

Simon stood up suddenly and his head crashed against the rafters; but he did not seem to notice that, or care. After a while he knelt down and fumbled for the boy's shoulders.

" Listen, Jarvie," he whispered hoarsely, " this time you're wrong. It's hard to explain how it is, but – Miss Leavitt, Charlot, is my wife. And she's a good woman. She's my wife, do you hear me? Like Eliza Snow was Brother Joseph's wife. We were married on the river after conference."

The boy did not move, and he did not make a sound. Presently his father said good-night and went down, his feet loud on the ladder through a great new silence. After that the night was endless. Endless and very dark.

Chapter XXXIV

Betsy and Beck sat stiffly in their little chairs, visiting like ladies. Charlot had just washed Mercy's hair and brushed it until it hung like black silk over her shoulders. She sang to the children.

" Hi-o, the sly young crow
Has been making fun of me.
Pdt – tick – fol de diddle
Sol de diddle
Di do! "

She stopped, listening.

" Go on, Mamma. Hi-o – "

" Sssh! "

" Sing, Mamma! "

" Sssh! " She could hear Jarvie's voice, lifted and warm. " I don't have to and I won't. That's Menzo's job and I won't do it."

" Jarvis Baker, you heard what your father said! "

Mercy's hands went to her cheeks and she turned off the side of her bed and found her slippers. When she opened the door wide she saw Jarvie's face, pinched and defiant.

" Jarvie! What's the matter? "

He looked at her. " Menzo's run off – he's always running

off and leaving me his stuff to do. I'm not going to do it."

"Oh, Jarvie, I'm ashamed, you talking back to Miss Leavitt like that! You do as she says – what do you expect her to do, with all the work she has? We'll see he does yours when he gets back, we'll see to it."

He looked at her and his fists clenched. Then he turned and went out of the door.

"I'm sorry, Miss Leavitt. That's not like Jarvie, not one bit like him."

"You shouldn't be up. You stop worrying yourself about things. I guess I can manage boys all right!"

"Jarvie's never been hard to manage, he never has. I can't think what's come over him. Yesterday about the wood and today –"

She went back to her room and finished the gay little song, but Jarvie's face stayed with her, nagging her. She could always tell when something bothered Jarvie, he showed his feelings so plain. He always cried easily, too, and got choked up, just like she did, when things went wrong. His face got white and pinched when he felt bad and he lost his appetite. Like after that Vic thing happened – surely, nothing like that again. Surely not. He understood so perfectly, Simon said.

When he came to say good-night, she took his hand and held it tight against the bed.

"What's the matter, Jarvie? What's wrong between you and Menzo?"

"Menzo's all right. He just forgets things, I guess."

He tried to turn away, but she held him. "Something's wrong, Jarvie, I can tell it. I want you to tell me."

"There isn't anything."

"You know, it's like Miss Leavitt said about Bert's trouble – it's better to get things right out of us."

"Oh, yes, sure. She's right about everything!"

His fierceness alarmed her. She tried to speak to him again, but he dragged his hand from her and bolted from the room. She heard him go rushing across the big room and outside, slamming the door. She listened anxiously, but it was a long time before he came in again.

"He's been out walking the way he always does when he feels bad about something," she thought. When Simon came she said: "Simon, what's wrong with Jarvie? Nothing's happened, has it – nothing else like that Vic affair?"

"No, nothing I know of."

She lay thinking. That fierceness against Miss Leavitt. Maybe Miss Leavitt had taken too much on herself and Jarvie resented it. After all, he had been in charge of things, and she did have a way of taking things up quickly, Miss Leavitt did. And it was bound to be hard for the children, having things different all of a sudden. There was Beck, for instance, crying all that one afternoon over Edy. But Edy was getting too big – you couldn't have a pig as big as that going in and out!

Charlot had said: "For heaven's sake, I can't imagine anybody having a pig in the house."

And Georgie, soberly: "She never makes a mess in the house, Aunt Charlot."

And Menzo defensively, his tone sharp: "We never had pigs in our house, Mother never did. But Edy was froze when she was born and had to come in the woodbox, and then she got used to sleeping on a pillow. She'll lay her head right down on a pillow and stay there all night and go and wake Betsy when she wants to go out in the morning."

"An awful smart pig," Bert said. "Smart as a dog, just about."

But of course Edy *was* getting big – you could see Miss Leavitt's point of view. Beck would just have to cry. Edy would have to be slaughtered before long, anyhow.

Mercy lay for a long time thinking of these things. And it came to her: "I've been here long enough. I've let myself lie here long enough – I'm all right, now, there hasn't been anything, not a sign of weakness for the last few days. Today when I got up, I felt strong, I could have done something. In the morning I'll get up and start in – maybe things will be different then, Jarvie will feel different, and we can iron things out and have some real *family* again."

When she went to sleep, she was oddly excited. To be part of the world again would be sweet – to churn and wash and sweep and smooth the covers in Sarah's cradle every day. And to bake bread and see it come out of the pans brown and good. And that cake with apple in it and currants and spice – she'd have Simon bring currants from the store if there weren't any and make that cake for a kind of celebration. Imagine, not even knowing if there were any currants in the house!

JARVIE jerked his bed closer to Menzo. "Listen," he whispered, "you can't work it like that!"

Menzo's mouth curled. "Damned old whore, her! She's a a damned old whore!"

"You and I've got to stick together –"

"I can't stand it, I can't stay around where she is, Jarv. I can't hardly swallow, it all comes up and stays at the bottom of my throat and I want to vomit every time I look at her. I can't stand it, I tell you."

"You can stand it if I can, and both of us can stand it better than Mother could. It's not going to help to run off like you did."

"When I go, it gets out of me some."

"I know, but it doesn't get out of the house, does it? It's right here when you get back. What we wanta do is make her quit – make her feel like we do, so she'll go."

"How?"

"Oh – ways. It comes to you through the day. Just don't

listen when she talks to you, don't pay no attention, just act like you don't hear. Then when she takes hold of you, tell 'er you won't do it."

"It's gonna make Father mad."

"All right, let it. And let it make *her* mad, too. Father can't stand things like that going on in the house. But we'll show him it goes on as long as she's here. There's not going to be anything make me feel any different."

"Me neither."

"All right, then. Don't you run off, you stay and make things as bad as you can."

"All right. But I can't hardly swallow, sitting across from her."

Jarvie stiffened. "Listen, Menzo, that's a good idea. *Not* to swallow. Anything she fixes – you and me don't eat it, see? Nobody can say much about that, we just sit there and leave it. Then when Father asks us, we say like you did, we can't swallow with *her* there."

"That's good, Jarv. Just not eating."

"And when she says something, just not hearing what she says. See? We just don't hear."

MERCY woke at dawn. It was a strange quiet dawn, coldly pink across the river. The trees were bleak and bare on the pink sky and that honey-locust – name of a girl and look of a pirate.

She lay luxuriously, watching. Poor Simon, he never rested, really. He was out already, without any breakfast, most likely. Then she remembered and sat up, thrilled. When he came in from the barn, there she'd be by the hearth making hoe-cakes! In that blue calico he'd bought himself and liked so much.

She stretched a moment, sighing, and then slipped out into

the cold. Trembling, she found her shoes and slipped into them. The dress – it seemed strange to be putting it on. She was afraid of being too big for it still, from Sarah and Mary, but found she was not. She was surprised to find how very thin she was. They had been so little, those two.

She braided her hair swiftly and bound it around her head, the way Simon liked it.

She opened the door softly and went in. Carefully, she stirred the coals in the fireplace and then laid a little log across the embers. It began to hiss almost at once and flames came alive in the coals, beginning to lick up.

The bed-ropes murmured a little and she stood very still. No use waking poor Miss Leavitt for a while – there was somebody else to make breakfast this morning! And Sarah cried last night again, till late. "Now I'm so much better," she thought gladly, "I can take the cradle by my bed –"

Someone sighed deeply and turned over. Mercy listened, uncertain, puzzled. And then she looked over in the shadowy corner where the big bed stood. Miss Leavitt's brief curls on the pillow, and – She moved closer, peering.

Familiarly, as they always did when she was distressed, her hands moved to her face, and she felt the cool fingertips as though they belonged to someone else. They were a sensation apart from that other sensation flooding over her – a bewildering nausea, a hot sickness that seemed to pour from her brain and over her, a cloak of nausea. Her fingers were pressing and cool.

"No, no, no. God in heaven, no!"

The door closed behind her. Softly. She thought only of escaping into the covers, she did not even think of the calico. And under the quilts she lay quivering.

It blinded her now, it was so clear. So clear. Eliza saying only a few days ago: "Brother Brigham is teaching it to many

Brethren now," and afterward, rising abruptly, and then saying that about the dog in the manger – that had been a meaning thing. And Jarvie, smearing his tears on his sleeve.

"Aunt Charlot – Aunt Charlot." It blinded her now, it was so clear.

Finally she heard them stirring in the other room. And Simon came in, tiptoeing; she could hear the roar of the fire when he opened the door. He dressed quietly, thinking she was asleep, and she kept her face to the wall and never moved. She heard him scraping at the hearth, knew he was building her fire. He went out again then, tiptoeing, and closed the door again.

Menzo brought her breakfast tray. He leaned down and kissed her, but she waited under the covers until he had gone away, and then she sat up and looked at the tray as she might have looked at a living thing. The napkin was very white, the egg well done, the bread browned by the fire and buttered, and there was wild-plum preserve from the big crock. This from Charlot Leavitt. All this. No wonder, no wonder, no wonder. It wasn't for her, not any of it, but for Simon. Charlot worked for Simon, cleaned for Simon, tended the children for Simon. Simon with his fair hair and his big arms and his slow kind voice and that singular charm that was Simon only and had never been in any other man in this world.

She turned her face to the pillow, and the egg cooled.

Charlot came to get the tray.

"You haven't eaten anything."

"I'm not hungry." Her voice was stifled and bitter.

"You feeling worse this morning?"

"No. Just – not hungry."

"You know," Charlot's voice was cheerful, "you need food to get strong again. Here, let me help you. If you're feeling weak, I'll be glad to help you."

Charlot picked up the other pillow and tried to lift Mercy's head to push it under her back, but Mercy cowered, holding the bedclothes against her chin. She was not ready for it, not yet.

"Please, I couldn't. Not this morning."

"If I start crying," she thought, "I will kill myself!"

"I'll leave it here on the table," Charlot said amiably. "Maybe after a while you'll feel strong enough to eat it. Seems like nobody in the house is hungry this morning; the boys didn't eat. I've been trying to think if there was anything yesterday might not have agreed with us."

When she had gone, Mercy gradually relaxed. She felt herself grow soft, as though she were dissolving in the feathers, but the nausea persisted and when she lifted her hand it shook violently. She tried to think and arrange her thoughts in sober consecutive order, but they broke fiercely into pieces and stayed in her brain in pieces, whole and jagged and piercing.

"I hate this country," she thought, "I hate it. I always hated it, really. It's too flat and terrible, there's no end or beginning to it, and the people are too flat and patient, taking things the way they do and believing them. To inherit the highest degree of glory – to sit beside Brother Joseph again, in another world, and to be commanded by that voice again." She knew suddenly that Simon belonged to them and not to her – he was flat and yielding and patient, too, Simon was. He wasn't living now, he was living forever.

The morning passed, somehow. And by noon, in the brave white light of noon, she knew what she must do. This Charlot Leavitt, so self-assured, so right, you could fight her because you belonged here and she was alien. It was all yours and they all knew it – they all belonged to you. Jarvie would stand close and help to fight her out of this house. And Menzo, she knew she could trust to Menzo. You could go and be strong again, you could be slim and white the way Simon loved you to be.

"Just let her dare shut the door again!"

The tray still lay there and she sat up and took it and ate everything on it. Then she got out of bed and picked the tray up and went to the door and opened it very wide.

They were all at the table, and Charlot was leaning over the kettle at the hearth. When Mercy stood in the doorway, Charlot looked up, surprised, and ran forward, reaching.

"Oh, you needn't, Mrs. Baker! I was just getting you a bowl of this hot soup — "

Mercy stood smiling. Charlot took the tray from her hands and she moved to the table and sat down, her knees trembling under her.

"I feel better," she said. "I've decided to get up."

She was aware of Jarvie's face, the full joy of it. And Menzo, smiling.

Simon rose and brought another chair for Charlot. When she sat down, he bowed his head abruptly and said: "Let us offer thanks." He asked the blessing himself, saying firmly: "We especially thank thee, O Father, for restoring the mother of this house to health, bless her and keep her. Amen."

Gratefully, Mercy smiled at him. It was a very wonderful occasion. Charlot was up and down, bustling and busy, and Mercy allowed her to attend to the service this time, because there was still that unreasonable weakness in her knees. That would pass. She scarcely looked at Charlot, but kept her chin firm, her head lifted, and the boys adored her with their eyes. When the meal was over, she went to Simon and kissed him as she had been used to do, kissing him on top of the head and then turning her cheek into his hair.

"It's so wonderful," she said. "I feel as though I'd been away a long time and had just come home again."

Charlot leaned to scrape the kettle, and the blood rushed into her full cheeks.

Chapter XXXV

MERCY stayed up all the rest of the day. Mostly she minded the children while Charlot did the work, and Charlot was very pleasant, full of chat and good nature.

"Your friends are going to be mighty glad to see you up and around," she said. "I never go to town or even out the door but what somebody's inquiring."

"They're good neighbors."

The hours went more rapidly than they had seemed to go in bed. She made the cake as she had planned; surely, there was more need for celebration than there had been when she first thought of it, and besides she felt a desperate need for active work under her hands. Before Charlot Leavitt, work loomed and she plowed swiftly and securely through it and left order flowing smoothly behind her. Her efficiency made Mercy's fingers fumble, even at familiar tasks. When she saw that Jarvie and Menzo left their tasks undone, she wondered if their fingers fumbled, too.

When Jarvie came in to wash before supper, Charlot spoke to him sharply and he just stood there drying his hands.

"Jarvis!"

He still stood there, drying his hands. Mercy looked up at him.

"Jarvis Baker," Charlot said shrewdly, "I'm no telltale and

never will be. But it's got to be told if those chips aren't in that woodbox before bedtime. There's one thing a Saint's got to learn to do, and that's his part. I've always said" – and Charlot looked at Mercy – "I've always said, if every one does his part, there won't be too much in this world for any one man to do."

He went to the fire and stirred at it idly. Then he took his book from the mantel, deliberately, and sat down on the bench and opened it in front of him. Mercy saw Charlot's hands clench, saw her face livid with an effort to maintain her composure. And, watching Charlot, she was glad with a fierce and savage gladness. She rose and went to Jarvie and sat down beside him, because she must be beside him and touch his side against her own. He looked at her, expecting to be reproved, and she saw that his eyes were hurt and haunted and she knew how deeply he was suffering. She wanted then to let him know she understood. But Charlot was there, her nails still pressing savagely into her palms, her face alive watching them, waiting for Mercy to press her discipline. But Mercy only sat there until Charlot turned away, and then she only said: "Menzo knows, too."

He nodded. Then he said swiftly: "I'm glad you're better, but you watch out lifting things."

"I will."

Abashed, he looked down at his book. "I've been reading this," he said, and showed her the page.

"Read it to me."

"This part." He began to read softly, the words flowing as they always had since he first began hanging onto his primers. You had a feeling he always knew far ahead what the words were and the whole sense of the words.

"How weary, stale, flat, and unprofitable seem to me all the uses of this world! . . . That it should come to this! . . . Hyperion to a satyr."

"After all," Charlot said stiffly, "there's supper to get."

But Mercy was looking at Jarvie, searchingly as a woman might look at her lover. "Do you think," she asked, "that Gertrude thought 'Hyperion to a satyr' – do you think she saw the difference?"

"After Hamlet told her; she must have seen it after that."

"If you were Hamlet," she said, "would you have told her?"

"Yes, but sooner. Right away. She deserved it, you know, being so stupid she couldn't see it for herself."

"Maybe –" She spoke through fear. "Maybe there was another reason for her doing what she did, so soon. There was being Queen, you know; maybe her husband would have wanted her to go on being Queen."

"He didn't. He came back and *said* he didn't."

She was surprised at the tempest in his voice.

"He couldn't have."

"Maybe you could peel these while you're talking," Charlot said, and laid a pan of potatoes on Mercy's lap.

"Of course, Miss Leavitt. I'm sorry."

"The chips are certainly getting low in this box," Charlot said.

SUPPER had a hedge around it, a prickly hedge. Menzo and Jarvie ate potatoes, and then the currant cake, making a great fuss over it. Conversation moved stiffly or lapsed entirely, and Charlot was beside herself keeping Beck on her stool because she *would* get down and go to Mother, who was a novelty at the table after so long. Mercy spoke to Beck, too, but gently, and cuddled her before she sent the child back to her place, so that soon she was back for more cuddling.

"It's always been my idea," Charlot said, "that when we play we play and when we eat we eat."

Mercy was aware that some sort of crisis impended and she

both feared it and desired it. Watching Simon so scrupulously polite to her and to Charlot, she thought: " It's all gone, all that's natural and easy and sweet; it's gone for him, too. There can't be somebody who doesn't belong, you can't just thrust them in."

When she had finished eating, she went to Simon and sat on his knee in the familiar way he had always loved, leaning back, one hand on the back of his neck supporting her. " Even this is a kind of malice," she thought, and wanted to go to her chair again.

" Tired? " Simon asked.

" Dead tired. I'd like to be taken to bed and tucked in, like Beck."

" You'd better be, then," Simon said, and lifted her. " Even this with malice," she thought.

Charlot began briskly to clear off the dishes.

Simon helped Mercy to get ready for bed, and she asked for the brush and sat brushing her hair for a long time. " I wish you'd come to bed early, Simon," she said. " You're tired, too; I can tell you're tired when you're so quiet."

" Me and Menzo are marking out a chest," he said. " We'd planned on doing it tonight."

" Not too long, then. I'll be waiting for you."

After he went away, she found her little trunk and searched through it until she came upon a ribbon, rolled into a ball and tucked into a box of lavender. Carefully she laced it through the eyelets around the neck of her gown and tied it in a bow under her chin. It was then she heard Charlot's voice.

" I think they could at least help dry the dishes – after all, I've done a day's work too! "

" Jarv! Menzo! "

" They're lazy. I made the mash myself – but I'm not going to fill up the woodbox! "

Simon spoke to the boys rapidly. Charlot came at once and

closed the door, and then there was only a fumble of voices, interchanging. Jarvie's voice high so that certain words came through, Menzo quiet, sullen as Mercy knew he could be. Then Mercy heard them going out and thought: "They'll get the wood, now." But clearly, from the shed, she heard the whip coming down, and knew.

It was an ordeal Simon Baker never forgot. They stood there, the two of them, and took all he could give them, took his whole strength out of him with boy-courage like bleak walls around them. He made it as hard as he dared and he made it long, but they vied with each other for courage. He knew they would never have been so brave apart.

Then he sent Menzo in to bed.

"Jarvis."

Jarvis stood quiet.

"You've put it into Menzo. I'm ashamed of you."

"No, I didn't put it in him. It was already there when I told him."

"I don't want any more of it, do you hear me? I don't want to have to do this again."

"Yes, sir."

"Do you promise?"

"No."

"Jarvis!"

"Yes, sir?"

"I said *promise*. I can't do this again, see? You're too old to act this way, you're old enough to face things now, the way they are. When things come up in your life, you take them, you don't fight them. It's time you learned that, you're a man now."

Jarvie stood silent.

"Now, what are you going to do? It's going to be different, isn't it, from now on? You and I understand each other."

The boy's face was white. "As they get bigger," he said deliberately, " I'll tell them. Every one of them. Bert pretty soon, and then Betsy. And then – "

" For God's sake, Jarvie! Do you think I'm going to keep it forever? Did you think I wouldn't tell them myself? It was for your mother, she was too sick for it – "

" She'll always be too sick for it."

Simon started at the passion in the young voice.

" She's getting better already. I'll tell her right away; Charlot and I were saying the other night she was just about well enough – "

" She already knows."

Simon stared at him, lifted his hand.

" No, I didn't tell her. She just knew. I could tell today that she knew."

Simon put the whip on the wall, limp and curling, and went into the house. He went directly to Mercy's bed where she lay in the darkness; he knew she was awake without asking.

" Now you're some better, Mercy," he said, and fumbled bitterly, " there's something – about Charlot – "

She let him flounder, because she could not speak. The wash of icy blood in her was already familiar, after one day, creeping into the fingers, down the thighs. It was a motion in her, a movement of thought through the body that she had never known before this day.

She heard him explaining, about Brigham, about circumstance, about necessity, about another world, about Brother Joseph himself. And as he spoke, she was thinking: " He hates this, he hates it. He always hated these terrible emotional things that tore at him. Especially he hates woman-emotion, uncurbed and hysterical; he's like other men, he gets out of the room before it, he shuns it, embarrassed. He hates this and he's afraid of what I'm going to do."

When he was quiet, she whispered: " I know, Simon. I already knew."

They were still and she was aware how shaken he was.

" Come here, Simon, come close to me."

He loathed woman-emotion, he shunned it, loathing. She knew that if she wept, if she cried out and accused and begged and chided, he would be sharp against her, and that she could not have, not now. Even here she could conquer. This morning she would have been incapable of it, but now there was a cunning in her made of pain and desire and of a new unfamiliar hate.

She took his head against her chest, fondled his hair.

" It was wonderful of you, Simon," she said, " a wonderful thing to do. There wasn't anything else to do, really, and you were thinking of me and all of us. A woman like that, so different from you, Simon – I know how you've had to suffer."

He stiffened, unbelieving, and tried to lift his head, but her fingers still moved in his hair.

" But it doesn't need to spoil everything for us, Simon; it can make things better for us, really, as you intended it should. There'll be somebody to take charge of things and I can go with you more, to conference and to the school dancing, and when we're together there won't always be somebody wanting attention. You know how we used to say after Jarvie came – right from the start he was between us, wasn't he, even before he was born? Demanding and demanding until we weren't like we had been at first. Now it can be like the beginning – just us. Just closing the door and forgetting everything but being together."

He sat very still, she only felt the brushing of his hair against her face.

" Charlot's wonderful," she said. " Just wonderful at so many things. She's meant to keep a house, and Brother Brigham knew it. He's so practical."

She was aware now that her voice was rising, with tension,

with pose, and struggled to bring it down and make it casual again.

" You used to say: ' Some day I'll hire a housekeeper for you, Mercy, and then you can keep your hands soft and pretty like they were when we were married, and there'll not always be a meal a-getting.' You said I could play the pianoforte again, that you'd bring it out for me. Now it can be almost like that, Simon! "

" I've got to be fair to Charlot," he said, lamely.

" Why, of course, Simon. I insist on it! "

He moved away, stood up. " You better go to sleep," he said.

" You won't be long, Simon? "

" Just awhile. Charlot'll want to know I told you."

When he had gone out and closed the door, she lay waiting and listening. She did not hear the boys, only Simon and Charlot. It seemed hours and she did not move, afraid to move lest she lose the sound of their voices, one and then the other, mumbling. There was sometimes a silence and then the wash of ice in her, thoughts that circled, wheeling. But not sleep.

Once, remembering a thing she had read from the great blind poet Milton, she found his book on her table and leaned to it, holding the candle to the pages while she turned them. Here had been a great man, surely, a great man, and if a thing is right one bears it, then, and seeks the good in it:

" It appears to me sufficiently established . . . that polygamy is allowed by the law of God. Lest, however, any doubt should remain, I will subjoin abundant examples of men whose holiness renders them fit patterns for imitation, and who are among the lights of our faith."

Brother Joseph might almost have written this; surely he had seen it.

It was just as Eliza had said once: " If you discount this from Brother Joseph, then you discount everything; if you fight this, you fight everything."

If you shook this, you shook what had become the foundation of Simon's life, brought down the star he was following.

Then again she waited and she listened. Finally, helplessly, she called to him.

He came, tiptoeing in his ridiculously heavy way, the floor shrieking every time he set his foot, and she watched him, his face wavy behind the candle he carried. When he climbed into bed beside her, she reached out and touched him.

" Did you tell Charlot I knew? "

" She said she knew you knew. Women are funny – you can't tell them anything they don't know."

She stretched her arm over him, and he yawned. She thought fiercely: " He's got to talk to me now, and she can take her turn listening and wondering what we're saying."

She began to pat him gently in a way he always liked.

" Mercy, you'll tire yourself out. You better get some sleep. You're not near so strong as you make out to be."

She lay still, arrested. " What makes you think that, Simon? "

" Charlot said she could tell you weren't. She said you were pretty brave, weak as a cat the way you are and trying to get up and help this way. But you don't need to try being brave, Mercy – no use hurting yourself. You know, that's the whole idea, getting you well again. That's Charlot's idea and mine, too, and things are going just fine without you."

So Charlot knew the way, too. Mercy could hear her: " Mercy is mighty brave to try helping the way she does, weak as a cat, doing things that don't need doing – " Letting him know what a little unnecessary help it was, and her fumbling with it.

" Please, Simon," she whispered desperately. " I'm all right. Really I am – it was something about having the babies and that's all over; it was slow but it's over."

" You be sure, Mercy. There's no hurry, you know. And it's

true—everything we've done would be undone if you'd start out too soon."

She knew he quoted Charlot. "I'm all right. Really I am, Simon, I never felt stronger in my life. It's months since Sarah and Mary came."

She stretched against him, agonized. To make up for the hours of listening to his voice in there beyond her, the words muffled through the door and beyond her as his words had not been these years and years. She wanted to enclose him and clutch surely for him and feel him alive and possessed, which was what he had come to mean and would not cease meaning in a day or a thousand days. He put his arms around her, sensible of her desire, felt the sharp width of her shoulders, ran his big hands along her body, and she quivered under them with the unrhythmic quiver of a reflection in a pool.

He said fervently: "God, Mercy, you're skinny! You scare me, you're so skinny."

Then he kissed her lightly and turned over and said: "You'd better get some sleep."

She lay still, listening, staring up, and knew when he slept. Then she moved from his back carefully and got out of the bed, took the candle from the lowboy and went to the dying fire and lighted it. Then she found four new candles and lighted these, too, in a bright circle. The mirror Father had given her, clear and round, with silver intricate around the glass, she took from the chest, unwrapping it. Father's note was still pasted on the back of the handle: "For one who is beautiful." And Mother's little note, too: "Beauty is as beauty does."

Then she leaned down and studied her face, intently. Shadows under the eyes and under the cheekbones and the suggestion of horizontal line on either side of the mouth. She moved one of the candles close to her face, moved it around, studying and hurt. Then she slipped her gown down from her shoulders and held the mirror back. It was true, just as he had said. A startling thinness and a pale blue over the bones. When she leaned down, crouched to the mirror, her dry little breasts fell to points, the sweet soft firmness of young breasts gone as though it had flowed away with her milk into younger bodies. Only in pregnancy and during nursing months had they ever been full and curving, and now even the hard youth in them had been pressed out and they were two useless little bags of flesh, without beauty and beyond function.

She saw that her bones stood plain under the white skin, and knew that within there was something that was not right, swelling the joints and catching at the breath and suddenly annihilating light as it had that day when she stooped swiftly for the log and lifted it. Within there, something. Gnawing and sucking at strength itself. She drew back from the vision of herself, and knew that she was afraid of it for the first time. She was afraid of dependence on it and aware of a strong physical repugnance to herself. This material thing that held her, it could give completely or withhold completely; there was nothing to be done, nothing to change.

She blew the candles out at last and went to lie at Simon's back, shivering.

Chapter XXXVI

Mercy steadied herself in the doorway. " It's a good wind, a good whipping wind. I like to hang clothes in a wind like that; every time washday comes I hope for a wind."

Charlot spoke amiably. " It's not good for the clothes, though. They don't get the benefit of the sun much and the wind wears them. Every time washday comes, I hope for some good quiet sun."

Mercy smiled because it was like everything between them, and very inevitability gave it bitter humor. " Maybe so," she said. " But all the same, I like to hang clothes in a good wind. And since some washdays are windy, I'd as well like it."

" Like it all you want, of course," Charlot said, " but that doesn't make it good for the clothes."

Mercy pinned the clothes carefully and strongly because the wind almost took them from her hands. For a little while, here with the wind blowing around her, she could be something past that she had not been for a long time. She was free here and untensed, like a bow loosened. The days inside the house, inert smoldering and every last little thing swollen into importance – they refused to come outside into the clean wind with her. They waited for her on the doorstep when she returned, she knew, and she would not have it different even though she suffered. Because the battle was sustaining her. There was a future thing to be fought for and her strength was holding to the task, miraculously, the way an ant's strength will persist at a mountain-crumb lodged imperturbably in its doorway.

A small thing – the waffle iron on a different hook.

"I always kept it here; of course, I keep looking for it, why shouldn't I? It was a place made for it from the beginning –"

"A waffle iron, I should think, would hang on a hook by the kettles."

"It was only that from the beginning –"

"It's a matter of principle, really. When the second place is better than the first place, you change, don't you? That's progress, the only way we grow is making changes."

The cups facing a different way on the hooks, the plates piled in a different corner of the cupboard; it was nothing and everything. The broom, even the broom – "If you would stand it on the handle instead of on the straw, Mercy, it'd last longer, wouldn't get crushed –"

Father's painting of the sea, the only bit of sea existing any more, and not a masterpiece, but the sea and Father's sea – even this must hang where it had never hung before, so that when you glanced up in the old way, needing to see it, it was not there. The place by the door where it had hung must be free for the row of pegs so folks could have their coats handy going out. Under protest, Charlot imperturbably carried the picture from place to place, her head on one side, considering. "You see how much better the light is from the north." And then there was the maddening conviction that she was right, and the remembrance of Father himself hanging it so, with north light on it. Then giving in, with words crusted and crisp.

"What boy wants a patch that sings out a mile at everybody?" So Charlot said, and wisely, ripping out old patches and cutting the undersides of pockets and underhem bits for new mending; when she stitched them intricately in place nobody would know about a hole at all without close looking.

Betsy said: " Can I go to Yeaman's before dinner – can I? "

Charlot answered first, out of habit, from weeks of responsibility. " No, Betsy, there isn't time before dinner."

Then Betsy looked at Mercy, snake-quick, seeking and begging. " Mamma, *can* I? Just for the littlest time, only for long enough – "

" Oh – " Mercy did not look at Charlot and it was agony not to look at her because she knew Charlot's look waited. " I don't see why not, if you're back instantly at twelve. That's not long, half an hour. Tell Mrs. Yeaman half an hour, Betsy." The insistence was half conciliation but half defiance, pressing home a seniority.

And then twelve o'clock came and Betsy was not back and Charlot set the table, Betsy's job, with elaborate haste, and the dinner got cold and Bert had to be sent to Yeaman's after his sister. And in Mercy then there was an unreasonable weakness, half shame, as though she had passed through a crisis. It was impossible, the little things that were continual crises, and each time a victor seizing triumph and laying it plainly in sight.

Not words always, but looks darting and dropping, and furtive eye-dabbing, even the boys' praise for their mother's cooking and their appetites, once so natural and wonderful, becoming significant beyond normal significance. Simon was carefully outside all this, but outside the way a man is outside his burning house, deeply involved in it.

The cool wet sheets lashed into Mercy's face and she loved the frankness of the battle with them, clutching them and subduing them with pins. She reached up richly, leaned to the basket with abandon, and the air was moving and tremendous everywhere.

She reached up again, and stood still, paralyzed. Then she sank down by the basket, leaning, her breath swift and unheard in the wind. After a time it was over, and she rose white-faced and finished the basketful. No abandon then, no full-bodied action, but a slow care and an intimate knowledge of ease. It passed. Walking slowly, leaning on things a little as she went by them, she came to the door, gripped the frame for a moment, and then went in.

"Oh, Mercy, I wonder if you'd mind kneading this a minute – I've got to see to that butter."

She went to the table and began handling the dough. She could feel the sharp thudding in her neck, but pressed her body hard against the table. It was a mass of dough, a mountain. She pressed her palms into it, doubled it, pressed again. When it was ready, she called Betsy to bring the pans. And the grease pot. Betsy helped smear the pans, helped press the dough into parts and roll each into its loaf. When they were finished, Mercy sat down and Betsy carried them near the fire for her and covered them to rise, in a long row.

"That's nice, Betsy. You're getting big enough to help with so many things. First thing you know, you'll make the bread yourself. Won't I be proud to have a daughter big enough to keep house!"

"Then Aunt Charlot can go home again," Betsy said pleasantly.

Charlot looked up and her eyes and Mercy's met, cleanly and sharply, understanding each other. Mercy almost said: "No, it was Betsy's idea this time, I didn't tell her." But of course such things were never said.

Charlot looked up at the clock. "It's eleven already!" and she ran for the basket to take to the cellar for vegetables. "Betsy, bring the pitcher and the big spoon." She called back: "Mercy, maybe you'd better be finishing that butter."

"Betsy –"

But Betsy had already disappeared, behind Charlot. It was fun to go to the cellar when there was skimming to do – fun! fun! fun! – over the big round pans. Mercy heard her gay little voice as she went around the house and then the muffled tune going down the steps and the abrupt close of it, underground.

Wearily she got up and walked to the churn. It was easy, really. And she took the handle and began lifting it up and down, up and down. Maybe if one could lean on something – it was too high to sit down. She looked at the table and leaned over to drag the churn across the little space. Of such a small thing to be bitterly afraid – but slowly, slowly, with both arms around the churn.

When Charlot and Betsy came back, she was half-sitting by the table, very pale, and her arms moved steadily and the cream splashed with the light rhythm of splashing around the heavy rhythm of the paddle. She could feel the butter coming.

THE GREATEST battle of all was preventing the small series of crises, the perpetual series, from becoming all she spoke about to Simon himself. At night the little things reared themselves and marched, an army in review.

" Simon, I have always – "

" It's having your ways changed, it's awkward for you! "

In spite of herself, the solution was suggested. " There's her house in Nauvoo – I'm so much better, Simon."

But such a suggestion did not exist for Simon. And she came to understand why it could not. He must not be the first to fail, or the second, even, or the last. With the word of God, one did not fail unless one could forget Brother Joseph entirely and his bitter denouncement of those who were not strong enough to bear the heat of the fire. The blessed were those who bore the burden in the heat of the day. A man could tell himself: " In this, Brother Joseph might have been mistaken, in this only. The great sharing is the truth I have felt to the marrow of my bones; the working together is beautiful and true; the eternal conquering of the personal man, from star to star, from world to world, from æon to æon, it is the only truth that does not carry death in the ultimate thought. Perhaps in this alone Brother Joseph was mistaken – this principle that brings sharing into every moment and every hour and forces even love to unnatural unselfishness." But then it came to you: " Why should love alone be allowed selfishness? " For a man it is even unnatural – did not most men cast their eyes on many women, suffering under their instincts and the burden of the other commandment? And did God smile on the rows of woman-bodies, unused and lonely? Did He smile on those others sitting by their windows with candles burning before them, and the men passing and looking and presently furtively tapping, and then the doors opened and the candles snuffed? Did He smile upon the smug wife passing by these houses with her market basket on her arm and her face averted with shame for her own kind? Before the first terrible misstep, a simple ceremony that gave sanction and invested pleasure with responsibility. It seemed a simple solution. Then *was* Brother Joseph wrong in this, was he wrong to try harnessing an instinct for the production of men, preventing it at the same time from doing shame to all men? Was he wrong then in harnessing an energy like that in Charlot Leavitt, energy being spent on a lone house and a lone body and spent in loneliness? Why should not this be harnessed and used in the service of mankind, as men catch the energy of a river and make use of it?

A man finds it hard to apply the ideal to the specific; the ultimate is remote from the immediate; this day is a small ingredient in eternity, but it seems very large. A man must project himself, he must think: " This also is the road and I am moving; there is no experience, after all, that is not part of the final experience."

It was of great importance to learn harmony, to seek it, to bring men together in this pursuit, in that pursuit, in play, in work, in building, in living every hour. Let a man lean on another man, break his first feeling of final isolation, teach him that Brother and Sister are everything. Make him see that Man Alone is likely to be Lucifer, but Men Together are God. If a man is alone and grows rich, he will lay his heel on his brother's neck. If he is alone and grows poor, he will starve and freeze and hate. He must feel Brotherhood – he must know: " We are all sons of a common Sire " – and then there can be neither rich nor poor. And he must know that the great paternalism is not spread benignly over one island or even over one continent, it is everywhere. Every Man and a Single Sire. No war, lest a man have a brother's blood on his hands. No contention, for would not every man have his brother clothed and fed? No arrogance, for is not one brother of the same blood as another brother?

Simon thought of these things and spoke of them tentatively to his family, sometimes stumbling over the vastness of their importance. Without every hand could the Temple have been built or even started? Without every hand how can the world be made perfect? World harmony, world perfection, is the ultimate destiny of this life for every man, and his strength and his intellect are part of a common store of energy. And when the world is made perfect, endowed with superior sight and a strength added upon with the use of long building, we must pursue the further destiny and perfect the structures of the stars.

All this pushed the day-by-day turbulence into a pitiless obscurity, for the time being. But sight is not habitually keyed to heights and depths; the real and the sudden obliterate everything beyond themselves.

" You can hold up a penny," Mercy thought, " and it will hide the sun.

" I am not All, I am only One. I am One and I suffer. I am One and I am in pain. I am One and I am afraid."

What had the cups and the plates and the broom and the

hurt look and the sharp tongue to do with eternity? Patience, Simon said, and without patience how can men hope to mend the world and own the universe? All day long he thought of these things while he worked hauling timber and making fences and doing the thousand things that used his body-strength and made him sleepy enough to drop into senseless satisfaction on his bed at night.

But around him, over him, the little things still reared themselves and marched, an army in review. Mercy watched for him to wake. Yet when they were spoken aloud, taken one by one, they sounded silly and bitter. And Simon had a way of listening with his lips tight and his eyes cold. Then he would say: "Well? What do you expect me to do about it? It's between you and Charlot, I should think."

Once he grew angry. "When things like this are in a house, we know who's moved in with us. It's Lucifer! I'd swear I saw him with my own eyes, going in the doors ahead of me or climbing in at the windows!"

"Oh, Simon, that sounds childish, you know better—"

"Satan's first trick is to make us think there isn't any Satan, and then we don't watch out for him. Then he can crawl right inside of us and we don't know the difference till it's too late."

"I only said—"

"Mercy, honest to goodness, I'd swear he'd crawled right inside of you, always finding fault, always telling tales, always complaining—"

He did not look at her or he would have started at the pain upon her face. But what he said only served to stifle her words, not her feelings. She thought, and longed to say it but dared not: "If the Devil's in this house, he came in with Charlot Leavitt. I never saw him here before she came."

Chapter XXXVII

Charlot stood motionless, looking into Jarvie's set face.

" I'll tell your father, Jarvie Baker, and he'll beat the stuffing out of both of you! "

She was hysterical today, which was strange for Charlot. In her voice was even a suggestion of tears, and Charlot was not one to cry.

" I'd rather be beat by Father than bossed by you."

There were no tears in Jarvie's voice. The strain that changed Charlot was changing him also, softening him when he was alone but encrusting him when he was with her, as though he drew a shell over himself for protection against the ways she could hurt him, and to harden the blows he could give back. Lately, like Mother, he had a feeling that a judgment was approaching, a final crisis built of perpetual small crises. Charlot's tears testified to it.

" Perhaps you'd rather be bossed by your father and beat by me? "

It was part of her hysteria, the way she turned to the hearth and seized the poker and ran to him, flourishing it. It was a thing the real Charlot would never have ruffled her dignity by doing, and when he seized her wrists in his hands and wrung them until the poker dropped, she stood there gasping. Then she lifted her foot, wildly, unreasonably, the way a girl fights in the battle of pretend with her young man. He caught her foot, too, and she screamed, hopping like an enraged hen. And Jarvie laughed, releasing her. He laughed until tears ran and he shouted with laughter and went red with laughter, while Charlot stood unbelieving.

She could have borne anything but such an affront to her dignity and power. Before supper-time she had gone. There was not even her bonnet on its peg by the door, or her big calico apron.

Jarvis himself told Simon, trying to keep the laughter out of the syllables.

Simon did not scold or even ejaculate. He simply got up and took his hat and coat and left the house and they saw him going down the bluff.

" It was her fault," Mercy said. But she was afraid, now that the crisis was over. She put the children to bed and tried to enjoy being alone with this task. And then Menzo sat working with his knife on the chest, intricately, adept among lines that would have confused another boy, and Jarvie read aloud. They did not speak of Simon, but all were waiting, and Jarvis read from the novel of *Clarissa* as though to ease them with a recital of another's troubles. Only Bert thought of sleep, and he sprawled on the hearth with his head on his two arms.

When Simon came back, he brought Charlot with him. And Charlot's bundles, just the way they had come the first night. He brought her to the fire and the two of them warmed themselves before he spoke. Then he said: " Jarvis, this is a matter between you and Charlot. I don't want it to happen again."

Jarvis said nothing, but Charlot looked at him. " I'm sorry, Jarvis," she said. " I was wrong."

" Charlot says she's willing to do her part," Simon said. And stung by the general silence, he said seriously: " I want Lucifer out of this house! "

Charlot went to Mercy and kissed her. Mercy did not move

or look up. It was so unexpected, the crisis they had worked for suddenly smoothed over like this when it had no right to be smoothed over, no possibility of being smooth in this world or another.

" I want to tell you," Simon said, " that Charlot is the one to be considered now."

He was almost pompous, but his fingers were nervous and he looked into the fire. " Charlot is going to have a child," he said.

Mercy's cheeks flared and she touched them with her fingers and then folded her hands in her lap, fearing betrayal.

Simon stood looking at Jarvie. " This child will be your brother or sister, an innocent child that deserves all our love and care."

Mercy thought: " He feels like God already." But she could not help seeing that Charlot, too, was pale and shaken.

" She's too old to start having babies! " And then Mercy thought, less bitterly: " It'll likely be hard on her."

SIMON prayed aloud and his family knelt about him as always. When they rose, Mercy sat at the table with her sewing and Jarvie sat close, using the same candle for writing, and Menzo worked by the fire and Bert and Simon tackled some problems. Almost, from all an outsider might see, as though nothing had changed.

But there was a tenseness which even the children felt. It was as though the circle that had flowed endlessly and easily, the circle that had been a whole and simple thing, had struck an encumbrance and had stopped turning, like a broken hoop. Even customary things were invested with a kind of awkwardness; as lovers will kiss, self-consciously and without passion, under eyes.

" She doesn't know," Mercy thought fiercely, " she doesn't

know what she's done to this. The calm of it, the peace, the utter whole peace of it. And Simon with shame in his face and even in his shoulders, the shame that won't let him look at me, that won't give us ease any more. She doesn't know."

And fairness told her: "She couldn't know."

In the silence the queer little whistle of the ferry was sharp and clear. Abruptly Jarvie stood up. They all looked at him, but he said nothing, only went out of the door.

"He can't stand it," Mercy thought.

Simon frowned down at the paper, but said nothing.

After a time Menzo got up as silently and went out. "They walk together," Mercy thought enviously, but she knew she would not go if she could, not away from Simon. Even with that crust of shame and darkness between them, he was Simon and her Simon and would always be. She would never be the one to leave what was left of the circle, charmed once and flowing peacefully.

❧ ❧ ❧

Charlot must not reach and Charlot must not stoop and Charlot must not carry. But Charlot herself laughed after the first weeks of nausea were over and declared that she had never felt better in her life. She grew as some women do with child, widening like a flower and with every quality of bloom in her—rich-blooded and bright-eyed and clear-skinned and obviously happy.

Mercy chided herself for jealousy. "Let her have the babies, now, let her have the waiting and the last pain and all of it." But then always it came to her: "And let her have the time just after and sit in the little rocker for nursing with her big white breast out of her dress. Let her have Simon coming to see his child and let her have the utter depth of rest and let her have the first time of laying her finger on a cheek incredibly soft and let her have the looking at a certain curve of ear and say: 'Simon's.' "

But she spoke no more to Simon of little things. Lucifer had apparently been chased from Simon Baker's house. He did not stalk the kitchen, at least openly. If ever he caught anybody's eye, it was from a corner, furtively. What Charlot had begun with her apology, her kiss, was the beginning of the Era of Man's Patience. Mercy described it in these words. The victor was humble, for in this battle the crown went to the humble; therefore the vanquished did not seek another battle, but was humble also.

The Era of Man's Patience. Mercy took her journal down and wrote: " Progression may be charted on its way. Here in this house on the bluffs of Iowa, we look over the world in which we have instituted the E. of M. P., and know our united energy moves the world toward Perfection."

Simon thought this very beautiful. Menzo thought it very obscure and Jarvie caught his breath over it, for some reason he did not mention.

But it was a few days after this was written that the Era of Man's Patience really began for her. She had been spinning for hours. Walking back and forth with the wool, barefooted, because nobody wasted good shoe leather, or wool socks, either, at spinning. The wheel droned and the thread stretched out.

Zeez, zeez, zeez. It was a song a woman remembered all night after a long day. Unusually often, today, the twist went wrong and had to be done over.

" Here, let me help you," Charlot said once, very kindly.

" I get sleepy, that's all."

" It makes a person sleepy. Maybe you'd better go sleep a little while."

" I'm all right now."

Zeez, zeez – It kept time to something in a woman, turning around hugely in her brain like flies in a sunny room. She was aware of a heaviness first, after the drawn weary joints which were part of spinning, and then she knew it was happening and tried to draw back with her hand out to prevent it. The twist was destroyed in her fingers and the thread followed wildly after the wheel for a moment. That was all, except Charlot running. And crying out.

Chapter XXXVIII

CHARLOT came to the door of Mercy's room and whispered: "Portia Glazier and Melissa Vermazon are here; do you feel like seeing anybody?"

"Portia and Melissa? Well – not both *together*, Charlot." And when Charlot had turned away, she thought: "There's something I get from each of them, but never when they're together."

Portia first, with her signet of sorrow. Looking up at her, Mercy saw her differently and it came to her: "This way a child sees grown faces, always from a little lower and they aren't the same." You saw this way that Portia had an uncertain chin that shook when she spoke, and you saw it rounding rather than long. You saw the under side of her bonnet, too, where clung a row of faded cloth violets.

"I'm sorry to see you down like this, Sister Baker. We'd have been to see you weeks ago if they hadn't of told us you shouldn't have comp'ny."

"I'm sure you would, Portia."

"After all, some of us are made for one thing and some for another."

Mercy did not help her, although she saw with what difficulty Portia spoke, desiring as she did to say just the proper thing and her real thoughts rising in her helplessly.

" What does Dr. Richards say, Sister Baker? We heard you were bedridden for good and all, and it was more than we could believe. I said I'd have to hear it from the doctor — "

" Dr. Richards is wise enough to tell other people more than he tells me, I suppose."

Portia's face reddened. " It's all hearsay," she said hurriedly; " folks *will* stretch things."

" Were they stretching what I just heard about you? " It seemed impossible to Portia, under the circumstances, that Mercy Baker could twinkle over a question, but she was twinkling over this one.

" Depends on what you've been hearing."

" About you marrying John Smith."

Portia's color gradually improved. " He's an old man, John is, and there's nobody to do for him since his wife died." Then she added: " John's been high in the Priesthood in his time."

" He's wonderful at his music now — nobody better."

Portia reached out and took one of the foot posters between her curled thumb and forefinger and ran them gently up and down.

" I believe," Mercy said, " that there's still a great deal of happiness in the world for you, Portia. Perhaps a person should never stop thinking so; he never knows."

" It's not a question of happiness," Portia said stiffly, " it's getting along. It seemed to me like I'd rather move now than wait till we all have to go and there's no place for us all to move into. And the Church the way it is, you never know how long there'll be a Church to turn to."

" You're not thinking very optimistically, after all, Portia."

" It's not thinking, it's knowing." The negative and then the quick positive were like Portia. " But I'm not marrying for the next world, Sister Baker, I made sure of that. With Charles it said *for time and eternity;* this one'll say *time*. We'll both have our firsts when we die."

Mercy smiled. " It's a good thing to make sure."

" Now, if Charles has a wife keeping him company till I get there, that's all right with me. I'm not one to be selfish, I hope. But I don't want any question about whose wife *I* am, over there. Charlie just wouldn't like it, me coming along in with Old John."

As their work would be continuous, so would their problems. Nothing, then, would be easy and solved, but only on another plane and defined with reference to new conditions. Mercy had heard many problems about heaven discussed weightily as though being of great immediate importance. If one man will rule over all his posterity, as God rules over us, what posterity will his sons have to rule over? If a woman inherits her husband's priesthood in another world, what shall the single woman inherit who has served faithfully and unselfishly? If a woman's children belong to the first husband, killed soon after marriage *in the Church*, what of the second husband who is loved with another and superior love and is flesh-father to those children? It was fascinating to consider eternity a practical problem – it had endless possibilities. It was better than planning a changed society in this world, even, because you started at scratch and nothing was impossible.

Brother Joseph, infallible authority on the qualities and conditions of another world, actually saw it all with his two eyes in vision and used to answer questions like this glibly and certainly. But there were questions that had occurred too late to be put to him, questions that had therefore no written answers in the Covenants. And Brother Brigham had a way of shaking his shaggy head and saying only: " You live the best you can in this world; everything will be all right."

But you did not *know*. Some folks did a deal of worrying over it.

" Maybe it would have been a good thing, Portia, if you had

been forced to learn to share Charles in this world – then the other one wouldn't worry you so much."

"Oh, it don't worry me, Mrs. Baker – I just wanted to be sure it'd just be Time with Old John. Charles was a mighty jealous man, he always was." This with pride. In Portia, it seemed impossible, but there it was. A man had loved her, loved her to the point of fierce jealousy, and it was still a pride in her.

"Now me, I'd not be jealous, like I said. If Charles has a woman keeping him company till I die, and after, even, that's all right. Like if you made a fuss over that lovely Charlot Leavitt – it'd be pretty ungrateful, now wouldn't it?"

"Like the dog in the manger," Mercy said, thinking of Eliza. "Only, Portia, it always seemed to me that there was something to the dog's side of it. A property right, really. Maybe the straw kept him warm even though he couldn't eat it."

Portia stared at her. Then she bustled about her gloves, which were tan and lace, apparently a relic of other times. "I'm overstayin' myself – Charlot said only a minute – said you were so unstrung lately."

She hesitated in the doorway. "All the same," she said with a puzzled air, "he *couldn't* eat it, could he?"

Mercy wondered at Melissa coming to this house at all. Because here, only a little while ago, the legend had been destroyed and the fairy godmother stripped of her mystery. There had been cold rain; the day before even freezing and rain together until the world for a few hours was a miracle of arrested dripping. But that night a south wind and water streaming from everywhere and the ground bogged and boot-printed. It had been nearly midnight, and Sarah fretful with the colic, when Mercy heard the Darling Lady: "Darling, darling, don't cry, darling."

There had been the sound of someone rolling heavily out of bed onto the floor, and Mercy had thought at first it must be

Simon. But it was Charlot's voice she heard when the door opened. " You go on home and mind your own business! The idea, coming around like that this time of night yelling in folks' windows! "

Then silence and Charlot scolding to Simon, who was dividing his nights evenly, now, in the manner prescribed for polygamist husbands. " The idea, that Melissa Vermazon! There ought to be a place to put folks when their heads stop serving them! "

It had been a pretty legend and a service of love to fill lonely nights with. Mercy kept thinking of the boy who lost the fairies because he went a-peeping. There is a penalty for curiosity – loss of the legend, loss of the fairies themselves.

But today it appeared that Melissa was not absorbed in herself enough to be humiliated.

" Your little girl," she said when she came in to Mercy, " she's better, now. And fat, like a baby should be."

" As soon as I stopped trying to nurse her, she got better. It almost seemed as if I were poisoning her, Melissa."

" It's hard to have just the one of them," Melissa said, and for the first time Mercy felt that someone else understood the full horror of the dismembership of Two. Once in a great while there are two creatures that do not really exist separately, but cease when they are parted, like the great lovers of antiquity. About the twins had been that feeling, and Sarah was never complete for her mother; there was always a blank at her side.

" Are you moving to Nauvoo when Portia goes? "

Melissa shook her head. " Nobody'll bother me, Sister Baker. There's nothing for the gentiles to take off me if they came. A bit later I'll plant me a garden."

About the Darling Lady, Mercy could not bring herself to speak, after all. But when Melissa turned to go, she said: " Come to see Sarah again, Melissa. And tell Charlot I said you were to hold her all you wished."

" It's hard, just having the one of them," Melissa said.

" But it's like Simon tells me, Melissa, I just lost one and you lost four – all you had."

Melissa's eyes were dry and bright, the yellow balls showing.

" Listen, Melissa, go over there where my Bible is and get me the papers under it. There's a Patriarchal Blessing there that Brother Joseph's father gave to Jarvie just before he died."

Melissa brought the papers and Mercy looked through them until she found the one she wanted. " I'll read it to you – I've read it a thousand times since Mary went, and it helps me. Maybe it'll help you, too."

As she read it, she could hear the quavering voice that had first spoken it, the sick old voice and its terrible sincerity. " You will live, if you abide by the Gospel of Jesus Christ, to see the day of resurrection. You will see the graves give up their dead. You will see the second coming of Christ, who cometh in a blaze of glory."

Jarvie had been young enough then so that the words were not so much idea as picture – the figures, the hill where the graves were, the last incline looking down over the backwaters dotted with yellow lilies; thunder, perhaps, and lightning certainly, because there must be an unspeakable brightness. And after Mary died, old as Jarvie was then, he read it with the picture still alive in it, but one figure standing plainer than the others, little and white at the crest of the hill. There was blood in her veins, a refined blood, distilled, indestructible, as Brother Joseph insisted, and she was coming toward the house along the path with her white feet barely touching the grass as she came.

Melissa wiped her eyes and blew her nose. Mercy hardly heard her say good-by, but she saw them going down the bluff, along the steep path, Melissa and Portia together.

" I've got a feeling," Portia said, " that Mercy Baker won't live to be much older than she is."

Melissa started. " I don't like such things said."

" Feel 'em, you might as well say 'em. All I know is she's lucky to have a woman like Charlot to leave her family with. You could eat an egg off her floor."

Melissa was silent.

Portia stumbled and gathered her skirts up to keep them from naked brambles along the path. " I declare, I felt up there just the way I felt the day of the Wolf Hunt in Missouri – a feeling like somebody in that house was going to die."

" Maybe the baby, then." Melissa spoke almost hopefully, thinking of Two.

Portia looked at her sharply.

" We'll see the graves give up their dead," Melissa said, almost casually.

" Melissa Vermazon, you're crazy as a loon."

" Sister Baker just read it to me."

" She did! " Portia stopped in the path and looked back up the hill, disturbed. " You see, we've *all* got the same feeling! "

Presently she said: " I've got some chicken boiling. When John comes, I'll send him on up with some broth for her supper."

It rained toward evening, and when Old John came uphill with a pot of broth from Portia Glazier, he was wet and Mercy insisted he sit by her fire and get dried before he went out again. He protested that he'd only get wetter after a while, but he was glad to sit for a mite of rest after that hill.

As he sat, the hands that knew the strings so intimately trembled on the head of his cane. At rest and unexcited by attention, age possessed him utterly. There was a quivering in all his limbs and a watery film over his eyes, which were very blue. The hair emerged from his chin in prodigal white abundance and red broken lines of skin stretched over his cheekbones. Between his fingers the skin was almost transparent, with a delicate purple coloring, and his nails had been cut to the quick with a pocket-knife and were thick as horn. His upper lip had fallen in where the teeth were lost, and appeared to lie in tucks, giving him the look of one who makes a wry face over a perpetual sour flavor. In him Mercy sensed a quality apart from the physical man, the indefinable quality of age that can lie upon an inanimate thing as well as upon a man of flesh and blood. John had seen the American Revolution, and he had seen Haun's Mill, too, he said — the first a war for the freedom of man and the second a massacre, a symbol of man's subjection. He did not try to reconcile the two any more, and he did not speak of them with emotion as a younger man speaks of the great events in his life, but rather with a mildness devoid of any feeling at all. The Revolution — it was apparently no more significant to Old John than the dinner he ate yesterday. Even of his own passing he spoke without real interest — " one of these days," he said, as though it were inevitable and therefore unimportant. For himself and of himself he had no more emotion. Occasionally a return of pride, but no more and quickly over.

It had occurred to Mercy in the first fear and uncontrollable anguish of knowing that she was caught within a body that refused to give her any longer what she still desired from it, that perhaps she was old already, that perhaps there was no real difference between sickness and age. After all, is not age merely a sickness of the body? What is the difference, after all, between swift change wrought by sickness and slow change wrought by years? Two bits of silk, one worn by use and the other by time — would not the sickness in the silk be the same, a loosening of threads, a breaking through?

She knew that, at least for a great time, motion must cease for her more completely than for Old John here, much more completely, and when motion must cease, there would be thinking swollen in importance to the sole excitement. She was to move from an active world into a passive one, except as she lived by proxy the lives of her children. It was a great transition and she bent herself to it with the emotion she brought to everything, an emotionalized intellect. First of all, the task of minimizing the body. It could not be obliterated when there was a cough that had nothing to do with the spirit but racked only the body — a midnight cough when the body was important beyond reasonable importance, stretched out full-length in the dark. A stricture of the throat, too, unless the shoulders and head were lifted against many pillows, and the body swelling itself out of proportion to its former size and importance, literally softening the joints with swelling. And there was nothing but the body when one must crouch upon the chamber and strain for difficult urine.

The body would not be obliterated. But it might be minimized with the pure excitement, even the pure gayety of thought. The eyes did not fail nor the ears nor the swift response to stimulus. Outside herself were a million things that had nothing to demand from the luxury of motion. Sarah on the foot of the bed playing with her string of buttons — there, look at that, there is a child, living and absorbed and making sounds that mean seeking, retrieving, enjoying. Before dawn, the loneliest time, the soft maple outside the window came suddenly alive and brimmed with voices. And then, after a while, a squirrel began a ceaseless pilgrimage up and down, never failing to pause on the window ledge to show her the spoils in his cheek. And there were Betsy's questions all day, questions to ponder over before answering sometimes. And evenings, the boys, Jarvie beginning now to talk out of himself.

She was thankful for Old John. Because she saw tonight that she was different from him, and her sickness different from age. True age was a blunting of faculties, a blunting of even the capacity for dread or pain. If it were not so, the sound of the old ones from their corners would fill the world and tear our hearts out of us. Some kind power had laid cotton in their skulls and turned their blood to milk. It left, for most of them, only the kind promise of waking and finding themselves young and fair and brave again.

It occurred to her that perhaps her sickness, of the two, was the more to be pitied, but she shook that thought away.

Just before John left, she said: " It's too bad you can't see my river – it's lovely from this window, daytimes."

She listened anxiously for what Old John would say, and when he spoke he said what she hoped to hear.

" Oh, the river – " Relaxed old voice, unstressed. " Guess I'm used to the river, never see it any more."

THAT night Melissa Vermazon died. Nobody knew exactly how it happened, but following her prints in the mud, there was a fairly clear story. She had gone on one of those wild excursions of hers, seemed like, and went past Baker's cabin. She hadn't made a sound – everybody testified to that, and Charlot Leavitt had been up with the baby, too, and hadn't slept most of the night, not feeling good herself. And then Melissa had gone on up the bluff and, starting down, had lost her footing above Stony Hollow and had fallen directly over the cliff. She must have struck her head many times, because it was badly bruised and one cheek was open and bleeding.

When Portia heard of it, she reverted to an old habit that should have been torn from her by an ancient conversion. " She the same as said it would happen," and Portia crossed herself.

Chapter XXXIX

It was a wonderful thing to go plunging down the bluff, not seeing the path or anything, digging heels in and the sensation of falling, yet not falling, stiffening the knees and digging the heels in. Jarvie went first and Menzo right behind him, and then Bert, still struggling with his jacket. There was one core of the night world, a blazing tower below them, and they moved to it in a straight line, tearing brambles and bushes before them and stumbling. There was only one sight, that fluctuating red, and the ground did not know it, but only the sky beyond there, billowing smoke and flinging sparks.

The ground leveled under Jarvie's feet and he bent his knees then, and ran with the feeling of abrupt descent still sick in his legs. Running through the tense red air was wonderful and he felt his heart hard in him and high.

Was anything ever like a fire in the night? Was anything ever?

People were running from all directions, the men and boys first, half-dressed, and the women struggling after with their hair half-braided and shawls and quilts thrown around them. Instantly a line of men was built from the blaze to the river and they handed buckets of impotent water along with incredible swiftness, from hand to hand. To one knot of nightgowns and hysteria the women went – to the Yeaman women, whose house it was that burned this night.

Nothing saved but the bed-quilts that were on the beds themselves, and didn't it serve Susie Yeaman right for saving all the good ones in her big chest and making the family use the old ones? Portia Glazier spoke thus, and a few others, but to some Susie Yeaman's face was a sight not to forget. Incredulous distress, a deprived child. And Snarl's ugly face screwed up like a rabbit's.

Even the ordinary bed-quilts were taken now by the men when the flames crept toward the outhouses. Once a thin angry streak began to climb the barn and they whipped it with wet quilts and it yielded.

" How'd it start? "

" When'd they find it? "

" How'd it get on so fast? "

Jarvie stood in the line, taking his turn at the buckets, his heart high and exultant with the glory of the red night. He was sorry; there was Snarl's stricken face and Susie looking the way a mother looks by a casket, and there was Polly Yeaman crying and throwing her hands like Ophelia, and it was a terrible thing to be happy – but all the same it was wonderful to see the pillar of red and the bluff waving eerily through the smoke and heat, and the river a sheet of melted brass. Even the birds were out, wild with excitement, going like rockets from tree to tree. He felt the broad wood handles of the buckets passing through his hands, the splash of water cold on his ankles, and the gradual drenching of his side. He heard the dull sound when a timber yielded and fell headlong into the flames and a new glory of tongues came up licking at the red air. It was all one sensation, a bright hour in time for all the tragedy implicit in it. He felt himself part of the fight against an enemy commanding fervent respect, felt himself part of a time lifted out of night and illuminated with terror and beauty.

" Like it was started from four corners at once! "

" All of a sudden it was all ablaze and it was all we could do to get out – "

The buckets kept moving, pathetic in inadequacy, while the roof sagged, groaning, and fell in. A high sound came from Polly Yeaman.

Susie sat abruptly on the ground and in her face was an intimate knowledge of all that was gone. A man never knows all a house holds, but a woman knows from the intimacy of use, she knows the feel of a thousand things in her hands and they are part of her hands and of her skill. In the smoke went her white shams and her table-linen, and out of the ashes her spoons would emerge, blackened and twisted. All the little things brought together gradually through years of progressing need. With every child another spoon, another pillow, another space for sleeping, until this whole blazing house had been minutely dedicated. Susannah and Huldah and Electa and Araminta and Eda and Sara and Polly and Charity and the boy. That Charity, this minute she ought to be in her bed with those sniffles and she ought to have her mouth slapped for talking so loud out of a smarty sense of importance.

" Kept dreamin' I was hotter 'n' hotter."

" I yelled at Father – "

" Mother said we'd got to get the chest out and Eda and me, we dragged it nearly to the door."

Jarvie could hear them, the sharp little tributaries flowing into the main stream of interest, feeding it. Every girl had her tale, taking her toll of importance, but Susie never said anything, staring at the house with the loss of a thousand things in her face. There were the piles of hopeful trousseau and the hours of stitching. Stitches every woman in the settlement had been anxious over, to make hers shorter and straighter, more even than anyone else's. Every quilt had been a finale of searching and collecting and planning and building; a tower of calico scraps in that one for Susannah, the big one that would touch the floor on either side of a double four-poster. And that other that Polly had dreamed of using in summer, silk that met the chin as cold as glass. Stitches and battings saved from scarce wool and calico and silk. Stars and flowers and little ships with sails of white silk and rings and patchwork put together with cat-stitch in bright colors. The one ardor Susie Yeaman had, packing quilts away in the huge chest Snarl had made a-purpose to hold them. There was other fancywork, too, from the agile fingers of all the Yeaman girls, shams with lace and initials, throws with crocheting five inches deep, colored embroideries. But mostly the quilts, Susie thought, and stared and said nothing.

There were no theories among the men, but one certainty. There had been a town meeting at Warsaw; the antis had come all excited and the first handy house got their torches. Some Brothers said belatedly how they thought they had heard horses going through. Looked like another blaze to the southeast.

Simon was quiet among them, because he knew certainly that this blaze had not been intended for Snarl's house, but for another house, up the bluff a little.

THE BUCKETS stopped and the house lay smoldering, a hot black heap of debris. Jarvis went closer, kicked at a log, and the charcoal gave to his boot with a crisp sound. Tomorrow when it was cooler there'd be searching for irons and ironware. He was curiously unwilling that it be over, his feet strangely slow about climbing the bluff he had descended so easily. And now he felt the strain of the buckets pulling his arms and he remembered how they had gone past him like feathers. There was a strength in you that slumbered except at high moments, slept except under excitement, smoldered the time it was waiting. It was not in your power to call it out for your service; some outer thing must do it, some terror or some beauty or some danger. Some pillar of flame in the night.

Again and again, the men prophesied bitterly to one another, this thing would happen. They must watch for town meetings and on those nights keep out the guards. It had been the same way in Missouri, and few Mormon boys but knew what it was to roll from their bunks and leap to the window and find their clothes in the reddened dark, their eyes like a cat's with excitement.

The gentiles called it wolf-hunting, declaring: "You either kill wolves or they multiply and kill you. And when you come on a wolf's den, you destroy it."

To Mormon boys old enough to experience fire, there was sharp glory in being on the defensive and innocent, and this they were never to forget. This was their first understanding of what the preachers meant on the stand when they spoke of revenge. It was their understanding of the Last Days, when the world would be consumed with fire and nothing remain but black substance, a mote on the sky. For the boys, the fires laid by wolf-hunters did not die in a night when the fuel was consumed, but lay in them always.

Something of this came to Simon when he opened the door and saw Jarvis's face, with no hope of more sleep in it. He touched the boy's shoulder and said: "You can help with the building – they're starting a new house for Snarl Yeaman tomorrow."

And Susie Yeaman, exhausted on a neighbor's pillow, lay thinking: "That red calico that's too little for Charity, now – that can be used for the circles."

Chapter XL

Charlot lay biting her lips, but making no sound. Once she took her Bible and read of Elizabeth and of Mary and of other women who brought forth men. "Now Elizabeth's full time came that she should be delivered; and she brought forth a son. And so it was that the days were accomplished that she should be delivered."

Reading finality for scriptural women, she saw that there was nothing of crying out, unless *time of travail* must cry out.

Mercy lay listening. Sometimes she reached out and touched the little heap in the cradle that was Sarah. The baby's buttocks were abrupt in the air – a strange way she had of lying with her cheek in the pillow and one hand under it, her knees drawn up under her stomach. The Baby would still mean Sarah, at least in one room of this house.

Charlot's voice, breathless but not complaining, and Mercy thought: "She's having it easy." Then Mother Turner, persuading and comforting.

Simon remained in the field until it was over. After all, there was much to be thought about these days besides women and getting babies. Being born is an incident, private destiny a small thing in a day when a city is threatened. Since Yeaman's disaster there had been others, and now a man didn't go out to his field without his gun hanging by him. He didn't get the length of a furrow from a gun, and he kept the tail of his eyes behind him every foot of the way up and down. Mormon crops were getting to be symbols of Mormon permanency, and Mormon permanency was growing into a menace. The state was slow to act, and the county was slow, so citizens could take things into their own hands, could they not, and see that a Mormon's corn did not tassel and see that his wheat did not bloom?

Simon came to Mercy every morning and the gun clanked at the bedside while he kissed her. This morning he had dragged Sarah's cradle in, early, and whispered: "You keep Sarah here until after."

Charlot was very brave, and her time was not so easy after all. Mother Turner told Mercy how Charlot was old to be starting and how the baby had such a wide head he was slow in coming. Never a sound, though, except the helpless sound with the last pains, and that wasn't a sound any woman could keep.

When Simon came home, he lifted his new son and looked at him closely, a great child with hands and feet large for his size and a square chin that already looked like a chin with some purpose.

Simon had the boys file by to look at their brother. "This is your new brother." And they looked briefly. When Jarvie went out to his mother, he whispered: "You don't have to go to school to learn it, Mother – half's not the same as a whole."

She was ashamed that it helped her so much.

In three days Charlot was up and about, looking gray under the eyes, but strong-voiced as always. And now there was a creature in this house that she loved, with a passion almost violent. The world was gentler for her and sometimes she even left the dishes on the table long enough to take up her boy and dandle him, singing.

SIMON was cultivating and heard the horses coming before he saw them. He called to Jarvie and Menzo, the way they had planned, just the word: "*Streak!*" They dropped at once into the furrows and moved unseen, wriggling along on their stomachs. Then under the fence into the elderberry bushes and buttonweed that grow rank along the edges of the fields and along to the abrupt descent of the Hollow. There was no sound but the crumbling of soapstone under their feet.

Simon clucked to his ox.

There were about a dozen of them, all on horseback, and one of them leveled his gun before he called out: "Hey, Mormon! Nice stand o' corn ye got comin'."

Simon paused, noticing how his hands were unsteady and limber on the reins.

"I hope it's all right," he called cheerfully. "A bit dry for it, so far." He could see his gun was no use this time, with so many, and they'd only take it over, so he leaned down and slipped it into the grass and started back down the furrow.

They dismounted and tied their horses to the fence; then they came toward him, careless of plants as they came. Simon started to speak of that, but checked himself, waiting. It would be time he needed.

They circled around him, and he saw that the leader's gun had gone into the holster, but a hand was kept on it.

"You'll excuse me," Simon said distinctly, "for entertaining you in my jeans this way – I've never had visitors come to my field before."

"Maybe they don't know it's your field."

The man who spoke was extremely thin and angular, with a sharp tilt to his nose and a quick shift to eyes as blue as a girl's.

Simon spoke slowly, against time. "I've my papers for it at the house if there seems to be any question."

" There're papers an' papers."

" I happen to've paid a good bit for these papers, and anybody who says different can take it to circuit court — "

" An' while the court thinks things over, the corn grows."

" I put in a parcel of seed," Simon said. " It ought to."

He felt dizzy with the desire to tear at the man who prodded him; his hands ached at his sides with desire. This was the way they usually worked, he knew, provoking, insulting, and then the quick scuffle when a man lost his temper.

" I understand," the man said, " you're a Mormon."

He made it a question that waited.

" Yes, I am. And have been a good many years now without any trouble."

" It's never too late for trouble, seems like."

" I mind my own business and let other folks mind theirs," Simon said, almost gently, " so I don't get into much trouble."

" When your land ain't your own, that's a good way to keep folks from payin' much notice."

It was a strange conversation, tense and bitter just under simplicity.

The man came forward with one of his fellows at his elbow. " We'll take over your job for this afternoon," he said. " You just go on home and have a nice chat with your wives; we'll tend to this corn for you."

He laid his hands on the plow-handles.

Simon did not move. The ox stirred and lowed gently. " I can tend to my own field," Simon said.

" A dozen can do more work than one alone — we'll likely have it all done in an hour." The man's fingers persuaded Simon's slowly toward the end of the handles, but he clenched his fists till the joints whitened. " There's no hurry, particular," he said, fighting his anger.

The two of them removed him, and one said, taking over: " We don't like corn up in here — this ain't corn land."

" It was mighty good last year," Simon said, and felt his arms held behind him. He noticed for the first time that John Peck was with these men, standing in the background, tense-faced. Simon was infuriated and strove with his voice, while he thought: " How far down are the boys by now? "

" Mormons and corn – they don't do so well on this land."

The man spoke to the ox, and the animal moved forward, the plow shifted so that it ripped under the little plants and leveled them.

" By God," the man said fervently, " this beats ordinary cultivatin' all hollow! " He moved down the row and Simon shook violently with his eyes on the even green, falling. He wrenched at his arms and felt the cool butt of a gun under his arm. After all, he could see, those Brothers familiar with all this knew how it ought to be handled. A number and you're covered – he could hear George Smith at the meeting: " Just stall while the boys bring the Brothers – there's no use of gun signals, or they'll work fast and you're dead when we get there."

He said brusquely, because a man does what he can for his corn: " Whoa! " The ox stopped, the great head turned.

The butt tightened under his arm, and after a moment the ox moved on.

" Old Hat Joe, he was pretty good talkin' fairy-tales, wasn't he? "

Simon nodded implacably. " Pretty good at most things," he said.

" But not so good at happy endings. Ol' Joe, he didn't live so happy ever after."

" I don't know. It's not ended yet."

The man jabbed with the gun. " You're pretty good, too, damned if ye ain't. A Saint, an' I'll bet *my* old hat on it."

They were all talking now, taking their turns at provoking.

" Come on, tell us a story. Who was the Indians' first daddy? "

" Has the Angel Moroni got whiskers or is he bare-face? "

"Did Joe eat off them gold plates *every* day or only on Sundays?"

Simon stood silent, watching the corn fall.

"Cat's got his tongue! Let's see if we'n find it." They lifted him and took him to the fence and stood him there with his arms out, binding them with strips of his shirt.

"Now, Jesus God-Almighty, tell us some more about Ol' Hat Joe."

Simon said nothing.

"When'd he go crazy?"

"How many wives you got, Jesus? You like fat ones or thin ones? You oughta let us in."

"Cat's got his tongue!" the fellow with the gun tilted Simon's head and pulled his mouth open, pushing the gun against his teeth and then against his tongue. For the first time abject terror went through Simon, a fork of terror that ripped him as it went and left him sickened.

"Now let's have it, the tongue's there all right."

The gun was withdrawn and Simon felt himself strengthened with fury and there was no sense left in him or any remembrance of the calm quiet procedure he had meant to follow, according to counsel. There was no room in him for thought, but only for fury, and the gun meant nothing to him suddenly, but only their faces circling around him.

"Do what you want to me," he said, and heard himself with his ears thumping, "but leave Brother Joseph alone. You've killed him – you ought to be satisfied."

They began to enjoy themselves.

"You a Mormon?"

"Yes."

"You a Mormon?"

"Yes! I said yes!"

"You a Mormon?"

He had heard of this, this was the thing to be avoided above all others, but he'd earned it, losing himself that way for a minute.

" You a Mormon? "

" Yes! "

They were ready with hickory gads, taking turns with him. Every time his acquiescence burst from him, the gads came down, and he felt them everywhere as though they must find every inch of his body before they were satisfied. And then there was no " yes " in him any longer but only a fierce nodding, again and again, with pride mounting and hate like sparks kindling in his veins and growing and bursting. This was the way with the others, then, who knew, and spoke so fiercely from the stand on Testimony Sundays. It could be put in you with words, but it could be whipped into you, too, it could be whipped deep into your hide with gads while your corn fell around you and you knew that to feel justified and innocent was everything and worth everything. Presently feeling was nothing and he stood because of the bindings on his arms and for no other reason. But he still nodded, again and again.

He did not know when the Brothers came, on their horses and shooting. He did not see the way the gentiles made for their horses or even how John Peck fell, sprawling, and lay dead with his eyes glassy against the freshly cultivated ground. He didn't know how the Brothers buried Peck in the middle of that same field. But when he was himself again, at home that night, he still knew the fervency of his last thought and told it to his family.

" It can be beaten into your hide, your religion. There's no taking it out of a man with beating or shooting or anything. Maybe you can make him *say* it – but what a man believes is inside of him, a strength in his muscles, and when it's been challenged, then it's inside of him as hard as his bones."

Chapter XLI

There was summer peace in the big room and no sound but flies buzzing and the abrupt kicking and grunting of little Simon in the cradle. Between the big room and Mercy's room the door stood ajar.

Purrmiew came across the floor, stretching himself amiably toward a pool of sunshine. He stiffened his legs a little as he walked and drew in his chin and then yawned an elaborate yawn. Purrmiew possessed a great purr and a great love of warm rubbing, and when he came close to Jarvie's legs he stroked them tenderly with his sides, turning back and forth for long deliberate movements. Without looking up from the book in his hand, Jarvie reached down and moved his fingers along the cat's fur. Purrmiew hunched his middle with pleasure and rubbed closer, the purr from his throat crowding out of him fervently.

Presently he moved off, across the room.

Charlot's baby kicked and grunted as he did all day, the perfect baby, without meanness or colic in him. The shawl over the cradle danced with his kicking and he reached for it confidently. And Purrmiew reached for the end hanging near the floor, his head tipped sideways in scrutiny and his paw catching at the woolly fringe. Presently he gathered his haunches under him and leaped, balanced a moment on the side of the cradle, and jumped soundlessly in. The baby reached out, enthralled, and sent his legs flying with excitement.

Jarvie looked up and half rose from the bench. Then he sat back again and watched, fascinated. The baby's flailing legs struck Purrmiew full center and sent him rolling to the foot of the cradle. He was up again instantly and leaped back to action, landing lightly on the baby's stomach. The baby reached out and took hold of the lovely spotted fur, gurgling ecstatically, and Purrmiew snarled. And dug in. For a second, the baby was silent, surprised, and then his voice came out in a great crescendo of indignity and pain.

Jarvis sought to control himself, but he could not; he began to laugh. And the baby screamed and fought, terrified of the thing that clung and clawed and made sudden horrifying sound.

Charlot came, like a she-buffalo, charging and heavy. She seized Purrmiew by the fur and he squirmed double in her hands and clawed at her, so she threw him, a whirling bundle of fur, half-way across the room.

There was the scrape of his extended claws over the floor and his body's impact against the table-leg, and then he was gone through the open door.

Charlot looked at Jarvie over the baby's ripped white thigh. He tried desperately to control himself, but could not.

"You did that, Jarvis Baker! You did it!"

He shook his head, found his voice. "No, I didn't. It – it was all Purrmiew's idea! It was for a nice friendly –" He straightened his face.

Charlot put the baby back deliberately and walked to the boy. Her voice was intense and low. "You did it, Jarvis, and you did it on purpose. Because you hate your own brother and you hate me. You did it! You threw that cat on top of him and don't you deny it."

Jarvie perceived that it was no longer funny but had somehow achieved the symbolic.

"No – I didn't *throw* him."

"Yes, you did. Don't deny it to me, I can tell a liar when I see one. And I can tell a sneak. Don't think I didn't see it, I was right there."

"No, you weren't, or you'd have got him out yourself."

"You threw him in."

"I didn't."

"Yes, you did!"

"I didn't throw him in – but I could have taken him out."

Charlot lost her equilibrium and began to cry. Because there was nothing else to do. You did not reach out and slap this big boy who could take your wrists and hold them. You did nothing but cry at him. "You hate me, Jarvie! You hate me and you hate my baby and everything that's mine and everything I do. Maybe you think I don't see it. But I do. Maybe you think you and your mother can get together and plan things out to hurt me and my baby. She told you to do that, didn't she? She told you!"

His face whitened. "Leave Mother out of it. She doesn't know anything about it."

"Oh, yes she does!"

"She doesn't."

"That door's open; if she has any ears she knows all about it. And don't you talk back to me, Jarvis Baker, or you'll get what you got before and I'll see to it."

"Oh, no I won't."

She knew what he was thinking because she was thinking of it, too. Simon himself had said it: "You can't beat anything out of anybody – you only beat it in."

He turned his back on her and sat down and she went back to her baby, clucking like a hen with all its feathers out. Presently he went into the other room to his mother and closed the door with finality. The afternoon was very still as it had been before anything happened, filling the house with summer laziness.

Mercy showed Jarvie the pointer-finger of her right hand, the nail bitten to the quick.

" You shouldn't have done it," she whispered, but he saw a gladness on her face. " After all, Jarvie, it's not the baby's fault."

She was thinking: " She can't do it, not with Jarvie."

And a great surging joy rose in her that made her feel buoyant, lying in the feathers.

Chapter XLII

" WHAT in God's name do they want? They got Brother Joseph, what do they want now? "

The Warsaw *Signal* was blunt with its threatening. " In Carthage and Green Plains, citizens are all in arms. Throughout the county every man is ready for the conflict. In Clark County, Missouri, they hold themselves ready to march whenever they are wanted. From Rushville, three hundred men have enlisted for the struggle. McDonough County is all alive and ready for command. In Keosauqua, Iowa, the citizens are in arms and from Keokuk and the river towns everybody is coming."

It was hard to believe what it meant till you looked again at the headline: " Counties Gather Strength to Cope with Mormon Menace."

The people asked one another: " Is it so in this country, then, that two men believing two things can't live together? Why did our grandfathers come here? What did they come for? "

Brother Brigham was gray in the face with it, and he answered no questions.

Eliza said as she had said in the beginning: " They might have let us build a city, but a kingdom – "

The steamboats did not stop so often late in that summer, but scurried by, hugging the channel. Nauvoo was still growing, but growing with folks from the outskirts, forced in. And life in Nauvoo was uncertain, with so many men pushed off their land

and lounging in the streets with their hands in their pockets and their families without adequate houses and without anything coming in for supplies. Then, suddenly, the cataclysm: the legislature met in Springfield and with one deft stroke cut Nauvoo's throat, unconditionally repealing the city charter. "To insure peace," the legislators said.

Brother Brigham heard it without words, but a pain sprang to his eyes that remembered Brother Joseph, and he said: "Nauvoo is already dying."

Tom Sharp, a shyster and a vagabond, was tried for the murder of Joseph Smith, but he was one out of many that shared the guilt and was released and acquitted. He said, and they put it in all the papers just as he said it: "The one who killed Joe and Hyrum Smith did his country essential service."

A mob of two hundred men, under arms, got started down in the southwest part of Hancock County. They rode in various directions, in groups, and pretty soon you could see the way they went from fires burning. It was as though the whole country was burning.

And while these fires burned, the workers on the Temple raised the first timbers for the tower. The framework of the roof was all up and the shingles ready, upwards of one hundred thousand piled on the ground. Around the lot a wall was being built that was eight feet high and five feet thick at the base, and all the stone was cut. When turmoil began in the streets and refugees from new fires poured into Nauvoo, the workers stopped and came down from the hill. But Brother Brigham turned them back with his whiplash of a tongue, and said: "Keep the work going."

Above everything the work on the Temple must go on. Didn't they remember the words Brother Joseph had said to the Temple workers in the beginning? "I say if you finish this work you will shine forth one day fair as the sun, clear as the moon, and you will become terrible, like an army with banners."

So they worked. But they saw every day how their numbers were shattered and more men had to come to replace those who were gone. William Smith, Joseph's own brother, disappeared with some of the people after him, to start a new colony. James Strang, black-bearded and strange and fiery, kept calling men to his new city up in Wisconsin. Lyman Wight, once so loving to the Prophet in his letters, took his followers up the Mississippi to the pine country where the Temple timbers had grown. " We'll build a Temple there," he said, " where it can stand forever." But there was not the spark in him that had kindled Brother Joseph, there was not the way of pushing men forward and making their arms strong under timbers and slogans, stone and prayer; so Wight's people were soon scattered.

All this was heavy in every household, and for those who were sick already, and sick at heart, like Mercy Baker, it was a constant lash at emotion. It was like the first days after Charlot's coming when she knew that a crisis impended.

WHEN harvest-time came, the men began working together, rushing like mad. Because they never knew when another field of wheat, ready for threshing, or of corn ready for husking, would burn in the night or the day. Sometimes no man had been seen on the guarded roads, and yet suddenly all hell was let loose in a cornfield. It was as though fire fell from the sky, so they knew that some of their own number were guilty, " in the pay," as they said. Again they recalled Brother Joseph's saying: " We can guard the gates, but how shall we guard within the gates? "

The fields were set cunningly, and burned from corner to corner and from the edges so that nothing availed to fight the flames. It was a strange and a terrible warfare, leaping rail fences and obliterating boundaries.

A man's thoughts stood at the edge of his brain, a man's nerves stood tensed on his skin. And Nauvoo looked forward bleakly to a winter of hunger. Brigham Young ordered all cattle driven into the city and there they were slaughtered and the meat cured and stored away in secret places. And he urged a quick harvest of fields yet untouched, and men went in crowds like grasshoppers.

❧ ❧ ❧

MERCY woke suddenly that night, about two in the morning, as a woman will when something is not right. She woke all at once, with no preliminary of swift dream or delicious dozing, and lifted herself half up toward the window. There was a light at the pane, a blazing light, and a face behind it, illumined.

For a moment she knew that terrible constriction of throat and the complete paralysis of emotion that is the first signal of terror; then the light passed, seemed to lift, to soar, and a soft thud obliterated it and the face with it. The window stood on the wall, all the little panes square and bronze as they were toward sunrise.

" Simon! "

She did not try to move, knowing that he would come.

She heard the boys tumbling down the ladder into the kitchen beyond her closed door, heard them shouting at each other, heard Charlot calling hoarsely. There was no sound then of either Simon or Jarvie, and she knew they were out after help already. She lay clutching the edge of the bed, hanging fiercely to the pillow and watching the spreading bronze that marked neat squares of pane. Deliberately she lay and marked them, numbering them.

Sarah began to cry, Betsy was screaming terrified quick questions. " What, Aunt Charlot, what, Aunt Charlot? " And Charlot's little Simon was demanding in his big voice above Sarah's wailing. Furniture was being dragged across the floor. " Menzo, hold the door open first and pull — "

The outside door came to, opened again, shut. They were outside, all of them.

Thought became a spasm of the brain. " It has come, then, and she'll be glad, she's going to burn me in here; she'd be glad if she could say it was too late and I was burned in here. She'd be glad, it would all be hers, they would all be hers."

The air was becoming acrid, smoke taste in the mouth and the nostrils. Still she lay for a time, waiting for Simon. And terror subsided in her and was a kind of strength, even, because it came to her that something could be done. Intense in her effort, she turned herself off the bed, seeing everything bright in her room as though lighted with millions of candles. She crept to the lowboy and fumbled in the drawers, pulling at things her fingers recognized. Then she moved to the chest, and the great lid was a weight in her hands, but opened when she stooped and bore up on it with her whole body. There was a suspended roaring in the air now that made her terribly anxious, but she took the things under her hands and laid them on the floor beside her, ready for Simon to carry. Really, some of the things were quite silly, just now. The wool shawl that had been Mother's, worn beyond any use but sentiment, those high pearl-button shoes meant for dancing, and the combs with imitation jewels set in butterfly shapes. The christening clothes there would be no more babies to wear, even the woolly shoes with blue tassels. Her journal and her Bible she held in her hands when the door opened behind her.

It was Charlot, still in her nightgown, her little curls bobbing. Her face was smudged and streaming, her mouth open, the under lip sagging. She looked big and frightened and ugly. She did not speak, but came to Mercy at once and picked her up like a plaything.

" Don't you pick me up, Charlot Leavitt! I'm no baby! "

Charlot turned to the door, but Mercy struggled and beat at her face. Charlot's mouth dropped and she drew back, letting Mercy slip to the floor.

" All right, walk then. But walk! "

Mercy stood in front of her, hardly understanding her own words. It was a necessary thing she said after the terrible experience of Charlot's arms lifting her. As though the featherweight in the big arms meant something.

" Simon will come for me."

" He can't, Mercy, he told me – "

" He'll come for me."

" You're excited. If you can walk, I won't lift you. But you're not waiting for Simon."

Charlot moved to her again, her face frantic.

" Don't touch me! You leave me alone. I won't stand it. You want him to think you're a hero! "

Charlot cried out before the flailing little fists, but she continued and stooped and tried to catch Mercy up again. Mercy was wild with revulsion, her lower teeth quite bare.

" She'll kill herself, fighting," Charlot thought, " she'll kill herself fighting me."

It was a mad moment that gathered together with its excitement and danger all the furious under-hate, all the unsaid things, and focused them in one emotion. So animals refused to be led from a fire, out of terror, balking at freedom; Charlot had heard it. In this sharp little face she saw pure hate, bare, for the first time. She thought: " When they hate enough to kill, that's how they look."

Quite simply, she reached out her big fist and struck. Mercy's eyes widened while she was sinking; if there had been time her eyes would have been incredulous, but it was done very quickly. Then Charlot took her up and carried her out through the familiar room, already half gone, while the fire reached out for her.

Chapter XLIII

A COMMITTEE from the state rode into Nauvoo, and behind them an armed force. If peace could not be had in Hancock County without state militia, state militia would step in and do something about it. So said the spokesman of this committee, the honorable Stephen A. Douglas.

The two sides met.

Brigham Young said: "What can we do? Let them tell us what we can do besides giving up our faith and prayers. We can't do that and no man has a right to ask it."

"All we ask," the gentiles said stubbornly, "all we ask is that you get out of the State of Illinois. There's not room for your church and for us, too."

Brigham faced it, unsurprised, weary. "We've been told that before," he said. "It's not new to us. But it's wicked; if I hadn't lived through it before now, I'd not have believed the government would allow it to be said."

"We can't promise peace unless you say you'll get out. We don't have any power over what's going on, or over what's likely to happen; there's no leader anybody can turn to. It's the people themselves that want you out of here. We can't promise any end to it unless you start getting out."

Douglas reminded them of the force at his command. "We can't take sides when two factions of a state are involved," he said. "Who's to decide which group of citizens is wrong and which is right? You're all guilty, and the state wants it stopped, the state wants the thing settled one way or the other."

"All right," Brigham said quietly. "I think the people will agree with me that we're sick to death of it. We're tired of your states that are so anxious for justice they won't take sides, and then stand by and see a minority driven like cattle. We'll be glad to go."

A shout went up from the gentiles.

"But in the meantime we want peace! From this time on, we want to get ready to go without trouble. There's got to be an agreement to that. We need food and we need supplies and we need wagons."

"All right." Douglas looked keenly around him at the faces that did not trust one another, at citizens who had no trust in other citizens or in their state or even in their country, at citizens who wore distrust and suspicion in their faces.

"The Mormons will leave Illinois, then," he said. "They will take steps that make it obvious that they are leaving. And the anti-Mormons will stop molesting them until their departure; persistence in a course of terrorism like that just past will mean forfeiting all the respect and sympathy of the state. I want the agreement of both parties in writing, duly signed."

"Are we agreed?"

"Agreed."

Brother Brigham's thin New England lips were set as he drafted his statement. When it was printed for distribution, every Mormon and every gentile household received its copy. It was very fine print, almost too small to be read by candlelight, and it was long and the words somehow ran together because it was a thing a man read with emotion.

"HERE, Jarv, you read it."

Simon handed it to Jarvie and the paper made a crisp new sound, going from hand to hand.

"What is it, Father?"

Simon looked up, slowly and heavily. "Read and find out," he said. "I want it read to me; sometimes you miss things, reading to yourself."

"Nauvoo, September 24, 1845. With regard to removing to some place where the peculiar organization of our church will not be likely to engender strife and contention, and, whereas it is our desire to live in peace with all men, without sacrificing the right of worshipping God according to the dictates of our own consciences, which privilege is guaranteed to us by the Constitution of these United States; and whereas, we have, time and again been driven from our peaceful homes, suffering all manner of hardships, even to death itself, as the people well know . . ."

"Be more quiet with it, Jarv," Simon said. "It won't do to worry your mother with it. Not just now."

Jarvie nodded and his voice sank almost to a whisper. "And whereas it is now so late in the season that it is impossible for us to remove this fall, without causing a repetition of like sufferings; and whereas, many scores of our houses have been burned to ashes, without cause or provocation and we have made no resistance, and whereas, we desire peace above all earthly blessings — "

He looked up quickly, almost afraid of what it might be going to say.

"— we propose to leave this county next spring, for some point so remote that there will not need to be a difficulty with the people and ourselves. It is a mistaken idea that we have proposed to remove in six months; for that would be so early in the spring, that grass might not grow nor water run, both of which would be necessary for our removal. But we will have no more seed time nor harvest among our people in this country, after gathering our present crops. By order of the Council, Brigham Young."

Simon's face was gray. He went to the door of Charlot's house, where they had been living since the fire, and out onto the porch where he and Charlot had stood when he first pointed out the bluff across the river. From here he could look down over the flat and up at the Temple.

"But there's nothing good in it, even in Nauvoo, when it's not safe from day to day. A man can't stand living if he's got to go to bed uncertain what will happen before morning comes again. A man wants peace and good neighbors that he can trust; if he's got to go a thousand miles, two thousand, any number at all, to get them, they're worth going after. Nauvoo here, she was going to be a citadel, wasn't she? At first she was going to be the Zion of the world, the haven for the oppressed all over the world, she was going to be a place where every man could lift his head."

And now – what was she?

"When grass grows and water runs." It came to be a chant through Nauvoo. "To a place so remote – *so remote* – "

Chapter XLIV

On the back of Charlot's cottage in Nauvoo Simon had built hurriedly two lean-to rooms, one for Mercy and one for the boys. Everybody said he was mighty lucky to have such a place to come into, and he knew that it was true, with Nauvoo harassed as she was and overcrowded.

But Mercy could not reconcile herself to living on Charlot's hospitality. For two weeks after the fire she was bitterly ill and could not, or would not, swallow so much as a spoonful of water. Even after Simon finally got some soup into her and she gradually grew better, there was a shell on her that nobody could push through. She was very quiet and never looked straight at anybody for long, and if visitors came she was seized with an alarming trembling. Even with Simon she began to develop a queer little monotone and a soft laugh that unnerved him and plagued him together.

Mercy's room stood wider than the house, so she could have a west window, looking at the river. It was almost as big as her other window. But she said such unreasonable things all the time, there was no joy in it for her or for anybody.

" I don't like the river from this side. The sun never comes up, it always goes down. I never see it come up, I see it go down every day. And the moon never comes up, either; it always goes down."

As if a man could order the sun to change its direction.

There were things for a man to be thinking about besides womenfolks and their queer ideas. Every hundred in Nauvoo had established one or two wagon-shops, and Simon's job was preparing timber for making wagons. The timber was cut and brought into the city green; hub, spoke, and felloe timber was boiled in salt and water, and other parts kiln-dried. Nearly every shop in town was employed at wagon-making, even the Nauvoo House basement, over Brother Joseph's head almost, and even the old Arsenal. Teams went to all parts of the country for iron; blacksmiths worked day and night. A man was ready for sleep when he came home of an evening.

One day when Simon came in for supper and leaned to kiss her, as always, Mercy said: "Simon, you're building."

He started, seeing her smile. He spoke the way he had begun to speak to her lately, humoring her as grown-ups will humor a child. "All right, I'm building. You might know I'd be building something."

She reached up and put her arms around his neck and he wanted to say something more, but did not, standing awkwardly bent over her, unrelaxing, with her arms tight.

"Do you think we can move back home before winter, Simon — before heavy winter? I'm so miserable here."

He looked at her, beyond her, frowning. "I don't know — there's no telling about these things, Mercy. Sometimes a job stretches out longer than you'd think."

She relaxed, looking up at him. He said lightly: "Here I thought you'd be glad to stay in Nauvoo, where houses are safe."

But she shook her head. "I like Nauvoo from the outside. From the bluff, Nauvoo is beautiful."

He knew what she meant. He had grown to love it, too, from the east windows of the cabin, the streets curving up the hill to the Temple, the houses like toys among the trees, the wood-smoke curling up in a blue haze. And here in the heart of Nauvoo herself, especially now, you were aware of her in the concrete, not in the abstract — in the reality, not in the dream. Charlot's house was too close to the street, and then there was the eternal bustle of building, and the dust. Simon was afraid for a time that Mercy knew it was the bustle of departing, not of living. But after she believed he was building again, she grew happier, except that she missed the full autumn.

Over the river, autumn had belonged to her and she to it. But here where the city lots had been carefully cleared, there were only a few trees and a few shrubs touched with the glory. Jarvie went to the woods and brought her what he could carry and filled her room with it, the blood-red of oak and the rose-red of maple, the mouth-red of buckberries, the grace of the wahoo. And the brilliance of bittersweet to poke in a dry jar by her bed where it could blaze the rest of the winter. But it was not the same; the leaves crisped and fell on the table and the floor.

One day the children went out and gathered their pokeberries and she helped them squeeze ink for the year at school, but she kept one branch for a long time unbroken. She said it was like a Chinese etching, with rough green wafers on red calyxes mounted on scarlet stems, and toward the base of the branch the wafer seeds purple, and then empty calyx, brilliant and patterned, like a second flowering.

She spoke sometimes of the hackberry that had stood just down the bluff so that she had looked straight out into its branches; it had kept berries all winter long and had been a rendezvous for birds until spring. Had it been hurt by the fire?

Jarvie brought hazelnuts, wearing their lovely pale ruffles, and elderberries in huge clusters, and woolly-leaved mullein.

Beck and George, seeing her pleasure, dragged in whatever they found by the sidewalks, wild hemp and cow's-tail and horse-mint. Mercy made a great fuss over the pale pink flowers of the mint and crushed them and let the children sniff of their spice-smell.

When Charlot came in to sweep and dust, she gathered up dried leaves and dropped berries without complaint. She and Mercy spoke little to each other. The night of the fire and the new status of Charlot as true mistress of the house they lived in stood between them, and neither sought to find a way around their feelings; some things are not spoken. But it hardly mattered, after all, now; Charlot seldom came in but for cleaning. The boys brought the trays, and Betsy was big enough to stand on a chair and brush Mother's hair and braid it, which she loved to do. That Charlot was in Mercy's consciousness constantly, absent or not, could not be helped, or that Mercy stood in hers in a mist of pity.

But one day Mercy called her. Unexpectedly. It was the day of the first snow, and the children were all at school but the little ones, who were out in it, happy as squirrels.

" Look – somebody's got to see."

On her face was a simple pleasure she seldom showed Charlot.

A pair of cardinals tipped and fluttered in the big elderberry that stood by the fence, every branch of it high with its burden of snow, every twig concerned with pure white. And the birds were startling against the world, their color on the white like a cry out of silence.

" They nest here every year," Charlot said.

Mercy whispered: " I've never seen them before, not in the snow."

" Ever since we came, they've come, too. The same pair, most likely."

When Jarvie came home Mercy made him promise to put crumbs on the window-sill every day, so they would visit her. They came to mean much to her, they were the only color in a white world. Usually the male flew down first, and then his mate, dun but for her bright bill. He would stand with his beak lifted and sing to her: "Sweet-sweet-sweet-sweet, oh" (his voice rising), and then: "Oh, sweet, sweet, sweet."

"They ought to go where there is long light and soft weather," Mercy thought. "I wonder why they stay here. Maybe because they know how beautiful they are when the snow falls. Maybe it's home to them. Sometimes home is in strange places, and we come to belong there without choosing."

THE GENTILES looked suspiciously at the growing Temple. "They're not going," they told one another. "Why should they finish that building, spending thousands of dollars, and then go off and leave it? It don't make sense."

And one night the Temple was lighted.

Simon said to Mercy: "You've got to see it," and he carried her to the north windows, pointing to it as he might have pointed to handiwork all his own.

It stood with its windows shapes of yellow candlelight, and, as Brother Joseph had said, it looked "indescribably grand." The hill itself seemed made only to contribute to that height and that dignity which had been placed with infinite pains upon it.

Mercy said: "It would look lovely from the bluff." And Simon sighed.

Every night after that the Temple stood lighted on its hill, and companies of people moved through the rooms, dressed in white. Ceremonies, passionate and reiterative, kindled utter faith and utter fear together. Those who had wavered went again into the water of the new Temple font and came forth with renewed spirit and new faith and fortitude. The ceremonies in the Temple were part of the preparation for a time of long traveling and homelessness and travail, a preparation as necessary and as desperately attended to as the swift building of wagons and the intense molding of bullets, and the day-long preservation of meat. For faith in the heart is stamina for the body and the spirit. Night after night Brigham Young led the way to the Temple with baskets of candles.

But the gentiles did not understand that this too was preparation for the journey. Passing on the river or on the roads, they asked one another fearfully what was this new thing the Mormons were doing every night, asked suspiciously: " Why? "

Some of them were bold enough to do some peering in at the windows. But the moving crowds of people, dressed in white with their aprons of bright leaf-green, the men with their strange little hats and the women with their veils, meant nothing to the gentiles, gave them nothing but an unreasonable fury at folks who could do things so sinister and mysterious.

" It don't make sense; nothin' these God-damn Mormons do makes sense. I'll be glad to see the tail-ends of 'em."

Chapter XLV

ALL in a night, the river was solid once more. Men began going in sleighs to the Islands to drag back their timber. There was not even the moving of the river to break the somnolence of the prairie world. And the whole prairie was no color but space-color as always in winter, and dead-color. It seemed to enclose Mercy, descend on her. Those accustomed to blue height and green height had better not live on the prairie; those accustomed to slate sea and blue sea had better avoid it. Because winter on the prairie is a thing made of ashes and powder. Death conquers it and it never fights death, but accepts it. The trees accept it, effacing themselves to mere shadow and lace on the landscape. Sometimes fleetingly a jay or a cardinal brings it alive, but even these are wary of their own color, as they must be, because they are too bright for a dead world.

For a few months Nauvoo became anonymous in the countryside, pretending serenity. There was the isolation of bitter weather with distances lengthened. Only the Temple, lighted till midnight or after, gave Nauvoo her identity.

Christmas broke her serenity briefly, as bells break a calm morning. Christmas was a brief time when men wondered, looking in other men's faces, what it was they distrusted. Cedar and mistletoe and bittersweet hung in the houses.

Menzo made dolls out of corncobs for Betsy and Beck, carving the faces, and Mercy cut off the ends of her braids to make hair for them, and dressed them in scraps of old silk. It was good, she thought, how Menzo could make even a corncob smile when he tried to. Water-guns for the little boys, from elder and cedar, and for the three bigger boys – Mercy was shocked when she saw this – there were real guns made by Jonathan Browning, with bullets and powder-horns. And socks and gloves for them all, days full of stitches carefully counted, and for Joey and Beck little mittens of rabbitskin with white fluff-tails stitched to the backs just for pretty.

All through Nauvoo spread an almost hysterical gaiety. There were carols at dawn, just as there had been that other Christmas, the last for poor Brother Joseph. There was a feeling, unsaid: "This is Nauvoo's last Christmas." There was a Santa Claus at Sunday school, giving the children popcorn sweetened with maple syrup. And all Christmas Day folks called back and forth, loud in their talk and their laughter.

For Mercy, everybody who called brought something. Christmas cake with citron and currants, jelly from ripe sloes dug in quivering spoonfuls from the brown crocks, wild strawberry jam, even chicken broth brought once more by Old John. His wife, Portia, he said, was in bed with a chest-cold.

He sat by Mercy's bed with the old fists on his cane hard as beetles.

"You ought to go in the other room with the company," Mercy said to him.

"At my age," Old John said mildly, "a man don't seek out company and company don't seek out him." He smiled. "Unless there's the singing wanted."

"Perhaps we could make company for each other, then," she said, and his ears, grown insensitive to the nuances of voice, heard no bitterness.

He sat there and she watched him nodding incessantly in a

way he was getting, a nod so small an ordinary glance did not detect it, but once it made itself known it was there, always, and one did not forget it but watched for it.

"I was a boy at Valley Forge," he said mildly. "We had music at Christmas."

Something Father had said kept coming into Mercy's mind as she watched him – Father who had deserted time before it could count him old: "Faith is for the old and for those who have always known, because they are not among those who ask questions. And philosophy is for the strong, only the strong, because nobody else can bear it."

"And what for me," she wondered, watching Old John complacent with his faith, "since I am neither strong nor old?"

"It was good you had music at Valley Forge," Mercy said. "Hard times aren't so hard when there's music."

"But at my age," Old John said, "it's a hard thing to move on again, music or no music. At my age a man wants to stay where he is."

She spoke gently. "I'd not let it worry me, John; things are better. You've been listening to Portia, and she has a way of seeing the worst of things."

"Portia sees what's in front of her," John said, "and she sees it square. She's younger than me, she can still face it."

"With the Temple finished and everything quiet –" she began.

"That's what the gentiles are a-sayin', M's Baker! And it's mighty dangerous, the way it's got them to thinkin'. They keep comin' in and sayin': 'By God, it was a promise! We've got it in writin'! An' it *don't* look like good business sense, finishin' up a million-dollar buildin' for strange folks to misuse."

"Things will be straightened out peaceably," she insisted again.

John shook his head. "There's nothin' but goin'. I've lived through it before an' I know."

He leaned forward confidentially. "What worries me is the old like me an' the sick like you. It's not just the next state this time, there's got to be a parcel o' country put between us an' other folks." He looked into her face. "I told Portia I'll quit the Church before I'll go. When it comes to the place where it's livin' or dyin', it's reason enough, God knows."

She was aware of the slight shaking, of the drama in his very lack of emotion.

"I even went right to Brother Brigham, an' I said: 'What about the old ones and the sick ones?' I said it with the words in the speeches: 'the old an' infirm.' He looked at me an' all he said was: 'John, we'll hope for the best. Get out y'r banjo, we'll be all right.'"

Old John stared before him.

"An' then I said: 'Brother Brigham, it wouldn't be so bad if a man knew where he was a-goin'.' I asked it, like it was a question, an' he said: 'No, John, it wouldn't.' An' that's all he said."

She did not speak, so Old John said bleakly: "He don't know himself."

He did not see that her color was heightened; his eyes were too old to be aware of nuances of color.

"An' your husband, this very night I said to him: 'You're not goin' t' take *her*, sick as she is?' An' he was just like Brother Brigham; he said: 'By spring, things'll be different.'"

Her voice was faint and her head came forward a little to listen. "Wherever they're going, John, the rest of them—Simon's not going."

His hard hands gripped the cane, he half rose upon it. His voice was incredulous and he leaned to her as one leans who would hear a choice bit of scandal.

"Is Simon a-leavin' the Church, then?"

She spoke quietly; he had no inkling of her excitement. A younger man might have noticed. "Why, John, he's building our house again — he couldn't be going anywhere, could he, building our house? "

John shook his head dubiously. " I didn't know," he said. " All I knew, he's a master wagon-builder, Brother Brigham says one of the best."

She shivered and looked at the hearth, thinking perhaps the fire had gone out, but there was a great log on it, blazing.

" It's the men who can build they want first," John was saying, " there's bound to be a parcel of building. An' like Brother Brigham was sayin' at Priesthood, the Gospel calls a man to do the thing he does best. If he's good preachin', he's called to preach. If he's a carpenter, then that's his call, and workin' with wood for the Church is as Godlike as workin' with souls."

" I think Brother Joseph would have said that, too. Wouldn't he? "

John rose, shaking his head curiously against his habitual nodding. " If the West ain't a call for Simon Baker, then I don't see as it's a call for me or for anybody else," he said.

SHE could not bring herself to speak of it to Simon — not directly or suddenly. But she watched him. When he came to say good-by in the morning, she said: " How is our house coming? "

" In bad weather like this, things go slow."

She was aware now of his averted eyes. Simon had always been a man of great honesty. And she listened for the sound of his footsteps, to hear the direction, and knew that he did not go to the river now. She could see the bluff from where she lay, very dimly, and sometimes she fancied she saw figures there; mostly she knew it was deserted.

But she had to ask.

" Jarvie " — it could be no one but Jarvie — " what is it about spring? Are they going, Jarvie? Everybody? "

He told her the truth as she had known he would, and brought her the paper with Brigham's name on it, and she understood why she had heard people saying hopefully: " It will be a long winter." When the river runs – when grass grows – some place *so remote* – She shared the refrain then that Nauvoo had sung since September. She waited for Simon to tell her and knew that he was afraid. When he came to her, she found things to say that might remind him and give him an opening. But he could not begin. She knew that he feared her resentment as he had feared it before, and feared her fear, perhaps, even more.

When he brought *Times and Seasons* she marked those advertisements that promised treatment of sickness. " LOZENGES: for coughs, for whooping cough, asthma, worms, CAMPHOR LOZENGES for nervous or sick headaches, heart palpitation, lasitude, and nervous affections. Persons traveling or attending large parties will find them really reviving, and importing the buoyance of youth. Used after dispensation . . ." She laughed, and showed this to Jarvie. " Used after dissipation they will restore the tone of the system and remove all the unpleasant symptoms arising from too free living. CATHARTIC LOZENGES, the best for removing bile from the system. SHERMAN'S POOR MAN'S PLASTER . . . for rheumatism, lumbergo, pain in the back, side, breast or any other part, only 12 hf cents. DR. W. B. BRINK, will treat CANCERS on the condition of no cure no pay and would say to those who are afflicted with cancers to call and try a remedy that has never failed, and I will pay fifty dollars for every case where it will not perform a permanent cure. A few rods west of the Temple."

Of this Dr. Brink she spoke to Simon. Of course, one did not know, but one had heard of the weakness, the pain, the gradual throttling.

" Dr. Richards doesn't do anything," she said. " He just comes and sits and sighs and goes off again."

" He says it's not cancer," Simon said.

" Did he say he *knew* or he *thought?* "

" Well – "

" Maybe he's wrong, maybe there's something new he hasn't heard about. This Brink man is new. It couldn't hurt, Simon."

Simon was dubious.

" I'd feel better to be trying something besides lobelia, Simon! "

He was impatient, he disliked to speak of these things. " All right, then, I'll take you up there as soon as you can walk. It can't hurt, I guess, to let him look at you."

Her voice was very little and cold. " Maybe I shan't walk. Couldn't he come here, Simon? "

He was caught by the reproach in her voice. " All right, then, if you want him." He looked at the advertisement again. " There shouldn't be any risk when a man makes a guarantee like that," he said.

" No. If I die, I can have the satisfaction of your collecting the money."

He glanced at her, surprised. First she was one thing and then suddenly another. " I wish you'd stop talking like that," he said.

She turned toward the wall. " It would be almost like being God Himself," she said. " When you sued him, I could look down and know that I was responsible for some of the misery in the world."

" Mercy! "

" Couldn't I? I want you to promise me something – promise if I die you'll make this Dr. Brink very miserable. Promise me, Simon."

" I will," he said soberly. " I will."

Then she laughed – the queer little monotone of a laugh she'd been developing.

" I wish you wouldn't talk about dying, Mercy. If you'd have a little faith, instead of thinking about all this medicine – "

She kept remembering: "Faith is for the old and for those who have always known."

She waited for a moment and then, her heart beating high with the importance of his response, she said: "If something isn't done, Simon, I don't see how I can be well enough by spring. Not by *spring*, Simon."

He forgot everything else, seeing that she knew, and dropped down beside her and looked at her, fully, for the first time in many weeks.

"Brother Brigham says you'll be all right, Mercy, and he ought to know. He says by spring the way will be opened for all of us. And God will be the one to open the way, not any quack gentile doctor without a paper in his pockets! That's what I wanted to tell you, just now – I've been trying to believe it as surely as I need to, and you've got to try to believe it too."

He saw that she shuddered, because now that he had said it, it became imminent and real. She asked small questions, covering her fear and her excitement.

"How many wagons will we have, Simon?"

"Our same two – and then a bed-wagon. If you're not well enough, see – I've had to plan on everything." He leaned to her anxiously. "There'll be so many ticks in it, Mercy, you won't feel a rut in the road."

She only looked at him, a look dry and unwavering.

"And not so long as our trip out here?"

"There'll be new things for you to see every day, Mercy. And this time you won't have the care of the children. I made the back low on purpose for you, Mercy, so you could see out."

She smiled. "And so the dust can see in?"

"There's the canvas," he said defensively.

All she wanted to say stood between them, but she was glad they had spoken together of this new thing, at last. It used to be they spoke of every little thing, no matter how little.

"I wanted to go back home," she said. "It was a rather childish idea I had, I guess. You made me think you were building."

"You mean I let you think it, Mercy. But it'll be home when we get there. It's always been home when we got there, hasn't it?"

"I don't know, Simon; home takes a lot of time, more time than just building. Sometimes I think twice in a lifetime is about all the time there is."

"I'll see that it looks east again."

"And going, I'll be looking east and the sun won't always be going down."

"That's a funny thing you said, Mercy. It's really quite an even show, you know, that coming up and going down."

"There's nothing but what you see, Simon, after all."

"That's not faith, Mercy. There's what you don't see, too, as long as you believe it."

He stood up, relieved, and remembered the night she had known about Charlot and the relief it had been to him. And now she knew once more and it was a relief again. A man shouldn't keep things, he told himself; it was a kind of cowardice in him.

"I'll try to be better by spring," she said. But that night, perhaps from the worry and excitement, she had a bad spell of coughing and for several hours Charlot labored with her to help her to breathe more easily. It was the worst spell since the fire, and she was not able to talk to anyone much for a long time. Until the day Dapper died and the whole family mourned together.

Chapter XLVI

For a time, in the West, a good dog was harder to find and would bring more money than a good milch cow. Folks watched their dogs as carefully as their dogs watched them. But after the family came to live in Nauvoo, Dapper would not stand watching any more. He was forever running off, and finally Bert tied him up till he should learn better. He'd be shot if he got to meddling round loose, or somebody would pick him up and take him off down river.

After he was tied, something happened to Dapper. All at once he began to grow old. He still stood anxious under caresses and still sat up when the boys bade him, but with a difference. With a droop in him, and his paws too lax in front of him. At night he always lay by the fire, and when he came in he would go to his place immediately and unobtrusively. Nobody paid much attention, everything was different, maybe it was natural for Dapper to be different, too.

One day he did nothing but lie down, so Bert untied him. And that night he came shaking the door like old times and Bert let him in. But instead of going to his rug by the fire he followed Bert to his chair. Bert touched the shaggy head with his fingers and fondled the ears in the way that used to set Dapper trembling with pleasure. Then the dog moved away and stood waiting by Jarvie, until Jarvie too petted him. Then Menzo and

George and Betsy and Joey, one by one. They did not pay much attention that night; it was the next day they remembered all this and it became a thing of significance.

Dapper went to the door and lifted his paw against it and whined a little, so Bert let him out. They all thought, they declared afterward, that he would be back in a little.

But that night he did not sleep by the fire, and next day one of the Cahoon boys brought his collar and said when he went to the Islands he saw Dapper lying on the ice, dead. He had got just west of the Islands, heading west, the Cahoon boy said. Not shot or anything, just naturally dead.

It was after that they remembered, and the whole family wept for days and Bert slept with the old collar under his pillow. They recalled everything Dapper had ever done, they recalled the game he played, the snakes he killed, they recalled his face and his bark, which had really been special, had it not? And they knew they would never love another dog so much.

BRIGHAM YOUNG stared into the faces of his Elders, his Priests, his Teachers, and his Seventies.

"Those with finished wagons," he said. "They give us twenty-four hours to get started."

They sat unbelieving and looked at him. Only those who were General Authorities already knew and sat with their eyes on their hands.

An Elder trembled to his feet.

"The contract said in the spring," he said. "When grass grows and water runs, it said, and the river's still froze over."

It had become a symbol of what permanency they knew, the frozen immovable river. Until such a time as it should begin to swell and roar and cast the fragments of its armor into the air, they could be warm in their houses and safe in Nauvoo.

Brigham knew this and his face was very set and very pale. But they sensed the finality in both his face and his voice when he spoke to them. " It's like I told the committee, if they knew how to keep a promise themselves they could believe we mean to keep ours. But they don't believe promises or contracts or the sign of a man's hand, because honor is a thing they don't understand. They don't believe anything but what they can see moving in front of them. The only things they'll believe are wagons on the move, and oxen facing west, and emptied houses."

" In two more months the grass'll be growing, and we'll leave according to the contract! "

" When a Saint finds there's no use talking," Brigham said steadily, " he does something else that there's some use doing."

" In two more months – "

The Authorities came to Brigham's rescue, grimly.

" In two months they're afraid the feel of spring will make a man want to start planting his land. Once a man has seed in his land, he's a fighting man, once he even sets his plow in it he'll fight for it."

" We promised no plowing – "

" They don't set no store by promises! "

" What difference do two months make to us, anyway? We've lived outdoors before, we've found holes to live in, like gophers. And those of us who were strong got to be all face, like Indians, and we were stronger than we ever were. And the ones that died – they were the spirits with weak tabernacles who were not meant for the work of the Gospel in this world."

Earnest finality lay in Brother Brigham's voice:

" We'll make winter quarters, and when the spring comes, we'll already be on our way, we'll just stop to plant for those that come after. I promised them a thousand families would leave tomorrow, and I've listed the heads of those families."

They called names. Brigham knew what men should go,

knew what men had finished wagons, knew what men had a talent for making home where home had never been before.

When his name was called, Simon Baker stood up, protesting. "I've three wagons finished — some of the Brothers can take them and welcome. But I can't go yet."

Brigham said simply: "We need wagonwrights, Brother Baker, and wheelwrights and carpenters. There are more things that we need in a good man than we can pile into a good wagon, and they're not things you can take from one man and put into another."

"I've a sick wife — a mighty sick wife, Brother Brigham."

"Sometimes — " and all of them listened, because many of them had reasons waiting for their names to be called — "Sometimes Satan has clever ways to blind us to the calls of the Gospel. Before the spirit that dares to defy circumstance, what is lack and what is plenty? When I started to England to open the glorious missionary work for the Gospel, I couldn't stand up in the wagon on my own strength to say farewell to my family. But I said farewell, with the help of Brother Haws and leaning on the side of the wagon. I hadn't a coat but a quilt from the crib of one of my children — but when I came home I had a hat and a coat and shoes and money in my pocket, and I'd sent thousands of Saints home to Zion! "

Simon stood listening, leaning his legs on the bench in front of him, and his knuckles were white with clenching. It had become a sermon, but he knew it was not only for him, it was for all of them.

"What is lack, I say, and what is plenty? And what is sickness and health before God? The Day of Healing in Nauvoo, I saw men and women rising under the Prophet Joseph's hands. Men who believed they had said their last words rose up and lived to haul stone for the Temple, lived to sit in front of me today, and will live to build another Temple in another land. If any reason comes to any of you why you can't perform the missions called for by your God in heaven, you'll know it doesn't come from God but from Lucifer. Dismiss any such reason, don't allow it to stay in your minds or come out of your mouths in words. If you feel uncertain about this thing, don't argue about it with me, but go home to your closets and shut your doors and have it out with God – ask Him! And don't expect lightning and thunder – He doesn't talk like that. He talks with a sweet peace and a knowledge that this thing must be done."

Simon sat down, humbled and shaken. They called more names. And the Spirit began to be manifest and men bore testimonies of times when the way had been opened unto them. Finally Simon himself stumbled to the front of the room and declared that he, too, had seen the Way opening before him.

After meeting, Dr. Richards came to him. He could leave the bed-wagon and one of the Brothers could bring Mercy after, at a more favorable season. In the meantime there would be other lone women who'd be glad of the company and the service, maybe Sister Eliza. There would be no more danger here; that was understood if a thousand families demonstrated the full intention, on the move. And without the children she'd be likely to mend faster.

But neither Dr. Richards nor Simon reckoned with Mercy herself.

❧ ❧ ❧

THIS time Simon himself told her, and at once.

She looked up at him with startled intensity. " Why should I stay, Simon? What would I stay for? "

He felt lame and weak with excitement, and then her eyes the last months had bothered him; they got bigger in her face and seemed more important as the weeks passed, under the sharpened line of her hair. As always, he wanted to escape without allowing her emotion to hurt him, or her accusation.

"You know – we thought by spring you'd be better."

"If I must be a burden on a long journey, I'd rather be on the backs of my own people, Simon. I don't see any particular reason to expect to be better by spring, anyway."

"I talked to Dr. Richards, and I'm just telling you he said –" He spoke tempestuously. "I tried to get out of going now, Mercy – I tried it, but you should have heard Brother Brigham. He made a whole sermon out of it – there's no excuse big enough to get out of doing the work of the Lord, because the Lord makes a Way."

She laughed the laugh that was so hard for him to bear patiently, little and bitter.

"There's no excuse for staying in one place, then, when the Gospel moves on – no excuse unless it's having died there, Simon?"

"That wouldn't even be an excuse," Simon said, and smiled a little. "If a man dies, he's just gone another place to do his part."

She tried to make her voice light. "Really, Simon, if you leave me here and refuse to let me do my duty, God might take it into His head to make me do some work somewhere else! That's quite ungenerous, Simon. I'd as soon do what I can in this world."

"I was only thinking of making things easier for you, Mercy."

"And maybe thinking of making things easier for Charlot!" She had not wanted to say it, but it came out.

"I wasn't thinking of that and you know it."

"Well, you can be sure Charlot is. And you can tell her for me, I'll ride very quietly – with all those ticks she won't hear so much as a bump out of me all the way, clear to Oregon if we go there!"

He looked into her face then and saw the excitement there,

a terrible excitement like that of a child who is up hours beyond his bedtime and has not the day-long quietude to bear exciting things. She looked very small, rigid under the coverlet, and her braids were lying along the pillow, twisting childishly when she moved her head. There was a look about her that he had seen about Betsy when something was broken that she wanted mended at once.

He thought: " I haven't been able to face her for a long time – she takes things so to heart." And he leaned down and laid his cheek against hers, losing sight of her with his face in the pillow because he could not face her, even now. Her hand lifted from the cover and she patted him gently.

" You see, Simon," she said, " I've got to go. There's nothing for me to stay for. If I shouldn't go – if I shouldn't be with you, just a little every day, even to see you from the back, driving, or riding by, maybe, I'm afraid I'd never get any better. If you weren't ever coming in at night and I knew you were getting farther and farther – I'm afraid of it, Simon."

" I didn't know that mattered."

" Oh, Simon! What else could matter? It's everything I've had, since Father. What else have I had? "

" I'm sorry, I didn't think of it like that. I was thinking about the best thing for you."

" How could I get better here alone? " Her voice struggled to rise, but she conquered it to hold him, spoke as softly as she could and yet make him hear. " Have I been happy here, Simon? "

" I thought so. For quite a while anyway. We were happy for a while, weren't we, Mercy? "

She remembered Georgie after they had all had smallpox and it had been weeks with everybody sick, looking up at her as a sick child looks and saying: " When is everybody going to be feeling good again, Mother? " Simon was like Georgie, asking his question.

" Of course we were happy, Simon — nobody was ever happier. Sometimes I lie here and think about it. You were doing things and I was doing things and at night we all told what we were doing and how much was done — "

" And some way," he said, stirred, " it was all part of something bigger, and that made everything important."

Her voice scrambled hastily then, as though afraid this time would be broken. " One time I keep remembering — I don't know why, but I even dream about it sometimes, just dozing, you know. We had the children over for the celebration, you remember, and we came home, after dark — "

He knew.

The first chilly night of autumn it had been, and the Indians had danced in Nauvoo and Menzo was wild with it inside of him as though (as Simon said) he had gone and swallowed the tom-tom. When they went home, up the hill at the last after a silvery-frosty ride on the ferry, Ginger ran up the hill with the plumes of her breath reeling out behind her. Then Mercy had laid a log on the fire while Simon unharnessed and bedded down the animals, had leaned over with Joey on one arm, asleep, and contentment had lain around her like a cape; and when the room was warm they all had milk, sitting on the benches by the fire with their shoes off, and she coaxed sleepy Joey to take his from a cup, and the fire seemed to go into them all, and they talked of the day, and then, one by one, slipped away to bed. She and Simon had been alone there by the fire, tired but wanting all the rest of love, drugged and exalted together with warmth and content.

" Times like that."

Then the school program that time when Cuddeback had put Menzo's papers on the highest row, with his curlicued writing spelling his name plain at the bottom. The program with its tenseness because of Bert's not being sure of his piece, but his getting through it with only one little stammer nobody else seemed to notice. Only pride then, and the good feeling among neighbors who looked indulgently at their own children and at others who had not done any better or any worse. Then fiddle music, by Cuddeback himself, who had rhythm in his insides and could take it out and hand it to you with a fiddle bow so that your feet answered without thinking too much of steps but mostly of music. Brother Joseph had come that night and shared the applejack and said jolly things about the stone schoolhouse being really one of the temples to God, for was not intelligence the glory of God? And shouldn't the schoolhouse be of stone as the Mayor insisted (though some Brothers said logs were good enough), when it ought to symbolize the good substantial things that children must learn to get ready for the stiff weather of living?

Simon had sat that night with his hand hard over Mercy's hand, so hard she felt her own pulse beating against her knee.

"Remember, Simon, we wanted to dance together that night so bad, and you said we'd better wait till after the baby. It was Beck I was carrying then, Simon."

She lay smiling.

"Remember, they got to singing songs around the fire and Peter played his fiddle and Old John his guitar. We sang *Harm Link*, remember."

She could hear the drawl of the syllables, the increased volume at the ends of verses when voices uncertain of the words caught on and joined in like belated marchers catching step.

"And when they played *Old Dan Tucker*, I wanted to die if I couldn't dance — "

She sang, and they beat their hands on the coverlet in time to the swift tune, and Simon sang with her. She even laughed, something he had almost forgotten she could do so thoroughly; it was not the hard laugh, brittle to breaking, that had been troubling him lately, but soft with remembering and with that indulgence with which folks sing the songs that belong to them.

Old Dan Tucker climbed a tree,
His Lord and Saviour for to see. . . .

"I always liked the ones that took your breath away," she said. "I liked to hear folks falling over their tongues!"

"You never did!"

He put his face on the pillow again, wanting to be there, wanting to be unoppressed by the weight of the suffering that had taken all this out of her for so long. He knew sharply that it had been between them this long time, that he had not been able to come to her around it, that it had destroyed ease between them. She had tried, once in a while, to force it back again, even around Charlot, especially around Charlot that one night. He could see that now, and knew how hard she had tried. But he had been afraid to look at her, and knew with his face in the pillow that he was still afraid.

"I like to hear you laugh," he mumbled. "And I haven't heard you sing since God knows when."

"Sometimes I sing for the children," she said. She was breathless with the importance of the moment, and afraid of it, too, so that she understood sharply why he could not look at her.

"We ought to sing all together again, sometimes," she said.

He was silent. Then he said in a strained voice: "When you've got to hurt somebody, Mercy-girl, it makes you hard, it puts a crust on you that's a kind of shield. It shouldn't, but it does."

"I know."

It was a time to remember. Broken from all time without warning, it came and rested in her hand unperceived until she felt the whole sweet weight of it. There were days like this moment, murky from dawn, with a moving ceiling of cloud and a depth of gray in every direction that the wind could not break but only encouraged, piling it and piling it in cloud-heaps that added to one another as though where clouds lived there was a never ending source of clouds. Then a burst, sudden as a meteor, and the full sun out of it, and down from it a slanting of widening white rays.

"It's been a long time," she said, and her eyes sought his, asking. But he said nothing more, and she spoke hurriedly, fearing to lose him.

"Simon, maybe I've just taken it too hard. Maybe I have. It seemed, for a while, all happening at once, it seemed like I was being pushed right out of the world. But they couldn't all be cheated the way Eliza was, I can see that. I've been trying to see it, how there had to be the little Simons, really — "

He caught his breath and his muscles tensed; when he spoke, his voice floundered and he was apart from her, removed and cool. "Brother Joseph couldn't help it," he said. "He was told what to do just the way we are, only directly from God. You and Eliza should remember this world is just a beginning."

"Oh, Eliza remembers, Simon. But it's true, she was cheated — "

Charlot came to the door and Simon stood up and Mercy knew that it was over. Awkwardly he moved away and she slipped over until her head lay in the hollow his face had left in the pillow. She reached out and touched him.

"We women like things we can touch sometimes," she said whimsically, but he moved from her as though he had become afraid of her fingers.

NOTHING but the grandeur of blank verse would do. Rhyme had a way of twitting when you didn't want it to; it was not for this prophecy.

Saturday Evening Thoughts.

First Eliza wrote the title, and then the surge of lines, unstopped by the exigencies of alphabets and sounds.

The pathway of the Saint, the safest path
Will prove, tho' perilous: for 'tis foretold,
All things that can be shaken, God will shake!

This Joseph might have said, and had said in his own words. Was there anything, any good thing, Joseph had not said? Zealot and dreamer, he saw a wrong and wanted to take his bare hands and wrestle with it. And when he failed to remake the world to the pattern of his dreams, finding life too short, then there was this for his own people: " Forsake evil and you will achieve immunity to the consequences of this wicked world. Set yourselves apart in righteousness; a Zion is your own if you build a wall around yourself and refuse to let the practices of The World corrupt you. Let it be said again and yet again, a man is his own governor; even Ralegh said it, so long ago, the apartness of mankind – 'In the great world man is a small and little world.' "

Then let me be a Saint, and be prepar'd
For the approaching Day. . . .

When she had finished it, she read it aloud as was her wont, and found it dignified and adequate. It would be a good poem to copy and give to the people to carry in their wagons; they would be wondering if Sainthood were a thing to be cherished, they would be wondering tomorrow when Nauvoo faded behind them. They would be wondering, even, some of them, whether a citadel of the spirit and a promise hazy with futurity could compare with the security of home, steady with the tangible strength of logs, of stones, of good red brick.

She spent most of the night making many copies. There would be keepsakes from friend to friend tomorrow; let this one serve to cast their eyes before them.

Chapter XLVII

Mercy could hear Charlot giving the orders, listing, planning, packing.

"The crane, the Dutch oven, the big trunk, that big kettle, what in heaven's name could we do without that? There'll be washing; won't it be months if not forever? The big board, it can hang onto the side, and both skillets, and all the bedding and the chest – one of the boys can sleep on it – or one *in* it, for that matter! – and both cows to follow, tied to the first wagon, there won't be too much milk, goodness knows, from either one of 'em when they start walking all day – and, well, it's all right with me if you take your cat, Betsy, if you carry him, but cats won't follow along the way dogs will. It's a pity Dapper – but he was too old to make it, even if he'd lived to start.

"I *said* yes, Betsy, though goodness knows where we'll get the milk to feed him. I should think we'd care for the babies first."

Charlot cried when the house sold for so little. "A sudden sale like this with folks leavin' anyhow, what can you expect in cash, take it or leave it!"

"For God's sake, there's plenty for sale hereabouts, you can take your God-damn house an' lot on yer wagon an' take it to hell 'n' gone, for all of me."

Simon was polite and considerate with the gentiles just now, and smoothed down the ruffled feathers of both buyer and seller. Yet Charlot signed with a snuffle at her nose.

"My inheritance," she said, "for a mess of pottage."

"Fifty dollars and four oxen are a likely mess of pottage just now," Simon said seriously. "Some aren't selling, aren't getting anything. We're lucky to get what we can."

Mercy heard everything, stiff in her bed. When she went to sleep, knowing the next day was the last in Nauvoo, strangely, too suddenly the last, she dreamed a long confused dream in which Simon piled stones endlessly, piled stones and piled stones, and as fast as they were piled as high as his head the wind leveled them. But he did not seem to notice, only went on piling and piling. Then she was under them and he was putting them on top of her, one by one, and she called out to him that he must not, but he piled on, imperturbably, and still the wind took them, like feathers, but upon her they were indeed stones.

When she awoke, he was sitting by her, talking in a low voice and patting her.

She tried to tell him, but she was breathless and began coughing. Then she tried again, and when he understood he shook his head and laughed, but she realized it had hurt him and wished she had not told it after all.

"It was just a dream, of course. I don't know what's the matter with me, dreaming such a thing."

He stayed a long time, patting her, and she slept again.

The dream came back then, and she woke once more with her breath difficult, with spasms of acute breathlessness that would not allow her to call out while they lasted, as though the stones, piled and piled, had really smothered her. Charlot came and rubbed her, and brought another pillow for her back, to lift her and make breathing more easy.

Again she slept, and when she woke she had no notion of what time it might be, but after dawn of a day as gray as yesterday.

There was a hard surge through her legs, a lifting and prickling that made them seem to grow, and she writhed, turning from side to side, to ease them. Yet even this motion did not help. The excitement, the dream, the imminence of leave-taking this day, she knew it was all a part of what she felt, and sought to calm herself. But her voice was above her, beyond effort, and she began to moan.

Simon was coming, she saw him pause in the door, looking back, and then Charlot's voice, clearly: " Remember, it's like Brigham says – it's just a trick to keep you from doing your duty."

The very words, plainly: " It's just a trick to keep you from doing your duty."

Fury rose in her, coiling up from her stomach in waves of nausea. She heard herself crying out, and Simon came to her. " Don't let her, Simon, don't let her say such things. How could she say – she wants you to hate me! "

He did not seem to understand, just started clucking to her to calm her, and said: " Shsh! Quiet, Mercy, it's going to be a long time before you can rest in your bed again all day. Try – "

" Don't you listen to her, she hates me. She's afraid you won't leave me, she's afraid you won't leave me."

He stood up. She could not see his face in the gray dawn.

She began to scream and was aware that she was being wild and incoherent, but there was the pain and the fury. She heard him call: " Charlot! "

He spoke swiftly to Charlot when she came, and then he went out. Charlot leaned over, seeking for the back of Mercy's neck, and began to rub gently, gently with her fingers.

" Lie quiet," she soothed. " Lie quiet, Mercy. He'll be right back, you'll be all right. He's bringing the Elders."

Mercy heard herself gasping. " You don't want him to think of me – you don't want him to think of anybody but you. You want him to forget about me, you want him to leave me here. But he won't leave me, he promised. He promised me yesterday. If I have to be carried, like Sarah – "

" He was thinking of you," Charlot whispered. " He's always thinking of you. That's all that's worrying him – it'll be so hard on you. Shsh. A wagon's not a house, he was just telling me that, a wagon's not a house, after all, no matter how good a wagon it is."

Mercy saw that Charlot's face was strained, that there were even tears on it. And she was glad.

" You want them all," she cried wildly. " All of them, mine and yours too. You want everything."

She lay staring for a moment. It seemed as though Charlot was not merely Charlot but a shape, something big and obscure towering over her, a shape that wanted everything, time and love and memories and all she had, even her children it wanted, and her husband and even the years she had looked to.

Charlot broke the illusion, whispering: " Shsh, try to lie quiet."

Her fingers were quick and firm, stroking, pressing the neck.

" You want everything – " Mercy struggled away from the hand. " But you can't have Jarvie. And you can't have Menzo. And you can't have Simon, either, because I took all there was of him and you'll find it out. I took it all, we were young enough – it's only his duty, I told him I knew it."

" Shsh." Charlot sought to touch her again.

" Shsh."

Simon came back, and when he lifted her she struggled against him, too, still talking wildly as though she suffered a blind terror and did not recognize him or anybody.

" She was all right yesterday," he said, agonized, and took her on his lap, holding her, speaking tenderly. She fell into paroxysms of coughing on his knees. Gasping, she saw the world a circle of caverns of varying colors, heavy-colored as though with great depth. Then she saw Jarvie, by the foot of the bed, his hands wrung together against his jeans and his face writhing. And the Elders, standing around her in a circle with their arms together.

Dr. Richards was with them, that doctor who still had a last resort when medicine and skill failed him. " A spiritual doctor," Joseph always called him, commending him.

She heard him plainly now. " It's a question, to be frank with you. Any extra strain, and she'll be out like a candle. I've only seen one like it before, I don't know. Nobody knows."

Strangely, she heard her own voice through his, whimpering. " If she wants to go, I'd say take her. But I don't know. To be frank with you, I don't know."

They were silent.

" Maybe God knows," Dr. Richards said. " But nobody else."

Simon had something in his hand, touched her forehead with it, anointed her hands. Holy oil. She thought of unction, but dismissed it; no, not with these simple Elders, not anything so solemn as finality here, but merely hope, the Spirit in all of us, struggling to unite in some of us, in the Priesthood to give power, to give healing. Perhaps healing, if there was faith enough. She lay still and listened now, because she was afraid and because she pitied Jarvie's face, and they took it up, one by one, around the circle. So simple. She listened. Like the day they had come to Jarvie, Joey's birthday. But then Brother Joseph had been with them. Looking at their earnest faces and hearing them imitate the words he had said so many times, she thought: " He is with them still."

" Our Father which art in heaven, if it be Thy will, look with compassion upon this Thy handmaiden and give her Thy blessing."

" Our Father, if it be Thy will, give strength again."

" In the name of the Father, the Son, and the Holy Ghost, and with the power of the Priesthood in me vested, I bless this

Sister and command her to rise and be made whole. In accordance with Thy will, in the name of Thy beloved Son."

It was never exactly the same, not like the sacrament prayers, but always different, as the Spirit itself dictated. Sometimes stumblingly, but always the Spirit stumbles in some men, sticking on their thick tongues. She even smiled a little as the thought came.

Simon laid her down gently and went out with the Elders, motioning to Jarvie. Then Charlot opened Mercy's gown and rubbed her with wide, firm, capable hands, rubbing the blessed oil into her skin. She lay still and felt the soothing motion of Charlot's hands, not thinking of Charlot or of anybody, but only of the comfort of words and of the comfort of moving hands, anointed hands now and without identity.

Chapter XLVIII

THE GENTILE came again to get his papers, and Betsy stared at him from a corner. She was surprised that he was exactly like any other man, except maybe more whiskers. When he came in she could smell stale milk on him the way she could on the boys and, very faintly, she was aware of the smell of manure. Just a man who milked cows and hauled manure and tended to horses, like anybody else, but she could see how Aunt Charlot despised him and how anxious Father was to get him out of the door. Once, she knew, he had sworn with big strong terrible words, saying the Lord's name in vain, but not since Father stood up to him and reminded him that Charlot was in the room. Now he seemed very quiet, and twisted his hat a little in his hands in a way she was familiar with, among the Brothers.

"You want to stay a few days account of your wife," he said self-consciously, "I ain't in *that* big a hurry – "

Betsy went out to the gate, Charlot's prim gate, and put her feet securely between the palings and began to swing back and forth, bending her body. She knew that yesterday or the day before, Charlot would have called to her, asking if she wanted, for heaven's sakes, to break the gate down, but today Charlot said nothing. After all, wasn't it this gentile's gate?

She saw her cat, Purrmiew, come down the fence, leisurely,

waving his tail through the air and stepping forward with great dignity. Sometimes the very tip of his tail jerked abruptly as though it were a thing apart with a joint of its own, and sometimes the whole tail wove upward in a moving curve that ended in air. When he came to the space between fence and gate, he leaped lightly, the gentle wave of motion moving down his body. Then he stood between the palings and her arms and the moment he felt the warmth of her sleeves, he began to rub and she was aware of the trembling his purr made in him.

" I should think we'd care for the babies first," Aunt Charlot had said. " Goodness knows if there'll be enough milk for the *babies* — "

This was a thing to make a lump in a throat, and the lump had been there all morning. Now it gathered together tighter than ever and from it came a stinging that spread back of the face, you would almost think a congregation of tears gathering like rain into a cloud and having moved closer and closer together, at last too heavy to bear.

Besides, had not this cat been achieved through a kind of personal travail, and so did he not belong to her in a *special* way and she to him?

Betsy sniffled.

The gentile was coming down the path, and she stepped from the gate hastily, gathering Purrmiew close. She saw that the gentile had spectacles and peered from them curiously, almost with kindness one might say if he were anything but a gentile.

" That your cat? " he inquired.

She nodded, sniffling again.

" He a mouser? "

She nodded.

The gentile stooped, peering at Purrmiew.

" He's a fine cat. You want to leave him here at the house, I'll take care of 'im. I'll be needin' a good mouser."

Betsy stood irresolute. Then she dared to look up very directly, straight into the eye-glasses. " I didn't know whether gentiles liked cats or not," she said.

He blinked, and his mouth trembled toward grinning. " If you mean Christians," he said, " I guess they like cats as well as anybody. Myself, I'm more of a Methodist, I guess! "

" Oh! " She regarded him with interest. " Aunt Charlot said you were a gentile."

" Some say gentiles are heathens and some say gentiles are Christians," he said mildly. " Maybe your aunt thought I talked like a heathen, an' maybe she was right. But Christian or heathen, I'm specially fond of cats."

She looked at Purrmiew with reverence, and he lifted a paw exploringly over the fabric of her sleeve and spoke his fervent little monosyllable. She felt the spreading of tears behind her nose again, wanting to sneeze or cry or something. Purrmiew yawned and then cuddled his nose into the crook of her elbow. It was almost too much because it was especially like a cat, a real cat-thing, and the gentile seemed to realize what she felt because he studied the palings of the gate with veiled eyes. After a moment he looked at her tentatively.

" You decide," he said. " If you leave him here in the house, I'll take good care of him."

He went through the gate and started up the street, and Betsy stood watching him. Impulsively then she trotted after him, and when he turned to her, inquiring, she said: " You'll want to know his name. It's Purrmiew."

He smiled mistily. " Purrmiew. I'll remember."

She went back to the house and sat by the fire on her little chair with Purrmiew contentedly in her lap. She felt the warmth of him clear through her dress, and he felt the warmth of the fire and began stretching at once, lying on his side and yawning, holding his paws out on rigid legs, his claws extended, sheerly luxurious.

When Eliza came to see Mother, the two of them were there by the fire. Eliza kissed Betsy and rubbed her finger around Purrmiew's ears.

"Eliza," Betsy asked with somber emphasis, "do you think it's all right to leave Purrmiew for the gentile?"

"They ought not to mind our *cats*," Eliza said. "They don't need to be afraid our *cats* will preach the Gospel!"

There was bitterness even in such a little thing and Betsy detected it. This had been a bitter day for Eliza, a day of many good-byes.

While Betsy sat by the fire, stroking Purrmiew and thinking: "He doesn't know I won't be here to cuddle him tomorrow," the gentile spoke seriously to his wife, puzzled. "Funny thing, that little girl with her cat – sort of made me think Mormons were folks, after all, folks like the rest of us, maybe."

"I've been reading this to all the families that are going," Eliza told Mercy. "Don't try to talk, just lie still and listen. I've been thinking especially of you every time I've read it."

She saw that Mercy's eyes were feverish, and when she spoke noticed that her voice was petulant and sharp.

"I want to ask you something first. Dr. Richards this morning – I heard him telling Simon something and I wondered if he'd told you. I don't think he believes I'll live to get there, Eliza."

"Oh, that's foolish! After all, Mercy, there'll be Elders all the way."

"Sometimes it takes more than Elders."

"It always takes more – you have to be with them. You have to believe along with them, Mercy."

She leaned over the bed anxiously. "You mustn't be afraid,

that's the first thing to remember, because there's nothing to be afraid of. It's a matter of faith."

Mercy sighed. "What were you going to read to me?"

Eliza thumbed hurriedly through the thin leaves of her Bible. "This is just what you need," she said. Then she read, as one reads who must have the whole poem and loves it:

"The Lord is my shepherd; I shall not want. He maketh me to lie down in green pastures: He leadeth me beside the still waters. He restoreth my soul: He leadeth me in the paths of righteousness for His name's sake. Yea, though I walk through the valley of the shadow of death I will fear no evil: for Thou art with me; Thy rod and Thy staff they comfort me. Thou preparest a table before me in the presence of mine enemies; Thou anointest my head with oil; my cup runneth over. Surely goodness and mercy shall follow me all the days of my life, and I will dwell in the house of the Lord forever."

"The only thing," Mercy said as though she had not been listening, "I feel as though I couldn't bear to be left somewhere on the prairie. It gives me a feeling I don't like; it always did. I feel out here as though I were in the middle of nothing, unprotected, and nothing flows all around me every direction. I'd almost rather be left right here, so I could be on the bluff, it's a little up, you know, and the river stops you — "

Eliza was very firm. "You've got to stop thinking about things like that. Anybody can think such things if he lets himself go, but you've got to hold yourself together. It's like checking a horse you're riding, you've got to pull back on yourself and keep your mind at a walk. Just think of ordinary little things, anything."

Mercy lay frowning.

"It's a matter of faith, really," Eliza said again.

Portia came in then, and Eliza read the psalm once more, rhythmically with the height of voice she never gave to prose.

" I'll see you again before you start out," she said. " But not to say good-by. Nobody is saying good-by – are they, Portia? They're all saying: 'See you out west'; it's a sort of silent agreement."

" Brother Brigham says we should even say it to Nauvoo, because we'll find a place and build it all over again."

" Not Nauvoo." Eliza shook her head. " Maybe another Zion, but never another Nauvoo."

" I'm not *that* sentimental," Portia said.

" I guess I am." At the door Eliza said soberly: " See you out west, Portia."

" See you out west," Portia answered.

" Are you and John going after all? " Mercy inquired when Eliza had gone. " John told me he was too old to go."

" He's not too old for anything I can put my finger on," Portia said. " He's gone every place the Church has ever gone, and there's no keeping him back now. He'll grumble till the folks in New Orleans'll think we're havin' a thunderstorm, but he'll go just the same. He'll go around singing all the way, too, and feel like a regular hero."

" It shouldn't be required," Mercy said. " It's like he said to me Christmas, the sick and the old shouldn't have to go."

" If John stayed here, he'd be dead in a month from having failed of his duty. He was born thinking about his duty and he's thought of it ever since. I tell him he grumbles just to make folks tell him how indispensable he is."

" Things *are* hard to do, sometimes."

Portia spoke briskly. " Like I tell John, it's all a matter of will. You don't want to give in to thinking something's hard. I've seen folks that took to their beds with too much thinking."

Mercy's hands gripped the clothes. " I don't think that's true, Portia. I can't imagine anybody *wanting* – "

" I've seen it plenty of times. It's a matter of either using your will or giving in. I guess I could've gone to bed after Charles died if I'd a mind to, but I didn't. I said to myself: ' It's a matter of will.' And I've seen the day that showed I was right."

" Eliza just got through saying it's a matter of faith."

Portia's long face twitched with eagerness. " Maybe it's the same. Anyhow, I told John I felt it was my duty to come and tell you what I thought. It's like some of the Sisters were saying the other day, we've all had as much trouble as you have and some of us more, but precious few of us go to bed over it! It's a matter of will, like I say – "

" Maybe – " Mercy's hands ached from grasping the clothes. " Maybe it's as well not to talk too much today, Portia. I didn't sleep well, and this morning – "

" That's why I came. John heard through Elder Pugmire. When women start having spells like that, it's in the mind, not only in the body. Once I knew a woman who had spells, and her husband kept running to the doctor in the night, till finally the doctor gave her husband a willow and said: ' You go home and spank her – that's all the medicine she needs! ' And she never had another spell, all her life."

Mercy began to laugh, weirdly and helplessly, and Portia laughed with her, wiping her eyes on her handkerchief. She rose, laughing. " There! " she said. " I told John I could do you some good."

Mercy nodded, laughing, but before Portia had reached the door, she had turned her face into the pillow, coughing.

" See you out west," Portia said gaily. And to John, waiting by the gate: " She'll be a different woman, I tell you; before I left I had her laughing like a girl."

A matter of faith.

A matter of will.

Surely not weakness, surely not merely lacking strength to lose Mary, surely not only inability to lose Simon, surely not these alone. Portia's Charles burning in the barn and her two children not lasting the winter – but Portia was a lean and a hard and a long-faced woman, like the lean trees that take wind easily. And Melissa – poor Melissa had walked the night with it. And the others. She reviewed them, one by one. Even Eliza, for all her talk about faith, after the martyrdom she was thinner and sharper. But somehow strengthened, too.

A matter of faith.

A matter of will.

Brother Brigham always said it, too – he always said: "The weak ones fall by the way."

JARVIE and Menzo climbed the bluff, and when they came to the place where the house had stood, a strange mass of unidentifiable shapes now under light snow, they stood there together, slapping their hands to warm them. And to make big confident sounds.

"I don't see why we came," Menzo said. "It's like pinching yourself where it hurts."

"I promised Mother I'd come."

Jarvie walked to the chimney, still standing, stone upon stone, like a monument. The hearth was there and the fireplace, gaping.

"They don't let the Indians come back much," Menzo said. "It makes them want to fight. Like one of the chiefs said, 'They don't like to see corn growing where their dead sleep.'"

"Say it all, Menz. I like it."

So Menzo said all he remembered, and as he spoke Jarvie was conscious of the same emotion out of Menzo that came out with his dancing. A litheness of syllable almost, feeling pressed out into words as feeling could be pressed out with rhythm of the muscles – feeling that advanced to meet one who waited.

"'We must find new homes and the white man will plant corn where our dead sleep. Our villages, the paths we have made, and the flowers we have loved, will soon be his. I have moved many times and have seen the white man put his feet in the tracks of the Indians and make the earth into fields. They will be glad when we have gone, they will soon forget the meat and the lodge-fire of the Indian, forever free to strangers. At all times the Indian has asked only for what he fought for, the right to be free.' "

"It wasn't any more fair to send them off than it is to send us," Jarvie said. "I see what you meant – it was theirs before it was ours."

"They liked it here pretty much, I guess." Menzo walked to the chimney and slapped at it, brushing away snow from the stones. "They liked the river and it was good ground for maize."

"It's not fair to send anybody off his land."

Menzo looked at his brother critically. "You talk like you'd just discovered that all by yourself," he said. "Like it had just come to you."

"Don't, Menz. The thing is, it's never come inside of me before, just like this. It's coming back here maybe, and then talking about them – it sort of cuts into you and gets clear to the middle. It makes you want to fight."

They wandered around, stirring the snow with their shoes, picking up charred wood and bits of stone and tossing them by again. They wandered out to the place where the pig-pen had been and the barn and then 'way out where the south field lay, still fenced, looking wide and still as though it waited patiently for spring again.

Jarvie pointed to the fence. "That's where they tied Father," he said. "Right there."

"More south, I think," Menzo said.

"There's where Ginger knocked the rail off the night of the fire, it was about there."

They preserved a lightness of voice, the two of them, not wishing to return to their feeling, a little ashamed of feeling so much. When they turned north again, they ran, kicking out and racing each other, finding high places to leap over, snow-covered clumps of sumach that their legs whisked through, shattering white design. They ran all the way to the river.

Chapter XLIX

ALL day the wagons moved into line, taking their places systematically as Brother Brigham had ordered. Clear from Young Street to the north, along Mulholland, Kimball, Parley, Sidney Streets, they came. One street and then another knew the rumbling of the big wheels, and as they passed, folks who were to remain behind came to their doors and followed to the bank of the river. And all day, from time to time, the band played, cheering them on.

The committee from Quincey rode the winter streets, waiting with guns handy. They saw the wagons packed and the children bundled, they heard the women call their men and boys inside for a last bite at their own fires. They were conscious, as they rode up and down, of the averted looks of men and women alike and of a smoldering disparagement that troubled them and made them sit their saddles straighter and talk louder to one another and occasionally to discharge a little powder from their guns, as though they required protection from scorn.

"Ho! *Ho!*" The teamsters kept their horses and their oxen in line, kept the cattle in order. Mulholland was alive as on a holiday, and Main Street was seething with folks leaving and folks bidding good-by, and clear to the river and across the ice moved a stream of wagons that seemed never-ending. Cows dragged from their warm sheds bawled dismally and excited dogs nipped at their heels. Great wheels churned the icy ruts into mud that deepened as the hours passed.

"See you out west! See you out west."

It was nearly dusk when the last company turned from the dooryards. Menzo strapped his canoe onto Baker's third wagon hastily. "It's good it's light," he said to Bert, who helped him, "or I'd not be able to take it." He was thinking: "There will be another river – not like the Mississippi, of course, because God never made two such rivers. But there will be a river, or maybe the kind of lake the Indians talk about, a wide still lake purple with mountains and green with trees."

Mercy sat up in bed and braided her hair with trembling fingers when Simon said: "Time, Mercy-girl." Her fingers fumbled among the locks of hair and she sought to control them, her teeth in her lips. A tide of feeling kept lifting in her, threatening her with tears, even with screaming. It was as though a hand gathered up her nerves, one by one, slipping them along like beads on a string, but closer and closer together until they lay in clusters, throbbing. She held her wrists steady and divided the long hair into three, outside over and under, other side over and under, over and under, over and under.

When she had finished, she left the bed and found her coat and put it on. She found her shoes and sat down and buttoned them slowly, clear to the top. When Simon came in, she stood up and laid her hand on the back of the chair, quite steadily.

"You don't need to get up, Mercy," he cried. "Jarvie and I were just going to take out the quilts, the wagon's all ready."

"I'll ride with you awhile, Simon," she said. "Isn't it better for me to ride out of Nauvoo the way I came in?"

He stared at her, incredulous, and a warm sense of power pervaded her as it had that day when she stood in the door with her tray in her hand, mistress of herself and of her house.

“ It’s wonderful,” he said huskily. “ It’s a testimony to start west with.”

She allowed him to help her a little, taking his arm, feeling very far above the ground and feeling it tremble under her strangely as her knees wavered. Jarvie came behind them, laden with quilts from her bed and with pillows.

In the kitchen Betsy sat stroking Purrmiew for a moment and then lifted her chin and pushed him from her resolutely and went out and closed the last door. He scrambled after her and, finding the door closed, mewed disconsolately, standing up against the boards. Helping Charlot bundle Sarah and little Simon, Betsy said soberly: “ You don’t think of cats when there are babies to think of.”

Charlot said nothing when she saw Mercy, nothing even when she saw that Simon helped Mercy to the seat of the first wagon. First wife, first wagon. When Simon came back to her and helped her onto the second wagon with her baby, she said brusquely: “ No use locking the door, they’ll be in before we can pick up our shadows behind us.”

“ No use,” Simon agreed.

“ I’d almost rather burn it than leave it to them.”

“ Brother Brigham said we’d leave like Christians, people are taught by example.”

Charlot sniffled and lifted her apron to wipe her eyes, even blew her nose on her first petticoat, which was unlike Charlot. Then she reached down to help Beck, and said: “ No Christian would get a good example from what I’m thinking! ”

“ Bert and Betsy can sit with Jarvis,” she said. “ And put Sarah in the cradle, Simon, she’s asleep already. Her mother needn’t be bothered with her yet.”

“ It’s going to be in the night, Jarvie,” Betsy said, as one who accepts recompense.

As the Baker wagons moved along the streets in their turn,

folks could scarcely believe their eyes, seeing Mercy Baker sitting high as you please beside Simon. And they called out and smiled and waved their hands. The word passed from one group to another.

"They had the Elders for her this morning."

It was a testimony to start west with.

Mercy heard the band playing once more, leading the way as though this were a parade going the length of Main Street, as though in a moment they would be passing Brother Joseph in his uniform, in front of the Mansion House. Yet there was the Mansion, its doors closed, impassive and unimpressed. The band was weary, the brasses lagging, but even a weary band serves to keep folks' spirits up.

"See you out west, see you out west, see you out west."

Eliza stood on the street near the river. She lifted her skirts and came running over the rutted snow, and beside the first Baker wagon she lifted her hands to find Mercy's.

"God bless you," she said. "We'll see you in the West, Mercy." Her voice, too, was weary from a day of difficult farewells.

Mercy's hands were very cold, even within her gloves. But she smiled and said: "Maybe it is a matter of faith, Eliza. I'll try to remember." And to herself she said: "And a matter of will."

Eliza stood watching, looking out over the river at the wagons full of people she knew, leaving homes she knew, and a poem began to shape itself in her mind, a poem for them to sing, of course, another poem for them to sing –

"Though we fly from vile aggression . . ."

She went hurriedly up the street and into her room and to the chest and lighted a candle with trembling fingers; it was too dark in here for writing, with the dusk falling and this one little window.

"Now what were the rhymes? Pray God I've not lost them –

aggression — profession — possession — oppression. The people will sing them."

Folks were beginning to light candles in their houses and to bring lanterns outdoors to follow the procession to the last wagon. When Simon spoke to his horses and they went down the bank and onto the river, the wagon leaned forward sickeningly and Mercy clung to the sides with frantic hands.

"Easy, *easy*," Simon's voice drew back on the syllables.

There was a great rolling sound, breaking of snow and grinding upon ice. The wagon-box leveled.

"You all right?" Simon asked.

"All right."

On the river the wind was strong and roared through the canvas. Ice crackled magnificently under the iron wheels. Mercy turned and looked back. A long narrowing line of wagons was following and alongside it were dots of men on horseback, captains of tens. And Brother Brigham rode tirelessly back and forth as he had done all day. The line was narrowed to a point now, and no more wagons moved from Nauvoo. The city lay blinking softly, along the swerve of her streets windows were marked and candle-lanterns moved in little circles on the snow. The Temple was only a shadow, but a colossal one, there on its hill. Later tonight, as Brother Brigham said, even tonight it would be lighted for work as usual, and it would be lighted every night as long as one Saint remained in Nauvoo. The last Saint remaining there would still climb the hill with candles and take off his shoes and pass through the great doors.

"It seems natural, looking back at Nauvoo," Mercy said.

Simon leaned to her and she repeated her words, louder because of the wind.

"In the morning," he said, laughing and remembering, "you'll see the sun come up!"

Then, while she watched from the river, something happened in Nauvoo. Something familiar and terrible, a sudden flaring, a red glow that spread almost instantly and then began leaping toward the sky.

" Simon! " Her fingers dug into his arm. " Simon, what are they doing? "

He saw that some of the wagons were turning a little, that all were stopping, that the men on horses were riding back toward the Illinois shore.

" For God's sake, they're setting fires! "

Like some of the others, he began to unhitch one of the horses, ready to ride back. But almost at once there was the sound of shooting and the wagons back near the shore began to move forward, the oxen driven with whips, the horses plunging and rearing. Men came riding along the train from the rear, shouting: " There's a mob come in – push on! Nobody's to go back – push on! Keep in line, keep in line, push on! "

Simon leaped to the seat again and took the whip from the socket.

" A big send-off," he said bitterly. " They don't want us to come back."

It was endless, coming to the Iowa shore, and then the wagon lifted madly, rolling, rearing forward and up, the wheels spinning, hanging on. Mercy did not speak but sat rigid, and when the ground lay level once more, she still sat with her hands clinging to the seat on either side. The sky was red now, and the last of the uneven line of wagons moved starkly on the river. Nauvoo lay brilliant, a brighter city than she had ever been, her home-candles obliterated by a wall of fire.

The wagons pushed on.

" Jarvie! " Betsy's voice was terrible. " I shouldn't have left Purrmiew, he can't get out."

" He'll be all right," Jarvie said. " They won't burn what's been sold 'em, they'll take good care of what's theirs, all right."

His voice was like Father's, authoritative, grown-up, and Betsy moved to him and laid her hand upon his knee.

"They could've let us go without that," he said. "We'd never have come back. God knows we'll never come back."

The red glare over the river showed plainly the front of Nunn's General Store, looming beside the road, center of Montrose, Joseph's Zarahemla. It looked curiously square and civilized. Joseph Nunn was a shrewd man with a simple creed to which his intact store testified. If your religion gets in the way of your business, maybe there is a better religion. If your friends do you no good, maybe there are better friends, maybe you'd as well shake hands with your enemies. A singularly peaceable man, Joseph Nunn, and here stood his store unmolested, firm and square by the side of the road, and his house beside it. All intact.

Simon looked at it infuriated, repelled.

Just beyond the store the little road to the bluff curved sharply off the main street. New snow was doing its best to hide it entirely and its ruts were white and undisturbed. You had to know it well to see it at all tonight.

Mercy did not speak and Simon let her be, thinking: "It's as well she shouldn't look; women are strange about such things. And especially Mercy."

They were not yet out of Montrose when she slipped quietly from the high seat and he cried out to her and dropped the reins to reach for her.

But when he called her name and bent to look at her, he saw that she had not forgotten the place where the road turned, after all; she had simply turned with it, and gone home.